OMG.
What a book.
Couldn't put it down
and didn't want it
to end.
  You learn so much
  from this book. A real
eye opener.
Enjoy every page -
    Claire J.

Immodest | L.S. Einat

Producer & International Distributor
eBookPro Publishing
www.ebook-pro.com

Immodest
L.S. Einat

Translation from the Hebrew by Susan Treister

Contact: einats58@gmail.com
ISBN 9798783965241

To my husband, with endless love

IMMODEST

L.S. EINAT

These shall be your fringes, and when you see them, you should remember all the commands of the Lord and do them. Do not stray after the thoughts of your heart and after the sight of your eyes, which you tend to stray after. Remember to do all my commands and be holy before your God. I, the Lord, am your God who brought you out of the land of Egypt to be your God. I, the Lord, am your God.

(Numbers 15:39-41)

ONE

The door to my bedroom opened slowly, letting in the hazy light from the bulb in the hallway. The door opened without a sound as only the day before the squeaky hinges had been oiled. Now for sure no one will ever hear, I thought. Before that, I'd had hope that someone would wake up and hear what was happening, but that was never to be. He came into the room as usual, hopping over the mattresses scattered on the floor, and like a tiger spotting its prey in the darkness, he came straight to my bed. As usual, I pretended to be asleep. My senses were sharpened, and every rustle or movement in the house sounded to my ears like noisemakers at a reading of the Book of Esther[1].

"Move over!" he demanded, and I made a faint snoring noise to convince him that I was asleep. The room was silent except for the monotony of the breathing around me. The realization that nothing would stop him even this time hit me hard, as had been the case almost every night that year.

I lay on my side and he lay close to me and pressed his body into my back. His adolescent hands started to grope me. First he stroked my legs, and gradually his hands climbed to my undeveloped chest. I felt something hard against me from behind and was afraid to move, lest I be hurt by this

---

1   The Book of Esther in the Bible tells the story of the rescue of the Jews of Persia from extermination by the villain Haman during the time of King Ahasuerus. This event served as the basis for the Jewish holiday of Purim. According to custom, when the name Haman is mentioned while reading the book in the synagogue, the listeners use noisemakers to drown out the name. It is also customary to wear costumes on the day of Purim.

thing. His hands chiseled into my stomach, pinching the skin mercilessly. His body moved up and down, rubbing and scratching my body and my soft soul. I was like a heavy boulder that even strong winds would not budge from its place. I closed my eyes tight, and clenched my lips in disgust, my whole body contracted and waiting for it all to end. As always, I heard a long, faint sigh. Afterward, the door opened and closed behind him, leaving me in tears and wondering exactly what had happened.

The next day, the usual morning commotion provided cover for the previous night's events, and it was as if nothing had happened. My mother was busy with the little ones, issuing instructions all around. Our home ran itself according to the long-standing familiar routine. Sentences were launched into the air: "Bring me your bag;" "Don't forget to pick up Yossele from daycare;" "I gave you sliced cheese;" "Don't forget to make a blessing before you eat." Each to his own concerns. Only I walked around looking down with a tremendous feeling of shame stuck in my throat because of an act that I didn't understand at all. We were nine brothers and sisters. He was the second after the oldest son.

The event that had repeated itself for almost a year scarred my memory forever. In time I realized what was going on in that dark room, and later learned to deal with what had happened.

We never talk about things that are even remotely connected with relations between a male and a female. It was absolutely forbidden to say—even in jest—words that might allude to a connection between a boy and a girl, or between a husband and a wife.

One day, while wiping my little brother's mouth, I tried to tell my mother about the nightly incident. I felt I could no longer keep it inside. I knew that what was being done to me was wrong, but our upbringing overrode any will or pain that I held in my heart. That morning, my mother was in a lighthearted mood, and even kissed my cheeks, something she usually avoided doing altogether. Her cheerful behavior inspired courage in me, and suddenly the words came out of my mouth without my first having rehearsed them. "Momme," I said, "Did you know that Baruch comes to my bed every night and does all kind of things to me?"

My mother, who usually moved slowly, turned around to face me in an instant. The sandwich she was preparing fell out of her hand, and her eyes flared a look I had never seen on her face until then. I was so frightened that I ran to the kitchen doorway in an attempt to flee for my life, but she was quicker than me and grabbed my arm.

"What did you say?" she flicked at me through clenched teeth.

My voice became a thin whisper. "Baruch comes to my room at night..."

Before I finished the sentence, her hand flew in the air and landed hard on my cheek. I was in such shock that I continued to stand in my place, planted like a tree whose little leaves had deserted it and left it naked. Her grip tightened around my arm, and she pulled me forcefully out of the kitchen, my cheeks burning. We reached the girls' room. She threw me on the bed, grabbed my arms, and sat me down, turning my face toward her. Her arms flung my body as if I were a rag that needed shaking.

"You listen to me!" she said with lips thin as paper. "And you listen good. Never—but never—are you to talk about that. Not with me and not with anyone else. Do you hear?"

When she realized I was not responding, she repeated herself. This time her voice sounded like that of the crow who woke us up every morning with its screeches. "Did you hear?" her arms again flinging my rag-like body. "Answer me when I talk to you!"

I felt his hands poking around my body and his hard organ pushed against my back. I experienced the nasty night over again, but this time it was morning and my mother was standing before me, threatening and bullying me.

"Promise me that you'll never talk about that!"

I nodded my head. That's all I could do at that moment.

"I didn't hear," she insisted.

"Okay," I whispered, and all I wanted to do was to lie back and close my eyes.

"Louder!" she commanded.

"Okay!" I yelled.

I couldn't bear her looking at my face. I pulled my arms away, pushed her back and left the room through the door whose quiet hinges prevented it from divulging the sins performed under cover of darkness.

The next night, and also the ones after that, he did not come into my room. Before I fell asleep, I heard my mother hurrying the boys to finish getting ready for bed, and then I heard the door slam and the sound of a key. My mother locked the boys' room and took the key with her.

Five years have passed since then, during which the acts were subsumed into a routine of instructions, rules, and conventions. Occasionally, the memory reared its ugly head in my thoughts, decisions, and mainly in my behavior. In the family, I was considered different. Also in the community. My name was pronounced in a mocking tone, followed by a shaking head and clicking tongue that attested wordlessly to that fact that my parents were to be pitied for having a daughter like me.

One day, my father called me and asked me to give him some of my time. That was his custom. "Perele," he said, "can you give me a few minutes of your time?" I was a teenage girl, in high school, with a head full of questions I had not found answers for. Confused, with no clear identity, and a tendency to argue about almost everything, I felt as if I lived on a deserted island, with water raging in and out, and each of the waves trying to pull me out with it. I worked with all my might to escape the endless trap around me. The loneliness had become an inseparable part of my existence.

Though I had several friends from school and most of the time I was busy, the feeling of loneliness lived inside me like another part of my body. I wondered if everyone felt that way, that, like a stomach or heart or intestines or diaphragm, we had a loneliness in our body. I was afraid to ask my friends about this, lest they make fun of what I was saying, like the other times I had asked them all kinds of questions. It wasn't acceptable to talk about falling in love or relationships. These words belonged to the secular world that we were supposed to distance ourselves from. Our lives were organized around instructions and rules that determine our daily routine; how we dressed; how to behave, whom to marry, whom we could and couldn't look at.

We were disciplined and obedient soldiers, at least on the outside. What happened in our hearts was something else. Despite the strict order and organization, inside we were confused. I learned that at a later stage, when I gathered up the courage to speak with a few friends about how I felt. I found out that they too were full of questions they had no answers for. That deep in their hearts they were scared, just like me. That they also dreamed of love and falling in love. Rachel even dared to admit that she didn't like that life at all. She spoke about how one day she was walking on one of the streets in the city and saw a couple that had stopped to kiss. She was floored by it but said that it looked really nice. That she also wanted that, to kiss with someone. Of course after she said those things, we were dumbstruck, and I envied her courage for saying her feelings out loud. A bit over a year after that conversation, Rachel was already married to someone she had met just the month before. When I met her after her wedding, she said that what she wanted then was to carry a baby inside of her, and after that another one and another one.

I went into the living room. My father was sitting, dressed in his *haletel*[2], his hands stroking his gray beard. He followed my movements until I sat down expectantly. The clock on the wall ticked away the minutes. The holy books crammed on the shelves of the cabinet behind my father were shiny and clean. The table we sat at was covered with transparent plastic to protect the cotton tablecloth underneath. My father smoothed the plastic, and his bowed head, deep in thought, accelerated my heartbeat. I knew this would be an important conversation. Always before important conversations my father hesitated before he got started, as if checking mezuzah parchment from the doorpost to make sure it was free of defects.

"Perele," he finally began, raising his head and looking me straight in the eye, "it's time for you to get married." I was so stunned that even after many minutes had passed, I still had not responded. My father interpreted my silence as agreement and continued. "You'll soon be seventeen. It's time to think about the future. Yesterday, I went to the matchmaker to ask about finding a *shidduch* [match] for you. It won't be easy, but we must be patient. Ultimately, it'll be all right," he tried to calm me.

"But Tatte, I'm still young, I don't want a shidduch."

My response surprised him. He raised his head, and his eyes were no longer warm as they had been before. "Perele, look around you. Most of

---

2   A light robe worn by men on weekdays

your friends are already engaged, and you have no prospects."

"But Tatte, I'm still a girl, I don't know anything..." I pleaded.

My father began to lose patience. "Perele, whatever you need to know you already know, and whatever you don't know, you'll learn when you're married. There's not so much to know, and it's time for you to get married."

"But Tatte..." Tears of fear and frustration streamed down my cheeks.

"Perele, I don't want to hear anything. I fixed a time with Mordechai for tomorrow and that's it. There's nothing more to talk about."

With that sentence, he ended the conversation. He got up from the chair, and without giving me another look, turned his back and left the room. I remained reproached and rooted in the chair that without warning had turned into a torture rack. My heart pounded, my stomach churned, my throat was dry and swollen, but mostly, my loneliness hurt. The "part" of my body more powerful than any other physical pain. Undisputed domination.

In the days following that discussion, I walked around dazed. I just went through the motions. I did whatever was expected of me. I got up at six in the morning, helped my mother with the little ones, took Yossele to day care, and Esti and Shmuel to nursery school. I met up with friends in school, went to class, wrote when I had to write and nodded my head when required to nod. In the afternoon, I picked up all the little ones and helped my mother make supper. Days passed like that, one after the other. My friends felt that something wasn't quite right, but they knew that sometimes I withdrew inside of myself and didn't ask what had happened.

The community is a bloc of people who must live according to agreed-upon codes that are protected by people in charge of making sure that everyone stays on the predetermined path. At school, we also had someone who was responsible for checking the length of our skirt and the length of our hair, measuring the appropriate space between the skirt and the knee, and between the hair and the shoulder. Everything had to be precise. Life is so easy, there's no need to think about practically anything. There's no need to decide. Any dilemma can be solved by consulting the rabbi. Even our clothing was determined for us. What we wore during the week, and what we wore on the holy Sabbath. Like solving a crossword puzzle, when it gets too hard, you can look up the answers. You can try to think, but if it's too hard, the answer is there with the wave of your hand.

In one of the conversations I had with a friend, I dared to say that I didn't like people telling me what to do. "I want to think for myself, I want to decide for myself."

Devorah looked at me as if I was out of my mind, and said, "But Perele, it's great that you don't need to worry about making hard decisions and there's someone who tells you what's the right thing to do." I didn't continue the conversation because I knew exactly how it would end. And that's indeed what happened. "Okay, Perele, you always were a bit strange..."

Until I was ten or eleven, I didn't know I was strange. I first found out that people thought I was different one day when I was with Devorah in the school yard. We left the classroom, and I told her that I really liked the teacher because she was really pretty. And then Devorah told me that she had on too much jewelry and things, and her mother had told her that that wasn't right.

"Why?" I asked naively.

Devorah shrugged her shoulders and said, "I don't know, but that's what my mother said."

"I actually think it's pretty," I decided.

Devorah looked at me, arrogantly, and said, "Okay, Perele, everyone knows you're weird."

"Why weird?" I asked her in an insulted tone.

"Because you always think the opposite of everyone else," she answered immediately.

"What do you mean?" I wanted to know.

I think that from that conversation I began to understand why there were people who stayed away from me or glanced at me dismissively. I'd always thought it was because of my appearance, but in that short conversation between classes, I learned that my direct sentences had become a wreath of thorns over my head.

Since that conversation with Devorah, I started to pay more attention to what the people around me said. I realized that none of my friends talked anything like me. None of them fired out their thoughts. Everyone had an active filtering mechanism. My mechanism didn't work. Everything that I thought came out, unfiltered.

When we got close to seventeen, the conversations focused on those who had already gotten engaged, on their husbands-to-be, on their aspirations for marriage, on children. Serious topics. We were already considered women on our way to marriage, and the old nonsense had left our heads, like in some kind of internal ceremony that happened deep inside of us that we had no control over. Nonsense until a certain age, after that disillusionment. When I spoke with the girls about how sometimes I wanted to be alone and sit and think, they would exchange glances and their eyes said everything they were thinking.

I felt the looks of the children in the neighborhood too. I also knew why that was, because sometimes when I left the house, I placed on my ear a flower that I'd picked in the abandoned yard next to our building. The little children would chase after me and try to snatch the flower with cries of contempt and snickering.

The fences that delimited our community stabbed me hard and hurt me terribly. I wanted to be like everyone else, to think like everyone else, and accept the rules as obvious. I just didn't know how to. Something inside of me wanted to cry out. To be heard. A private, personal voice, a separate one. I didn't want to be different at all. That was difficult and complicated. I didn't like the mocking looks I got, or the pitying stares directed at my parents for having me as their daughter. I saw everything. And despite my seeming indifference, my soul was consumed from the inside like a burning bush. I felt bad for my parents, but I couldn't help them. I knew exactly why my father was in such a rush for me to meet with Mordechai the matchmaker. He was concerned that as time went by, my chances of getting married would diminish.

I lived in a city that was not far from the sea. Walking quickly, you could reach the beach in twenty minutes. Along the shore were tall, beautiful residential towers, and among them were one-story houses facing the sea. I lived further inland in an area with old neglected four-story houses. If a nonreligious person would have come to our neighborhood on a holiday, he would surely have thought that he had landed on another planet. We were different in our dress, in the posters hanging on poles along the sidewalk, in the products sold in the neighborhood grocery store. In just about everything.

I remember how one Purim I was walking around outside with my father. Out of the blue, he noticed two women wearing jeans and tank tops. It was a very hot day. My father, who was still holding my hand, turned his head the other way. That's how it always was. Fearing that a man's gaze would meet a woman's gaze, and provoke unworthy thoughts, men would turn away from the sight of women.

In front of our house was a large yard where we ran around in our childhood without fear of passing cars. Behind the house, across the street, a few minutes' walk away, was a field next to an industrial zone. The field served as a garbage dump, and the business owners who operated around it tossed their scraps into it. No one complained about the mess, and the piles of trash multiplied. It was in this filth that I found comfort. I knew that no one would come there and turned it into my own. In one of the corners of the field there was a small mound that I love to sit on and look out from, forward into the nothingness, and to the side, to the small businesses that looked like matchboxes standing one right next to the other. I loved that limited world. I could put my arms around it and feel as if I were embracing something that belonged only to me. It was a wonderful sensation, and the only one where I really felt like myself. A feeling that I had something that no one could touch or take a piece of. The junk-strewn field was like a kingdom for me. I accepted with love the chrysanthemums and dandelions that grew haphazardly, I loved the abandonment, and blessed the indifference that people had for that place. I admired it for managing to overcome in its yellow-spotted beauty the objects discarded into it so casually.

One day, I went to that place. It was a spring day. Neither hot nor cold. The sky above me gathered the field up to it and wrapped it in a soothing blue. An almost imperceptible breeze moved the tips of the stalks, and they nodded, first to the right, then to the left. I felt the movement in front of me like a silk sheet being shaken out. I straightened my arms and the field tickled my palms. I closed my eyes and felt that I too was being wrapped up and hugged by the sky. Suddenly, an unfamiliar noise broke the calm.

My closed eyes refused to open. My body was warm from the thought that someone there loved me, taking me close to him without judgment. I didn't want to pull myself out of the so realistic feeling, but the beats that penetrated my consciousness became stubborn and rhythmic. "Takh, takh, takh..." a pause, and again. "Takh, takh, takh..." I could turn the beats into music playing in my head, but now there was a human voice. Someone shouted and someone else answered. And then someone shouted out an instruction and someone else objected, and this happened over and over. A fragmented conversation, incomprehensible. A nonviolent duel of words. I opened my eyes and looked toward the industrial area. Dark heads raced around this way and that. The grating of an electric saw pierced the tranquility, and metal panels were unloaded from the back of a truck. I got up reluctantly from my mound and looked at the activity taking place just under my nose. I quickly understood that another enterprise was joining the row of businesses. More garbage, was the first thought that went through my mind. I shook out my skirt and straightened the pleats. I took a quick look at the newborn business and left my refuge.

As soon as I stepped foot in the house, I knew something had happened. My father was sitting in the living room, and my mother came over to greet me. Her fingers pressed the apron tied around her waist, and she looked down as soon as her eyes met mine. The bathroom door opened and a man I didn't know exited, mumbling a prayer. The man walked past me. My father was silent, his lowered head staring at his hands. When the stranger left the house, my father got up from where he was sitting and called to me, "Perele, come sit!" Tension was evident on his face.

"That man just now was Mordechai the matchmaker..." he began.

I took a deep breath and said nothing.

"He found you a prospective husband," my father said. And his voice suddenly seemed hoarse.

"But I don't want to get married, Tatte," I pleaded.

"Perele, this is the way of the world. You've come of age and now you need a husband." He spoke as if reciting a verse of a poem.

"I don't want to. I don't want to!" I yelled.

From the corner of my eye, I could see my mother leaning on the wall and peeking at what was happening in the living room. She didn't get involved.

My father clenched his hands and his knuckles whitened. He looked up and then said, "On Tuesday, God saw the world was good twice [from the biblical story of creation], and that's when we're meeting the prospective groom's parents. Just your mother and I, and then we'll see..." I saw he didn't have the energy to deal with my opposition. He stroked his long beard, sighed, got up and left me with a bubbling stew of feelings of anxiety, fear, frustration, and of course, loneliness.

In the days that followed, my father and I exchanged not one word. As if nothing had happened. But inside I counted the days until Tuesday evening. My father came back from the *yeshiva* [3]where he taught and immediately went into the bathroom. My mother sat at the dining table, her head in her hands. About an hour later, my father walked out of his room. His beard was neat, and he was wearing a new yarmulke that he had purchased especially for the occasion. I couldn't help but think how nice he looked with his height, his graying hair, and his beautiful clothes. That whole time, my parents didn't look at me or say a word. Just before they left the house, my father turned to me and said, "May this be successful."

One hour. Just one hour after they left, they returned home. My mother went straight into their bedroom. My father sat on the couch in the living room, removed his hat, and scratched his shining forehead. His yarmulke fell to the floor. He bent over, picked it up, and put it on his head. He did all that with his eyes averted. He said not a word to me. Many minutes passed in silence, until I realized that he had no intention of talking to me. I left the room and went into my bedroom. His heavy movements and downcast look made me feel pity for him. I almost hoped the meeting had gone well, just to make him happy. I didn't like the bitter disappointment scorched on his face like tar on a burning hot road. I understood that the meeting had not been successful. I was happy, of course, but I was also sad.

---

3   An orthodox institution of higher education that teaches Torah.

Two

By the end of the school year, Nechama, Hadassah, and Rivky were all already engaged. Rivky walked around like a proud peacock. Her groom was a scion of a very important family in the community. I knew who he was. He was small and ugly. I would never be willing to marry such a creature, even if he did belong to the royal family. Rivky never stopped extolling his family tree. She kept talking about his virtuous and generous parents and how he was known as a Torah prodigy. Nothing was ever said about his looks. I felt sorry for her. I was pretty sure that deep inside of her she was terrified. Maybe a little disgusted by him. But the deal was signed and the words she had to say were adjusted for appearances' sake.

Gone were the days when we sat and dreamed together. The days where we allowed ourselves to speak about forbidden subjects. Then we felt special and courageous. But everything had changed. The engaged girls were in another world and spoke only about topics related to their wedding; about the dowry they would receive, the preparations, the apartment being rented or bought for them. I felt how gradually the distance between us was increasing, like a ship moving away from a familiar shore. They also felt the space being created. I would find them whispering secrets to each other. When they noticed me, they'd flash a smile of confidence mixed with pity and condescension. They were relieved when I always found another excuse why I couldn't take them up on their invitation to join them. The language between us had changed. They were moving in a direction that I refused to go.

One day, my mother sent me to a tailor. His shop was outside the neighborhood. It was hot and humid outside. The thick nylon stockings covering my legs were itchy. The jacket covering my long-sleeved shirt pressed my chest like forceps. My hair stuck to my cheeks, and the end of my hair stuck to my tongue with the salty taste of perspiration. I couldn't carry my body, which felt heavy and worn out. I had to cool off, unwind. I wanted to take off my jacket, roll up my sleeves, and get rid of the thick ugly stockings. I felt like an old lady whose seasoned body had become happy enough with its appearance and wasn't looking forward to anything new. I didn't want to feel like that. I was just seventeen and a half, full of dreams, but at the same time, petrified of them. My steps were slow and heavy. Then I felt a cool breeze. My tired eyes looked up and I saw that I'd passed by the public library. I'd never been to a library before. My father forbade us to read anything but holy books. There was a bookstore near our house, but I'd never been inside. I looked around to make sure there was no one around who knew me and slipped inside. At once I felt totally different. A special unfamiliar smell surrounded me, something that was a mix of old and new. I looked around a large room and saw people sitting at tables, heads bent over open books. On either side of me, bookshelves stood tall and straight, peacefully stacked with masses of books. There was no way to count how many books were there.

I was mesmerized. I'd never seen so many books in one place. Some stood straight, others leaned on the books standing nearby. I couldn't tear my eyes from the scene. I felt my heart pound and couldn't explain what was happening to me. It was an unfamiliar and incomprehensible excitement. I imagined the books hugging me and pulling me close to them, exactly like in my dreams of romance. At that moment, I knew I had fallen in love. I inhaled the intoxicating scent and drew it deep into my lungs. I wanted to fill my body with it so that all the unpleasant things there would be pushed out for lack of room. The jacket that had constrained me before let go and hung lightly on my shoulders. The stockings stopped itching, my body was refreshed and ready. For what? I didn't know yet. I took a deep breath and strode into the hall. I wanted to immediately become part of the world that was laid out before me. It drew me in as if it were returning me to my natural surroundings. None of the people bent over reading at the tables looked up to see the foreign invader. From their point of view, it was just normal for me to be there. I felt happiness. I was just normal. Normal, me? I continued toward the shelves and walked down the rows. My fingers patted the books as if making their acquaintance. I wanted to meet each and every one of them. To get to know their internal world. To introduce them to mine. I wanted to make friends with them, to spend time together. To have joint experiences. I wanted these things, and standing there, I knew I would do it.

The library became my first home. I visited once a week, sometimes more often. I gulped down the books as if they were nectar. The words turned into my friends instead of those that had all but disappeared. Each week I dove into a new world, which opened up another world and another. I met characters that I hadn't known existed, was introduced to relationships that in my parallel world were forbidden, and that suddenly became proper and natural. I met strong and bold women who didn't give up. I met figures, with some of whom I could identify. Others I rejected. I discovered that the world wasn't just one big herd streaming in one direction, but a diverse assemblage of people with different opinions. My soul raged, and the confusion increased. I asked myself what was right and what wasn't. Was it possible to live in two opposing worlds at the same time? Was what was written in the books only a sequence of worlds from the writer's imagination, or was it somehow connected to reality? The questions whirred inside my mind nonstop, and the more of them there were, the more they interested me. I looked for answers. I wanted to be able to conform, to know exactly where I belonged. I wanted a simple answer, one way or another. Black or white. Left or right.

And then the message came in. My world, protected by the secret I carried with me, was suddenly shattered. It happened one day when I had spent many hours at the library. I had been cut off from time and the world around me, and for those hours I'd been in another world, which accepted me unconditionally. There I had been truly happy. I was so immersed in reading that I didn't notice that I was the only one left in the hall. A hand touched me softly. "We're closing in another few minutes," said the librarian who had unbeknownst to her, become my anchor. I felt her gentle touch on my arm as a caress. I lifted my head to an understanding and sympathetic gaze. "I didn't want to bother you," she continued, "but we're already supposed to close the library."

"Oh, excuse me, I just hadn't noticed what time it was," I apologized.

"No problem," she said. Her warm eyes looked at me softly. "Next time you come, I'll show you the new books we've purchased."

I smiled at her awkwardly. Until then, I hadn't known that anyone had noticed my presence. I would come in, march straight to the bookshelves, and sit down in a corner of the reading room.

"Thank you," I managed to say and got up. I could feel her gaze on my back as I made my way to the door.

On the way, the librarian's gaze accompanied me home like a friend. I felt that she knew things about me without our having spoken about them, and that was fine with me. I was even happy about it. But the joy was cut short the moment I got home.

"Mazel tov, congratulations!" my mother approached me and planted a kiss on my cheek. My father came over to me and his face shone as if the sun were shining straight on it. My little brothers and sisters jumped up and became part of the merry occasion, though they apparently didn't know what it was all about. I stood in the center of the room as if I were watching a horror movie. My arms hung at either side and tears flowed uncontrollably. My father, who had misinterpreted my reaction, came over to me. He had words of encouragement.

"Everything will be all right, Perele," he said with a smile. "We found you a groom, a learned boy, from a good family. Everything will be good."

Inside of me I thought, what's he talking about? What's all the happiness for? Didn't he know? Did he forget? I despised my father at that moment. I couldn't look at him. Did he forget our conversation? Why was he ignoring what I'd said, what I wanted? What kind of father was he? I turned around and fled from the house as fast as I could. I couldn't bear the way my parents were looking at me or their fake joy. I knew that inside they knew the truth, but were choosing to ignore it, and me. I ran to my little hill in the open field. My body trembled from anger and fear. The sky above was gray and threatening, adapting itself to my situation. I imagined that it was shrinking and getting closer and closer to me, until it almost touched me, and I put my hand up high to stop it from crushing me. I felt terrible. Defeated. Weak and panicky. I knew my fate had been decided. The deal was done. Hands had been shaken in agreement. At that moment, I was returned again to my dark room, submitting to the inclinations of my big brother.

My mother and sisters worked all week, polishing and purifying the house. Every corner was doused with cleaning chemicals. Even the walls were polished, and my father had painted all the stains that had accumulated on them over the years. My mother bought a new tablecloth that this time wasn't covered with glossy nylon but glowed with gold and festive decorations. Two days before the event, she took me out shopping. She negotiated with the saleswoman, who was surprised at my apathy and lack of involvement in choosing the clothes. And me? I moved like a robot. Nothing interested me. I walked around the world like a doomed person; no whimper of resistance on my part would change my fate.

The terrible day arrived. My father went to the *yeshiva* but returned earlier than usual. He was excited. My mother spent the whole day in the kitchen. The aroma of the foods she had made that usually pulled me into the kitchen just nauseated me. At five in the afternoon, the bell rang. "*Shoilem aleychem*!! Welcome," my parents greeted the visitors. I remained standing on the side with my head down, so my eyes wouldn't meet those of my intended groom, and I would commit the sin of lack of modesty. My parents invited the intended groom and his parents to sit, and we sat across from them. Despite my contempt for the whole event, I was curious to see the face of the person I would be spending the rest of my life with.

I sat, my arms next to my thighs, and gradually, without their noticing, I lifted my head. The first thing I saw was the end of a copper beard. I lifted my head up a bit more, and the copper was still burning across from me. I couldn't make out the facial features. The orange hair covered them entirely. He was quiet too, and let his parents conduct the meeting without interrupting. We sat like two stone statues, cut off from what was happening and from each other. I wished I could have made myself disappear. I wished I were a pesky fly. I could have moved from one to the next and bothered them. I would land on the end of their noses or on their mouths and not let them sit there and decide my entire life clause by clause, as if I had nothing to do with it.

The meeting was almost over. Our parents stood up to shake hands, and without their noticing, I lifted my head and looked for the first time at the person who was supposed to be my husband. I saw narrow lips and an eagle nose, but my heart accelerated at his eyes that looked back at me with no embarrassment. Narrow eyes, surrounded by smile lines, or more correctly, smirk lines. They contained no sign of anything good or comforting. They had something that was hard for me to define. I shrunk into my chair and felt I wanted to shrink down to nothing and disappear. Why? I didn't know. But one quick glance at those lines managed to arouse aversion in me, without my knowing why.

A week later, my father said that I could meet with Menachem Mendel alone, for a short time. He came to the park near where my family lived, and we sat on a bench at the appropriate distance from each other. At first we said nothing. Then I asked him how old he was, and he answered that he was twenty-three. My heart sank. Twenty-three was an old age for marriage. Many questions ran through my head. Why hadn't he been married until now? Had he ever been married, was the family hiding something, were my parents hiding something from me? Despite the storm raging inside of me, I fired the first question that came into my head. "Were you ever married?"

"No," he answered and didn't elaborate.

"So why haven't you gotten married until now?" I continued.

I knew that it wasn't right to ask such questions at the first meeting, but I couldn't stop myself. The questions shot out of me like a bullet from a rifle.

"And you?" he shot back, "Why haven't you gotten married yet?"

"Because I didn't want to," I answered defiantly.

"I didn't either," he answered. The smirk I saw at our first encounter joined his narrowed eyes in a kind of mocking and warning look.

"When we're married," he said suddenly, "you'll lengthen your dress."

"What?" The changed direction of the conversation took me aback.

"Your dress is too short," he said and looked more serious.

"My dress is fine!" I protested.

"You'll lengthen it!" he said, as if he had made the decision and there was nothing further to be discussed.

"What about children?" he shot out.

"What about children?" I didn't understand the question.

"How many do you want?" he clarified.

"I don't know. Three, four," I answered cautiously. "Why?"

"I want more. My mother had thirteen."

"I don't want so many children. I want to have time for other things too."

"What things?" he wanted to know. His head was tilted to the side.

Suddenly, I lost my confidence. I wanted to tell him "books," but a feeling inside stopped me like a traveler walking in a dark desert feeling like each step was liable to bring him closer to his end. So I said nothing.

His mustache stretched like an accordion when he smiled. "Let's go," he said.

I got up and walked behind him, his red smile with me the whole time. Even a week after that meeting I couldn't lose the image of his hairy smile stretched like a gaping pit in the ground.

We met twice more, and both times were like the first meeting. Already at those meetings I became familiar with his response to ideas he didn't agree with. The orange smile. The narrow stripe stretched under his mustache. I wanted to go over to him and pick up his rusty hair to expose what was under it, but of course I didn't do that. An uncomfortable feeling made me think that under that reddish grove hid a terrible secret, but I immediately dismissed that thought by thinking that the books I read had made me imaginative and melodramatic. I was very angry with my parents but trusted their love for me. Their ideas were different from mine, but their love was true and secure. This thought soothed me somewhat.

I acted as if none of this had anything to do with me. I spent every free minute at the library. It was easier for my mother to not have to see me hanging around her. She was uncomfortable seeing my disgust and frustration with the event that was being forced upon me. I also repressed what was awaiting me, as if nothing were about to change. And I too, like my mother, knew that inside of me everything was about to change, and nothing would ever be the same.

"Tomorrow you have a meeting with the bridal counselor," my mother informed me a few days later.

"What for?" I asked.

"What's that supposed to mean, 'what for'?" she repeated my words. "Every bride meets with a teacher before her wedding to receive explanations on all kinds of things."

"I want **you** to explain those things to me!" I said.

"I can't," she said, and her neck reddened a bit.

"Why not? I want you to teach me! I don't want to speak with someone I don't know who doesn't know me," I insisted.

"Why are you like that, Perele? Why is everything an argument with you?" her voice sounded whiny.

I kept my mouth shut. I felt bad for her for having me, as I was. It would've been a lot simpler for both of us if I had just walked in the groove that had been set out for me, but the stormy surging bubble that was who I was could not skip over my parents, and usually touched them right at important junctions in life. So many times I'd decided to take their path. To agree. To understand. To keep quiet. But at the moment of truth, I didn't manage to live by those decisions. Instead of saying, "good, okay," the word "no" came out of my mouth even before I'd managed to understand what they'd wanted from me. Obviously, I ultimately met with the counselor.

I entered a bare room. Except for our Hassidic leader's picture on the wall, a table and two chairs, there was nothing there. The room was austere. I sat across from the rebbetzin[4], her hair wrapped in a scarf. Her small brown eyes peered at me from behind her old glasses. Her round stomach stretched her shirt so far, there were small holes in it. There was nothing pretty or attractive about this rebbetzin, but as soon as she opened her mouth, the river of her voice was like light ripples over the sea. It was calm and relaxed. Her eyes looked at me sympathetically, and all her attention was on me.

"Are you excited?" she asked.

"A little," I lied.

---

4   Wife of a rabbi who teaches marital law to brides.

"It's pretty frightening, this whole hullabaloo of a wedding," she said warmly.

I still hadn't decided to trust her, so I just nodded.

"Today, I'm going to talk with you about things that may scare you a bit..." she put her hand on my arm and moved her body closer to mine. Her movements forced me to look into her eyes. I couldn't escape her gaze. "Today we'll speak about relations between you and your husband," she added.

That shocked me, and I said nothing.

"Do you know what sexual relations are?" she asked in a quiet voice, as if someone were waiting behind the door and liable to hear the secrets we were sharing.

I shook my head.

"So, after the wedding, you are permitted to your husband..." she continued.

"Permitted?"

"Yes. This means that you and your husband can try to bring children into the world. Because after all, that's what we were created for. "Be fruitful and multiply and fill the Earth..." she quoted from the Bible, and a slight smile distorted her lips. "Well," she continued, "today I will teach you how the commandment of be fruitful and multiply is performed."

The rebbetzin put her hand toward the end of the table and pulled over the Bible that was lying there. She rested her right hand on it, and then in a quiet voice, started to describe what was going to happen the night of the wedding. As she spoke, a black screen slowly closed over me. The words she used were foreign, threatening, and disgusting. I felt sick and wanted her to stop.

"He'll put his sex organ, which is below his stomach, inside of you. You'll need to open your legs and help him put it inside. As you do that, you'll think about how you are a partner to carrying out this important mitzvah[5]. After you feel that he's finished, you'll put your nightgown back in place, and he'll return to his bed."

I had no idea what she was talking about. What's that supposed to mean,

---

5   Religious commandment

that he'll lie on me? How could she commit such a sin in talking like that? What kind of rebbetzin was she? All our lives they talked to us about the value of holiness. To stay away from anything related to sex, more strictly than what religious law actually states. They spoke with us of separation even between husband and wife. They always warned us against contact with people of the opposite sex. In school, there were constant lectures warning us to stay away from boys. Even from our cousins or brothers. A year ago my cousin got married. My mother didn't let me go to the wedding, lest I sin with my eyes. I'd never seen my parents touch each other. I'd never seen a naked body, not even mine. The fear of touching, even of sinning in our thoughts, was with us our entire life. Now I was sitting across from someone disguised as a rebbetzin who was telling me that I was commanded to allow my husband to touch me and penetrate my body. Her words and exact descriptions mingled in my head like bees in a hive, and my nausea grew until I could no longer tolerate the horror, and I got up and ran to the toilet. I vomited my guts out and the fluids emitted mixed with my tears and the tremors of my body. When I came out of the bathroom, the rebbetzin was waiting for me and gave me a cup of water. "Perele, I know that it's all a big shock for you. Lots of girls react this way. It's as if we're contradicting everything we've taught you until now. But it's not like that. To bring children into the world is a big mitzvah, and this is the only way it's possible to do that. Gradually you'll understand and get used to it. What's important is that you think the whole time about the mitzvah and the rabbi who directed this holiness out of the wish to protect the spirit and not be tempted by the drives of the body. As the Baal Shem Tov[6] said, 'where a person's thoughts are—that's where he is.' You must be very careful with your thoughts, because thoughts are liable to lead to actions. If you want, come to me after you've fulfilled the commandment and tell me how it was. You'll see that it's not so terrible..." She paused for a moment and then said, "That's enough for today."

I ran from there as if a frightful monster were chasing me. My legs carried

---

6   A public leader in the 1800s in Eastern Europe, considered the founder of the Hasidism.

me to the field. I felt terrible shame. I couldn't stand other people looking at me. The very conversation planted in me a feeling of sin. I was completely confused. I lost my grip on solid ground; the solid ground of harsh rules that on the one hand made me resentful and on the other hand created order.

I kneeled on the damp ground, leaning my head on my knees, and tried to calm down. I started to review what had happened during the past hour. The sympathetic rebbetzin who'd created an atmosphere of calm. Her soft touch on my arm, her full attention on me. I couldn't understand how everything had changed in an instant. How all of a sudden terrible, forbidden words and sentences had been flung in the air and whacked me like a carpet beater. And then, as if out of the depths, my brother's image was before me, and with it arose the question, whether my brother had been performing some kind of mitzvah when he did what he did.

The bewilderment was too much for me. I just wanted to sleep. I sprawled out on my back and used my arm to shield my eyes, that just wanted to close.

THREE

Someone was touching my arm. At first I imagined that it was the hand of the rebbetzin before she stabbed the air with what she had to say. But this hand was rougher and different. I opened my eyes, and shade was bending over me, surrounded by the light of the sun. I quickly sat up and my hands sunk into a layer of wet soil. The blurry figure started to become clearer, and I was looking into the eyes of a young dark-haired man, who was looking at me with true concern.

"Are you okay?" he asked.

"Yes," I answered tersely.

I put my head down and smoothed my skirt.

"Can I help you get up?" he asked and reached out his hand.

"No, thanks," I ignored his outstretched arm. "I must go," I murmured.

I pushed my body up with my arms. For a moment I almost slipped, and he was quick to grab my elbows and keep me from falling. I shook my arm away from him, muttered 'thank you' again, and ran off as fast as I could.

The days before the wedding caused me to forget the encounter with the dark-haired guy. I was completely disoriented at the wedding. If anyone were to ask me what happened there, I wouldn't be able to answer. My body was there, but my thoughts wandered far away. Except for some flashes that included lots of black points jumping up and down, terrible noise, smiling mouths emitting the words "Mazel tov, congratulations!" and mainly a for-ever recurring image of a thin line with orange hair above it that caused my heartbeat to accelerate as a kind of warning signal, I remembered nothing.

I woke up from my befuddlement at night, when we got to the apartment that had been allotted for us. It was a modest apartment that his parents had arranged for us. On one of the walls in the living room was a large picture of the Hassidic leader. Alongside it were smaller pictures, of other rabbis.

Menachem Mendel entered the apartment before me. I didn't know if I should go in after him or wait for him to tell me what to do. He disappeared in the bedroom, and then I heard his voice calling me. Was he calling me? In fact, I heard, "Psssst." At first I didn't understand what was happening and continued standing where I was. And then I heard "Psssst" again. Menachem Mendel stood in the doorway to the bedroom and motioned with his hand for me to go in. The walls of the bedroom were white and bare. Two beds stood on either side of the room, far from each other. They were covered with white lace embroidery bedspreads. I imagined that Menachem Mendel's mother had seen to that.

When I walked into the room, he motioned with his hand for me to take off my dress and held out a white flannel nightgown that had been resting on the chair at the end of the room. And then he went out, saving me from embarrassment as I undressed. I sat on one of the beds and looked around. The first thought in my mind was of a prisoner entering his cell for the first time and starting to take in the fact that that narrow place was to be his home from then on. I felt as if I had invaded a place that belonged to someone else. A stranger. Somehow, I knew for certain that I'd always feel that way.

I managed to get out of the wedding dress, and put on the nightgown, which came down below my knees. Menachem Mendel came into the room. The panic was evident on his face. His eyes darted around, and he avoided looking at me. His eyes were red as if he'd had a shot of alcohol.

"Sit on the bed!" he commanded.

I sat down and lowered my head. I didn't remember a thing the counselor had taught me. My head was empty like a deserted hall. Menachem Mendel turned off the light. I felt as if my heart would shatter any second. As if I were circling on a giant wheel that had gone out of control. I felt my cheeks burning, and my hands were nervously tugging at the fabric of the nightgown. In the dark room, I heard the rustling of fabric, and understood that he was taking off his clothes. The room became completely quiet, and then he instructed me to lie down on my back. The fear of what was about to happen nailed me to the spot. Menachem Mendel raised his voice a bit. "Lie on your back!" he commanded.

I lay down on my back. My arms lay lifeless at my sides. I held my legs firmly together. Menachem Mendel stood over me. His shadow was projected on the wall and I saw the ritual fringed garment covering his upper body.

"Open your legs!" he ordered.

"Menachem Mendel..." I began.

I wanted to tell him, to ask him, to beg him to wait until tomorrow. That we didn't have to do it that day.

"Open up!" he commanded. "Lift the nightgown and open your legs!"

I closed my eyes and pulled the nightgown up above my waist. Menachem Mendel got on the bed and his scent of fear, or maybe it was the smell of my disgust, filled my nostrils like trash compressed into a garbage truck. The closer he got, the stronger the smell. I was afraid I'd throw up any second. I closed my eyes tight and held my breath. Menachem Mendel bent over me and tried to force his organ into my body. At first it seemed that he was getting lost, as if he didn't know what or where. Suddenly I felt strong pain, as if my body were tearing. It hurt so much that I let out a scream. I opened my eyes to ask him to stop, but he looked forward to the wall in front of him, and I, who was lying underneath him, had become invisible, someone not even worthy of a glance.

Then everything stopped. Menachem Mendel was no longer above me and the pain stopped. The physical pain.

The next day it was as if nothing had happened.

My other life had begun. A new routine was born. Menachem Mendel was almost never home. He was at the *yeshiva* most of the time. When he returned home, he continued sitting and learning, of course not before he sat at the dining table and received his expected meal. Twice a month he came to my bed. Once on the night I had gone to the ritual bath, and once on Friday night the following week. Then he would lean over me silently and return to his bed. That was his routine, and it seemed he was satisfied with it. There were almost no conversations between us. There was a lot of silence in the apartment, which became a familiar presence, and wrapped me in desolation and a terrible sense of loneliness.

One day, when I felt I could no longer stand the silence, I decided not to make supper and to suggest to Menachem Mendel to walk around outside a bit and buy something to eat. When I heard his steps, I opened the door, and with a smile that I had chosen especially for the occasion, I told him that we would be having a special day. Menachem Mendel raised his eyebrows.

"Today we'll take a walk and get something to eat." I said.

He didn't respond.

"Menachem Mendel, let's make ourselves a different day, and do something special. Something we've never done before."

"What about supper?" he interrupted me.

"Well, I haven't cooked today. I want to walk around a bit and eat out." I felt my voice tremble.

Menachem Mendel was quiet for a moment, and then said quietly, "You want to." Again I saw the narrow line of his mouth stretched in a smile that made me strangely fearful. "And I want supper at home," he muttered, and the tense smile was still there.

"But Menachem Mendel, since we've been married, we've hardly left the apartment at all. Let's do something a little different today." Fear had been added to my trembling voice.

Menachem Mendel walked to the kitchen and opened the dish cabinet. He put his hand in, took out a dish, and hurled it to the floor. My body bounced back in panic.

"Menachem Mendel!" I yelled, but he didn't hear me. He took another plate and threw it to the floor, and then another and another. The kitchen floor was covered with shards of plates, along with the shards of my life. I never made any suggestions again. I let Menachem Mendel's routine become mine. A boring routine. Empty. Black.

I lost myself. All the thoughts that I'd had before were suppressed and covered under a veil of fear and apprehension. For months I didn't go to the library, and for weeks I didn't visit my little hill. Whenever I felt like doing either of those things, the fear always raised its head and warned me not to. I mainly spent the days at home. I rarely visited my parents because

I was ashamed. I was afraid they would find out about the secrets of my marriage. It seemed to me that I was mainly afraid they would find out to what extent their rebellious daughter, the one that had always resisted and argued, the one that had her own opinion on every subject, had turned weak and submissive. But mainly I was disappointed in myself. I had given in to fear. I had turned into what I hadn't wanted to be. I despised myself for becoming obedient. For lowering my head, for not having the courage to go out and do what I wanted to do. I had turned into my husband's shadow. He had become my undisputed ruler. Full days I sat at the kitchen table, my head in my hands, thinking how far I had fallen. Where are you? I would ask as if there were another me. I spoke with my reflection and got angry at it. At its weakness. Because a few plate shards had turned my former courage into paralyzing fear.

Weeks went by until I had decided "no more." Like a drowning person who reaches the bottom of the sea and does everything possible to raise himself up. Gradually I felt how the self-contempt shook the courage from its slumber and pulled it up, and one day I decided to do something about it. I knew that Menachem Mendel would arrive late that day. After the *yeshiva*, he was supposed to go to the *shtiebel*[7] where there was supposed to be a meal. He wouldn't be home before ten.

The moment he left, I threw on a pullover that covered almost my entire body, put on my wig[8], and left. My head down, I walked quickly past people so as not to give them a chance to recognize me. I was invisible. I passed the neighborhood limits, crossed streets, and still made sure that no one saw my face. Finally, I reached the door of the library. I went in and undid my cloak. In a second I turned into myself, into someone who existed. The usual librarian looked up from the counter and looked me straight in the eye. A few seconds passed before her mouth turned into a warm smile. She got up and came over to me.

"How are you?" she asked, "I haven't seen you here in a long time."

---

7   Small synagogue/social club

8   According to Jewish religious law, married women cover their hair for the purposes of modesty.

I felt my body melt. My muscles, which had been tensed for months, relaxed. Heat spread all through me. I smiled at her awkwardly. I wasn't used to people showing interest in me, especially people I didn't know.

"Come," she said when she saw I wasn't moving. "I have a surprise for you." She lightly touched my elbows and motioned for me to follow her. We went into one of the rooms behind the long bookshelves. "Look," she said, and pointed to a pile of books on the table. I looked at her and didn't understand. "This is for you; I saved them for you."

"For me?" I asked, not understanding what she meant.

"Yes," she said with the same warm smile on her face. "I saw what you were reading and I'm sure these books will interest you. I didn't let anyone else check them out, I've been saving them for you."

"All of them?" I couldn't believe that someone would talk about what I liked or wanted or would make a special effort for me.

"Yes," she nodded, "come look at them and decide which ones you want to check out."

"Check out?" I whispered. "I can't borrow them."

"Why not?" she asked innocently, "You don't have to register for a library card, I trust that you'll return them."

"I can't bring the books home," I explained. When I saw that she didn't understand I added, "In my community, we don't read books like these."

At first she didn't respond, and then she looked me up and down. Slowly her surprise was replaced with comprehension, and then she said, "I understand."

There was silence in the room. The librarian whose name I didn't know patted the books on the table with one hand. She went over each one of them with her head tilted to the side, and it seemed like she was trying to come to some decision.

"You know what?" she said. "These books are still for you. I'll leave them in the room, and when you come, come here and choose one of them. When you finish, return the book to the pile and take another one. How's that?" she turned to me.

I nodded. A faint smile spread over my face.

The librarian went out of the room and left me alone with a pile of new adventures, and all I had to do was decide which one I wanted to experience first. I dismantled the tower of books and scattered them on the table, which became a sea of titles, characters, and words. *Jane Eyre*; *Wuthering Heights*; *A Tale of Two Cities*; *David Copperfield*; *The Little Prince*; *Anne of Green Gables*; *Daddy-Long-Legs*. I looked at the words and didn't know which one to choose. I wanted to read them all at once. I was afraid that if I chose one, the rest would disappear. I wanted to bring them to my chest and wrap my arms around them. Ultimately, I chose *Daddy-Long-Legs*. The rest of the books I piled into a tower and moved them to a corner of the table. On a whim, I tore a sheet of paper from a notebook that was on the edge of the table and wrote "Perele" on it and put it on the top book on the pile. I breathed a sigh of relief. Now I was somebody, not just a rag doll but a real flesh and blood person with a name and, concealed behind her was an entire world.

Hours passed without my noticing. Page after page after page after page. The evening colored the windows black, and only when the lights in the library flashed on and off, as the signal that it was closing soon, did I understand that the hands of the clock were far ahead of my sense of time. It was almost eight at night. I closed the book and went into the room with the open door. I put it on the top of the pile. I left the room, closed the door, leaving it open just a crack.

I made my way back with measured steps. I wasn't really in a rush because I knew that Menachem Mendel still wouldn't be home. When I got to our street, I glanced quickly at our apartment. My heart sank into an abyss. The lights were on all over the apartment. A lump of fear stuck in my throat, and my legs stopped moving. I stood still and didn't know what to do. My head was empty of thoughts, completely hollow, but the rapid beats of my heart served as a warning notice.

I forced myself to continue walking. I put my ear to the door but heard nothing. The door handle burned the palm of my hand as if it had just come out of a fire. When I went in, the silence echoed around like an alarm bell. The kitchen was lit up and clean. Nothing prepared me for the scene I found in the living room. Menachem Mendel was leaning against the wall stroking his beard that had grown over the months. His eyes scanned the floor. When

I entered, he said nothing. Laying around him, like slaughtered bodies, were broken pieces of furniture. The table was completely separated from its legs. The chairs lay dismantled. A vase that had decorated the table was smashed to bits. There was no part of the living room uncolored by gigantic shards of rage. The only piece of furniture left whole was the cabinet containing the holy books.

For a moment we stood quiet. Neither of us said a word or moved. Suddenly Menachem Mendel thrust his body from the wall, came close to me, and with one hand clutched my cheeks and squeezed them hard. My face was distorted from the pressure and the pain. I tried to say something, but an incomprehensible murmur came from my mouth. His pressure tightened, and the pain was unbearable. He brought his face closer to mine until his beard burned my skin and from his stretched lips came the sentence that would be etched in my memory forever. "I could kill you if I wanted."

The sound that came out of me was foreign to me. It was meaningless but completely understandable. Menachem Mendel smiled. His eyes were close to mine. They contained contempt, disgust, and satisfaction. His control of me gave him pleasure. He enjoyed tremendously the fear in my eyes. His grip on my face began to loosen. I felt as if two holes had been bored in my cheeks. And then he moved away from me, raised his hand, and before I realized what he was doing, he landed a punch that threw me back and knocked me to the ground. I was so stunned that I stayed sitting like a scarecrow, surrounded by broken furniture and bits and turning into one of them.

Menachem Mendel didn't speak. He didn't ask anything. From his point of view, I could have been at the neighbor's or on an errand related to the apartment. Just the fact that I hadn't been home when he got there was reason enough to "educate me."

From that day, I almost never left the apartment. My mother asked why I didn't come to visit them, and I evaded the question, saying I had a lot of housework. For some reason, she didn't try to find out more. I passed my days walking from room to room. The only sound I heard was the echo of my steps. I was the queen of the apartment. I was in charge of everything having to do with managing the home, but at the same time I was a prisoner within its white walls.

A few weeks later, Menachem Mendel came home and informed me that a meeting had been set up for us with the rabbi.

"Why?

"Because of the children."

"What children?" I asked in amazement.

"Ours," he answered with his usual indifference.

"I don't understand..." I mumbled.

"We need to ask the rabbi why we have no children," he explained, emphasizing the word "we."

"Maybe we should see a doctor?" As soon as I'd asked that, I realized that it was a foolish thing to say.

The leering smile filled his face. "Be ready. We're leaving in an hour," he said and left the room.

The rabbi didn't waste words. He asked Menachem Mendel a few questions and ignored me almost completely.

"How many times a month?" he asked.

"Twice, Rabbi," Menachem Mendel answered.

"Is there difficulty with penetration?" he asked, and I felt my ears redden.

"Yes," Menachem Mendel answered tersely.

The rabbi mumbled to himself and stroked his gray beard. "Is there intention? Are you concentrating on the right thing?" he asked suddenly.

Neither of us answered.

"Is there intention?" he asked again, and this time he looked at me.

I looked at Menachem Mendel, and since he didn't answer, I nodded my head and whispered, "Yes."

"I couldn't hear you," said the rabbi.

"Yes, there is intention," I repeated.

"Good."

The rabbi opened a drawer and took out a tube. He offered it to Menachem Mendel and directed him to apply it before performing the mitzvah, and then he turned to me with familiar contempt. "When performing the mitzvah, you should think of other things. Don't look for enjoyment. You must be concentrating on the mitzvah of being fruitful and multiply and fill..."

What was he talking about? I asked myself. What enjoyment? How was such a brutal act connected with enjoyment? For me, the twice a month was a nightmare. To see Menachem Mendel's face so close. Sometimes he drooled while moving, and I felt like vomiting, and held my breath so it wouldn't happen. Enjoyment? Torture. Even without his telling me to, I thought of other things. I imagined myself in the field I so missed, the wildflowers that adorned it in green and yellow; the little hill that was like a throne for me. I even missed the trash among the flowers, and in my eyes it seemed exactly in the place where it should be. The scene was so natural, primitive. No human hand had tried to change it or make it beautiful or clean. In that place, I felt I could think freely. I could imagine forbidden thoughts without anyone knowing about it or stopping me. I was free like a person on a desert island, far from the prying eyes of other people. I was *me*. Me. Me. A word that I repeated many times, but it had begun to disappear in a routine of violence and oppression.

FOUR

On 13 Av according to the Jewish calendar[9], Menachem Mendel informed me that he was traveling abroad. It was the best birthday present I could have asked for.

"I'm traveling," he said and added, "my mother will come and visit you occasionally."

He of course meant that she would check in on what I was doing. I didn't know if he shared what went on between us with his parents, but even if he did, he surely didn't tell them the whole truth. I didn't know why he was traveling, for how long, or with whom, and I didn't ask him. The day he traveled was a celebration for me. I didn't show anything outwardly, but my heart leaped with nonstop joy. In my head I was planning what I would do while he was away. The tower of books was waiting for me at the library, and like longing for a loved one who had been away, I looked forward to our reunion. I even missed the librarian. The quiet hall, the anonymous heads, bent over whatever they were reading. I missed the soft fluorescent lighting, I missed walking on the carpet that swallowed every rustle. I missed the shushing by those whose sleepy rest had been disturbed. I missed the hushed voices, the tapping on the computer keyboard. My heart raced, filled with an old joy that I'd almost forgotten about.

The day I went to the library, I walked up to the librarian's desk to say hello. I'd never done anything like that, but the happiness in my heart and the liberation I felt as a result guided my actions and made me fearless.

---

9   During the yeshiva's summer vacation.

The librarian smiled warmly, got up from her chair in my honor, and said to me, "I'm so happy to see you, but I don't know your name."

"Perele," I answered. "My name is Perele."

"Perele," the librarian rolled my name over her tongue, "I like it," she said, "a pearl. You really are a pearl." She said my name again and laughed, revealing two rows of perfectly white teeth. "I'm Sophie," she said and returned to the desk.

I went into the room behind the shelves. My books were resting exactly as I had left them. On the top of the pile was the paper with my name on it. I smiled to myself with satisfaction, and sat down on one of the chairs, when suddenly there was a knock at the door. I looked up and a swarthy head emerged from outside. "Excuse me," he said, "the bathroom?"

"What?" I asked.

"Where is the bathroom?" he asked again.

"I don't know," I answered.

"You don't work here?" he wondered.

"No, I'm just reading here," I answered.

"You look a little familiar," he said and pushed his head in a bit further.

I started to feel uncomfortable. We don't usually have conversations with strange men. I looked down and didn't answer.

The guy seemed to be waiting for a response, but when he realized that I didn't plan to answer, he took his head out of the narrow door opening and stepped back. When I was sure he'd gone, I looked up. I knew him. I knew exactly who he was.

That day, when I returned home, I met my mother-in-law on the stairs. "Where were you?" she asked before she'd said hello.

"I was out on errands," I answered immediately. To prove it was true, I took out some cans and other food packages from my bag. I'd actually brought them with me to the library in case someone took me by surprise. I smiled to myself with delight. When I got into bed at night, I shed tears for what I'd turned into: a fearful, submissive woman, scheming in order to survive in a world I didn't want to be in at all. I knew that if I accepted my place, I'd just disappear. Sometimes I was so angry that I had let fear control me, that over and over I decided to speak with Menachem Mendel when he returned, but then the violent fear returned and spread its wings and laughed scornfully at me. It knew full well that I didn't have the courage necessary to stand up to the man that I'd been forced to marry.

One summer day, when the sun was cooling down and its rays weren't so strong, I decided to go to the field. I put *A Tale of Two Cities* by Charles Dickens in an opaque bag and walked confidently to my place of refuge. The streets were crowded. There were children running all over, mothers pushing strollers with curious infants; pizzerias with chairs scattered randomly on the sidewalk serving slices to children who munched on the crust and licked dripping strings of cheese. It seemed like a festival. I passed people like a ghost. No one turned to look at me. I was invisible.

When I got to the field, I saw that it looked totally different. No more yellow blossoms, but dry thorns that made crackling noises under my feet. I found my place and cleaned broken stalks and thorn branches from it. I spread out the sheet that I'd brought with me and sat down slowly, stretching every moment and every movement of my body to enjoy the fleeting feeling of freedom. I lay on my back, extended my arms and legs, and closed my eyes. I let the sun caress my face, and the warmth of its rays penetrated my clothes and warmed my body.

Suddenly I sensed movement near me, and then I heard, "It's you!" Even before I sat up I knew who it was.

"I was sure we'd met, but I couldn't remember where. When I saw you from a distance, I remembered," he continued.

I didn't know what I should say, so I didn't say anything. The silence continued while he stood above me, blocking half of the light of the sun.

"Can I sit next to you?" he asked.

"I'd rather you not," I answered immediately.

"Okay, so can I stand next to you?"

Though I didn't look at him, it seemed to me that he'd said that with a smile. I nodded.

More silence. "So," he began, "that's how it's always going to be between us? I'll speak and you won't?" again I knew that he was smiling. "That's no way to build a relationship, it has to be mutual. Sometimes I talk and you answer; sometimes you say something, and I nod..."

He moved and his shadow blocked the light above me.

"I don't understand what you're talking about," I whispered. My head refused to turn and look at him.

"What's not to understand?" he answered. "About our relationship, of course." He stopped.

"What relationship? I don't know you at all." I felt fear sneaking into my voice.

He apparently also felt that. "I'm just kidding," he tried to calm me, "I'm just joking with you."

"Ah..." I grunted.

"Do you need help getting up?" he asked suddenly.

"No, I'm okay."

I got up. Now we were standing next to each other.

"Any chance of your lifting your head so I can see your face?" This time he was serious.

I felt really awkward but lifted my head. My eyes saw a dark shirt, and from so close I could see the black stains all over it. Oil stains, I thought.

"Hey," he said, "I'm here, up here."

I lifted my head up a little more, and my eyes found his black eyes. Around them were little smile lines, and since he was smiling at that moment, they widened.

"That's much better," he said, with no trace of irony. "This is the second time I've seen you here, in the field. Do you come here a lot?"

I nodded.

"Why?" he didn't give up.

I had no good answer for him. What could I say without revealing that that place was my sanctuary? After one question, there would be more, and the answers to them would reveal the story of my life, which I didn't intend to reveal. I said the first thing that came into my head. "I love the wide-open space here, the view, the yellow flowers..."

As soon as I said all those things, I regretted it, because the only things blossoming there at that time were thistles and other thorn bushes, some of which were crushed under heaps of garbage. He was quiet for a moment, and then surprised me by saying, "Do you want to see where I work?"

"No!" the answer slipped out of my mouth, and then I said more softly, "I have to go, I'm late."

I picked up the sheet from the ground, mumbled "thanks" and walked off quickly.

On the way, as I was shaking the sheet and folding it up, I thought how strange and impolite my behavior must seem to him. And, I thought further, that I had just spoken with an unfamiliar man who was not from the Hassidic community, and nothing had happened. If I weren't so worried, maybe we could've had a normal conversation without thinking the whole time about malicious intent or hidden thoughts. How nice it would be to just talk with someone, about things that weren't related to what's allowed and what's not allowed. Just like that, to say what you think, ask a question, smile and stay relaxed, without worrying about a disaster about to happen. In my life, in the community that I belonged to, fear was the gatekeeper. It was with us everywhere; with everything we did.

The days after that I spent in the library. I woke up early in the morning, tidied the apartment, bought what I needed, and ran to the library. I became a fugitive. I took advantage of the window of opportunity that was diminishing, closing in on me. I knew that when my regular life came back, I wouldn't be able to touch *Wuthering Heights* or *Anne of Avonlea*. I had to exploit this opportunity to the maximum. I ran to the library and got there exactly when Sophie, my friend the librarian, sat down in her chair behind the desk. "Good morning," I greeted her, as I continued on to the back room. I sat down and chose another book from the big pile. I'd finished Dickens at home and returned it to the library a few days before. I figured that Sophie had put it back on the shelf. As always, the time passed without my noticing. I was so absorbed in reading that I didn't look up until a hand touched me.

"Perele, you've been sitting here for hours. You're all bent over. It's not good for your back. Do you want to drink something before you go?"

"I don't need to go yet," I told her, "there's more time."

"But I need to go," she answered. "I need to close up," she added gently, with a warm smile.

"What time is it?" I asked in wonder.

"Closing time, dear. Look up and see, it's already evening."

As always, the imaginary world I had been visiting had me completely enthralled. I walked on stone-paved streets. I watched children rolling a wheel. I visited orphanages, was angered by evil, and overjoyed by kind-heartedness. I loved these books for their innocence, that sadness and happiness were mixed together in them, and mainly I loved the taste of optimism they offered me. I let out a long sigh, stood up, straightened the tower of books as always, turned off the light, and went out into the dusk. I took the remaining time until it was really dark and walked slowly, enjoying every step, breathing in another world, different from my own. A couple in their fifties passed me. His arm on her shoulder, their bodies touching. We could never have such closeness in my community. My father always walked first with my mother a few steps behind him. They never walked side by side; their bodies were never close together.

I turned back to look at the couple, and was surprised at the simplicity of their steps, the casual intimacy they shared in the street, in public. I turned back around and felt my cheeks redden and my heartbeat accelerate. I didn't understand what was happening to me. I felt goosebumps, the kind that come from the sweetness found in something forbidden but fun. I imagined myself walking in the street with a man's hand resting naturally on my arm, and I am looking at him so as to better hear what he's sharing with me. Just like that, in the most normal and natural way. Without noticing it, I tilted my head to the side, as if he were leaning on my shoulder, and my ears tensed to hear what he had to say. I invented a nice conversation between him and myself on what I had done that day, on the book I'd read. He listened, asked questions, told me what had been going on with him.

I could walk around the streets for hours and make up strange stories that had nothing to do with my world, but the apartment appeared in front of me and a soft darkness enveloped the street. Here and there, voices were coming from the other apartments. A woman leaned over the balcony railing to hang laundry, a young *yeshiva* husband hurried home with careful steps, and when he passed me, he turned his head away. I got to my lonely apartment, turned on the lights and looked around. How nice it would be if I could hold a book and read it without worrying that someone would come in and catch me in my iniquity. I always had the feeling that a big eye was monitoring my deeds and reporting them to my husband, the counselors, and the rabbis. Deep inside of me, I knew I would be punished for something. My Judgment Day would ultimately arrive, and the heavenly angels would decide my fate. I was living on borrowed time. I was living in fear lest someone read my thoughts. Lest someone find out what I really wanted and would know what I wanted to get away from.

FIVE

Menachem Mendel returned two days later. He came into the apartment as usual, as if returning from a regular day at the *yeshiva*. The day before, I'd spent extra time preparing his favorite foods. I made him a carp head, which he so loved to suck the bones of. When he ate, he would concentrate on the fish and make sucking noises until I couldn't stand watching him. I prepared him hot chicken soup, goulash, and finally served him a sweet kugel. Menachem Mendel sat as usual at the head of the table. That's what he always did, even though it was just the two of us sitting at the table. It was his way of declaring that he was the undisputed head of the household. That didn't change anything for me. Even if he sat across from me, he would still be the head of the household. In his weakness, he felt the need to demonstrate control and ownership, but I only understood that at a later stage.

After he was done and had said grace after the meal, he went off to his bed and slept until the next day. That whole time, I stayed at home. I was afraid he would wake up and be angry that I wasn't there. I busied myself with housework, though everything was clean and shiny. I cooked more food that we didn't need and sat for a long time and imagined myself at the library, in the sheltered room behind the shelves of books.

Menachem Mendel very quickly returned to his routine. One day, I went out shopping. Menachem Mendel was at the *yeshiva* and was supposed to return toward the afternoon, to eat his meal at the usual time. He had changed his habits and returned home every afternoon, and then returned to the *yeshiva* until the evening. At the grocery store at the end of the street there were several other women crowded in there at the same time. We squeezed in, right next to each other, to leave room for the produce piled in heaps around the store. Outside was a heat wave, and the store was stifling. There was no air left to breathe. Sweat dripped from my face and from that of the other women. The atmosphere became more tense when one of the women started asking the checkout clerk questions. We started to stir impatiently. I had items in my arms, and the woman in front of me was making great efforts not to knock over the pile of food that was next to her pregnant tummy.

"What's happening?" I heard someone ask behind me.

"I don't know," another answered.

In any case, the line didn't move. I felt the fear slithering into me like a snake. I knew that if Menachem Mendel came home and the food wasn't out on the table exactly on time, I would feel the sting of his hand. The precise lifestyle he demanded, the fixed time periods for each action, served as security walls for him. The moment something did not happen as he'd expected, he would turn into a volcano. The lava would boil, and only cool down when his mouth spat poison and his hands hit hard.

I felt the tension spreading in my body and wanted to leave without making the purchase, but at that moment the shopkeeper asked me to move forward. I lay the items on the counter and started to look for the money in my wallet. I paid the amount he requested quickly and didn't wait for change. I left the store quickly and began to run. The shopping basket rocked back and forth in my hand making loud noises like a clock warning that there was only a certain limited time remaining until the eruption.

Menachem Mendel was at home when I got there breathless. I went straight to the kitchen, opened the cabinets, turned on the stove, put the pots on the fire, and then, like fluttering angels, printed white papers flew all around me. At first, I didn't understand what was happening. I was so busy shortening his waiting time, that I didn't even look up. When I finally did, I saw Menachem Mendel, and his eyes, two burning flames. His beard was suddenly a fierce orange, as if on fire. His chest heaved and his hands were frantically ripping the pages of the book he was holding. For a second, I thought he was ripping one of the holy books, and I was horrified, but then I recognized the cover of the book and my horror grew. I was sure I'd returned that book to the library. I'd brought it home and read it day and night when Menachem Mendel was abroad.

"What's this?" he asked through tight lips.

I was paralyzed with fear. I couldn't answer.

"What did you bring into our home?" he asked and came a bit closer to me.

"Those books are an abomination. Are you bringing non-Jewish books into my home?"

"Our," I said stupidly.

"What?"

"Our home," I repeated.

I have no idea why it was so important for me to emphasize our partnership in this regard. Maybe it was a desperate attempt to preserve some proof of my existence.

The fist that thumped me crashed me to the ground and a hot pot of soup spilled on me. I heard screams next to me. My arm burned as if someone had thrown me onto a bonfire. I shook my legs in a fit of madness. I didn't know what to do with the pain. I weaved right and left and screamed my guts out. Then I opened my eyes and found myself in a white bed, drugged and bandaged. I didn't remember anything else. They told me that I'd fainted, and when I got to the hospital, they gave me painkillers. I looked around and saw my mother, sitting at the edge of the bed saying prayers from her Book of Psalms.

"Momme," I whispered.

My mother looked up and came over to me. "How do you feel?" she asked.

"I don't know," I answered. "Tired."

"You need to rest and get stronger." For the first time since I'd gotten older, she put her hand on my bandaged head.

"What happened?" I asked. "I don't remember anything."

"You made lunch for Menachem Mendel and then a pot of soup spilled on you..."

"How did it spill...why?" I was deeply medicated, but something in the depths of my consciousness did not accept her simple answer.

"Menachem Mendel said that you turned around for a second and apparently your shirt got caught and pulled the pot handle and the soup spilled on you and then you fell and hit your head."

"I don't remember having my shirt get stuck on the pot." I whispered in an effort to remember what had really happened.

"Rest, Perele, Tatte's coming soon," she promised. Though I was drugged, I felt her awkwardness.

When I woke up, my father was in the room. He paced back and forth, stroking his beard, mumbling to himself.

"*Vos hert zich*[10], Perele?"

I smiled instead of answering.

"It's lucky that Menachem Mendel was at home," he said, and I felt dizzy, my blood rushing.

"Why?" I asked.

"Imagine if he hadn't been at home. Who would have helped you? Who would have called an ambulance?" he said the obvious.

A hammer pounded my head. My father's words were logical, but from within the fog wrapped around me, I knew that they were not correct.

"Tatte, I think that Menachem Mendel was the one who caused it."

My father looked at me with pity and said, "Perele, you're talking nonsense. Menachem Mendel saved you!"

I decided to let it go.

Menachem Mendel came to the hospital once and stayed by my bed about five minutes. I breathed a sigh of relief when he left.

My recovery was slow. The doctors told me that a scar would remain on my hand, but that it would fade in time. After I returned home, my mother came three times a week to help me with the cooking and cleaning. The first time she came into the apartment, after she'd been there only once before, she was surprised to see that we had replaced the furniture.

"Why did you replace the furniture?" she wondered.

I waited a moment before I answered. I finally said, "It was old."

Old? she mumbled to herself, though didn't really expect an answer. "Let's heat up some chicken for you. You must gain some weight, Perele," she said, deciding to avoid getting involved in whatever the issue really was.

---

10 How're you doing?

SIX

Menachem Mendel did not calm down; his abuse of me just became more proficient. No more punches that threw me down and might cause other people to get involved, but things that would not leave signs over time and were masked by words, instructions, and orders. As time went on, I started to feel how I was gradually disappearing. Dying out. The library was like a dream that grew fainter and fainter. The field, the only place where I felt like I existed, also became distant and unreachable. From a defiant girl who'd had no problem expressing her opinion even when it was the opposite of everyone else's, I'd become a shadow of my former self, docile and dejected.

Where are you, Perele? I asked myself for the millionth time. Where did you disappear to? I looked for myself and tried to figure out what had happened to me. Was it the fear of the punches? Was it because no one understood me or supported me or came to help me? Had I just changed and become different because that's what happens to every woman after marriage?

I didn't like the person I had become. I despised myself for the fear, for my reconciliation with the situation. I knew that deep inside of me was hidden another Perele, that other Perele who did not accept the obvious, who opposed what she didn't agree with, and didn't go along with the herd with closed eyes. And here, now I had become a prisoner of my fears and weaknesses, especially in the hands of a person that I despised with all my heart, and my hate for him grew stronger and had now reached epic proportions.

One day, I felt I couldn't take it any longer. The loneliness that had been forced on me was impossible to bear. I decided that I didn't care what would happen, I had to leave the apartment. I put on my dark cloak of concealment and left the cold apartment. In my head, I thought how much time it would take to get to the field, sit there a half hour, and return home. I reached the conclusion that I would be home long enough before Menachem Mendel would come home for lunch.

The field received me like an old friend. It was still dry and thorny. The ground was cracked and gray, and the familiar garbage all around had increased. It was as if the sky felt the need to color the field and had lit it light blue with feathery touches of white paint. How I loved that place. For me, it was even prettier than any stylish dress, luxury apartment, or landscape from overseas. It was just before noon on a weekday. The air was full of banging hammers, the irritating noise of a saw, and the vague sound of people talking, all of which were drowned out by a motor revving.

Those noises would have disturbed some people, but they gave me a feeling of sanity. Of life. In that place I felt the most real, the most me. I felt that I existed, even if no one else noticed me. There I enabled the memory of that whom I used to be to surface. In that place I admitted that I hated my life. There I also told myself that inside of me something was seeking to burst out. I looked forward at the horizon, to the place where blue met gray, and said to myself that I could get there. That I could fly, spread my wings and navigate myself forward, pass the visible horizon, and create another one and then another one. My thoughts were courageous, free of any obstacle or fear.

My eyes stared forward, cut off from the sounds around me, until I felt I wasn't alone. I turned my head and met the look of the man with the black eyes.

"Where've you been?" he asked with half a smile. "You didn't tell me anything. I looked for you here, asked about you at the library, but the librarian didn't know anything."

"You were looking for me?" I asked in amazement.

He hummed and smiled a little smile.

"Why?"

"Why?" he repeated. "You know what? I don't have a snappy answer. I just wanted to see you. Strangely enough, I had gotten used to looking up and seeing you, and now for a long time, you haven't been here," he explained, scratching his head and tousling his hair.

I was embarrassed.

"I embarrassed you," he said.

"A little, yes." I pushed a recalcitrant lock of hair into the scarf on my head.

I got up, so I wouldn't have to stretch my neck, and stood a bit away from him. "I have to go," I said because that was the first thing I thought.

"Are you sure? I wanted to invite you for coffee."

"Why?"

"You say 'why' a lot, huh?"

"Why?" I said, my face serious.

He said nothing and then smiled. "You're joking, right?"

"Yes," I answered, and smiled an embarrassed little smile.

"So what do you say, Ms. 'Why'? Will you come see where I work?" he repeated his question.

That moment I thought of nothing. Not of Menachem Mendel, not of fear, not of time pressure, of nothing. I answered exactly what I felt I wanted to do. There were no rules. So as not to, lest... caution... punishments. My thoughts were empty of anything that tied me to the life I had outside of my thorny oasis. We walked together. Every once in a while I stole a look at him, but he was deep in thought. His head tilted to the side, and his eyes gazed at some point on the ground.

"What are you thinking of?" I ventured.

He looked up and said that he was thinking of a problem they had at work.

"Ahh..." I said.

We left the field behind us and approached the place where the sounds came from every time I visited the area. The pounding of the hammer was stronger than ever. The voices of people that I heard from afar became clear, meaningful sentences. The blurred figures became real people. I realized that I didn't see any women. Only men were walking around there. Most of them wore dark coveralls. Here and there I saw men in regular clothes, and I figured they were customers or managers or chance passersby, like me. A few heads turned toward me and caused me to feel uncomfortable. I wanted to leave, but on the other hand, I very much wanted to stay. Something in the atmosphere of the place made me curious. Made me excited.

"Why are they looking at me like that?" I asked the guy walking next to me.

He thought a bit before he answered and then said, "Because you're a woman, and as you see, there are not many women here, but mainly because of how you look."

"Do you mean my clothes?"

"Yes," he answered. "You're not dressed like the women who walk around in places like these."

"So what can I do?" I asked awkwardly.

"Nothing," he answered quickly, "just continue to walk and behave as always."

"Is it dangerous to walk around here?" A slight fear crept into my mind.

"Not at all. It's just curiosity. Nothing more. You have nothing to worry about," he promised. "We're here."

A few men were checking something deep under the hood of a car. When we came into the garage, they looked up at me for a few seconds. Two of them looked down immediately and continued with what they were doing. Others looked at me and him, and then at me, and then at him. I saw question marks on their faces and an expectation of an explanation, but the young man next to me ignored them and looked at me.

"Come see what we're doing," he said and touched my arm lightly, leading me forward. We passed the people and went inside. Though a few fluorescent lights were on, the place was pretty dim.

Something was happening in my body. A great fear was mixed with excitement that I didn't understand. I didn't know whether the palpitations were caused by fear or excitement. I ignored the feelings and continued walking after him. Suddenly we stopped. "Here, I'm working on this one now," he said, and it seemed to me that a trace of pride had slipped into his voice. When I looked down, I was standing next to a car with no hood. It had no windows, and many other parts were missing from it.

"What happened to the car," I asked, "an accident?"

He chuckled. "No, we're building something for people who want a special car."

"What does that mean, a special car?"

"A car that's been discontinued. There are no more models like it on the road," he explained.

"Why would someone want a car that didn't exist?" I asked, puzzled.

He laughed before he answered. "You're right. Only a crazy person would want a car that's no longer being produced, and really, the people that we're putting the car together for are completely crazy."

"And what about replacement parts for the car? What if something broke and they're no longer making it?"

"Good question," he agreed. "There are small manufacturers in the world that make replacement parts according to the original model, using old-fashioned technology. In England, for example, there is a workshop where they make wooden steering wheels. They even use the same wood they'd used, and the method is exactly the same as in the olden days. There are a lot of original parts around the world of cars that died ages ago. And that's exactly part of it," he said.

"What's part of it?" I asked.

"I told you that these people were crazy for this. Some of the craziness is in finding original parts. That's what drives the people, what puts adrenaline in their body and soul." He spoke quickly and excitedly and that's when I understood that he was one of those crazy people.

"So what do you say, 'Why,' is it interesting?"

"Yes," I said. And then I added quietly, "Very much."

Suddenly I noticed that the people at the front of the garage had disappeared. There were no longer any voices in the background. "Where is everyone?" I asked.

"Ah, they went out for lunch," he answered and bent over to check something in the exposed engine.

"Lunch break?" I asked in panic, "What time is it?"

"It's almost one in the afternoon."

What an idiot I am, I said to myself, and quickly started to run out of the garage. He lifted his head, surprised. "Hey, 'Why,' where are you going?"

"I have to go," I grunted and started to flee.

"Wait a second, I'll come with you!" I heard him call after me, but the panic that gripped me along with the sudden awareness of what I had been doing during the past hour shook my body like a Lulav[11] being used for its

---

11 Palm branch used on the Jewish festival of Succoth and taken as part of the four species, along with the Etrog, myrtle and willow for commandments of the day.

ritual. I ran as fast as I could, ignoring the thistles tearing my socks and forgetting the dark cape I'd used to protect myself from the curious looks of my gossip-loving neighbors.

I got to the apartment, and just a few minutes later, I heard Menachem Mendel come in. I was still breathing heavily, trying to calm down from the running and fear. Menachem Mendel gave me a look of contempt, went to the bathroom, ritually washed his hands, and sat down at the table. The food wasn't warm, and he had to wait a few minutes. During that time, I saw him look around the room and felt his glare on my back while I was busy warming up the pots. Two thoughts went through my head simultaneously. One was defiant and twistedly wanted to knock him out of equilibrium so that he would get angry and hit me, and the other, more familiar, was afraid. I was so angry at myself for not protesting, that I believed I should be punished. Punished for something unknown. Maybe for my weakness, maybe for the evil I'd done to my parents, that I wasn't like everyone else.

I thought about the visit to the garage the entire week. I was surprised to reveal that I didn't think about the young man, that he'd touched my arm by chance or that I'd been alone in a place where there were only men. Mainly I thought of my excitement when I saw the car with the missing parts. Something strange attracted me and made me curious. I saw the car before my eyes, and around it, people trying to find solutions for the re-assembly, to make it something whole. The wonder of creation. Like a fetus that gets a new body part every so often, until it turns into a perfect human being.

The look of the car body with the missing parts wouldn't leave me. I had to return to the garage and see it again. I kept thinking about how the parts could be assembled and it would be complete. I'd never driven a car, nor had my father. I'd had no connection with cars except for my few trips in buses. The sight of the car flashed in my eyes like a pulsating star that could pull me to it in the firmament, far from the treacherous ground. I waited for the opportunity to come.

SEVEN

It was a cold and rainy winter's day. The air was filled with irritating humidity. Rain came down intermittently, disturbing, irregular, and surprising. On those days, the streets were already empty in the early afternoon, and people went home, escaping the early darkness of the street. Menachem Mendel told me that he wouldn't be returning for lunch because he didn't want to run around the rainy streets. A small ball bounced in my heart with pleasure, and it grew into happiness mixed with excitement. Outwardly I showed indifference, and told him if that were the case, I wouldn't cook that day.

Menachem Mendel narrowed his eyes studying my face, and then he turned and left, slamming the door behind him. I knew he was always suspicious of me. When he came home, he would look all around, searching for a hint of some evil deed I had perpetrated. Sometimes he walked around the rooms and checked, picking up a chair cushion, passing his hand over the furniture and opening drawers. Only after he was satisfied did he continue with his normally scheduled activities. And me? I was as careful as I could be. I myself looked over every spot in the house every day, making sure he had no reason for suspicion or anger. I had adopted the lifestyle of a battered woman to the point that my eyes were always running around the apartment, looking for a hint of an accidental sin committed in good faith. I hated myself for that, but always took comfort from my reflection in the mirror. This life is temporary, I told myself. It wouldn't last forever. Something in me promised me another life.

At eight in the morning, I was already ready to go out. Even if Menachem

Mendel changed his mind and came home in the afternoon, I would already be home. I picked up the big umbrella, took one last look around the rooms, and went out into the wet streets. My shoes clattered on the wet sidewalks, splashing the thick nylon socks that modestly covered my legs. Few people were on the street. Mainly husbands hurrying to the *yeshiva*, their brimmed hats covered with plastic. The rain grew stronger and turned to hail that scattered chunks of crystal on the sidewalks and streets. I walked faster. The faster I went, the faster the rain stuck to my clothes. My shirt was plastered to my chest, and my skirt to my stockings. The wind blew suddenly, folding my umbrella like flapping hair. I wrapped myself in my coat and held it tight to my body with my free hand. I was cold and uncomfortable, but nothing stopped me from heading toward the wonder that had captured my heart at first sight.

I crossed the field. Mud, with its intoxicating smell of fresh earth, stuck to my shoes. My pumps turned brown and looked like someone else's shoes. Finally, my feet reached the asphalt expanse around which were scattered garages and small businesses, like precious stones in a crown. For a moment, I didn't remember where I was to go, but then I noticed that the garage was right nearby, at the end of the asphalt, closest to the field. I continued walking without further thought, but when I got close to the garage, I slowed down and started to listen to the sounds mingling in my head in a disturbing cacophony. One of them was the voice of Menachem Mendel. Another was the voices of my parents, and the strongest of all was my own voice. What are you doing, what are you doing? This is not my world, it's the world of disgusting men. And what if they do something bad to me? And if someone finds out, and if someone knows? It's forbidden, a terrible sin!

It was suddenly clear to me that if I continued in that direction, things would never be the same again. My life would change and become much more dangerous. Was that really what I wanted? Of course not. But something stronger than me or the voice of reason pushed me forward, into a dark, enticing, intriguing hole, and I had to know what was in it.

"Hi, what are you doing here?" I didn't see him and jumped in fright.

"I didn't mean to scare you," he apologized. "Suddenly, I looked up and saw you..."

The words got mixed up in my head and I couldn't manage to organize them into a logical sequence to answer him.

When he saw that I was not responding, he again touched my arm lightly and led me into the garage.

"Come, sit," he said and dragged in a plastic chair that had once been a different color, and directed me to sit down. "You're completely soaked." He sounded a bit worried. He disappeared for a second and returned with a small electric heater. He plugged it into the wall and put it next to my feet. He then disappeared again and returned in a few minutes with a cup of tea.

"Thanks," I said and brought the steaming cup to my lips. I put my hands around the warm cup and felt how they were starting to defrost. I blew into the hot mug and steam rose to the garage ceiling. That whole time he stood above me silently.

I felt my body warm up. Blood started to flow and thaw my frozen extremities. My thinking began to clear, and I knew I had to explain my presence there.

"I just wanted to see the car again," I said, as if we were already in the middle of a conversation.

He raised his eyebrows in surprise and waited for me to continue. When I didn't, he asked, "Why?" and we smiled at each other.

"I don't know," I answered honestly, trying to explain something that I myself did not understand. "I really don't know; something drew me here."

I saw his eyes open and a smile crease the corners of his eyes.

"What." I asked, "Why are you smiling?"

He looked at me a second and then became serious again.

"I don't know," I tried to explain, "but I was curious what would happen to it in the end. How you'd manage to overcome the difficulties and problems. Where you'd bring missing parts from and how you'd put it all together. What if you'd bring a part and find that it wasn't suitable? How would you make it run? And after you put it together, how would you make it look nice? How would you decide what to buy, what color to paint it?"

I stopped the deluge of words and waited. My honest enthusiasm caused me to forget the rules. What was permitted and what was forbidden. I was completely careless. If I'd have stopped for a second and thought about what I was doing, I would have understood that I was digging a deep pit for myself, into which I was liable to fall with no possibility of return.

The young man looked at me. He had a strange expression on his face. He offered his hand to me and said, "Dan." His outstretched arm was left unanswered, like a baby bird crying out for the touch of its mother's body. And then he said, "Oh...sorry" and returned his arm to the side of his body.

"So what do you want to do now?"

I looked around. Wires and cables were hanging on hooks. In one of the corners of the garage, a small sink was attached to the wall, its white porcelain rim peeking out like teeth in the dark. In another corner were two men in dark coveralls talking to each other with lively hand gestures. Every once in a while they snuck a glance at me, and when our eyes met, they quickly looked away. I couldn't hear what they were saying. To my left and right were piles of tires and other parts in perfect disarray. The dominant color was black. Even the young man's hand was covered with black motor oil. I thought that if I shook his hand, my hand would also be covered in black, and that thought did not bother me at all.

"Can I see what you people are doing?"

"Are you sure you want to? You're liable to get dirty," he warned.

"I'll be careful," I promised, mainly as a warning to myself.

Three men leaned over the empty space where the engine was supposed to be. Once in a while they too glanced at me and at the man, who for some reason I had trouble calling by the name he had used to introduce himself. To call him by his name was too personal, as if I would be admitting that there were some kind of closeness between us. As long as he remained anonymous, the distance remained, and the foreignness was convincing protection from my thoughts and fears.

While I was there, they mainly spoke among themselves. They exchanged ideas, debated, argued. Every once in a while, they remembered I was there and became quiet, sometimes they moved away from me when a random closeness was created and again, they returned to their involvement with technical matters. It seemed like the young man had forgotten me, or maybe he'd gotten used to my presence. He was completely engrossed in the work. Once he went off and came back with a diagram, maybe of the engine, and the four of them became completely involved in their conversation. Sometimes they patted the drawing, looked at it for a while, and added imaginary lines with their fingers. Then they put it aside, until the next time. And me? I was hypnotized. My body was tense, and my ears tuned in, so I wouldn't miss a word. I didn't understand most of the words, but the depth and the debating, the thought they put into everything, their hand movements, all mixed into a perfect musical creation in which each one had a different role and musical scale. Together they created wonderful harmony.

The hours flew by. The clock became my enemy. The black hands became head-chopping hatchets, and the racing time became a ticking bomb. Tick-tock, the voice of Menachem Mendel thundered in my ears. I knew that if I didn't run out immediately, I would never be able to return. I lifted my head, mumbled "I'm going," and rushed toward the field. I ran, ignoring the rain dripping on my face, getting delayed against my will when my feet sank in quicksand-like mud. I had forgotten the umbrella at the garage, and when I got home, I was soaked with rain and mud. It was five in the afternoon, but outside it was already dark. My knees trembled as I climbed the stairs. I knew that my fate would be sealed when I opened the door. For better or worse. I opened the door and inside was gloom and darkness. I understood I'd been saved. He hadn't come back yet. I ran to the room, took off my wet clothes and wanted to get into the shower. How wrong I was. Menachem Mendel stood at the doorway to the room, leaning on the doorpost, his hand stroking his long beard. I knew it. I saw in his eyes the familiar insanity. I stood in place for a second, naked as the day I was born. It was the first time he'd seen me like that. He reached me quickly, grabbed my forearms, and threw me on the bed as if I were an object. "Menachem Mendel..." I tried to plead and get up from the bed. But he was already on top of me. His tense pelvis pressed my pubis and his hands held mine like clamps. His eyes stood fixed on my chest for what seemed like forever to me. I was paralyzed with fear.

"Don't you dare move," he warned me. His deep and threatening voice had its effect. I lay like a corpse on the mattress, felt the pain of his weight on my body. Without warning, he grabbed one of my breasts and squeezed it tight. A yell of pain came from deep inside of me, but he didn't hear and continued squeezing. Like a boy who had been given a new toy that he didn't know how to play with. Menachem Mendel did the same thing with my other breast. I screamed with pain and begged him to stop, but he didn't listen and saw nothing. He was in a world of his own. A world in which no one else was important or of any value at all. My pain did not penetrate his mantle of madness. Then there was relief from the pressure. He got up and started to take off his pants, his gaze not releasing my eyes. And then he climbed on me and started to push his erect member into me. The pain was unbearable. I was dry and my muscles were tense and refused to open up my body for him. The more difficult it was, the more violent his attempts became.

"Open your legs!" he commanded.

"I can't," I wailed.

"Open your legs!" he repeated as if he hadn't heard me.

I spread my legs to relieve the pain. He lay on me with all his weight. His beard scratched my face like wire. I cried, first quietly, and then loud and louder.

"Quiet!" he ordered.

I tried, but I couldn't. My body howled its pain without my managing to restrain it. His right elbow thumped my face intensely and for a moment I was dizzy. His mouth approached me, and his teeth bit my lips mercilessly.

"Stop...stop!" I screamed, tasting my blood in my mouth.

He ignored my pleas and his movements became faster and more aggressive. I wished I could cut myself off from my body and look down on it from above, but every part of me was reacting to the pain. Finally, everything was quiet. The weight on my body was eased. Menachem Mendel went into the shower, and when I heard the running water I got up from the bed and my feeling of disgust turned immediately into a desire to vomit. I went to the toilet and emptied my insides. Since I hadn't eaten that day, only yellow gastric juices came out, and filled the toilet with all the loathing I'd felt from the touch of the hands and body of my vile husband.

I went into the shower after he left it. I looked at myself in the discolored mirror and saw my bruised and bleeding face. My lower lip had a long bloody slit, and my eyes were covered with blood. That's it, I'm leaving! I said to myself. I'm not staying for another minute. Menachem Mendel sat in the living room and read from one of his holy books. I passed by close to him and he didn't even look up. As if nothing had happened. Life had moved on. I wouldn't have been surprised if he'd asked me to serve him supper, but he said nothing, totally engrossed in the holy words that had absolutely no connection with his deeds.

I packed a bag with some clothes, took off my shoes, and went toward the front door. Menachem Mendel sat bent over, his body swaying up and down as he read. The door didn't creak when I opened and closed it. In the front hallway, I put on my shoes and straightened my clothes. Before I ran out, I saw the innocent gaze of a young girl about my age who was standing in the doorway of the apartment opposite, watching what I was doing. I'd never seen her before. Our eyes met for a few moments, and for some reason, I felt that we had met before, but where I couldn't remember. I lowered my head and ran away quickly.

Outside it was dark. The streets were quiet and deserted. It wasn't a normal sight, a woman walking alone in the street at such hours. But I wasn't thinking at that moment what was okay and what wasn't. I just wanted to get to my parents' house and calm down. I wanted to be in a safe place. My steps became more rapid until I was running. The bag hanging on my shoulder shook heavily, but I didn't think to stop once. Even if I lost it, I would continue running. My legs carried me far from the place where I'd turned into a valueless object.

I knocked on the door of my parents' apartment. I was wiped out, and I felt I was about to collapse. The power that had carried me there was gone. My mother opened the door, and I fell into her surprised arms. She almost fell together with me. A cry came from her mouth, "Perele!" and a few of my brothers and sisters gathered around us, followed by my father. When my father saw that my mother could barely drag me, he helped her and both of them pulled me to the couch and put me down just as I felt. Like an object. My father looked at me, and then told my brothers and sisters to go into their rooms.

"Perele, what happened? What are you doing here, where's Menachem Mendel?"

I had no words. The crying burst out in loud and endless sobs. My mother wrapped her arms around me and pressed me to her chest, and my crying only grew louder. My father also sat down on the sofa and they both waited for me to stop crying. It was a long time before I calmed down and could tell them what had happened. I didn't know where to start. I was stammering and unclear.

"Perele," my father tried, "we can't understand what you're saying, speak slowly."

"Menachem Mendel," I said.

"What about Menachem Mendel?" my father asked.

"He hits me," I finally said.

There was silence. My parents looked at each other and said nothing. Then my father asked, "Since when?"

"From the beginning," I answered.

My father got up and started to pace around the room. I knew what he was thinking. What do we do with that information, how do we handle it so no one in the community hears about it? How do we keep the good name of the family? In our community, no one washed dirty laundry in public, no matter how foul. With us, everything stayed in the family and was covered with thick layers of concealment, so that there would not be even a single little crack that would expose what was underneath.

"*Vas maken du*?"[12] my mother said to my father.

I thought to myself, wait a second. Talk to me, first of all soothe me, console me, be with me in my pain. Let the practical things wait a bit. Show me that it hurts you too. But my worried parents were already deep in the future. The present would wait for them to get around to it.

"Come, Perele," my mother urged me. "Come, rest a bit."

She lay me down on the couch in the living room and covered me with a wool blanket she'd gotten from one of the rooms.

"Stay with me a little, Momme," I requested.

My mother sat above my head and stroked my face, which still had visible signs of tears. I closed my eyes and tried to calm down from the sound of her "shhh... shhh."

---

12   What are we going to do?

When I opened my eyes, dawn had come. The house was still quiet. I knew that soon my father would wake up, and indeed I soon heard water running in my parents' room, and my father came into the living room. "Perele," he said to me when he saw I was awake, "I'll go speak to the rabbi today. We'll see what he has to say."

"Tatte, I don't want to go back there," I pleaded.

"Shhhhh... let's see what the rabbi says."

A little while after he left the house, my siblings came into the living room. The older ones looked at me, and when they saw my wounded face, they continued with what they were doing. I understood them. I looked frightening, and the answers to the questions that had come into their heads would be even scarier. They preferred not to deal with the difficulty and just ignored me. To keep the fear in their hearts and continue on. That's how we were brought up. The little ones, on the other hand, whose world was still innocent, stopped and studied my face with no shame. Shloimeh, one of my younger brothers, ran to my mother, and in a frightened voice, told my mother that Perele has darkness on her face. After him came Yossele and Esti and the three of them looked at my mother as the person who had all the answers.

"Everything's fine, go get dressed fast and come drink and say the prayer, it's getting late."

Her answer satisfied them. They ran to their rooms, and as happens with children, something else had already caught their attention. The darkness they saw in my face was already forgotten. From the room came carefree laughter.

After everyone had gone out, just my mother and I were left alone. My mother was in the kitchen working on her usual chores. Pots clattered, the fridge opened and closed, the chicken soup boiled, and my mother's footsteps chased each other like a queen bee controlling her kingdom with clear awareness of her authority.

"Momme?" I called her. "Come sit with me a bit."

"Perele, I have lots of work to do," she answered immediately.

"Momme, a little. Please."

There was silence in the kitchen and then she came to the living room, wiping her hands on an old towel that bore years of exhausting work. She sat across the table from me.

"Come sit next to me, Momme."

I needed her to be close to me. Someone to console me. An understanding and tolerant heart. I demanded it of her by force, despite her clear reservations. She stood up from the chair wearily and came to sit next to me on the couch. I brought my body close to hers. At that moment, I desperately needed contact. For almost a year, the only touch I had had was that of Menachem Mendel. He had no tenderness or affection or any other positive emotion. He had evil, pent-up lust, contempt and violence.

"Momme, hug me," I requested.

My mother put her head down and her fingers pressed against the dirty towel.

"Momme, please."

A few seconds went by, and then she got up from her place and said, "I'm sorry, Perele," and ran off to her room.

I remained alone in the living room, in the noiseless house. I was filled with loneliness, stronger than ever, and to that was now added the insight that here, in my childhood home, I would not find what I was looking for. The thought filled me with deep sadness. "I'm alone," I said out loud, and imagined that someone had heard me. The tears ran down my face in streams, and my body trembled. Self-pity flooded me like a river overflowing.

Eight

In the evening, my father came home and said that tomorrow we would meet with the rabbi, and he would tell us what to do. And then he added casually, "Maybe you'll return home, Perele? Menachem Mendel is probably worried."

I was so shocked that I couldn't say a word. My father sat down in front of me and continued, "Look, Perele, every couple has its problems. Menachem Mendel is not a bad person. He's probably sorry about what he did. A woman needs to be beside her husband. Go back home and tomorrow we'll go together to the rabbi."

My rage was so strong, I found it hard to respond. "Tatte," I began after I'd calmed down a bit. "Do you want to know what really happened?" I saw that he was embarrassed and that he preferred not to know. I decided not to have mercy on him.

"Tatte, do you want to hear what happened?" I persisted.

He shifted uneasily in his chair. I was engulfed in my emotions. I didn't want to take his feelings into consideration. I desperately wanted a little understanding from him, a little hint of unconditional fatherly love, but all I saw across from me was a Hassid who had a problem or who didn't want to deal with an incident that undermined the tranquility of his life governed by the special strict laws observed by our community.

My father was silent. The two of us sat for a few minutes in silence. When I realized that he wasn't planning to answer me, I got up and without saying anything, I left the place where I had had the mistaken idea that I would find consolation and refuge. On the way home, thoughts ran through my head. I walked slowly and for a moment I was tempted to leave everything behind and continue walking to where my legs would take me. To leave the neighborhood, my disappointing family, my violent husband, everything that hugged me in a vise grip, and check whether outside of that life there was another life. Deep inside I knew there was, but I still wasn't ready to check it out, and certainly not ready to join it. Outside the field, outside the library, which was a kind of borderless parallel universe, a world of imagination where everything was possible—there was nothing of value or meaning in my world that made it worth my staying there. The uncompromising rules and regulations, the constant fear of transgressions and sins, the family, the relationships, the great fear of touching the opposite gender and temptation—all these filled me with great sorrow. Inside, deep, deep inside of me, I knew that I was destined for something else, but my cowardly consciousness prevented this recognition from rising to the surface. The feeling of missed opportunity filled me, though I didn't know what exactly I was missing.

The apartment was dark when I got back. For a moment I hoped that Menachem Mendel wasn't there, but the snoring that came from the bedroom shattered my hopes. He had gone to sleep as if nothing had happened. His sleep was not disturbed by a troubled conscience or worry. I tiptoed into the room. Menachem Mendel lay on his back and the hairs of his mustache waved up and down to the rhythm of his breathing. Just the look of him disgusted me. The thought went through my head that if I'd only decide, I'd be able to end all that suffering with the thrust of a knife. The thought upset me so much that I quickly left the room. I went into the quiet living room, upset by the thoughts passing through my head. Perele, I said to myself, what's happening with you? Where have you gotten yourself to? And as the questions multiplied, the rage pent-up inside of me increased. I felt that I had to release it, that if I didn't, I would explode. I grabbed the first thing next to me and hurled it at the wall in front of me. I took the fruit bowl that adorned the table and hurled it to the floor. The shards of my life were scattered all over the shiny floor, an expression of the pain and fracture I felt inside.

Suddenly I felt I wasn't alone. I turned my head. Menachem Mendel stood in the doorway to the living room, leaning on the doorpost. A narrow smile graced his face. He said nothing, made no noise. The scornful, contemptuous smile stretched across his face like a sword stuck in my heart. At that moment I felt so humiliated, weightless, and worthless. His smile widened a bit and his eyes shot poison arrows that penetrated my armor. The contempt in his eyes met my desperation and what little self-respect I had left. I bent down and grabbed a sharp pottery fragment. I ran to him and raised my hand to hit him, to stab the pain that I'd carried for almost a year. Actually, for years. The stares I'd received in my youth, the dismissive attitude of my teachers, the distancing of my friends, my differentness, and the feeling that I had been born in a place that I didn't belong to and that was wrong for me. I wanted to get revenge on the pain, to feel the relief that comes after revenge. I wanted to feel life, my life, my heart beating and my muscles stretching. I wanted to return myself to myself.

I raised my arm and brought it down straight into his hand which grabbed it hard. His eyes burned from something. From passion, hate, a feeling of absolute control. For seconds we stared at each other and our looks were full of emotions mixed like a stew in a boiling cauldron. Finally, he pushed me down to the floor with both hands like a sack of potatoes. My hands, which I used to break my fall, were injured. Blood seeped out and stained my white shirt. My hands were slit, and red welled in the cracks like veins on a leaf. Before I knew what was happening, my hands still red with blood, Menachem Mendel lay down on me and raped me again in his madness. His eyes did not meet mine and the movements of his body were like a hammer forcing a nail into its intended place. The pain was unbearable. I screamed, kicked, yelled his name, but nothing stopped him until he spilled his sperm, got off me, and disappeared into the bedroom.

I couldn't stay there, in that hurtful and painful place. I got up from the floor, leaving blood stains where I'd lain, staggered toward the door and went out. The cold air met my burning face and cooled it a bit. I took a deep breath and drew a little cold air into my anguished soul. I walked down the silent dark street, my head empty of thoughts. I walked and walked. At first with no direction or destination, and then after what seemed to me an eternity, I reached the open empty place where I felt more at home than anywhere in the world. I had no idea what time it was, if it was still evening or already night. I ambled up to my little hill and sat on the damp earth. The city lights I'd left behind sparkled not far from where I was sitting. I looked left at the garages. Here and there, dim lights were on. Most of the area was dark. I put my hands on the damp ground. The cool dampness relieved the pain in my hands a bit. I hugged my knees to my chest and leaned my head on them. The pictures and sounds of the previous hours haunted me and pounded in my head at an uneven, deafening pace. Like thousands of hammers. My helpless parents, my evasive older brothers and sisters, my violent husband. Is this how my life would look from now on? I asked myself again and again.

I took the Perele that I knew and put her in front of me, and wondered where she had disappeared, where my real personality had sunk, and how I would find it again. I found myself talking out loud. Since there was no one next to me, I looked up to the sky and asked the Almighty why he had put me in such a confusing place. Was he trying me? Was there an objective that would become clear later on? Was he testing my capabilities? My head was bursting with questions that I had no answers for. I was like a fish swimming in a stormy sea, and passing by me were remnants of objects and scraps of food, half-eaten fish, filth that had spilled, fragments of shipwrecks—and he didn't know what all that meant. 'Why?' I jumped at the sound of the voice.

"What are you doing here?" He sounded truly worried.

The transition from loneliness to being in his presence was too sharp for me. He came over and stood above me. He put a coat on my shoulders and offered his hand to help me get up.

"Come," he coaxed.

I put out my hand, still silent. I didn't feel any fear or embarrassment from his touch and didn't try to avoid it. He helped me get up, hesitantly wrapped my shoulders in his arms, and when he realized I was not resisting, he began to walk us toward the garages. That whole time we said nothing. He opened the lock and lifted the rolling door, and then gently led me inside and turned on the light. From the surprised expression in his eyes when he looked at me, I understood that my face looked bad. He looked down and saw the bloodstains on my shirt. He disappeared and then came back with a cup of water and a dark work shirt.

"Drink." he commanded.

I gulped from the cup and felt my trembling body start to calm down.

"Take off your shirt and put this on, it'll warm you up."

"Thank you," I mumbled.

He turned his back and waited for me to change my soiled shirt, and then he brought a chair and sat in front of me.

"Do you want to tell me what happened?"

I said nothing for a moment, not because I had any problem with his knowing, but because of the shame I felt over my weakness.

"Some other time," I said. "Not now."

"C'mon," he insisted.

"It's something to do with my husband," I said cryptically.

He continued to sit on the chair and look me straight in the eye, as if my story were written on my eyes and he was reading it now. After a while he got up and went where I couldn't see him. Minutes passed until he returned. There were drops of water on his face and I understood that he had washed it.

"So what are you planning to do now?"

"I don't know," I answered. "Tomorrow I have a meeting with the rabbi, we'll see what will be..."

"You're going by yourself?"

"No, my father's going with me."

"I see."

"I'm going," I said after an awkward silence. It seemed like there was nothing left to be said. Every sentence would seem silly and superfluous after the intimacy of those moments.

"So come, I'll walk with you," he said. When he saw my surprised expression he added, "At least until you cross the field."

I nodded. After he locked the garage, we walked silently side by side. Every once in a while, his shoulder touched mine and I would move a bit away from him.

We got to the edge of the field, where the street joined it to the edge of the neighborhood where the apartment was. I stopped and whispered, "Just up to here. I'll continue alone."

"Are you sure?" I heard real concern in his voice.

"Yes, it's okay, I live very close to here."

"Go, I'll wait for you a while."

I smiled weakly and started to move away from him. I turned around once and saw him standing in the same place, without taking his eyes off me.

I smiled to myself without understanding why. My mood was different from when I had left the apartment a few hours earlier. When I went inside, Menachem Mendel was fast asleep. At that moment I thanked the Almighty for the prohibition of sleeping in the same bed. The meter and a half that separated our beds turned into light years between me and the figure sleeping with me in the same room.

Nine

The next day, I met up with my father and we went together to Rabbi Weiss's office. A woman whose hair was covered with a high turban greeted us at the door and led us to the rabbi's office. The room was modest, with no superfluous objects. The table the rabbi leaned on was in disarray. On the wall above his head, hung a picture of the Hassidic leader who looked down on us. A gray metal filing cabinet stood next to the rabbi, and in front of it was a window covered by a curtain. One of the curtain rods was threatening to leave the wall.

We sat in front of the rabbi, on the other side of the table. The room smelled musty like the inside of a cave that had never seen the rays of the sun. The rabbi cleared his throat and said, "*Vos frage*[13]?"

"Rabbi," my father said with his head down somewhat, "*Dos* Perele[14]."

"*Vos mit* Perele[15]?"

And then my father laid out the problem. He said that it had been hard to find a husband for me because I had all kinds of modern thoughts in my head, and finally they had managed to find a boy from a good family, a learned Torah scholar, who was now learning in the *yeshiva* and was meticulous about observing even the most stringent commandments.

"*Gut*," approved the rabbi.

"But," my father continued, and it seemed that his voice was getting

---

13 What's the problem?

14 This is Perele.

15 What's with Perele?

weaker. "Sometimes he gets angry at her and hits her. Here, see, honorable Rabbi, yesterday he hit a lot." My father turned to me and asked me to pick up my head and allow the rabbi to have a look at my injured face.

The rabbi looked at me for the first time. Before that he hadn't looked at me at all, as if I didn't exist. He looked at my face a few seconds and looked back at my father.

My father was silent. The rabbi thought a few minutes with his head bent over a paper that was laid on the table in front of him and ruled, "You must be more *nochgeber*[16]."

"What?" I asked.

The rabbi ignored me and continued speaking to my father. He said that a woman must be more sensitive to the needs of her husband. If she sees that he's in a bad mood, she should not talk to him. If he is very hungry, serve him food on time. The husband must be in a good mood for his learning. When he comes home, the house must be clean and organized and the woman must receive him pleasantly and be devoted to him. He was sure, he said, that my husband had no evil intentions. It was possible that on that day something had disturbed him greatly, and my behavior had been insensitive, and that's what had caused the harsh reaction.

"Honorable Rabbi," I interrupted him, "in any case it is not permitted to react like that. And besides that, I did nothing bad. He doesn't talk to me at all; he doesn't ask me anything. He…"

I suddenly felt my father's hand on my leg. He tapped it in an attempt to stop me from talking.

The rabbi was quiet and waited for my father to get me to be quiet. He finally got up and said, "*Men zol heren nor gute bsoirois,*[17]" and left the room.

I stayed in the chair, stuck like cement.

My father got up and urged me to get up. We left there with nothing. The woman with the high turban wasn't there when we left.

The next morning, I felt like I had become a few inches shorter. My back was bent, and my head was facing down. I had no energy to stand up

16 Forgiving

17 We should hear only good tidings.

straight. My body was heavy as lead and my steps became slow and weary. I'd aged before my time. I was just eighteen and a half, but I felt like an old lady whose past and present left little room for her future. I was in despair. My father's submissive face when we sat with the rabbi bothered me greatly. When he'd suggested we consult with the rabbi, that had given me hope, maybe a solution would be found for my situation. But what happened at that meeting filled me with desperation.

The next day, my mother came for a visit. That was maybe the second or third time she'd come to the apartment specially to see me. Her movements were clumsy, and I saw that she was very uncomfortable.

"Come, Momme, sit. Do you want some tea?"

She nodded.

I brought her a cup of tea and she put it on the table. She held a white handkerchief that she was rolling between her fingers. I put my hand on hers and she stroked it firmly. "My Perele," she said suddenly, and heavy tears flowed from her eyes. This was the first time I'd seen my mother cry. She'd always been strong and tough. She'd never shown weakness or revealed pain. I was scared. I wanted her to be strong and in control, but at the same time, I wanted to see in her vulnerability and compassion. I was perplexed. I waited quietly for her to regain her composure.

"You were always different," she began. "From the time you were born, I could see that you weren't like the other children. When all the other little girls played, you would run and play with the boys, and as much as we tried to dissuade you from that, you persisted just to spite us. When you got a little older, we would criticize and be angry at you, but your behavior only got worse. You would escape the apartment without our hearing and join the neighborhood boys. People started to comment to us about your behavior, and one day even the rabbi scolded us. But the angrier we got, the more you persisted. You would leave home for school and fold your skirt up, to make it shorter. The teachers got angry and called us several times to come into the class, but that didn't bother you. You continued doing whatever you wanted..."

I tried to read between the lines of what she was saying. Did they feel only anger, guilt, disappointment and frustration, or maybe, just maybe, appreciation was hiding somewhere in some abandoned corner?

"One day, when you were about fourteen, Pessia the matchmaker came to our house. If you remember, she was our neighbor from one floor down, until they left the neighborhood. She asked to speak with me alone and she said that we had to take really good care of you, because if you continued the way you were, there wouldn't be a good match for you. 'People are already talking,' she warned me. Her words distressed me greatly. And then we started to argue a lot, you and I. Everything you did seemed to me to be against the Torah and our way of life, and I was very angry at you. The whole time I was thinking about the shame you were bringing upon me. When I walked in the street, I put my head down so that people wouldn't talk to me. I was so embarrassed. I started to leave the house as little as possible. Because of that, I would send you, the older children, on all kinds of errands. So that I wouldn't have to explain and make excuses."

Her crying became stronger. She wiped her tears with a handkerchief until it was completely wet.

"Stop, Momme, that's enough. You don't have to talk. Everything's okay." It was hard for me to bear her crying and distress. I felt a vague pain in my stomach and then I understood completely the anguish I had caused my parents, especially my mother. The thought flashed through my head that I was a selfish person. I thought only of myself without seeing how my behavior affected others.

"Stop, Momme, you're right... I'm selfish. I didn't think about you at all... I promise that from now on, everything will be all right. You won't suffer from me anymore..."

"Shushhh Perele!" she said.

I looked at her and what I saw in her face completely amazed me. There was compassion, understanding, and reconciliation. I saw no anger or disappointment. I kept looking at her in wonder and waited in silence for her to say something. I didn't want to ruin the moment. I wondered if I saw in her face what I thought I saw.

And she went on. "I always spoke with the Holy One, Blessed Be He, and asked why he had made you like that." Was he putting me to a test? Had I done something bad? For years I thought I had sinned and tried to find out what that sin was. There were days, Perele, when I hated you. That I was sorry I had given birth to you..."

I couldn't stand her words. I burst out in loud crying and hid my head between my knees. Her words stabbed me like nails. All the pain and rejection I'd felt over the years, both from my family and my friends, came out now. I was releasing the pain I had carried with me ever since I could remember myself. The endless internal war that took place inside of me between my internal desire and the need to be part of the community. The thoughts and deeds that had hurt the people most important to me. The inability to compromise for very long. Everything was coming out then, with my mother crying there. Our tears mixed until I didn't know where her pain began and my pain ended. The future suddenly seemed impossible.

"Perele," I heard her voice from the other side of the screen of tears, "*meine sheine tochter*[18]."

I looked up and was submerged in a loving look I had never before seen on her face. At that moment, I remembered one of the Torah classes where the teacher Leah went over again and again the verse from Ezekiel, "...and make yourselves a new heart and a new spirit...[19]" She had us repeat the verse after her maybe ten times. It was after she had been forced to scold us again and again for the noise we made in class. My mother had changed right before my eyes. No more distance and tight facial muscles, but softness and love. As if her locked heart had opened and invited me to step inside. I kept looking at her, refusing to believe what I saw, and thinking I was mistaken. She took my hand in hers again, and this time put it on her wet cheeks.

"I'm sorry, Perele," I heard.

"What?" I whispered.

"I'm sorry and am asking you to forgive me."

"Momme?"

This wasn't my mother. This was another woman holding me, who was strange and unfamiliar. I was a little afraid, and a little hopeful.

---

18 My beautiful daughter

19 Ezekiel 18:31

"Perele, my little girl. I have done you a great disservice. All the time I asked you to be someone different that would be easy for me to live with. I never thought about you. I thought only of myself. I was afraid of what they'd say, afraid of the rabbi, the truth is, I was afraid of everyone. But it's not your fault. I wanted to change you so it would be easier for me. And you, *mein zol*[20], you tried. I know you tried, but fear controlled me, and I didn't see you at all."

She stopped and let out a long sigh. She rested my head on her chest and covered it with her hands. We sat like that, wrapped in a hug that was foreign to me but suddenly completely natural. I also let out short sighs. One of pain, another of concealment, another of confusion, and another long one of relief.

---

20 My soul

Ten

One evening, a week after my mother's visit, Menachem Mendel informed me that we had a meeting with the rabbi the next day. "For what?" I asked and felt my muscles tensing. For a moment it seemed that he was going to leave the room without answering me, but then he turned toward me and said, "Because you are not managing to have children."

"We've been there already. How will the rabbi help now?" I asked him and looked right into his cold eyes. After my mother's visit, I'd felt more daring, like a turtle whose head was emerging from his armor when he felt the threat against him had been lifted. Menachem Mendel walked toward me and then stopped, as if backing down. "The rabbi will tell us why you cannot conceive."

"Maybe it's you who cannot have children?" I protested, ignoring the coming danger.

The blow was quick and sharp. My face flew to the side, and my lips trembled from the momentum of his hand. For a moment I rocked in place, and then I put my hand on the wall and stabilized myself. My husband's face was covered with red dots of rage.

"So you're a real *giboyre*[21]," he hissed and then left the room.

The next day he came back from the *yeshiva* earlier than usual. The meeting was set for the early evening. Outside, the world went on as always. People went in and out of stores; mothers stood on the sidewalk and rocked strollers, trying to calm their cranky babies; buses went by trailing behind

---

21 Heroine

them the sounds of escaping exhaust. We crossed the busy street. Menachem Mendel took quick steps in front of me and I trudged behind him like a servant after his master. He held an opaque bag in one hand, and in the other, he directed the drivers to slow down while we jaywalked across the street. When we entered the rabbi's office, a different woman greeted us from the one we had met the last time. She smiled pleasantly at me as I passed her, and completely ignored Menachem Mendel who had entered before me.

The rabbi instructed us to sit. The room looked darker to me. Like the last visit, the rabbi ignored me and turned his face and body toward Menachem Mendel.

"*Vos gishein*[22], Menachem Mendel?"

"Children," Menachem Mendel sighed.

"*Vos mit kinderlach*[23]?"

"My wife hasn't gotten pregnant," Menachem Mendel continued.

Also this time the rabbi asked how many times a month we had marital relations, and Menachem Mendel answered twice a month, not on the unclean days of course. "How is it done?" asked the rabbi, and I felt my cheeks burning. The conversation on what was happening in my bedroom was held between two wheeler-dealers. There was no feeling or discretion. Everything was revealed to the rabbi. There was no border that stopped him from discussing the most intimate deed between a man and a woman.

Menachem Mendel described to the rabbi how we had relations, and the whole time the rabbi nodded his head and stroked his long beard, as if thinking about some matter in the Talmud. Suddenly he turned to me and asked the same question that he'd asked at our first visit. Did I have relations with full intention. His question caught me by surprise, and a few seconds passed before I regained composure and nodded my head. The rabbi was not convinced by my answer and asked again if I thought about the commandment that I was doing when we had sexual relations. Whether I fulfilled with all my heart the way of the Hassidic leader. Before I answered,

---

22 What's happening?

23 What about children?

I suddenly heard the loud voice of Menachem Mendel. "She doesn't!" he yelled. The rabbi and I turned to look at him. Menachem Mendel picked up the opaque bag he had brought, opened it, and took out a blue man's shirt. I felt an earthquake under me. My face burned and my body shook. It was the shirt I had received from Dan, who'd tried to protect me from the cold on that awful day. I had forgotten about it completely.

"Honorable Rabbi, I found this shirt in the house!" he announced. He was quiet for a few seconds and then added, looking at me, "and it's not mine."

The rabbi looked back at me. There was revulsion and contempt on his face. "Mrs. Friedman, is what your husband says correct?"

"No." I managed to whisper. The rabbi waited for me to continue explaining.

My indecision lasted only a few seconds. I felt my body stop shaking. My cheeks still burned, but the heat that spread through my body strengthened my determination to reveal the things I had kept to myself. "Honorable Rabbi, Menachem Mendel raped me," I hissed with determination.

The rabbi looked back at Menachem Mendel. It seemed to me that during that fraction of a second, they shared a hidden smile. I turned off my wild imagination and continued describing the events of that day to the rabbi. The rabbi listened to me. From time to time, he put his head down and then looked up at me. From time to time, he exchanged glances with Menachem Mendel and then again looked at me. I was so engrossed in describing that day and the rising pain, that I didn't notice the hints flying around me like flies swarming on piles of garbage.

I didn't feel the tears making tracks down on my cheeks until I stopped speaking. There was silence. The rabbi cleared his throat, looked at Menachem Mendel, and then asked, "And the shirt?"

I had completely forgotten about the shirt. I had been so imprisoned in the memory of the rape that I'd forgotten it had all begun with the shirt.

"After what happened," I tried to explain, "I fled from the house. Someone had pity on me and gave me a shirt because it was rainy and cold outside."

"Who was that 'someone'?" asked the rabbi, and he stressed the word someone. I felt a hint of mockery, but I ignored it.

"Someone that I don't know," I replied weakly.

"And you were willing to wear the shirt of a man you didn't know?"

I realized that the conversation was totally not about the rape. The rape had become a side issue. The conversation was about me and my behavior. Nothing I could say would open his blind eyes and sealed heart to see my pain as a woman and a wife. That wasn't the place I would receive compassion and understanding. A husband raping his wife? Complete nonsense.

I looked at both men. Their contempt for me floated around the room even in their silence. I got up, snatched the shirt that was sitting on my husband's knees, turned around, and left. I don't know why I took the shirt. It was a mistake, because it gave the rabbi absolute proof that I was a rebellious wife. Everything that Menachem Mendel had said about me was right. It was a childish act, I know, but I had to feel, if only in some small gesture, that they hadn't wiped me away completely.

I walked home indifferently. My feet carried me. I didn't see people looking at me. I didn't see people hurrying home, and I didn't hear Menachem Mendel's steps walking behind me at a safe distance.

I entered the apartment and headed quickly for the bedroom. I put the blue shirt on my bed and lay on it heavily. I was worn out and felt empty of pain and feeling. I closed my eyes and fell asleep immediately. In my dreams, I met angels that circled around me, white wings spread. I heard the beating of their wings, and the sound made me calm. As if someone had wrapped me in soft white down and hugged me with endless love. When I woke up, I noticed that my arms were hugging my body. I remembered in a panic that one of the angels who approached me more than the others was in the figure of the young man. The owner of the blue shirt.

Menachem Mendel's bed was empty. The apartment was quiet. Even the refrigerator that would sometimes make crackling noises was silent. I got up from the bed and walked quietly into the living room. It was empty. I turned on the light in the kitchen. The table was clean and tidy. Menachem Mendel was not in the apartment. I hadn't heard him come in and didn't know he had left. I breathed freely. I made myself something to eat and made a decision.

Menachem Mendel didn't come back in the morning. Apparently, he had gone from the place he had slept at night straight to the *yeshiva*. I walked the familiar and beloved way, and in no time arrived at my favorite place, the library. Without hesitation, I approached the librarian, my friend. She was giving an explanation to one of the library members, and when she looked up, she had a warm smile on her face.

"Perele!' she said happily. My name played on her lips like a favorite song. She got up, walked around the counter, and hugged me with her thick arms. I so needed that hug that I didn't control the tears from running freely down my face. What a wonderful place, I thought.

"Why are you crying? My dear, did something happen?" she asked with concern.

I shook my head no, and then said, "I'm just happy to be here." After a few seconds I added words that I'd never said. "I've missed you."

"Me too!" she answered immediately, took my hand in hers and pulled me after her. On the table in the back room, there was a new pile of books. "These are yours," she said and pointed at the tower. "These are old books that I discarded from the library and now they're yours."

"Mine-mine?"

"Just yours," she emphasized and smiled. "Sit down here. I'll close the door so you can have privacy, and no one will bother you."

At that moment I understood the meaning of the word "happiness." The feeling that filled me was the complete opposite of the feelings I'd had the previous day. Openness vs blindness. Love vs hate. Caring vs indifference. I found out there was a universe different from the one I'd lived in since my birth. A world that I'd always heard was bad, that they'd turned into a monster. My body still lived in the familiar world, but one foot had crossed a line and had passed into another world, foreign, threatening but tempting. Frightening, but at the same time instilling hope.

The closed door made me feel confident. I looked around the bare white-walled room. Except for the table with the piles of books and the chair next to it, there was nothing in the room. I stretched out my hand and stroked the books I so yearned for. I could sit for hours and just look at them and subsist on the enjoyment I got from the feeling that they were mine and only mine. I could read them, I could rip the pages, throw them on the floor, or hug them. I could do whatever I wanted and no one had the right to say anything about what I did. Because they were mine.

Finally, I picked a book that was on the bottom of the pile. *Little Women* by Louisa May Alcott. It was an old copy with a mostly ripped binding and ends worn away. I leafed through the yellow pages and brought the old book up to my nose. It had that old book smell. The smell of years of dust build up, but for me, it was the smell of citrus flowers that came from the last remaining trees at the end of the neighborhood where my parents lived. I breathed the old fragrance deep inside and sneezed a few times from the dust. I laughed out loud and opened the book to the first page. Time, which sometimes stands still, flashed by like a ray of lightning quickly crossing the night sky. There was a knock at the door, and my friend the librarian told me that it was already evening. I was so absorbed in the book that I couldn't put it down. I asked if she could wait a few minutes so I could finish the chapter.

"Of course," she smiled.

Even before she closed the door, I was again deep in the house of the March sisters. I could imagine how each of them looked. How they were dressed. The color clothes each one wore. I imagined Laurie, their besotted neighbor. I was completely carried away into that period and into the sisters' house. I shared moments of pain and happiness with each one of them. I was jealous of the love they received and for a moment thought that loves like those described in the book did not exist in real life. I closed the cover on the world I had drifted into and returned to my threatening world, knowing that I had committed the sin of curiosity, and aware that retribution would arrive quickly.

Before I opened the apartment door, it seemed like I heard voices inside. I went inside and was surprised to find Menachem Mendel's parents sitting on the couch in the living room.

"Where were you?" Menachem Mendel asked before I could say hello to his parents. "You see?" he said to his mother. "I told you!"

His mother got up from the couch and came over to me. "Perele, we've been waiting for you for a long time," she said. The accusation burst from her words like a fish jumping out of a calm sea. I chose not to respond and asked, "What are you doing here? Do you want something to drink?"

"No, thank you," she answered. "Come, sit with us, we want to talk to you."

"Just a minute," I answered and went into the bedroom.

I stood and took a deep breath. My arms hugged my body because there was no one else who would do that. I stood like that for a few seconds until I felt more relaxed. I took another breath and went back to the living room. Menachem Mendel's mother patted the couch, indicating that I should sit next to her. Menachem Mendel and his father sat across from us, on the other side of the table.

"Perele, Menachem Mendel tells us that you sometimes disappear from the house, like now, and he doesn't know where you go. You know that it's not okay for a married woman to disappear without telling her husband where she is. At this time of day, when he returns from the *yeshiva*, there should already be food on the table."

"And what else does he tell you?" I asked and looked her right in the eye.

Out of the corner of my eye I saw that Menachem Mendel was shifting uncomfortably in his chair. I knew without looking at him that his lips were stretched into a narrow stripe and his hands were white from the effort to remain calm.

"What do you mean?" his mother asked.

"Did he also tell you that he hits me every chance he gets? Has he also told you that he smashes objects in the house? Has he told you about his violence toward me in the bedroom?"

Until that moment I hadn't paid much attention to his father, who'd sat quietly from the time I came through the door. Suddenly he got up and went out of the apartment, slamming the door loudly behind him. In the living room there was silence. I looked at Menachem Mendel. He rolled his eyes and then gave me the familiar look that said, "Just you wait..." His mother remained seated, as if she hadn't heard what I said. Her head was down. She didn't look at her son at all.

"Chana," I asked her again, "has he told you that? Did you know?

Chana picked at her head. I could see the tears welling in her eyes. She stretched out her hand and squeezed my arm firmly. Then she got up, took a quick glance at her son, and left. It was just the two of us in the threatening silence. Finally, Menachem Mendel got up, walked around the table and approached me. With one hand he grasped my cheeks and pressed hard. My face was contorted from the squeeze, but my eyes stayed dry. He brought his face within millimeters of mine. My eyes saw only the mouth that so disgusted me, and that mouth was threatening me, saying that I should be careful, because there was no one who would protect me.

"I can do whatever I want to you..." he hissed, and his grip tightened until I felt like my jaw was almost coming apart. His lips tightened to the size of a sheet of paper, and then he let go. My twisted mouth slowly returned to normal. I knew that in the morning I would find two purple bruises where his fingers had dug into my face. I threw my body on the sofa and waited for the pain to pass. Only then did I remember that I had gone to the library to tell the librarian about my decision, but the excitement from the pile of books waiting for me had put that out of my mind completely.

I would need to go there again, I told myself. I knew that neither the pain in my jaw nor the threatening look would hold me back.

ELEVEN

It was the beginning of the Hebrew month of Adar. The winter moved on in favor of spring. Expectation was in the air. Maybe only I felt that. Once again there was no need for heavy jackets, and the body felt light and airy. Nice weather hugged those who left their homes. People talked to each other in the street. The stores were open until the late evening. A sense of cheerfulness pervaded the streets and infused the heart with hope.

That morning I decided to return to the library to speak with Sophie, but my decision changed when my foot hit the pavement. Instead of turning right toward the library, my legs took me in the opposite direction. A strange excitement gripped me and hastened my stride. I ran across the street and continued like that, until I got to the field. The familiar beloved colors greeted me happily. Yellow flowers, some without petals, and scalps of white hair above green stalks—all these created a spectacular dense carpet. I stood and breathed in the view before my eyes. I looked forward and continued walking. I crossed the field, careful not to run over the upright flowers, until I got to the garage. I hadn't thought about how I would justify my visit. My legs carried me inside. I stood in the doorway to get used to the dim light inside. Someone passed by me and mumbled casually, without looking at my face, "He's inside." I walked in.

He looked up and smiled immediately. "I've been waiting for you," he said. I felt as if that was the most natural thing.

I went over to the car. His friends nodded their heads hesitantly at me and continued talking among themselves. I stood next to him as if that's what happened every day.

"How do you feel?" he asked so that only I could hear him.

"Okay, now I'm okay," I answered and then asked what they were doing.

"We're trying to find a solution for something."

"Why?"

"Well, this car was manufactured in the 1970s, and it came without air conditioning. We're trying to find where we can position the air conditioning compressor under the hood. We had a few ideas, but they didn't work out."

"Show me the compresher," I said.

"Compressor," he corrected me, with a mischievous smile.

"Do you see here? This part is called the alternator. It charges the car's battery. Here, this is the battery," he pointed at a rectangular bloc. "The alternator is connected to the battery with this cable and now we're debating how to connect the compressor..."

I followed his hand movements. I saw the parts he was pointing at, and suddenly recalled a present my parents had brought us when we were little. We didn't receive many presents when we were children, so I remembered that present well. It was a block, and on it were squares in different colors. It was called a Rubik's cube. We had to arrange the squares according to the colors, such that each side of the block would have only squares of the same color. I remember my father handing the block to my brother and I grabbed it from his hand and ran to the stairs. I sat there and within minutes had managed to arrange the cube into six separate colors. My brother, who tried later to arrange the squares, did not manage to do it until I taught him how. Like then, when I looked now at the parts of the engine in front of me, I knew exactly where each belonged.

"Maybe you could move the alternator to the other side of the engine, and then mount the compressor where the alternator was? And then connect this belt to both the compressor and the alternator so that it operates both of them..."

"What? Wait a minute... Motti, come here quick," he called to someone who was on the other side of the garage. When Motti came, my young man repeated what I had said.

"I don't believe it... why didn't we think of that?" said the young man with a smile. "How did you come up with that?"

"It wasn't me... she did," he said and pointed at me.

Motti looked at me in appreciation. "Great job!" he said.

"Thank you," I answered and felt my cheeks blushing.

"What's your name?" he asked, and I saw Dan staring at me. Both of them awaited my response.

"Perele. My name is Perele."

"Nice to meet you, Perele, I'm—"

"I know, Motti," I said and smiled at him.

I noticed that Motti did not offer me his hand; he accepted my answer and didn't ask any more questions. I thanked him for that.

"Very, *very* nice to meet you, Perele," said Dan, "but it seems like 'Why' suits you better..."

I smiled at him.

"So, you find all this stuff about cars interesting?"

"I guess anything that has parts that need to be arranged interests me. Somehow I see the big picture in my head, and I know where everything goes."

"Great, so you have a great reason to come here sometimes," he smiled and then looked serious. "The truth is, I thought about you a lot," he said.

"Why?"

"I was worried about you."

I knew what he was referring to. The last time we'd met, he'd seen me in the depths of my humiliation. Bashed up and in pain. I looked down. For some reason, I felt responsible for what had happened. And maybe to some extent that was correct.

"It's all right," I said, attempting to avoid the subject. I preferred to keep my different worlds separate. I didn't want to mix them. When I was in the garage, I felt great, and didn't want to ruin that feeling. The apartment, life with Menachem Mendel, belonged to a completely different world. Separate from this side of my life. There's a world where I suffered, and a new world, of other people, interests, curiosity and a tiny feeling of self-esteem. "I prefer not to talk about it," I said, and turned my back to him.

I looked all around. The place was clean and dirty at the same time. The combination of the two was for me two halves of the same whole. Sometimes there was quiet talking and sometimes yelling. Sometimes there was silence, when the guys bent over the car and thought how to continue with the work, and sometimes there was a loud noise, when they operated the tools. The contrasts between all those things were very interesting to me. They connected with my life, which was also full of contrasts. Something there completed me. I didn't want to leave, but my time was limited, and awareness of that forced me to go.

"Come again!" the young man called after me, and his voice faded as I walked away.

I got home on time. I went straight into the kitchen and started to prepare lunch. Menachem Mendel liked to eat fresh food every day. Once I had given him food from the previous day, and he got angry and hurled the plate to the floor. After that, I made sure to prepare him fresh food every day.

*

On Wednesday, before I left the apartment, there was a knock at the door. It was my mother. In one hand she held a shopping cart, and in the other, she wiped the sweat flowing from her face.

"Momme, what are you doing here?" I wondered aloud.

My mother was a pretty heavy woman and climbing up the stairs caused her to breathe heavily and perspire. I took the shopping cart and helped her come in. She sat right down on the couch and waited until she caught her breath. I brought her a glass of cold water and a towel for the sweat. That whole time, she said nothing. When she was breathing normally, I asked her again why she had come. My mother took a deep breath and said she had come to ask how I was. "I'm worried about you," she said and looked right in my eyes, as if looking for answers to questions she didn't dare ask explicitly.

"I'm fine," I assured her.

My mother looked at my face and I knew that she was looking for marks. Since she didn't find anything, she felt a little better.

"Momme, why didn't you tell me you were coming? I would have helped you with the cart."

"It's okay. I was just at the market and decided to come visit you."

Of course I was very happy she had visited, but there was still something strange about her behavior. Something that made me uneasy. Since that day that she'd asked my forgiveness, we'd seen each other two more times when I went to visit them. Each time, my father went out to take care of a few things, and we were left alone. Both times she asked how I was and when I said everything was fine, she continued working in the kitchen. Now she was sitting with me. I noticed her fingers moving restlessly.

"Momme, what's going on?" I asked and felt anxiety creep into my heart.

My mother was quiet for a few seconds and said, "It's Tatte."

"Tatte?" I asked in panic, "What happened to Tatte?"

She sighed and her round belly rose and fell like a pump. "Tatte said that you shouldn't come anymore."

"Shouldn't come where anymore? Where?"

"To us," she answered.

I felt as if I had been kicked in the stomach. "Why?" I asked and my voice became hoarse.

My mother sighed again and said, "He's afraid you'll influence the children."

"I don't understand."

"He's afraid of your modern ideas."

"And what about what Menachem Mendel does to me?"

"Tatte says that you're a married woman now and you have to work it out with Menachem Mendel."

I couldn't believe what I was hearing. "Momme, but Tatte knows that he hits me, he saw!"

My mother was quiet for a long time and said, "Tatte went to Rabbi Weiss, and that's what the rabbi said."

I put my head down. I felt like an innocent prisoner whose family was deserting him without giving him an opportunity to make his case. My father had abandoned me. He, who had begot me, carried me on his shoulders when I was little, provided my sustenance. The one who had found me a husband. He was abandoning me and leaving me to my fate.

"And what do you say, Momme?"

My mother started to cry. I sat next to her quietly and waited.

"What should we do, Perele, what should we do?" she asked.

"I don't know, Momme, what should we do?"

"I'll come to you," she said.

The insult was so powerful that I felt a terrible burning in my throat. "So I shouldn't come to visit you anymore?" I asked, about to burst into tears.

"I'll speak with Tatte," she promised, "I'll convince him."

We both knew that she wouldn't do that, and the promise was empty like a dry stream.

After she left, I sat in the living room and reflected on things. On the one hand, she wanted to support me. She loved me and was concerned about me, but the rules she had been brought up on and lived according to all the years were so deeply ingrained in her that her motherly love was no match for them. To some extent I even pitied her, but only for a moment. Because the thought immediately impaled my head that the children needed to be first. I wasn't a mother yet, but at the base of my being, I knew that a mother was supposed to put her children before anything else. My mother had submitted to fears and demons that haunted her. She allowed them to control her and direct her life as they saw fit. She allowed them to wipe out her personality, her desires, and they controlled her thoughts to the point that her words and lifestyle were theirs. She carried out what had been determined for her without challenging it.

Sadness came down upon me. I knew that my mother wouldn't have the strength to stand by me when I needed her, and the thought intensified my loneliness. It was eleven in the morning. I knew that in two hours, Menachem Mendel would be home to be served his fresh mid-day meal. I would wait until he ate and returned to the *yeshiva*, and then I would go out. In the meantime, I began to organize my orderly home. I moved pillows, rinsed a glass that was in the sink and took out the bag of trash. When I went out, I heard a nearby door slam. I looked up and met the eyes of the young woman that I'd seen a glimpse of a few months before.

"Hi," she greeted me.

"Hi," I returned.

"I'm Sara," she said.

"Perele," I said and started to walk down the stairs with the bag of garbage.

"Do you want to come in for a cup of coffee?" she asked.

I was inclined to decline, but then I said with a smile, "Tea?"

She smiled. "I'll boil the water before you get back."

Warmth. That's what I felt when I entered her place. The blinds were open, and curtains covered the windows, muting the rays of sun that insisted on coming in. Rugs in shades of red and brown were scattered everywhere. Bigger and smaller ones. The furniture was of a dark wood, and on the table there was a vase with fresh flowers that gave off a delicate fragrance. At first I thought that our apartments had different layouts. The walls were cream, and not the usual white. Sara invited me to sit with her in the kitchen. On the white table was a glass with tea for me. The kitchen cabinets, refrigerator, and all the rest of the furniture and electrical appliances in the kitchen were white. In contrast to the dim living room, the kitchen was flooded with light.

"I've seen you several times before, leaving the apartment, but you were in such a hurry, I didn't try to stop you.

"Ohhh..." I murmured and swallowed the warm tea. I didn't know how to have a conversation with someone I'd just met, but it seemed like Sara had no problem with that. She told me about when she'd come to the neighborhood and about the place she had lived before. She spoke with great love about her parents and siblings, and finally she told me a little shyly that two weeks before, she'd found out that she was pregnant. A wide smile warmed her face and revealed beautiful white teeth surrounded by perfect lips.

"And what about you?" she asked.

"Me?"

"Yes, when did you move here, and where do your parents live?"

I told her where my parents lived and how many brothers and sisters I had. That was the easy part. I was afraid she'd ask more personal questions and I started to feel a little uncomfortable. I quickly finished the tea and Sara begged me to try the cookies she'd baked that morning. I took one in my hand and promised her that I'd try it at home. I got up and started to walk to the door. Sara came close to me and before I left, she hugged me and said she was really happy that we'd gotten to know each other, because she had the feeling that we'd be good friends. I smiled and left.

At home, I organized the afternoon meal. I put out a plate for Menachem Mendel and warmed up the food that I'd prepared earlier that morning.

He arrived at exactly one o'clock. As usual, he went to the bathroom, ritually washed his hands, and while he was still mumbling the appropriate prayer[24], he came into the kitchen and sat at his usual place. All that without greeting me or asking how I was. The meal went the same way every day. Menachem Mendel waited for me to serve him, and then he ate in silence. Between courses, I leaned on the counter and waited for him to signal that he was ready for the next course. After he finished, he said grace after meals, wiped his mouth with a towel, and left until evening. Alienation was like a beacon in our apartment. It stood upright and illuminated from afar.

As soon as he closed the door behind him, I put on a sweater and went out. I got to the library in less than ten minutes. I went inside and, as always, the feeling of home surrounded me immediately.

I went up to Sophie, whose head was bent over a notebook, and said hello. Her face lit up when she saw me. As always, she got up from her chair, walked around the counter, and hugged me.

"How are you, Perele?" she asked.

"I'm great," I answered and then asked her the question that had brought me there. "Sophie, can you help me find information about courses to take?"

She lifted her eyebrows and then smiled and said, "With pleasure."

She took my wrist and pulled me to the other end of the library. On the way she asked one of the other employees to fill in for her at the desk. We sat down at a computer. For me, that machine was like the horizon. You can see it, but it's unattainable. I'd seen computers everywhere, but never, not even once, had I typed on a keyboard. For some reason, I was afraid of the computer. I'd always felt that they were meant to be used by people who

---

24 Asher Yatzar - a prayer of thanks and praise to the Holy One who made our body wisely, so it could rid itself of wastes through its orifices while the essential and useful materials remain. The hands are washed and dried before saying the prayer.

were very, very intelligent. Sophie asked me to bring my chair closer and look at the screen.

"You've never worked on a computer?" she asked when she saw my hesitation.

"No. We have no computer at home, and we didn't at my parents' either."

"I see," she said. In that case, I'll explain everything to you as I go along." She typed quickly on the black keys and I couldn't follow her hands. The effort made it hard for me to listen to her explanation. "Google is a search engine," she said. "Tell me what you want, and I'll search for it on the computer.

When she saw my hesitation, she turned her body toward me and asked if I wanted her to find me seminars for school and nursery schoolteachers. I shook my head no.

"I just know that most of the women who work in your community work in those professions," she explained, and when I didn't react, she added, "I see you want something else."

I nodded. It was still hard for me to say what I wanted.

"Maybe make-up classes? Or psychology studies?" she tried.

"I want to work in a garage!" I blurted.

"In a garage? What garage?" she asked, her eyes as big as two bubbles.

"A garage for car repairs."

There was silence for a few moments.

"Are you serious?" she asked finally.

"Yes," I said in a barely audible voice.

"Where'd you get that idea? Do you know someone who works at a garage?"

"Yes and no..." I answered ambiguously.

Sophie waited. She looked at me in silence. She was sensitive enough to know that she had to enable me to find the words that would explain my unusual request.

"You're right, most women in our community—the ones who work—do work as nursery school or schoolteachers. But it never interested me to work with children. I always dreamed of something else. Work that I could do with my hands. Something that required creative thinking. Otherwise..."

Sophie folded her arms and looked at me for a long time. And then she said, to my surprise, "It's not easy to grow up in a place where you're considered different."

Her words surprised me greatly. She'd touched on the exact most painful spot of my existence. I didn't answer, and just smiled weakly. She freed her hands and squeezed my arms. That simple gesture moved me. I swallowed the tears that threatened to burst like a raging cascade, and took a deep breath. It seemed that Sophie noticed how I felt, because she said abruptly in a practical voice, "Let's start searching."

She typed quickly. Pages came onto the screen and went. Sometimes she moved quickly through pages, and sometimes she read them carefully. It almost seemed like she had forgotten I was there. She mumbled words to herself that I couldn't quite identify, said "No, that's not appropriate" a lot, and sometimes got angry at herself.

Finally, she looked at me. "Here, I've found three places that might be interesting for you. Two are in the area, and one is in Tel Aviv. What do you think?"

"No, not in Tel Aviv. I can't go that far," I answered.

"Okay, so these are the places. Here, write down these two telephone numbers."

She gave me paper and pen, but I didn't take them.

"Do you want me to call?" she asked gently.

I nodded.

In fifteen minutes, I had all the information I needed. I left the library, my hands guarding the pocket that calmly held the information I had received. I felt as if I were guarding a rare stone, and was careful that my body not touch or rub against anything. I knew I had taken the first step. Now I had to think how to continue, as every step had to be taken carefully, without anyone around me knowing what I was doing.

TWELVE

On the 13th of the Hebrew month Tammuz, I found out I was pregnant. I remember that day well, including the exact time. For the weeks preceding that day, I'd felt terrible. I'd thought it was because of the cold I'd had in the middle of summer. Outside it was burning. With the wig on my head, the thick stockings and long sleeves that covered every bit of skin, it was impossible to walk around outside, especially in the daytime. I stayed home most of the time and read over and over the paper with all the information I needed about the study programs. Until that day, I hadn't dared to register, plus I needed money. To my dismay, I saw how the dream I'd woven was falling apart. My bad mood and bad cold made me want to vomit. Several times a day, I ran to the bathroom, but nothing came out. On the other hand, staying home alone was good for me. But it meant I was very lonely. There were times when I thought about visiting the neighbor, my new friend, but her good mood and the light in her apartment were not right for me at that time.

That day, I'd thrown up for the first time. I had unbearable stomach cramps and needed something to relieve the pain. I went out to the neighborhood pharmacy. There were a few women in front of me in line. Two of them looked pregnant. I watched one of them make circles on her belly with her hand, and when I looked at her face, I saw that it was smooth and calm as if nothing in the world could affect her mood.

The other obviously pregnant woman was indifferent to what was going on around her. It seemed as if she only wanted to take what she was buying and run out. Suddenly, I trembled. I put my palm on my stomach and the understanding slowly sank in. When it was my turn, I asked the pharmacist for a pregnancy test kit and left quickly. At home, I threw my handbag on the floor and hurried into the bathroom. After I'd read the explanations on the package, I sat on the toilet and, stick in hand, followed the instructions. The time that passed until confirmation of my pregnancy seemed like a lifetime.

I sat on the couch and tried to take in the new knowledge. I did not feel exaltation, like most of the women say. On the contrary, something sad took hold of me. The happiness that something wonderful was happening inside of me drowned somewhere in a puddle of sadness. I said nothing about the pregnancy for another two weeks, until I decided it was time to tell my family about it. I decided to ignore my father's instructions and went to visit them. When I got there, both my parents were home, but as soon as I came in, my father left on the pretext that he had to be somewhere in particular. My mother hugged me lightly and led me to the living room.

"Should I make you something to eat, Perele?" she offered, and when I didn't answer, she continued, "I have something that you love."

"I'm not so hungry."

"But this you won't turn down," she promised and went into the kitchen.

She came into the living room with a plate of sweet kugel, that normally I would have gobbled up and demanded more of, but I'd lost my appetite and was hurt to the bottom of my soul by my father's reaction, that he didn't even say a single word to me, and preferred to disappear. My mother, who was well aware that my father had left, tried to maintain a cheerful atmosphere, as if everything were completely normal.

"Momme, come. Sit with me for a while," I asked her, and, as always, she spoke to me from the kitchen while she cooked.

She must have heard something in my voice because she left everything and sat down right away.

"Momme, I'm pregnant."

At first it seemed that she didn't understand what I was saying, but suddenly she got up, pulled me from the couch, and started to kiss me. Tears of joy flowed down her face and her round body jumped like a cricket.

Then she left me and ran to the window that faced the street. "Avram, Avram, come up!" she called.

I couldn't believe what I was hearing. My father had been right downstairs that whole time, waiting for me to leave. He hadn't even bothered to go somewhere else, if only to be true to his lie that he had things to take care of somewhere else. In her excitement, my mother had forgotten their collusion, and urged him to come home. Even before he had come in, she called to him, "Avram, our Perele is pregnant!" The word "our" grated on my ears like a fork scraping the bottom of a pot. My father's face lit up, as if all the problems of the world had been solved in that moment. He came over to me, and in an unusual gesture, hugged me and said, "It should be in good time!" And me? I wanted to run from there. I was overcome by his hypocrisy. I released myself from his hug and dashed out of their apartment. I heard my mother's voice call out to me, but my ears closed, and my heart bled from the insult.

I continued running and didn't stop until I got home. My face burned from the effort and the heat, and my skin was covered with sticky sweat. As soon as I entered the apartment, I took off my clothes piece by piece and got into the shower. I felt I had to shed the feeling of rejection. My mother's two-facedness did not make it easy for me either. I let water flow over my body and mix with my tears. I was deeply disappointed by my mother who had cooperated with my father's lie. I'd tended to think that she was unconditionally on my side, but my mother tried to have it both ways. She did not take a courageous position. She tried to find a way to keep me, without paying the price.

The cold shower soothed me a bit. When Menachem Mendel came home, I was ready to tell him about the pregnancy. When he sat down at the table and started to eat, I casually admitted, "I'm pregnant." Menachem Mendel held the fork outside his mouth, looked at me for a second and said "*Zol zein in a mazeldikker shaw*[25]," and then put the fork in his mouth and continued eating.

The days that came after that were dreary. I stayed home to be near the bathroom. Every once in a while, I vomited, but mainly, I sat and thought

---

25 It should be in good time.

what I would do with my life. The hope that had been keeping me going had become an illusion. Thoughts of studying, determined decisions I'd taken upon myself; everything had been cut off like a flower cruelly picked, leaving after it a piece of stem that would dry up and wither away. All the plans that I'd built in my head were wiped out. Now I just had to wait patiently for the birth and become a dedicated mother who spends most of her time taking care of the children.

As the days passed, I felt how my thoughts were being painted black. The future that once had seemed so promising and interesting became devoid of intrigue and satisfaction. Day after day passed and a little bump stuck out of my flat stomach. I stroked the little bump but felt nothing. Not happiness, not sadness. One day, Menachem Mendel's parents came over for a visit. His mother said congratulations and hugged me tight with both arms. "Can I get you something to drink?" I asked.

"No, I'll make it! You sit here and I'll do the work in the kitchen," she answered.

She got up, made drinks for everyone, and came back into the living room and sat close to me. She took my hand in hers and said that now I was a queen. That I shouldn't work hard or bend down or drag heavy things. "Now there is someone else for you to take care of, and with G-d's help, everything will work out fine."

In my innocence, I wondered if she was only referring to the pregnancy. As my stomach grew, my mood changed. I was irritable and impatient. Everything made me angry. My movements became sharper, and sometimes words came out of my mouth that I really didn't mean to say. One day, Menachem Mendel returned from the *yeshiva*. Winter was coming and the days were gray. The sky was gloomy, like my mood. After he ritually washed his hands, he sat at the table and waited for me to serve him his meal. But I hadn't made anything. I sat in the living room and read the newspaper, *Hamodia*[26]. At first I heard nothing from the kitchen, but then a chair scraped, and Menachem Mendel came into the living room.

"What about the food?" he demanded.

---

26   A Haredi Jewish newspaper associated with Gerer Hassidim.

"I didn't make any," I answered indifferently, with my head in the newspaper.

"Go make it. Now!" he commanded after seconds of silence.

"Why can't you make it yourself for once?" I challenged him.

I heard each of his breaths. First slow, then faster and faster. "Get up and go to the kitchen and make supper!" he commanded again. His voice got louder.

"I'm not getting up," I dared talk back to him. "Did you forget that I'm pregnant? Your mother said that I'm a queen and that I need to rest." I felt my heart accelerating. I looked like I didn't care on the outside, but inside I was all panic.

Menachem Mendel turned and returned to the kitchen. I made the mistake of thinking he had surrendered. Suddenly I heard the kitchen cabinets opening. Dishes broke one after another on the floor. I stayed seated, my eyes running aimlessly over the newspaper page. I waited for him to stop. Then it was quiet, and I made the next mistake of thinking the tantrum had ended, but he came into the living room, snatched the newspaper from my hand, grabbed my arm and threw me to the floor. I was so shocked I couldn't say a word. I just looked at his gray face and heaving chest. My silence only increased his wrath. He would have preferred I ask his forgiveness and beg for mercy. His eyes were fixed on me in deep bitterness. He came closer and kicked my leg. I looked back at him in silence. His uncontrollable indignation and rage were evident. He pulled my arm, stood me up with one pull and threw me against the wall. The blow to my back took my breath away. My legs hit a chair and dropped it on my stomach with great intensity. And then he punched my face again and again until a black screen came down in front of me and I lost consciousness.

When I woke up, I found myself in a pool of blood. The apartment was dark and quiet. One side of my body was leaning diagonally on the wall, and my open legs were spread out like two logs thrown randomly. When I tried to move myself, pain attacked my entire body. I felt as if someone were stabbing me with sharp spikes. I tried a few times to straighten myself, until I finally managed to push my body forward. I wanted to get to the telephone that was hanging on the wall in front of me. I got on all fours and crawled toward it. Every inch forward meant massive pain. I especially felt the pain in my lower abdomen. I pulled down the phone receiver and dialed my parents. My father answered, and in a barely audible voice, I asked them to come.

"I need an ambulance," I said.

An unknown period of time passed until my parents came in. "Perele," I heard my mother and then I fainted again. The next time I woke up, I was in a snowy white hospital bed, bandaged and connected to machines. My mother stood near me and monitored my every movement.

"Perele, how do you feel?" she asked with honest concern.

"Okay," I answered in a strange voice. "The baby?" I asked weakly.

My mother shook her head. I turned my face to the wall and stared at it. I saw a gray stain that seemed like someone had wiped their finger on the wall. Here and there were other dark points. I counted the points again and again. It seemed that I heard my mother's voice calling me from far away. My head refused to turn. I wanted to close my eyes and sleep. Not to see or hear anyone. The repeated counting caused my eyes to close until I fell asleep again. The next time I woke up, my father was standing at my bedside, praying. He didn't notice that I had already awoken, so I was able to watch him without his knowing. His face looked etched with wrinkles. His beard, that he always kept tidy, was unkempt and dirty. His clothes were what he'd worn when I called them to my apartment. He looked up and his eyes met mine.

"Perele," he said in a hoarse voice, "I'm sorry."

I didn't answer, I just kept looking at him. He apparently interpreted my silence as an accusation because he started to explain his behavior.

"I didn't know he was like that. His parents said he was a genius and was strict about commandments of all kinds. The matchmaker said the same things. I didn't know."

"It's okay, Tatte, I'm not angry..." I barely whispered.

"You're a good girl, Perele..."

After two weeks, the doctors said I could be released from the hospital. My mother suggested I come stay at their place, but I refused. My father said that Menachem Mendel was living with his parents in the meantime, so the apartment was empty. They brought me home. The apartment smelled of cooking. My mother cooked my favorite foods and had bought enough groceries for a large family. They helped me get in bed, made sure that everything was neat and organized, and left. The quiet that prevailed after they left wrapped me in warmth. The apartment without Menachem Mendel was more than bearable. All I wanted at that time was to sleep and rest. I felt very weak. During the days that followed, my mother came over in the afternoon and served me lunch. I sat and waited for her to heat and serve, exactly as Menachem Mendel had always done. It was possible to get addicted to that, I thought to myself. After a week, I felt I could no longer stand doing nothing and depending on my mother. I felt stronger and told her that she didn't have to come every day. It looked like she was relieved.

"Are you sure?" she asked, and then I promised her that I felt much better, and she left saying she would be in touch soon.

The thought that Menachem Mendel was liable to return at any minute did not leave me for a long time. For weeks after the incident, it seemed that I heard his steps and I expected the door to open and he'd be standing there. But time passed, and to my great happiness, Menachem Mendel stayed away from the apartment. One day, when I was preparing my breakfast, I heard a knock at the door. I tensed up and felt how my body suddenly turned to stone. I didn't move and hoped that the unknown visitor would give up and go. But there was another knock and then I heard a familiar voice.

"Perele, it's Sara."

I debated whether to open the door for her or keep quiet until she went back home. Finally, I opened the door and invited her in. Sara looked as if she had just come from a beauty salon. Her clothes fit perfectly. Her appearance conveyed wealth and contentment. She was wearing a long dark skirt with a pink shirt. She had a thin white scarf around her neck, and a silver chain adorned her shirt. Her face was made up gently, and her lips were colored in soft pink. She came up to me and gave me a light hug, as if she were afraid I'd break.

"How are you, Perele? I haven't seen you in a long time."

I debated for a moment how to answer and then said, "I'm okay now. I had a miscarriage a while ago and was in the hospital. But now I'm okay."

"I'm sorry," she said, and without meaning to, stroked her prominent belly.

"Come, sit," I invited her. "Can I make you some coffee?"

"Yes, thanks."

It was the first time that I had invited a friend in for a cup of coffee. Life with Menachem Mendel had not been conducive to making social connections. Thoughts about life with him blocked my heart from the little pleasures of life, like spending time with a friend, walking in the street for fun, or buying clothes for myself. His absence from the apartment had softened my heart. Gradually, I felt my muscles relax and my movements become lighter. I noticed that my tone of voice had also changed and was less gruff. I didn't have to think twice before saying anything. The fear that had dwelled in my head and heart slowly left room for a feeling of freedom and daring. Even my breaths became lighter.

"How are you feeling?" I asked Sara.

"I feel wonderful," she said.

"And how does your husband feel?" I challenged.

"My husband? Why?"

"I mean, how does he feel about the pregnancy. Is he happy?"

"Oh, very, very happy. He's always warning me not to work too hard, not to lift heavy things. As if pregnancy were an illness." She laughed broadly, and her belly moved as if it were laughing too.

A small stab of jealousy stung me. I looked at her as if I were looking in a mirror. Her pretty clothes reflected my old clothes, and the look on her face, my tired face. Her happiness reflected my grief and her hope distanced mine.

"Does he sometimes help you around the house?" I continued. I guessed to myself what her answers would be, but something inside of me insisted on emphasizing to what extent her life was the reverse of mine.

"He helps sometimes, but not a lot. If I ask him to put the folded laundry in the cabinet, he'll do that. Or put a nail in the wall. Things like that. Though sometimes I prefer he do nothing, because after he does something, I need to clean up after him..." she said and again laughed out loud.

For a moment I wondered to myself what it would be like to burst out in such laughter. I couldn't remember when I had done that, if ever. To just laugh and not worry about a thing.

Then her face became serious and she asked, "How did your husband react to the miscarriage?"

I didn't have an answer ready for that. She saw that I felt awkward, and suddenly told me how clean and tidy the place looked. "Sometimes I don't have the energy to straighten things up, and then I just leave everything all over the place," she said. I appreciated her efforts to help me out of my embarrassment.

I smiled at her, and simply said, "Thank you."

In time, I learned to trust her. We were very different from one another, but it seemed that our differentness made us closer. Neither of us tried to change the other. She loved her life but didn't try to make me live like her. I didn't tell her about Menachem Mendel. When I did mention him, which was very rarely, it was just by the way, and on general subjects, so she couldn't find out very much about him. In her sensitivity, she understood that there was something not good in connection with him, and she didn't push me to tell her about it.

THIRTEEN

Months had passed since Menachem had left. My parents told me that he was still living with his parents, and that he was meeting regularly with Rabbi Weiss. I hoped he would stay there forever. I got used to the quiet and my independent lifestyle. The thought that he would return to my life was threatening, devastating for me.

When I felt stronger in body and soul, I decided to take advantage of the freedom and return for a visit to the garage at the end of the field. So many months I hadn't been there, and the memory of the solution I had found for the problem they had, and the appreciative looks I got from them, were often in my thoughts. I'm embarrassed to admit that the features of the young man's face, of Dan, were also engraved in my memory, and I thought of them once in a while, especially during quiet moments when I leaned my head on the wall and allowed my thoughts to flow freely.

I put on a coat and boots that came up to my knees. I didn't want to drown in the mud in the field as I had the previous winter. I saw the garage from afar. It was black like the sky. For a moment I thought that maybe no one was there, that maybe it was closed because the rolling door was shut, but when I got closer, I heard voices inside. Light rain started to fall, and it quickly began to pour. Thunder and lightning shook the sky. I knocked on the metal door, first with one hand, and when no one opened it, I pounded on the door with two hands. The door started to slide up and legs popped out from under it. Slowly a whole body was visible, and my young man was standing in front of me. At first he didn't recognize me, but after a few seconds, when I took the scarf partly off my face, he took my hand and pulled me inside. Then he rolled the door back down, and it banged down onto the floor.

It was pleasant inside. A few space heaters were on in various corners of the garage and gave off an orangey light. The other guys whose faces I'd already started to recognize, looked at me and then continued with what they what they were doing, as if my being there were something routine.

"So you have some kind of habit of going outside in stormy weather and frightening people, yeah?"

I smiled and started to take off my coat and scarf. Dan was watching me, and when I had exposed my entire face, he said with a smile, "Yes, it's you... I guessed right."

I rubbed my hands together to warm them, and Dan brought me over to one of the heaters.

"Perele, you disappeared for a long time. I thought you'd never come back."

Then, without warning, a sentence came out of my mouth, that if I'd thought for a second, I never would have said. "You wanted me to come?"

He was just as surprised as I was. His eyebrows rose, wrinkling his forehead. Right after that, his mouth stretched into a smile, and his laugh shook his Adam's apple and pulled my heartstrings.

"Come," he said, "I want to show you something."

I followed him, looking around. I was very excited. The farther I went inside, the more I felt new energy flowing inside of me. I loved that place. The darkness created a mysterious feeling that in turn created in me an expectation of something vague and unknown. We got to the car they were working on.

"So, what do you say?" he asked, stroking the metallic body.

I looked at the car and also reached out my hand to touch it. I felt its rough texture and saw that its previous color was now painted over in black. Here and there were rust stains.

"We scraped off the original paint," he explained.

I nodded and looked into the internal workings of the car. The seats had been taken out of it, leaving a big hole that made me feel a hidden and incomprehensible fear. I looked away, and Dan directed my gaze to the engine.

"We listened to you," he said, and pointed to the place where the compressor was attached.

"I see that you have made progress."

Yes, we've been working hard these last few months."

"When the engine's ready, what will you do?"

"It'll take a bit more time. We're always trying to improve the car's performance. The car's owner would like it to reach really high speeds."

"Isn't that what everyone wants?"

"No, some people want the car to look good and authentic, so we invest work mainly in paint and accessories. Others, like the owner of this car, prefer of course that it look nice and special, and have especially good performance statistics too. He also wants every part to be an original part of this particular model, and therefore the work progresses very slowly. To buy original parts is a whole job in itself. The search, the verification, the ordering, the purchase—the entire process takes a long time."

"Yeah, I got that."

"It really interests you?"

"Why do you ask?"

"Again why," he muttered with a smile. "Because it's pretty unusual for a girl to be interested in this stuff." he answered, and then said, as if to himself, "Of course there aren't so many men that are interested in it either. And besides that..." he continued and then stopped.

"Besides that what?"

"Forget about it. Let's not get into that."

"Beside that what?" I didn't give up.

He cleared his throat and then said, "To see you here in the garage, it's a pretty unexpected sight."

"Because I'm very religious?"

"Yes."

"So?"

"Your behavior is very confusing."

"Look, on the one hand, you won't shake hands, but on the other hand, you're with a group of men that you don't know. You're in a very masculine place, but you walk around freely. You come here when you feel like it, hang around with us, and suddenly disappear with no explanation, for a very long time. Though we've met several times, I don't really know anything about you. You appear and disappear, and then appear again, and disappear again."

"Does that bother you?"

Before he answered, he thought for a while and then said, "Sometimes, yes."

"So do you want me to stop coming here?"

"No!" he said sharply. "I want you to come here more. But I also want to talk with you about things besides cars. I want to get to know you."

This conversation with Dan echoed in my head for a long time after I'd left the garage. He was right, of course. He understood the confusion that I myself felt. I was like a driver making his way to an unknown destination, getting onto a street and finding that he had made a mistake, driving backward and arriving at a different place, sometimes continuing on and sometimes going the wrong way and retracing his route. I wanted to touch the world beyond mine, but sometimes I was afraid I'd get burned and withdrew back inside. How could I explain to him my contradictory behavior, my strong desire to free myself from the shackles, alongside the fear of doing that, the touches of his world and my disappearances full of fear at what I had done? If anyone in my family were to find out about my connection with this man and his world, I would be ostracized immediately. Even the suffering I'd been through would not be counted in my favor.

I was becoming more and more confused. I was living in two worlds at the same time. One familiar, known, and to some extent comfortable, with laws and conventions that regulated life in well-defined little boxes, while the other was attractive and tempting in its vagueness and lack of boundaries. In one was a violent man, and in the other a sensitive and intriguing man. My heart and mind were pierced with small holes through which were starting to pass some unprocessed and very confusing thoughts and feelings.

Fourteen

A week later, my mother visited me after first calling in the morning and asking if she could come over. Something in her voice sounded strange to me, but I didn't say anything about it and told her I would be at home. When I opened the door for her, I noticed that she was very pale, and asked her anxiously if she felt okay. She didn't respond to my question, walked into the living room, and sat right down on the couch.

"Come, Perele, sit next to me," she said.

"What happened, Momme? Is Tatte okay? Is it the kids?"

"Everyone's okay, Perele, relax."

I sat next to her on the couch. She took my hand in hers and said, "We met with Rabbi Weiss yesterday."

"With Rabbi Weiss? Why?"

"Please let me finish, Perele," she said, and I felt an anxious tingling all over my body.

"He said that Menachem Mendel had met with him many times and they spoke about everything. He said that now Menachem Mendel knows that he hasn't been behaving properly, and he wants to come back home and continue with the marriage."

"*What?*"

"My dear Perele, I know you've been through a lot, but now everything will be okay. Menachem Mendel will continue to meet with the rabbi every once in a while, and you'll see that everything will be just fine..."

I could hear the emotion in her voice. She was appealing to me to just let her return to her comfort zone, so she wouldn't have to explain to her friends why Menachem Mendel had left home, what was happening with Perele, and why she was suddenly living alone. But in my head were only flashbacks. Flashbacks of punches, smashing of furniture, hateful glares, and an orange beard.

"Momme, I don't want him to come back. He hasn't changed at all."

"How do you know, Perele? Rabbi Weiss said that he's changed. And anyway, what were you thinking? That you'd continue to live alone? You're a married woman! You have a husband."

"Husband?" I spat. "I have Haman at home, not a husband. That's a husband? You saw me, how I was with that husband."

"Perele, calm down."

"I will not calm down. I know he hasn't changed. Do you want me to die? You won't understand until I'm six feet underground?"

"Perele, don't talk like that, it's not nice."

"Not nice? Of course it's not nice. I live with him, you don't. He's a bad man, Momme."

"Enough, enough, come on…" She tried to shush me, and then thumped me with a sentence that hurt more than any punch of his ever had. "Tomorrow he'll be coming home, and you'll see that everything will be good."

After these words she took her hand from mine, got up, and walked toward the door. Before she went out, she turned around and promised again that everything would be just fine. The door shut after her with a little bang. I could imagine her sigh of relief that she had completed her mission.

*

He came the next day. In one hand was the suitcase he had left home with, and in the other was his prayer book. When he passed me, he shook his head slightly and went straight into the bedroom. His presence filled the entire apartment, like a balloon inflating until it becomes a giant bubble. I felt I had no room to breathe. I put on a sweater and went out. My feet naturally took me out to the field. I sat on the damp ground like I always had and let myself relax. Thoughts and decisions ran around my head like annoying flies. What do you want, I asked myself; what do you really want?

Inside of me I already knew that the time would come when he would return home. The illusory independence of the preceding months had been just a temporary gift, one that I took full advantage of, to avoid thinking about the day when I'd be forced to make a decision, one way or the other. With or without him. With him, that meant with everyone. With everyone and with a lie.

It was like I was on a stage. I was somebody else. Someone who had a role that she had to play to convince others of her authenticity. Now I had reached the crossroads where I had to decide which direction to turn. Suppressing the two had assisted me in postponing the choice I now held in both hands. I lay down on the ground and felt its coolness. Where do I belong…where do I belong? The sentence came back and echoed in my head nonstop. Whoever doesn't belong to one place, does he belong to another place? I asked myself. Must one belong to something or someone? And how do we know what we belong to, and can we change that belonging? And anyway, why do I need to belong to anything? I'll just belong to myself.

This is how I kept thinking. The decisions came and went. For a moment they were strong, and then they just got weaker. The confusion and fear of what awaited me left me limp and exhausted, until I fell into a deep sleep haunted by demons that warned me, and scattered promises. Sometimes they smiled, and then suddenly their faces became devilish. I wanted to ask them what would be, what I needed to do, but I remained mute, no sound came out of my mouth. I woke up and around me everything was black. It was already night. I shook the sticky sand off and made my way to the apartment. Before I left the field, I looked over at the garage. It seemed to me that I saw a pale yellow light emerge from it, but I didn't know if it was closed because the workday had ended, or if the door was closed just to keep it warm inside.

When I got home, I found Menachem Mendel reading one of the books that filled the big brown cabinet in the living room. When I came in, he looked up. The detestable look that I knew so well was spread over his face, but when I looked back at him, he looked down and returned to the big book. I went into the kitchen and fixed myself something to eat. It was late. I wondered if he'd eaten. I went into the bedroom and started to undress. I thought to myself how life would be with him from then on. It just wasn't possible that we would live under the same roof and remain silent. The apartment was small. We couldn't each take a corner and stay far away from each other. Our paths crossed constantly.

And then I made my decision. I put my clothes back on and went into the living room. He was still sitting in the same position.

"Menachem Mendel, we have to talk," I said in a weak voice. He didn't look up, and I thought for a moment that he hadn't heard me. I raised my voice and repeated myself.

"Speak," he said, and his head was still bent over the book.

"Can you look at me please?"

I saw his mouth clench. His knuckles whitened as he clutched the book. I knew exactly what he was thinking. From his point of view, I had gone too far. Since when did I ask him to look at me? But to my surprise he lifted his head and looked me straight in the eye.

"Now that you're home, after you've spoke with Rabbi Weiss, maybe it'll be different between us…"

I paused for his response. He kept his eye on me, stroked his beard which had grown long, and then he said one word. "Sure."

I waited for him to continue, but he looked down again and went back to reading. I sat across from him another few minutes, and finally, when I saw he had no intention of continuing the conversation, I stood up and went into the bedroom. Even before I got into bed, I knew nothing had changed.

FIFTEEN

The rain began to recede. The sun popped its head out of the clouds every once in a while and warmed the unwelcome chill. It was Sunday, the beginning of the week. The days after the "discussion" with Menachem Mendel were quiet. We said almost nothing to each other. The old routine returned. Once in a while, I would try to get him into a conversation. Sometimes he answered me with a word or two, but usually he nodded his head or was totally incommunicative.

That day, Sara invited me to visit her. "For a cup of coffee," she said. I readily agreed. The long days during which I had been sitting at home were starting to weigh on me. I was bored by the housework. I didn't know what women like me did during their long hours home alone, before they became mothers. The water had already boiled when I entered her apartment. She invited me to sit down and put two cups on the table. She made coffee for herself, and tea for me. She went in the kitchen again and returned with two pieces of cake. "I just made this now, it's still hot," she said. Just like the previous time, this time again the apartment was scrupulously clean and pleasant. I didn't manage to avoid comparing her apartment to mine. Her place was bright, not only because of the wide-open windows, but also because of something in the atmosphere. The atmosphere was created by her strict attention to each and every detail. Little doilies that she had apparently crocheted herself were laid out on the living room and dining room tables. At the center of the table was a new glass vase with yellow silk flowers that looked very real, and next to it were two giant silver candlesticks. Also on the sideboard that contained holy books, she had laid out a white tablecloth, and on it a silver box. Every detail had its exact position, to the point that I felt I had to be careful not to move any item from its place so as not to ruin the perfect harmony she had created.

"It's so nice here," I told her as I came in.

She thanked me and asked, "So how do you feel? After the miscarriage, I mean," she explained after she noticed the bewildered expression on my face.

"Oh. I'm fine," I dismissed her concern.

"I saw your husband yesterday..." she said cautiously.

"Yes, he came back," I said noncommittally.

"I see that you don't want to talk about it."

A battle was going on in my head. Should I share it with her or not? I didn't know her well enough to know whether I could trust her. On the other hand, it would be so nice to tell someone instead of suffering with it all alone.

"Menachem Mendel hit me and that's why I miscarried," I said finally.

Sara covered her open mouth with her hand, and tears began to run down her face. "I am so, so sorry. That's terrible! Why did he do that?" she asked with the innocence of someone who'd never experienced rejection or violence.

"Because I hadn't prepared his food," I said with false indifference.

"That's the reason?"

"Yes. He's used to my serving him his afternoon meal immediately after he comes home. That day, I hadn't felt like cooking, and I told him to make it himself, and he became angry and hit me."

"Was that the first time he'd done that?"

For a moment I hesitated, and then I told her about the other times.

Sara was astounded. "I don't understand that. So, what are you going to do?"

I raised my hand to show that I didn't know.

"But you can't continue like that," she said heatedly. "Do your parents know about this?"

I nodded.

"And what do they say?"

"He's met with the rabbi several times, and now they claim that he's changed and everything's fine."

"Is that what you think?"

Instead of answering her, I asked, "If heaven forbid, something like that had happened to you, what would your parents do?"

"They would send him packing," she answered without hesitation.

She got up and pulled her chair up close to mine. She took my hand in hers and looked at me with her big innocent eyes. "So what are you planning to do now?"

"I don't know, I'm pretty confused. One day I decide that I'm getting up and going, and then the fear freezes me, and I stay."

"Has he hit you since he's been back?"

"Actually no. But he's not talking. Our apartment is very quiet. We are like two shadows passing in the night without touching or speaking."

"You poor thing," she said and stroked my hand.

The next day, I decided to make a special meal, using a cookbook I'd bought in order to learn how to make new dishes. I went to the sideboard. Since we were married, Menachem Mendel and I had an agreement that he would leave me a certain amount of his income in a can in the cabinet, to be used for running the household. Usually, the amount he left would be enough to cover our modest needs, plus a little savings that I accumulated without his knowledge. I put my hand in the tin can and opened it. It was empty. I was surprised. I looked between the books on the shelf above, but there was no money anywhere. When Menachem Mendel returned home, I asked him what was going on. I thought I saw a little smile peeking out from behind his mustache, but I ignored it and asked again where the money was.

"There's no money," he answered.

"What's that supposed to mean, there's no money? You don't receive a salary at the *yeshiva*?"

"I do."

"So?"

My mind refused to understand what was happening. I continued to look at him and waited for an explanation.

"From now on, you'll have less money to waste."

"So how will I buy food? What will I use to make you your afternoon meal?"

"I'll eat at the *yeshiva*. I won't come home in the afternoon."

"But I need to eat too, no?"

The hint of a smile I'd seen before had turned into a big smirk. "You'll need to make do with less now, and not waste it on nonsense."

His enjoyment of this confrontation was clear. His absolute control over me gave him tremendous pleasure and gratified his evil inclination.

"You'll get exactly the amount you need and no more," he ruled, and then sat in the kitchen and waited for me to serve him the food.

His last meal at home passed in silence. I put the plate in front of him and left the kitchen. I went and sat on my bed and waited for him to finish eating and leave. So that's how he plans to continue, I thought to myself. It didn't bother me at all that maybe I'd be a little hungry and couldn't buy anything for myself. What bothered me more was his ability to control me. In the past, it had been through physical violence, and now it was through money.

After he left, I returned to the kitchen and washed the dirty dishes he'd left. He'd never once thought to put the empty dishes in the sink. After he finished saying grace after meals, he got up, shook out his beard, and left. After everything was back in place, I put on a thin sweater and went out. All the way to the library, I thought about what I was going to do. I hoped the plan would succeed, if only for the need to have some control over my life.

Sophie greeted me with a little hug. "You haven't been here in a long time," she said, "Have you started studying?" she asked hopefully.

"No, no, I'm not studying," I answered and thought to myself, not yet... "Can I speak with you for a second?"

"Of course."

She got up and pulled me to the inner room, which was still waiting for me with my pile of books. I sat on the only chair in the room, and Sophie sat at the end of the table and waited for me to start talking.

I took a deep breath, and then I said, "Sophie, I'm looking for work." She sat up straight and waited for me to continue. "I need money. Not a lot, just enough for me to buy some things at the supermarket, and some other small things."

"Does your husband work?" she asked abruptly.

"He studies at the *yeshiva* and receives a certain amount from them." I stuttered.

"I see," she said. "And you want to work here at the library, right?"

I nodded.

"Have you ever worked?"

I shook my head.

"Look," she began, "I don't know. I'm not in charge of this area. I can only make recommendations."

I lowered my head because I understood this to be a refusal, and then I heard her say, "But of course I'll recommend you." She smiled at me and promised an answer soon. "Call me in two or three days, and we'll see."

I put her telephone number in the small bag on my shoulder, thanked her, and left there with lots of hope, but also with fear at the unusual step I had just taken.

"Two or three days" were just words, but for me the answer I would receive then was like a life-or-death sentence. The hours seemed to purposely slow their steps like an old person whose life burden was unbearably heavy, and whose steps were cautious and slow. The clock was my enemy during those days. When I looked up at it, its arrogant hands stood in place, and looked at me defiantly. One day passed, and another day began. To pass the creeping time, I scrubbed the floor, and the walls, and cleaned dust from places I'd never gotten to. I washed the floor several times a day and occasionally I looked up at the clock ruling over the room. And then two days passed. It was eight in the morning. I stretched out my arm and put the phone receiver to my ear, but then a divine voice whispered in my ear to wait until the next day, so they wouldn't think that I was too interested. Control yourself... But I really am interested, I answered the voice.

I hung up the telephone, took the bucket and rag, and cleaned the shiny floor again. Three days passed. I took out the paper with Sophie's telephone number on it and dialed.

"Library hello," I heard her familiar voice.

"Hello," she said again when I didn't answer.

"Sophie, this is Perele."

"Perele, how are you? I thought you'd call yesterday…"

I didn't say anything.

"Perele, are you there?"

"Yes."

"Good, so I spoke with the person in charge, and it's fine."

"Fine?"

"Yes, you can start to work. For now, only three days a week. If in the future they need more time, then there might be the possibility for more hours. Is that good for you?"

"Yes," I whispered, and wasn't sure that she'd heard me.

"It seems to me that I heard 'yes,' right?" I could imagine her smile.

"When should I come?" I finally managed to ask.

"Whenever you want," was the immediate answer.

"Today?"

"Today."

I hung up the telephone and sat down on the couch. I felt as if I'd run a few kilometers and needed to catch my breath. I was so excited, my legs shook. My breaths were deep and fast. I got up and sat down again. I walked into the kitchen and wiped down the counter and went back to the living room. My body was restless, and I couldn't stand still. I had to move to calm myself. I was going to work! I said it to myself, and then whispered quietly, "I'm going to work!" My voice became surer of itself with each passing moment and finally I yelled out loud, "I, Perele, am going to work! I, Perele, am going to earn money!" I started crying uncontrollably. Crying of release, excitement, expectation, victory. Of all these things and more. I took the mop and started to sponge the floor while singing. I danced as if the mop stick were my partner. I spoke with it and smiled at it, and I swore I saw it smile at me. I threw it high in the air, and it landed on the couch after brushing against the wall and leaving a black mark. I laughed at myself and to myself and decided that that was the happiest day of my life.

SIXTEEN

About six or seven years ago, I invited home a friend from my class. Her name was Michal. We weren't really good friends, but here and there we spoke at school. In the evening, after she had left, my father called me over for a talk. He sat me down on the couch and sat on a chair across from me. He looked very serious when he said, "Perele, please don't bring Michal here anymore."

"What? Why?" I asked. I decided then that I would invite her over again.

"I just want you not to do that, and that's it," he decreed.

"But why?" I demanded to know.

"Just like that," my father answered, and I decided that not only would I invite her, but I would do it very soon.

I remember that when I got up from the couch and turned my back on my father, that his sigh sounded like sawing on steel. The next day I came home from school with Michal. I saw the surprise in my mother's face, and when my father came back from the *yeshiva*, his eyes bored through my face like two nails. In the evening, after Michal went home, the house was silent. No one spoke. Even my younger brothers and sisters felt the tension and stayed quietly in their rooms.

The week after, I invited her over again. When we came in, my mother was in the kitchen clearing the table after the little kids had finished eating. My mother came out right away and greeted Michal warmly. "Come, come, Michali. I've just prepared something that I'm sure you'll love." She took Michal by the hand and seated her in the kitchen and continued chattering around her as if she were a princess from a faraway land. She served her the food, asked her how it was, whether she wanted more. Even though Michal didn't answer, she added another portion to her plate. Michal was completely overwhelmed. First she was embarrassed and very quiet, then she cooperated with my mother, and they both giggled about things that I couldn't hear. She kept complimenting my mother on the cooking, and my mother seemed to take delight in her every word. I sat on the side and looked from one to the other. I was so confused by the change in my mother, that I remained speechless and got a bit angry. I was angry at my mother and father, who when he came home a little later also showered Michal with affection and exaggerated hospitality. From that day on, I didn't invite Michal over, and my connection with her ended a few weeks later.

I don't know why I recalled this incident just when I was taking my first steps in the library as an employee. Maybe because of the confusion I felt, or maybe because of the rebellious act I'd committed in both cases. My negativity in childhood that my parents had often been forced to deal with had reared its head again.

Later I learned that Michal's family had been outcast in the neighborhood. They were considered too liberal, plus one of her brothers had gotten divorced, and another had left the Hassidic community. My parents didn't want to catch anything from this ostracized family. When they saw that asking nicely didn't work, they decided to capitalize off my rebelliousness, and were successful in this case.

I stood in the doorway of the library and couldn't find the courage within myself to go inside. Sophie saw me, and in her usual sensitivity, spoke softly to me and told me how exciting and frightening it was to start a new job. "I remember myself on the first day of work," she told me. "The moment I got there I wanted to run the other way. I told myself that I wasn't good enough for it and would certainly not manage to learn the job. But you see? I'm still here, and more than fifteen years have passed." That whole time she held my hand and led me gently, without my noticing, further into the library where people sat, and my panicky self was of no interest to any of them. To them, I was totally invisible.

Sophie paired me with a young woman named Natalie who taught me how to arrange the books on the shelves. She taught me that the non-fiction books were organized according to the Dewey Decimal system. I didn't un-derstand much of what Natalie was saying. What she said was talking and h That's how I felt in the library, with words sounding in my ears and turning into mute lip movements. Natalie's mouth opened and closed, and I just saw the black hole inside. Finally, she said she'd give me time to digest it all, and in the meantime, I could gather up the books from the tables and put them on the gray cart.

After four hours, Sophie came up to me and told me that was enough for that day. Before she let me go, she explained that I had to open a bank account so that my salary could be deposited into it directly. "Go home and come back the day after tomorrow. I know that everything's mixed up in your head now, but soon everything will get straightened out. Don't worry!"

Don't worry? Why wouldn't I worry? I understood nothing of what I'd been told. Natalie probably thought I was a complete idiot because I only nodded my head. I didn't even ask her any questions. When she asked if I wanted to ask anything, I shook my head. I was afraid to open my mouth so I wouldn't ask a stupid question. I looked up and encountered the smiling face of the big clock on the wall. I mumbled "Thanks" to Sophie when I passed her and ran from the library to get home on time. I didn't want anything to darken my first day of work, and I certainly couldn't accept the possibility that Menachem Mendel would foul the new world I had entered with his words.

In the afternoon when Menachem Mendel returned to the *yeshiva*, I went to the bank that was near the library and far from my neighborhood. I asked to open an account in my name. The clerk was very nice and didn't let me go until I'd signed all the pages. When I left the bank, I felt as if I'd grown an inch or two. I had my own bank account, in my name only. From then on, only I would decide what to do with the money in it.

Two days later, I again went to the library, and so on the week after. I gradually started to understand what I had to do. Natalie was very patient, and she graciously repeated her explanation from the first day.

One afternoon, I collected all the books left on the tables and put them on the cart. So it would be easier to arrange the books on the shelves, I sorted them first on the cart. I organized the non-fiction books by their Dewey

Decimal numbers, and the fiction books by the authors' names. I already knew that Dewey had invented the method for classifying books according to subject, and that every category had its own number. For example, the number 100 represented philosophy and psychology, 200 religions, 300 social sciences and so on. In time, I learned by heart what each number represented, and was able to reshelf the books faster and faster.

That same afternoon, I finished my tasks pretty quickly. Sophie said that I could take a break because there wasn't a lot of work, and that in any case I did my work fast, so I deserved a prize. "Go to the room and read to your heart's content," she said. I smiled at her in thanks, especially for the compliment she snuck in there which filled my heart with great happiness. The fear I'd had in the first days was replaced with satisfaction and contentment. I deserve it, I sang to myself, I deserve it, I sang again, as if the whole song was made up of just the chorus.

I sat in the inner room, took out a sandwich I'd brought with me, crossed my legs and leaned back on the only chair in the room. As usual, I passed my free hand over the pile of books that stood like a statue in the center of the table. I was in love with that room because being there gave me a feeling of boundless freedom. I could laugh there, dance, curse, think about my life, make decisions with no limits or fear of punishment. I could be defiant. Any emotion or thought that came into my head could be expressed out loud as I wished. Now I smiled to myself. I got up and began to dance around the table. Mysterious music played in my head, and my legs moved to its beat. My body swayed and my eyes closed. I moved first to one side and then the other, and I felt as if I were floating in an endless expanse, my unconfined body controlling the air around me and moving it all around in perfect harmony.

Suddenly there was a knock on the door. At first, I wondered if the knock came from the music playing in my head, but the door opened a crack and a familiar head peeked inside with a slight smile.

"Am I disturbing you?" he asked.

I didn't answer at first because I needed to catch my breath. I felt my cheeks burning.

"No... yes..." I stuttered.

"Should I go?" he asked.

"No, no," I answered, "You can come in."

"Hi," he smiled.

"Hi," I answered awkwardly.

"Am I keeping you from something?"

"No, I was just being silly."

He came in and stood on the other side of the table from me.

"How are you, Perele?"

"I'm fine, and you?"

"I'm fine too."

There was a strange silence. Not of embarrassment and not of openness, but something in between.

"Sooo?" he said after a while.

"What?"

"That's how we'll continue, to speak in monosyllables? Maybe we can also speak in full sentences?"

"Maybe..." I smiled.

"What's up with you?" he continued.

"I'm fine, and you?"

"Likewise."

We burst out laughing. The smile lines I'd noticed before filled his entire face. Around his mouth, on his forehead, beside his nose.

When we stopped laughing and the awkwardness had passed, he asked why I hadn't been coming to the garage.

"I don't have so much time," I answered.

He lifted his eyebrows and waited for an explanation.

"I'm working!" I declared proudly.

"Working? Where?"

"Here."

"Here, in this room?"

"Here, in the library."

"Really?"

I nodded.

"Great!" he said, and I knew that behind that word were a few other questions. There was silence, and then he asked, "And how does that fit in with your life?"

I thought a moment before answering, and then I gave the most honest answer there was. "It's a secret."

"I understand," he said seriously. "Until when will you keep it a secret?"

I wondered for a moment if he was referring only to my work at the library.

"I don't know," I answered.

"Perele," he said suddenly, and his voice caused my muscles to quiver. "I think about you a lot."

I wanted to ask why, but I decided not to. We stood facing each other with only the table separating us, but his penetrating gaze and my accelerating heart created the feeling that we were connected to the same body. After a long silence, he turned around, left the room and closed the door behind him, leaving me completely confused by all the emotions spinning inside of me. I sat on the chair, ignoring the tower of books standing in front of me like a flagpole. My thoughts came and went like waves bringing questions and parts of words and taking them deep into the sea. It was clear to me that something was happening inside of me, something that I couldn't name or describe clearly.

SEVENTEEN

"I think about you a lot." That sentence echoed in my head relentlessly, from the moment I left the library, and over the entire weekend. What did he mean? I asked myself. Does he think about me because he was used to seeing me once in a while or because he didn't know anyone like me, and I intrigued him? Or maybe he said that to break the silence? Something fluttered inside of me, exciting and frightening at the same time. I knew it was forbidden for me to feel what I was feeling. Even without that, I broke conventions and ignored rules. Being with him alone, having personal conversations, his touching my arm by chance. All those things were just not done. If someone were to find out that I'd been hanging around alone with a man who was not my husband, there would be an earthquake. My parents would be looked at askance, my siblings' chances for good matchmaking would be lost, and Menachem Mendel would have every reason to return to his previous behavior. No one would come to my defense. I believed that even Sara, my new friend, would condemn me for my behavior. People from the community distanced themselves from people like me, lest they catch a fatal illness.

A month had passed since I'd started working at the library. I sometimes noticed Menachem Mendel's amazed look. Every evening when he came home, a meal awaited him as always, despite the fact that he didn't leave a cent for me to buy food. At first, he'd walk around like a peacock, with an expression of victory that began to disappear as the days passed and nothing had changed. He'd expected me to beg him for money, and he was disappointed when that didn't happen. The trick he'd planned did not succeed, and he didn't like that. When he came home early one day that week, and found me in the kitchen preparing the meal, he started checking in the rooms as if the answers to his questions were written on the walls.

I knew it wouldn't be long before my secret would be revealed. And maybe that's what I wanted. I knew it was a very cowardly way to reveal who I was. Instead of getting up and publicly announcing that I wanted a different life, I waited for something to happen that would create a justified reason to do so. It was clear to me that I wouldn't be able to go on like that for too long, but I still wasn't ready to make my battle public. The connection with Dan both frightened and attracted me. His face that smiled when he spoke with me, his light sense of humor, and the respect he had for my world that was so different from his, all that was affecting me in a way I didn't seem to have any control over.

Menachem Mendel continued to monitor me. One day he arrived very early but lucky for me, I was at home. It was a day I didn't work. But I was on borrowed time. I still liked to see his wondering look when he found me at home, and the expression of frustration when I served him his meal. His eyes rolled around in their sockets looking for any bit of evidence. As time went on, he showed clear irritation. One day, when I put a plate in front of him with chicken cutlet and mashed potatoes, he put his nose right on the meat and suddenly threw the plate from the table and the food flew all over the place. "This stinks!" he grunted. "Make me a new one!" For a moment I wanted to refuse and tell him to do it himself, but I knew that that was exactly what he was looking for. I bent down, picked up the food from the floor and fried him a new cutlet. Once in a while, without his noticing, I took a look at him. His tightly closed fists resting on his knees served to absorb the rage waiting to erupt from inside of him. His loss of control over me drove him crazy. I figured that it wouldn't be long before he lost control of himself, and all the fury pent-up inside of him would come out at once.

And that day arrived. It was Wednesday. I was supposed to finish working at six and hurry home. Usually I left a few minutes before with Sophie's permission, and I got home a little before Menachem Mendel returned from the *yeshiva*. But I hadn't foreseen the unforeseeable. The street I had to cross was closed because of a suspicious object. The police allowed no one to cross it, and time, which sometimes hesitates, charged quickly, like an animal escaping a predator. The watch on my wrist burned my skin. If I could only have turned the hands back. When the street was reopened, I knew well that there was only one option open to me. A road with no exit, and maybe it was just as well. I again thought about the dark room where I froze when my brother did to me what he did. Why was I playing the game according to the rules set by the man I so detested? Was working at the library a victory, or was it a tiny improvement designed to disguise my cowardice? Who was I fooling? These questions drained the last remaining bit of my self-respect. I felt like an inflatable doll, now deflating, wrinkled and twisted. My steps became slower, and my thoughts more frightening.

I didn't want to fight anymore. Not myself, not my thoughts, not my family, and not Menachem Mendel. I just wanted to leave. To leave everyone and everything behind and just go. But to where? To whom?

The silence erupting from the other side of the door gave no evidence of what had happened there. I opened the door slowly, and the sight revealed shattered all at once everything that I had imagined was liable to happen. Menachem Mendel sat on the armchair in the living room, his body was tense and his arms in repose on the armrests. A smile was frozen on his face as if someone had sculpted his features from tar. He moved not a muscle. It was like he was a doll in the shape of Menachem Mendel. When I turned my face from his frozen figure, I saw that the floor was covered with pieces cut from the rug. The couch had also been cruelly murdered and a white material similar to cotton peeked out from the fabric that had once covered the entire chair. The glass doors of the cabinet had turned into shards, and the table that stood next to it had been hit with a heavy device that created unfixable holes and dents. But what surprised me the most were the holy books. They were strewn all over the floor, wounded by the glass shards and embedded in the fabrics and broken pieces of furniture. The wrath that had burst from him was so great that he had not managed to separate the holy from the profane. The books that were so dear to his heart, that he stroked and nurtured with cautious reverence, had in his ire become as worthless to him as anything else. The fury pent-up in his tight fists had been released.

I walked in and avoided meeting his eyes. I passed him by, but I wasn't careful enough. He grabbed my arm and forced me to stand still. I tried to shake off his grasp, but he was stronger than me.

"Where were you?" he hissed, and maintained the frozen pose, his face fixed on the wall in front of him.

"Let me go!"

"Where were you, I asked."

"At the library."

"What library?"

"The one in the center of town."

"What were you doing there?"

"Working."

My answer made him curious. He turned to look at me and in doing so, I saw how his face changed from questioning to understanding.

"So that's where you have money from...," he mumbled to himself. "And who said you could go to work?" he asked suddenly.

Until that moment, fear had controlled my body, but when he asked that question, my feeling changed from fear to the desire to speak the truth, without caution or avoiding answers that he wouldn't like.

"I had no choice, right?" I looked straight into his eyes.

"Why didn't you ask me for money?"

"Would you have given me any?"

In the strangest way, we were having a quiet and open conversation of the type we had never had before that. His grip loosened, and he finally let go.

He stayed sitting and I made my way to the bedroom. Under my bed, the brown suitcase was waiting patiently. I took it out and started to fill it with clothes.

"What are you doing?" he stood behind me, blocking the doorway with his body.

"I'm leaving," I said.

"No, you are not!"

"Menachem Mendel," I said. I thought about taking advantage of the narrow window that had opened to conduct one last true conversation. Maybe, I thought to myself, maybe we'd be successful. "You know that from the beginning it wasn't working out between us. It was not a good relationship. That happens sometimes. Let's just say goodbye, and each will go his own separate way."

"No one is going anywhere!" I heard him say that, and I knew the window had closed.

In the following days, Menachem Mendel stayed home. He informed the *yeshiva* that he was sick and used the broken living room table for his studies, after he had collected the holy books and returned them to the cabinet that was barren of its doors. I left things as they were. I didn't bother to clean up the remnants of his fury and spent my time in the kitchen. I cooked and cleaned and sat, I thought about my situation, but I also knew that the opportunity would come. A strange peacefulness fell over me. I didn't lament the situation, and I also didn't feel impatient. I was relaxed and I knew that my time would come, because Menachem Mendel could not stay home forever. The decision was made, and I was filled with a feeling of completeness. As the days passed, I felt how I had been getting stronger. I preferred not to think of what would be, and I planned nothing. I was afraid that the fears would make me weaker and I would change my mind. I waited patiently for the right time, but unfortunately it came earlier than expected.

Eighteen

"Perele, come quick, Momme fell."

It was one of the rare times that my father called me. I took a taxi to the hospital and I got there ten minutes after the ambulance. Momme was unconscious. She was sent immediately to intensive care, and they told us to wait. My father paced the hallway saying Psalms, and two of my brothers did the same. When they saw me, they nodded hello and continued praying. A half hour later, one of the doctors came out and told my father that he should go inside. They told us to stay in the waiting room and explained that they couldn't let more than one person into the ICU. My father came out a few minutes later, and for the first time in my life, I saw him cry. He held the prayer book, kissed it, and his tears stained the black binding. My brothers and I looked at him and waited anxiously for him to say something.

My father came up to me, ran his hand over my head, and told me to go in and say goodbye to Momme. Goodbye? I didn't understand what he meant. I continued to stand there waiting for him to say something else that would explain what he meant. When that didn't happen, I went through the automatic doors and was swallowed up in a cold, quiet hall. Only the beeping of the devices attested to the remnants of life remaining there. I looked around and didn't know which way to go. The covered figures on the beds had no identifying signs. All of them looked exactly the same. I tried to find a familiar sign that would direct me to the figure I'd known since birth, but I found no hints. A nurse approached and asked me who I was looking for. When I answered, she led me to one of the beds. An unfamiliar woman was lying in the bed. A woman I didn't know. I stood and looked at the silent figure. One tube came from her nose, and a thicker one came out of her mouth. Her face was smooth and yellow, her expression blank. But the most disturbing thing was the silence around her. There was no beep or other sound. The machines were there, but they, like her, had become silent. I stood planted in my place like Lot's wife and looked at the figure I had once called "Momme."

"Momme?" I whispered, "It's me, Perele."

"Momme?" I said again. "Answer me..."

I took her hand, but it was already cold. Her face had started to take on a purplish hue and her cheeks were sunken as if the flesh had begun to evaporate. I was scared. I wanted her near me, to tell me it was all right and not to be afraid. But she didn't answer and remained distant and quiet. A hand touched me.

"Come," I heard. "Your mother is no longer with us."

I was gently led outside. My father looked up and when he saw my eyes, he understood. "Hear O Israel, the Lord is our God, the Lord is One," he said, his voice drenched with tears. "Blessed be the name of His glorious majesty forever and ever... Hashem is God...Hashem is King, Hashem always was King. Hashem will reign forever and ever."

My father repeated the prayer several times, and my brothers after him. His voice filled the waiting room, and the few people who were there stood up from the bench and they too repeated his words. Afterward, the strangers who were there walked up to shake his hand and say the outrageous statement, "may you know no further sorrow." How can you say to a mourning man in pain, that he shouldn't know further sorrow? Is that what would console him? I didn't wait for my father and ran out of that place that emitted the smell of death. I couldn't stand the cold or the smell that was so final.

I knew I had to go to my parent's home, but I couldn't. My grief was not their grief; it was only my grief. I was grieving for her leaving, that she would no longer be present, but mainly I felt the pain of the unfinished business between us. That we hadn't managed to grow closer, as I had wanted. I grieved over the rift that we hadn't managed to repair. I mourned her inability to choose me, her daughter, absolutely. I mourned the fears and anxiety she'd had over the years, which I'd only added to with my behavior.

More than anything, what hurt was the finality, the lack of hope, the lack of any chance to change anything. The period of Momme was over for me.

A terrible thought passed through my head, and I threw it out right away, because you weren't supposed to think that way. Maybe it would be better for it to have been my father and not my mother. With my mother, there still could have been a chance. My relationship with my father wouldn't change, and his opinion wouldn't change, not even for me. I walked around aimlessly for hours, until nightfall. Cars drove by and their headlights shone over my face. I was wiped out. My legs could barely carry me. I noticed that the few people who passed me were stealing glances. Finally, I got to my parents' home. A memorial candle was already lit. People, some of whom I didn't know, filled the house. A few of them were whispering with my father. Someone came up to me and told me not to worry, that she would take care of everything for the *shiva*, the week of mourning. "You take care of the little ones," she said.

The mirrors in the apartment were covered with sheets, and mattresses were placed on the floor. I walked around as if I were sleepwalking. Everything was mixed up in my head. The people, the voices, the faces, some of which seemed familiar but not really familiar. My father was swallowed up somewhere in the funeral arrangements, and he also seemed to me to be lost. He didn't know how to manage a home. He only knew how to study and teach. The neighborhood women took command and managed things confidently.

I barely remember the funeral. In my head spun a wheel of unclear voices and sights. People who said that we shouldn't know sorrow, and that they were with us in our sorrow. My father walked behind the wagon, held on either side by two men. "A woman of valor who can find, her price is far above pearls..." I heard, and next to her grave the men mumbled "...in the world which G-d created. May G-d's majesty be revealed in the days of our lifetime..." and again I sank back into myself. "Blessed be G-d's great name in all eternity..." "May the One who makes peace on high, bring peace to us and to all Israel, and say Amen."

"Amen."

That's it, it's over. Momme was laid in her grave and covered with dirt.

As was the tradition, stones were laid on her new resting place, and she was marked by numbers and letters. She was no longer Momme, but a row and a column.

The mourning week began. Madness. Coming and going and snacking and eating. Unfamiliar women cooking and whispering. Oy, I hear. Tongue clucking. "What will he do now?" "Who'll take care of the children?" "After all, it's Perele who this, who that..." and I was walking around between everyone like an outsider. Not connected to anyone. Sometimes sitting and sometimes getting up to go to the bathroom and sitting again and shaking hands and nodding. And then... Sophie. And then I started to cry. Sophie, the one from my other world, that no one knew of its existence. She came.

"How did you know?" I asked.

"You didn't come in, and you didn't call, so I checked the forms you filled out and there was an address, so I came. You live here?"

I shook my head. "This is my parents' home."

"I'm so sorry, Perele, I was worried about you."

I got up from where I had been perched on the floor, and she opened her arms. I leaned on her chest, closed my eyes, and rested. Only then did I feel how tense I had been. My rigid body relaxed, and I sunk completely into her embracing arms. When I opened my eyes, I saw that people were sneaking glances at us. No one came over to us, and no one said anything. My father, who looked at us out of the corner of his eye, didn't say a word. But his squinting eyes and stare drew a big question mark on his face. Our hug created an island that people didn't cross.

"Come sit down again," she said gently, and helped me find a place. She found a low chair and brought it over to me. "When did it happen?" she asked.

"The day before yesterday," I answered.

"Had she been sick?"

"No, it was a complete surprise."

"So why didn't you come to the library before that?" she wondered.

I was silent.

"Did something else happen?"

I nodded and my head moved in the direction of my husband who was sitting within a group of men. Sophie followed my glance until her eyes crossed those of Menachem Mendel. The two exchanged looks for a few seconds, and then she looked back at me. It seemed to me that there was no need to explain anything to her, as if she could read my thoughts. Her eyes were fixed on mine, and they were full of infinite softness and understanding.

Menachem Mendel came to my parents' home every day after the *yeshiva*, in time for evening prayers. He didn't hide his discontent and didn't take his eyes off me and Sophie. If he could have, he surely would have gotten up and moved her away from me. His white knuckles, so familiar to me, were a measure of his anger at my other life, about which he knew nothing.

The mourning week ended. The people left the apartment, the sheets came off the mirrors, the mattresses and chairs were taken away, and the apartment returned to be as it had been, but without Momme. The kitchen was desolate. The cooking smells were swallowed in the cold air. The children went to school, my father to work, and I remained alone, wondering what I should do. How to continue? During the entire week of mourning, Menachem Mendel said nothing to me. He came, prayed with everyone, and went home.

I left my parents' place and within a half hour, I was at the library. Sophie stood up and hugged me hard. She took my hand and brought me to the inner room.

"How are you today?" she asked.

"A little better."

"How's your father?"

"He went back to work."

"So the house is empty."

I nodded.

"Let's hear it," she said.

I picked up my head in surprise but put it right back down. I wrung my hands and swallowed. I didn't hesitate whether to tell her. I was debating how to tell her. Where to start, and how to present things so that she'd truly understand them. So that she'd understand that the problem wasn't Menachem Mendel. It had to do with decisions I'd made or hadn't made. I didn't want Menachem Mendel to turn into the center of the story.

"When I was a little girl, I made my parents' life very difficult. I argued with them often and would do the opposite of what was normally done and acceptable. There were lots of fights at home. I was a little like a boy. I liked to hang around with the boys in the neighborhood, and I stayed away from girls. I remember that once..."

I went into a long story and tried to bring her as much as I could into our community life. I told her about the harsh rules and conventions, and I tried to give them some rationale. "Our rabbi tried with all his might to unite the community after it had fallen apart during the Holocaust. He thought the only way to do that was to return the situation to what it had been before the Holocaust in Poland, with clear instructions and rules that would separate the community from other Hassidic communities. He believed that people had the ability and potential to find within themselves the powers to recover from what had happened and build something new on the old ruins. To some extent, he apparently wanted to bring Poland to the land of Israel."

"But didn't the people ever ask why that had happened to them?" she stopped me. "After all, a period like the Holocaust could cause a religious person to stop believing. What do your leaders say about that? How do they explain what happened to the Jewish people?"

"The truth is that the rabbi lost almost his entire family in the Holocaust. His wife, son, daughter, son-in-law, and many of his students were murdered. But only rarely did he speak of that. I think that he treated your question like a subject that had no answer, and therefore believed that it was better not to speak about it."

Sophie rolled her eyes. "Okay, so you said that in order to unite everyone he made all these rules; that means what?"

"They determine what is permitted and what is forbidden in everything related to relations between a man and a woman. And mainly," I added, "emphasis on what is forbidden. Which is a lot. The thing is that many of the men took it very far. Like my husband for example," I added in a whisper. "The rabbi demanded that men adopt the very strict behaviors that in Poland only a few people lived by," I continued. "In some way, I think that that gave people here the feeling that they were special, that the rabbi believed in them and in their ability to observe these demands. My father was also strict in everything related to his relations with my mother. We never saw him show any affection toward her. He certainly didn't touch her in front of us, to the point that he didn't even call her by her name. If he wanted to tell her something, he either said "Pssssssssst..." or asked me or one of my sisters to call her. That made me very angry, and I told my mother so, but she laughed and said that I was just getting angry at nonsense. I had a childish wish to change the rules at home with my contrarian behavior, but of course I didn't succeed."

I continued talking for a long time. I told her about my minor rebellions, which only distanced me from my parents and sometimes created an unpleasant atmosphere at home. For some reason, I also wanted her to know about my combative side. It was important to me that she not have the impression that I was weak and cowardly.

"When I was about eleven..." I started and then stopped. This time I looked into her eyes. I think that I wanted, for the first time in my life, to face what had happened without the need to put my head down and be ashamed of what I had been put through. "My brother would come to my room at night and do something to me," I continued bravely. "Until a few years ago, I didn't understand what he was doing, I'm not sure that even he understood."

Sophie's eyes squinted, and her hands held mine more tightly. She didn't say anything, just looked at me, and her eyes sent waves of warmth. "Except for Momme, I've never told anyone that until today. I was so ashamed. I knew that there was something bad about that, after all, he did it at night, quietly, so that no one would hear. When I tried to tell my mother, she got angry at me that I was talking about it, but she also made sure that it stopped happening."

I continued talking without stopping, until I got to the time that they matched me up with someone that I didn't know at all, and didn't want to marry, or didn't want to marry at all. I told her of the shock I experienced on the first night after the wedding, and what happened on the days that came after that. I told her about the hospitalization and about my mother's attempt to get closer and make things up with me. A fragile reconciliation that put my mother in a very uncomfortable position.

"What helped you to manage with all this for so long?" she asked.

"The books, the library. You. That I had my own outside world. You understand that in this marriage I completely lost my identity? The Perele that once was, completely disappeared on me. I was like... like the stuffed doll I had when I was a baby, but without its stuffing. Just the upper part, depleted and shabby. That's how I felt. I kept trying to resist, but then the beatings came and turned me back into a worthless creature. The truth is that the beatings didn't hurt me as much as my damaged self-esteem. I was always asking myself what had happened to me. Where had I disappeared to? I was much angrier at myself than I was at him. I didn't even try to talk to him, it was impossible to have a conversation with him. I mainly talked with myself. I would sit alone for hours at home and think to myself. There were times when I thought I'd go crazy, but then I came here, and the books started to gradually change things. The old Perele started to come back."

"And he knew nothing about it?"

"At first, no. But once I forgot one of the books at home, and then I was hospitalized."

Sophie nodded.

"And he knew about your working?"

"Not until recently. He didn't leave me any money to buy food and he went crazy when nothing was missing at home as a result. He didn't know, and that drove him nuts."

For the first time since I had started to speak, I smiled. I thought of the amazement on his face, his eyes looking all around for clues what was happening.

"And then?"

"And then I decided to leave, but my mother died." I expected her to hug me, after all the things I'd told her, but instead she continued sitting in silence. Her eyes looked at me, but I saw that she didn't really see me, but was thinking about something else.

"And what now, Perele?"

I took a deep breath and said, "I'm leaving!"

"Are you sure?"

"Totally... totally."

Now she smiled.

"I'll stay at my parents' place for a while, and then I'll leave."

"To where?"

"I don't know yet. I need to decide," I said ambiguously.

There was silence. Each of us pondering something and then she said, "I want to help you."

I just looked at her.

NINETEEN

In the days following that conversation, I didn't return home. I called Menachem Mendel and informed him that I was staying with Tatte to help out. I didn't explain or provide details. I decided to take time for myself to think and look into what I should do. My father took my presence in the apartment as a matter of course, but when weeks went by and I still hadn't shown any sign that I ever planned to leave, he started to make comments like "Menachem Mendel surely needs you at home" or "Perele, a woman should be beside her husband."

Finally, he said explicitly, "Perele, I can manage now. Go home to your husband."

One day I answered, "I'm not going back!"

"Oh, Perele, Perele, *az men zicht chalo, farlirt men derveil dos broit*[27]."

"Tatte, I have nowhere to go back to, don't you understand?"

"*Narishkeit*," he hissed.

"It's not nonsense," I yelled.

"Is he hitting you?"

"No!"

"*Nu, den, was vil sta?*[28]"

"I don't want to be with him anymore!" I continued to scream.

"So what do you want to do?" he asked again.

"I want a divorce!"

---

27 You're looking for challah, but in the meantime, you're missing out on the bread.

28 So what do you want?

"*Gut hilf mer.*[29] "Divorce? We don't divorce. Go to the rabbi and get help from him..."

I decided to be quiet. Exchanging verbal blows wasn't going to help. I was upset, but I knew very well that he would never be able to give me his blessing. Even if he knew deep inside how much I was suffering.

"If Momme, may she rest in peace, were here, she'd know what to do," he muttered.

I sensed his helplessness and even felt a little sorry for him. As time went on, it became clearer to me that the best way for me was not to expect his blessing, but to tell him of my decision and hope he'd be able to live with it in the future.

While I was staying at my parents' place, I went to the library several times. Some of the time I worked, and some of the time I spent in conversation with Sophie. Talking to her helped me focus my thoughts. I knew what I didn't want, but it was hard for me to decide exactly what I did want. With Sophie's help, I found a tiny one-room apartment for rent not far from the library, which I could afford if I started working more hours. Together with her, I planned how to act, when to leave, and how. The more I spoke with her, the more I felt my courage returning and filling me with energy. The plan was to go home when Menachem Mendel was at the *yeshiva*, pack clothes and other items that were most essential to me in a suitcase and leave behind whatever wasn't important.

*

It was midweek, 9 a.m. Most of the married men were at the *yeshiva*. It was a clear day. A perfect day for starting a new life. I was leaving my parents' place feeling great excitement. The apartment was quiet and neatly organized. Food was ready for the afternoon when the children would return home. As always before I left, I looked around, pleased to see that everything was in place.

---

29 God help me.

Weeks after my mother was gone, I still smelled her scent. In their bedroom when I cleaned, on the service balcony, where I'd hung everyone's laundry. Everything I did came with the thought that her fingerprints were there before mine, in every corner, and I was touching them. On the clothesline, on the old broom, on the rag that she used to wipe the kitchen counter, even on the toilet brush. Every corner and every object were imprinted with her hand or footprints and her sighs from whenever she'd bent down to clean or got tired, and the "oh" came out of her mouth just like that. Sometimes I would stop and stroke the so very familiar objects, put them by my nose, and inhale the scent that was so full of the difficult life she had, the life that was based on the female tradition of cooking, cleaning, automatic sighs and accepting the rules that had been determined long before she was born. I missed her so much. Everything that had been or hadn't been between us had evaporated in thin air, and only the pain of her absence remained. Suddenly now it didn't matter whether she supported me or not. Whether or not she kept her promises or fought on my behalf. I wanted her back, as she was. With the fears and anxieties, with the hesitations, with the attempts to convince me to change my ways, but also with the rare hugs. I was mainly missing the love that I'd always known existed, even if it wasn't expressed in the way that I'd wanted. When she was alive, I was often angry at her, I yelled my disappointment at her loudly. But when she was no longer, none of that seemed important. All I had left was the memory of her character, and a terrible longing.

I got to the building that I hadn't been to in weeks. I looked at it and saw the plaster peeling on the building facade. It had never been refurbished. On the front of the building, near the balconies, were rows of hung clothing that weighed down the clotheslines. A woman was hanging up her wash. She had a clothespin in her mouth, and her skilled hands straightened the clothes on the line. Once in a while, she took a quick look at the street below her, but quickly continued with her task. She had many more tasks, and no free time. Garbage piled up on the sidewalk. The full garbage containers did not manage to hold all that had been brought to them and were overflowing. People walked around the garbage and continued on their way indifferently. Someone passed by and threw a wrapper on the sidewalk that was already so dirty. I looked around me and realized that until that day, I hadn't seen the neglect and wretchedness of the street and the building. I'd always entered with my head down. I'd also never felt like I belonged — not to the street, not to the building, and certainly not to the apartment.

I went into the entrance lobby which was also neglected and dirty. No one cared that his way out or in was full of all kinds of packaging or mud that had stuck to shoes, or objects some of which there was no need for, and others, like old bicycles or baby strollers piled on top of each other and almost blocking the way through. I made my way to the second floor. On the door to our apartment there was no identifying sign. Not a sticker with a name or a piece of metal with the family name, like Sara the neighbor had. I took out the key from my wallet and pushed it into the lock, but the key wouldn't go in. I tried again and again and again. I pressed the door handle and pushed the door, but nothing happened. It just refused to open. I checked the key in my hand, but I was not mistaken, it was the key to the apartment. Only when I pushed the door again with my body and made a few more unsuccessful attempts to insert the key in the door did I understand that Menachem Mendel had changed the lock. Tears filled my eyes. Tears of anger. I kicked the door once, and again, until I heard the door open behind me.

"Perele, is that you?"

"Hi, Sara."

"Perele, where did you disappear to? I was so worried about you." She came closer to me and continued asking where I had disappeared to. "I was crazy with worry about you. I didn't know who I could ask. One day I knocked on the door and your husband opened. I asked him where you were, and he told me he didn't know and closed the door."

"I'm fine," I tried to calm her.

"But where were you? Where did you disappear to?"

"Momme passed away."

"Oh no," she blurted, "what happened?"

"She just fell and died... in the kitchen."

"I'm so sorry," she said and sounded so sincere.

"I can't get into the apartment. Menachem Mendel changed the lock."

"Wait a second, I'll call Yedidya, he's home," she said, and disappeared into her apartment.

A few minutes later, I met a nice-looking man with a short neatly trimmed beard. He nodded to me, and his face looked just like his name, friendly. He had brought tools with him and started to use one to bang on the door handle. With a screwdriver he took apart the lock and then pushed the door with his body until it opened wide.

"Thank you," I said, a little embarrassed.

I imagined that Sara had told her husband about me and Menachem Mendel. The thought that he knew about us embarrassed me. In any case, he smiled and even asked if I wanted him to come in with me. His question warmed my heart and made me feel guilty for not trusting Sara enough to share more of my life with her.

She came into the apartment with me. I saw her eyes examining the rooms. Maybe she was looking for hints of what I'd already told her. The apartment was cold and dark. The shutters were closed completely. There wasn't the tiniest opening to allow even a bit of light to come in. To Menachem Mendel's credit, it must be said that the kitchen was clean and tidy. It turned out that he knew how to wash dishes, though he hadn't done it even once when I was home.

I went into the bedroom and took out the suitcase from under my bed for the second time. With Sara's help, I filled it with clothes in a few minutes. From the bathroom I took a toothbrush and toothpaste, a face towel, and a bath towel. I didn't want to take anything that wasn't absolutely essential. I had just one more thing to do. I went to the bookcase in the living room. The container in which he was supposed to leave me money was empty and abandoned. I took it and looked at it and shoved it in my suitcase. Sara helped me close the stuffed suitcase and we both left the apartment. I didn't look back. Sara asked if she could help me with anything.

"Let me help you, Perele," she pleaded.

I went over and hugged her. "You've helped me a lot, Sara. And tell your husband thanks again."

"Where are you going, to your parents' apartment?"

"No. I've rented a small apartment in the center of town."

Sara looked at me in amazement. "Really?"

"Yes."

"What courage you have," she said, looking at me in admiration.

"So tell me where it is. I want to visit you."

"I would love that," I answered honestly, "but let's wait a bit. After things get organized, I'll get in touch with you," I promised.

Sara hugged me again and I started to walk toward another, unknown future, scary and intriguing at the same time.

After walking about an hour, I arrived at the little apartment. I'd decided to go the distance by foot, despite the heavy suitcase I was carrying. I wanted to extend the time that separated me from leaving the familiar life and entering my new life. I wanted to think, to be with myself. To test whether fear would manage to send me back, something that had happened many times over the past few years. But it didn't happen! Despite great anxiety, I had not a single regret, nor a moment's hesitation. I knew for sure that I didn't want to return to life with Menachem Mendel. But I knew more than that. I was sure that I also didn't want to return to the life I'd had without Menachem Mendel. The revulsion I felt from the life I'd been born into was stronger than my concern for the future. I tried not to think too far forward, because I knew that the uncertainty, the loneliness, and the struggles to come with the unfamiliar were liable to discourage me. I didn't want just to leave, I wanted something more, something that I didn't know how to define at that time.

The apartment was truly miniscule. It had one bedroom defined only by a drywall partition. The kitchen and living room were one unit. The bedroom was on the other side of the drywall, and in it was a bed, and a small cupboard with one door. You could take in the entire apartment in one glance. But the highlight of the apartment was a tiny rear balcony with room for two chairs and a small table. The apartment was old, and it seemed like the landlord had invested nothing in its maintenance. Some of the floor tiles were crooked, the walls needed painting urgently. Two or three tiles from the baseboard were thrown on the floor and revealed a wall covered partly with green stains. A few cracks were starting to appear on the drywall, and the kitchen needed a good scrubbing because a sticky layer covered the countertop, and in the sink there were stains of fat and old food. I saw everything, but there was nothing I saw that would cause me to retrace my steps.

I worked tirelessly the following days. I rubbed and scrubbed. I poured bleach everywhere possible. With the little money I had, I bought a small rug to hide the crooked tiles. I cleaned the closet and stuffed everything I had brought in the suitcase into it. Gradually, the apartment started looking like a place to live. The first night, I didn't manage to fall asleep. Every noise I heard jolted me out of bed. My thoughts also disturbed my sleep. I fell asleep shortly before sunrise, but I soon woke up when the buses and the honking of cars insisted that a new day had begun. I got out of bed, washed my face, put on the kettle, made myself some coffee, and went out to the balcony. Only then, when I was finally alone in my own apartment with no one watching, criticizing or threatening me, did I allow myself to breathe a sigh of relief and unwind.

TWENTY

"So," she said with a big smile, "how's the apartment?"

"Great," I smiled back at her.

"Come tell me about it," she said. She took my hand and led me to the back room.

"How did Menachem Mendel take it?" she asked.

"I don't know."

Sophie raised an eyebrow.

"He wasn't home when I left," I explained.

She took a deep breath and looked me straight in the eye, my hand in hers. "Do you think that's the smart way to leave?"

"Otherwise he wouldn't have let me go."

"Got it..."

We stayed a few more minutes in the room, and then she said, nudging me, "Let's go, it's time to get to work."

We got up and went back to the main room. I'd never even thought of leaving a letter when I went, but now that Sophie had mentioned it, it suddenly seemed like that's what I should have done. I had no doubt that when he saw the broken lock and found the empty closet, he'd know that I'd left. It was also clear to me that my actions would put him in such a rage that it would be impossible for us to have any kind of logical conversation. I knew that there was nothing that could mitigate his response or calm him. I saw proof of this just a few days later.

It was Thursday, almost the weekend. In the world I'd left, that was the day I would have been busy mainly with cooking for Shabbos. This time, I wasn't racing anywhere. I preferred to work that day and stay in the apartment on the weekend. I walked between the shelves and arranged the books that were waiting on the cart. I stood between two bookcases, completely hidden. I was so absorbed in classifying the books, that at first I didn't understand what was happening. Books started to fall from the shelf to my right. Some fell on the floor, and some hit my body first. Like a storm whipping up anything in its way, the books fell one after the other, individually and in bunches. At first, I thought that the shelves together with the books were about to collapse on me, that maybe it was an earthquake, and I needed to run away fast. But then, like a drawing being revealed gradually, the face of the man I had escaped appeared. First only the hat, then the eyes, and then the beard with the familiar smile. As my shock increased, the smile widened.

"You thought you could run away," he said, a cynical look on his face.

I froze. What was he doing here?

"Now you're wondering how I found out you were here," he said with a ridiculing chuckle. "You'll never manage to hide from me. I'll always find you."

"Menachem Mendel, let's go outside," I asked, after I'd pulled myself together a bit. I didn't want to make a scene at the library. I wanted to move him out of there, a place that was not connected to him in any way. But he was enjoying my fear of a scandal, and purposely lingered.

"Maybe I'll tell everyone what a whore you are?" he said.

He'd never spoken to me like that. What I'd been afraid of had arrived. The rage and insult that I'd left were so great; he didn't care what he said. He didn't care about anybody or anything. He just wanted to humiliate me and hurt me, like I had hurt him. It was the only weapon he could use to get back a little of the honor I had taken from him.

"So, suddenly you have nothing to say, huh?"

"Menachem Mendel, please let's go out and talk," I pleaded.

His smile widened and his pupils ran around in their sockets like a bug trapped in a jar. I started to walk out of the library and hoped he was behind me. I got to the hall's entrance and turned around to make sure. I saw him at the desk, his head down, his hat almost touching Sophie's face. I saw his lips moving, but from where I stood, I couldn't know what he was saying. And then he stood up and followed me out.

"What did you tell her, Menachem Mendel?"

"I didn't tell her anything, I warned her that if she got involved in our life, it would end badly for her.

"You threatened her?" I felt my blood surging with the shame, anger, and hatred I felt toward this man who was standing with me, his face glowing with victory.

"Go home right now!" he commanded me.

I didn't answer right away, and he interpreted that as agreement.

"Go get your things and come home with me," he said in a slightly more conciliatory tone.

I took a deep breath and said, "You listen well, Menachem Mendel. I'm not going home ever. I want a divorce. I don't want to be married to you anymore. So let's do it peacefully. Let's go to the rabbi, tell him that we want to divorce, and get the process moving. Each will go his own way and it'll be over."

Again that smile. And then he surprised me by saying, "Okay, we'll go to the rabbi. I'll leave you a message at the library when to come to the meeting with him."

"Great," I said. "It's best that way," I added and felt elated that I'd managed to convince him to conduct things peacefully.

He turned around, and I watched his black-robed body until he disappeared from sight.

I went back into the library and went up to Sophie. "I'm sorry," I told her.

"Don't worry about it," she calmed me.

"What did he say to you?" I couldn't resist asking.

"Oh, nothing special, don't worry." And before I could respond, she continued, "Go, straighten up the shelves, there's a big mess."

I rushed to the bookshelves and picked up all the books that had been thrown wildly to the floor. I arranged all of them neatly on the shelves. Despite my shame and concern when Menachem Mendel was in the library, I was happy that he'd agreed to go to the rabbi to take care of the divorce.

That evening, I took the time to fix myself a meal like those I used to eat when I lived with my parents. An omelet with vegetables and cheese on top, a fresh roll I'd bought on the way home, and a cup of tea. It was a simple meal, but for me it was special, because it reminded me of my mother, may she rest in peace. It was the meal she loved. When the apartment was quiet and organized, the kids and my father in bed, she would turn off all the lights except for one in the kitchen. Then she made herself a meal and ate it slowly, enjoying every forkful she put in her mouth, as if it were a meal fit for a queen.

One of those evenings I didn't manage to fall asleep and got out of bed. I thought everyone was asleep. I went to the bathroom and then I noticed a light coming from the kitchen. I wanted to turn it off, but then I saw my mother sitting and eating leisurely. She hadn't noticed me and was completely absorbed in every bite she took. Once in a while she lifted her head and looked forward, to the wall in front of her. Her eyes were fixed on it for several long seconds, until she looked down at the vegetables again and put another forkful in her mouth. I backed up without her noticing me and went back to bed. I lay awake for a long time and wondered to myself what she had been thinking about. What had been going through her head. Were they good thoughts or bad thoughts? Had she been thinking of us, the children, my father, or maybe about herself and her life? I remembered that the sight of her having chosen to be alone at that time changed something in me. Never before had I seen her as an entity separate from her children or husband. Suddenly she had turned into a distinct person, with thoughts that didn't necessarily have anything to do with any of us. I thought maybe she'd been thinking about herself. Whether things were good for her or not. That maybe she wanted something she didn't have, or maybe she just wanted to be somewhere else, without us.

I remember that those thoughts had scared me. It was much easier to see her as just Momme, with a clear and defined role, than as a woman with thoughts beyond her motherhood. I think that was a moment that had a big effect on me in my adolescence. And later I found myself in the same situation. Eating her food and thinking about my life separate from my husband and my family. A week later, Sophie had a message for me.

"Menachem Mendel called," she said, and I felt all my muscles tense. "He said he's arranged a meeting with the rabbi. Tomorrow at 10 AM."

"Thanks." I said.

I wanted to ask if he'd said anything else, but I was too afraid of what the answer might be. I thought about how instead of calling me, he'd chosen to leave me a message at the library.

At exactly 10 AM, I was at the rabbi's office. Menachem Mendel came a minute later. We sat across from the rabbi who finished saying the blessing over bread and swallowed the piece of bread he held in his hand. We remained quiet until he finished eating, and only when he shook the crumbs from his beard did he look up and say to us, "So..."

Before I'd managed to respond, Menachem Mendel opened his mouth and what came out of it caused me to want the earth to open up and swallow me whole. My face reddened, and I didn't know where to hide the shame.

"Honorable Rabbi," he began, "my wife is a deviant. She does not observe the laws of the Torah. She behaves like a prostitute. She's always pushing to have marital relations, much more than is permitted. She doesn't go to the *mikveh*[30] after the unclean days. She does not act in the bedroom in a way that is worthy of a Jewish woman." He stopped, sighed and shook his head in distress.

"What exactly do you mean?" the rabbi asked, and I decided to run from there, but my legs didn't listen to me. I remained petrified in the old metal chair and was forced to listen to the lies and inventions of the man that everyone called "my husband."

"She wants sex all the time. She shamelessly waits naked in bed and does unmentionable things. She touches all kinds of places on my body and hers and uses her mouth to act like a street whore. We've argued endlessly about this, but nothing helped. The woman is rebellious. Who knows? Maybe she learned these things from other men," he said, as if to himself, and again shook his head and stroked his beard piously.

The rabbi listened to him without moving his eyes from him. It seemed to me that maybe Menachem Mendel was describing his own innermost

---

30 A bath or pool where, according to Jewish custom, one goes to wash off impurities, such as after menstruation.

thoughts to cover up the sins of his fantasies. Embarrassment surrounded me from all sides, but anger was also building inside. I could no longer keep silent.

"Your Honor, there is not and has never been any truth to these words. For months there have been no marital relations between Menachem Mendel and me at all. Your Honor knows that this man has trouble controlling his inclinations. He's shown me the back of his hand several times, and recently even decided to starve me. He left me no money to buy food..." before I could go on, Menachem Mendel cut me off.

"She went out to graze in the pasture of strangers. She went to lewd secular people and learned their ways."

I decided not to respond to what he was saying, though I did want to get up and punch him until he bled. With all my strength I remained calm, and only my hands, resting in my lap, trembled in rage.

"Honorable Rabbi," I continued, "I want a divorce!"

"Just a minute, Mrs. Friedman. Not so fast. Every couple has problems. Small ones and big ones, but there's nothing that cannot be solved peacefully."

"Honorable Rabbi," I cut him off, "this is not the first time we've come to hear your advice. Your Honor has been aware of our problems for a long time. We've tried to overcome them. Menachem Mendel has not changed and will not change. There is no love between us, Honorable Rabbi. I would like to undo this marriage."

"Dear Mrs. Friedman, please, calm down. The question of marriage is not a simple matter. You don't just go and annul the vows. It must be checked what can be done, and every means possible must be used to save the marriage."

"Your Honor," I interrupted him again. "I want a divorce. There is no possibility that I will continue my life with Menachem Mendel. From the beginning of the marriage he has been violent. Your honor knows that, as he's come to you for discussions. When he returned home, he continued with his ways—"

"Has he hit you?" This time the rabbi interrupted me.

"No, he hasn't hit, but..."

"So, Mrs. Friedman. The treatment helped. You need to see the good things before the bad ones."

"Honorable Rabbi, hitting is not always with the hands. One can also hit without hands. Menachem Mendel held back food from me. He didn't leave me money to buy things at the grocery store. He would eat at the *yeshiva* and leave me without food."

"Liar!" Menachem Mendel yelled suddenly. "So how was there always food in the apartment?"

"Because I went out to work!" I yelled back at him.

"You see, Your Honor? I told you that the woman went out to strange pastures. She went out to work with secular people who influenced her." He had a look of victory on his face.

When I was seven or eight, the circus came to town, set up not far from our neighborhood. It was one of the few times that my father took us out for that kind of activity. I especially remember the clown. To make the crowd laugh, which included many children my age, he walked a certain way in long black shoes, hit some kind of obstacle, and fell and rolled on the ground. Then he got up, again walking the same way, hit the same obstacle, and again rolled. He did this several times. The children roared with laughter, and the poor clown continued to bash himself up by falling. I remember that I was one of the few people who didn't laugh. I looked around and felt anger and sadness that one person's pain was the source of enjoyment for another.

Now, with the rabbi in front of me and Menachem Mendel next to me, I felt that I was in the clown's shoes. I tried every possible way to justify my request to divorce. I gave examples, spoke logically, told of things that had happened, words that were said, about the hate and distance between us. I expressed my pain in every possible way but like the clown, I tripped again and again. In one last desperate attempt, I went over the same words in the hope that I could elicit an emotion from one of the men who was sitting with me. But my pain meant nothing to them, and its place was taken by feelings of power and pleasure. When I saw that nothing would move them, I stood up. Without looking at them, I left the room. In the background, I heard the rabbi calling me, but I was already outside. I had to take a deep breath, to fill myself with clean air. I felt defiled in a room packed with prejudice and stereotypes, condescension, customs and laws invented by men.

I walked quickly toward my modest apartment, but then changed my mind and went toward the big field that I hadn't visited in several weeks. The field waited for me, neglected and spacious. As soon as my feet walked on it, it was as if I had come to a warm home opening its arms to me. I looked around and breathed in the feeling of liberation the field brought to me. I kept looking around toward the industrial zone at its edge, and in a moment's decision, rushed toward it. Three men were bending over a car. Dan was in the middle. When I stood in the doorway, my body blocked some of their light. All three raised their heads at once. A few seconds passed until Dan recognized me. In a sharp move, he turned toward me, and in seconds he was at my side.

"Perele..." he said my name. It seemed like he wanted to do something with his arms, because he held them stiff and close to his body. "Where've you been?" he asked. "You must stop disappearing on me like this." Suddenly he turned to the others and said to them, "I'm going out for a little while." He said to me, "Come, let's go sit somewhere."

He walked in front of me, and I was a few steps behind him. He turned around and said, "Why are you walking behind me? Walk next to me."

His request seemed strange to me, as in my community, husband and wife did not walk together. Usually, the woman trailed behind and kept a distance between herself and her husband. I moved faster and caught up to him. He looked at me and smiled. I smiled back a bit tensely. We got to the expanse behind the garages. We walked farther away from them, and Dan suggested that we sit on a flat boulder. No one was there, and again I named to myself the sins I was committing. Secluding myself with a man who was not my husband. Sitting next to him with no one else around. My shoulders touching his elbow in a random movement without shrinking away in panic. I especially thought about the ease I felt around him, about the quiet he brought me with his very presence, and how this intimate time together seemed so natural and right to me.

He turned his face toward me and said with a familiar smile, "So what's been happening with you the past few weeks, Perele?" I felt he said my name differently.

I took a deep breath and announced, "I've left home."

His eyes looked into mine and he waited. "I rented a small apartment not far from the library," I added, and he continued looking at me in silence. "And that's it." He shook his head slowly and asked, "And...?"

"I don't know what will be. I only know that I'm not going back. I also know that it'll be very hard." I said, my voice weakening.

"Perele..." he whispered my name and his hand rose and turned my face so that I would look right in his eyes. The touch of his hand on my skin felt like tons of tiny prickly pins, and that hurt and delighted at the same time. I looked in his eyes and saw that they weren't as black as I thought. They had green flecks, like fallen leaves decorating the ground with color. We looked at each other in silence for a long moment, until I looked down in embarrassment. Then I heard him say in the same velvety voice, "I'll be with you, Perele."

It was nice to hear what he said, but I also knew that I had a long battle ahead and wasn't sure that his promise would withstand the test of reality.

TWENTY-ONE

The days passed one by one. I knew that Menachem Mendel would never let me live my life as I wanted, and every day that passed without something happening was a pleasant surprise. I felt I was living on the edge, putting my feet on safe ground but looking just a bit farther into the abyss. I worked in the library four days a week, and on the fifth, I did things I'd never done before. One time I went to the beach. It was a hot day at the beginning of the summer. I was dressed in my long clothes with a scarf on my head. I got to the beach after a long walk. There was almost nobody there, except for a few people walking on the shore and a few others lying on the sand.

I looked out at the sea, thoroughly permeated with fear. Never before had I been so close to the water. We'd only gone past the sea a few times, when we rode on the bus or walked with my mother to the outdoor market. The sea was next to us, but I'd never really looked at it. It had been like a background image. I remembered that once my father had also come with us, to buy things at the outdoor market, when suddenly a girl exercising caught my eye. She made all kinds of strange movements with her arms. She stretched them forward and looked ahead, beyond them, and then lowered her head and stretched her arms back. Every movement she made lasted a few moments, and during that time, she stood motionless, concentrating. I couldn't take my eyes off her. Her movements fascinated me, but what especially caught my attention was the calm she radiated. Even standing at a distance I could feel it. She moved slowly, as if measuring every move. When she found the right pose, she held it for several moments, until she had received the full benefit from it.

I was hypnotized and didn't hear my father telling me to move on. It turned out that he'd called me several times, and when I didn't respond, he came back to me, took my arm, and dragged me away. I didn't remember exactly what he told me then, I remember only the anger in his words, and his spitting, that I remember well. He spit to the side, mumbled something, and pushed me forward. I understood then, as a ten-year-old girl, that what the girl was doing was bad, and that I shouldn't even look at her. Now, I stood by the sea, and my father's warning echoed in my head. Inside of me, there was a storm. Should I get close to the shore or turn away from it? Should I cross a red line, or heed my father's warning?

I kept walking through this internal battle. My mind struggled endlessly with the thoughts, but my legs moved in complete freedom. Like a moth attracted to flame, despite the warning signals, I continued to walk, and my feet sunk into the sand. I walked and walked, as if the sea were calling me, until I got close to the water. The sea was pretty still. Light ripples swayed the water and white foam drew a line all the way across them. I stood there and my eyes followed the waves that appeared and disappeared. I wondered if it was the same water that returned or if it was new. Where did the water that was here before disappear to? What a neat movement. Water coming and water going. The same pace, the same movement. What clarity. How easy to know where you need to go, how long to be in the place where you are, when to retreat. A hand touched my shoulder. I jumped.

"Sorry, I didn't mean to startle you. I thought you were probably hot, so I brought you some water."

The girl speaking to me was almost completely naked, except for two small pieces of fabric that covered only what she obviously thought absolutely needed to be hidden. I looked at her and didn't know whether to take the water from her or ignore her and move away. Finally, I put out my hand and took the plastic cup from her. I drank it all and said, "Thank you."

"Do you want more?"

"No, thanks, I'm fine."

She smiled and walked away. When I was home and thought about that short encounter, I smiled to myself. If someone had looked at us from the side, he would certainly have wondered about the strange meeting between two women, one almost naked, and the other completely covered from head to toe. After the young woman had left, I sat on the hot sand and looked forward into the distance, to the horizon, exactly as I always did in the field. At a certain stage, I started to count the waves that came and went. And then the sun set. I sat by the waves for hours and felt more relaxed than I had in many years. As if the water had entered me and purified my disturbing thoughts, undesirable memories, fears and worries.

When I got home, it was already dark. My shoes were full of sand and my body covered with sticky sweat. I took off my clothes and got in the shower. The water caressed my body and removed the stickiness and salt, and something else that I didn't know how to describe. Though I'd only gone to the shore and looked at the sea, for me it was much more than that. I did something else that my father had warned me not to do. I wondered if I'd made a step toward something, or whether it was only a momentary caprice.

The next day, at the library, the feeling of calm that I'd felt when I sat at the beach for hours was still with me. Every once in a while I would smile to myself when I remembered the nude girl who'd so naturally offered me the cup of water, and I hadn't run from her. Nothing happened to me as a result of my contact with the "secular whore," as my father would have referred to her. But the calm was shattered at once when I returned home. The apartment had been broken into and the door was wide open. At first, I thought to run back to the library and ask for help, but then I dismissed that idea. I entered the apartment slowly. I could see everything in one glance, as the apartment was very small. Nothing had changed. Everything was whole, in place, and spotless. The apartment was completely tidy, exactly as I'd left it in the morning. With a little more confidence, I moved inside. Except for the broken door, there was no change in the apartment. Nothing was missing. And then I understood. He wanted to show that he could get to anywhere I was, and that I had no chance of running away from him.

The next day, I called Sophie, and told her I'd be late.

"Is everything okay?" she asked, concerned.

"Yes, everything's okay, I just have something urgent to take care of."

I went to the rabbinate building. The old building was graceless, its facade cracked. No one had bothered to improve its appearance. A metal sign read: Rabbinical Court. A heavy wooden door greeted those seeking to enter. I pushed it with my whole body and went inside. On both sides of me were long corridors, with walls painted white. I debated which way to go, and then chose to turn right. I passed one room with a closed door, and another one that was empty. In the third room was a clerk, concentrating on her computer screen. I knocked on the door and stuck my head in.

"Excuse me," I said, "where does one open a divorce case?"

The clerk looked at me and asked, "Have you come here alone?"

I nodded.

"Do you have a rabbinical pleader?" she continued.

"I don't understand," I stuttered.

"It's best to have a rabbinical pleader to represent you," she explained.

"Does that cost money?" I whispered.

"Yes."

"Is it possible without a pleader?"

"It's possible, but it's more difficult."

I was silent, ashamed of my ignorance. But then I decided that if I'd gotten that far, it wasn't the time to turn back. I'd postpone the rabbinical pleader for the meantime.

"So what do I have to do?" I continued.

The clerk opened a drawer and took out some papers. She organized and stapled them together, and then motioned for me to come closer.

"You need to fill them out and leave them here, with me. In a while, you'll receive a notification when to come for the first sitting."

I thanked her and went out into the corridor. My heart pounded. Finally, I was doing something official on the way toward my final break up with Menachem Mendel. It was obvious that he'd make trouble. He didn't want a divorce. He wanted to continue humiliating me to maintain his feeling of control over me. My renting a separate apartment and moving away from him had only increased his hatred and desire for revenge. He had to win. It was clear that he would use anything he could to represent me as promiscuous and a rebellious wife. It was possible that if he hadn't threatened me, I would have continued my life as it was, but the broken door reminded me that as long as we were tied together by law, I couldn't do anything against him.

The following months were exhausting. We had three hearings that left me
drained and frustrated. Menachem Mendel came to the first hearing with a
rabbinical pleader and his father. He told the three judges about my alleged
sexual iniquities, more or less the same things he'd described to Rabbi Weiss.
Like then, I sat embarrassed by his baseless descriptions. Two of the three
rabbinical judges were hanging on his every word. The third judge glanced
at me occasionally, and it seemed that his face showed compassion. But
that may have just been wishful thinking on my part, since I'd come to the
hearings alone and was representing myself. Menachem Mendel walked
around like a king. When he passed me in the hallway, he didn't look at me,
and neither did his father. I felt bad for his father, who was forced to hear
the sexual descriptions that filled the court room.

At the second sitting, I was called to the stand. The first question I was
asked was how it happened that I had left home and was living alone, without my husband. In response, I described to the judges the violence I had
suffered at the hands of Menachem Mendel. I told them that I had been
hospitalized as a result of a beating from him, and about the miscarriage.
Two of the judges asked me questions regarding our marital relations, and
I was forced to respond despite my embarrassment. Once in a while they
asked me to speak louder. They had no compassion toward me, and the
questions they asked were intrusive and far from the point. When I described the blows, they asked what I thought had brought him to act like
that, and then they checked my behavior. It was clear to me that they were
completely biased from the outset, and that nothing I could describe would
change their mind.

Every once in a while, when I couldn't stand Menachem Mendel's lies, I
closed my eyes and imagined that I was in another place. Most of the time
I thought about the sea. I imagined the waves, as if I were in them and they
were caressing my body and soothing me. Occasionally, I would see the
young woman who had brought me something to drink, and the knowledge
that there were other people in the world, not just evil men and rabbis, made
me smile. I also thought about Dan. About the warm smile on his face when
he looked at me. About his promise to be there to help me. Thinking of him
relaxed me and gave me hope for a different life. I implored myself to believe

that not every man was like those sitting there with me. Dan was different, and the ones in the garage also seemed different from them. Even the ones who came to the library and politely and respectfully asked for my help were different. With all my heart, I was careful not to be caught in despair and not see the world in black and white. I had to hold onto hope, as without it, I'd have nothing left.

From the third hearing, it was hard for me not to leave in despair. Menachem Mendel's father got on the stand and supported his son. When asked by the third judge, the one who had been quiet most of the time, how he knew all the details, as it wasn't normal for a son to share his marital relations with his father, he answered that his son had consulted with him often, and they'd discussed how he should act. "Did you ever speak with your daughter-in-law about this?" he asked him, and my father-in-law answered that it wasn't a subject that was discussed with a woman. "My wife tried to make peace between them, but she also failed," he responded without batting an eye.

Occasionally I berated myself for not having brought in a rabbinical pleader. On the other hand, I had a need to manage this battle myself. I wanted to represent myself but was concerned that I wasn't doing it well. As time went on, I realized that the situation was not working in my favor. The judges were convinced that there was room to work things out and were inclined to send me for talks with the rebbetzin, who would teach me how to act like a married woman and how to please my husband, the *yeshiva* student. They understood that no one had prepared me well enough for married life, and that the problems were all a result of that. Therefore, they said, what had to be done was to teach me the religious laws of the home and marriage. It's hard to describe my feelings during those moments. It was a mixture of shame, frustration, despair, a degree of reconciliation, and tremendous loneliness. I felt that I was alone in the world. My father knew about the hearings but had chosen not to attend them. I wasn't in the right kind of relationship with any of my brothers and sisters that I could ask any of them to join me. And girlfriends? I didn't really have any girlfriends.

The last sitting was to take place two weeks later. When we left the hall, Menachem Mendel walked past me and bumped into me, ostensibly by accident. I tripped a bit and saw how he grinned smugly. After the door of the hearing room closed behind us, I sat on the bench in the hallway and asked myself what Menachem Mendel really wanted. He didn't love me; he didn't even know the meaning of the word "love." What was behind the show he was putting on? What was motivating him? The simple answer that came up immediately, and which I'd already known, was the feeling of victory. For that feeling, he was willing to sacrifice a lot. To achieve it, he gave up any modicum of privacy, and was prepared to tell everyone about his marital relations, his personal problems, and the story of his life.

TWENTY-TWO

The day before the last hearing, I felt scared. I felt that I could not go through it by myself. Outside it was cold, but I was burning with fever. Sophie asked me what had happened, and I answered that I didn't feel well. She ordered me to go home and get into bed. At home, I couldn't rest. I lay down in bed and the high temperature caused me hallucinations in which I saw myself in front of the rabbinical court judges and heard one of them order me to return home. I screamed with fear and rage. I told them that they were sentencing me to death, but they were indifferent. I even saw that they exchanged glances that showed they felt sorry for Menachem Mendel that he had to deal with a woman like me.

I went to shower and let the water cool my burning body. Gradually, I started to feel better. When I returned to the room, I realized that the bedding was partly on the floor. The sheet was drenched with perspiration. I changed it and lay down in bed again, but after a few minutes I felt I could not stay alone in the apartment. I got my wallet, put on a sweater, and went out. In a little while, I reached my hated apartment, but instead of going into it, I turned to the door on the left. I knocked and heard the shuffling of feet. The door opened, and Sara, in all the fullness of her pregnancy, stood in front of me. I hadn't seen her for many weeks, and now the slim woman with a little bump was standing there with a gigantic pregnant belly. I couldn't resist and asked her with a laugh, "What happened to you?"

"A volcano, that's what happened to me," she answered, joining me in laughter.

"Where have you been?" she asked and invited me in.

"Here and there," I answered ambiguously.

"Perele, stop disappearing on me. I want to know what's happening with you. You said you'd invite me to your apartment sometime, and I'm still waiting for an invitation."

"Don't be angry, Sara. I've been through a lot of things," I said and suddenly started trembling all over. I'd left home with only a sweater, and outside it was very cold.

Sara saw me tremble and pulled me into the living room, where a large electric heater was blazing.

"Sit!" she commanded and went to the kitchen. Within a few minutes, she came back with a mug of hot tea and put it in my frozen hands.

"You are completely frozen," she said, and disappeared into one of the rooms. She returned and wrapped me in a warm woolen blanket.

"Better?"

"Yes, much better."

"So tell me, what have you been through?"

I told her everything, from the moment that I found the broken lock until the last hearing at the rabbinical court. I told her about the lies Menachem Mendel had told the judges. About his father who supported him without question. About the mocking looks of the judges. About my feeling of being a nobody at each hearing.

"So why didn't you take someone to represent you?" she asked wisely.

"Because I'm stupid," I answered. "I thought I could fight for myself. But it's actually not a question of fighting. It's a lost war in a system made up totally of men who see me as someone who's not worth listening to, and certainly not worth having her opinion considered. Do you know what lies he told them? And they listen to him as if he's God Himself. He and his father. Two devils lying without batting an eye. I'm sure that the rabbis know that they're lying, but they act as if they're telling the truth and I'm just some stupid woman from the street."

"You poor thing..." she murmured and patted my shoulder, and then asked, "How can I help you?"

At first I was silent, and then I said, "You could come with me to the last hearing. I don't think I'll be able to stand there alone."

"Of course I'll come. Why didn't I think of that myself?"

"Yedidya won't be angry?"

"Why would he be angry? He also feels bad for you. He said that I need to help you. That Menachem Mendel shames the entire community."

"He said that, really?"

"Yes. He thinks that people like Menachem Mendel should be banished. That he takes advantage of his power over you, that you are a poor thing that no one defends, and therefore I need to help you."

The tears came spontaneously. From the beginning of the hearings I hadn't cried. I'd held myself firmly and hadn't allowed myself to break. But here, covered with the warmth of words I never thought I'd hear, the dam of my tears broke, and flowed down my surprised face.

"You'll come with me, really? With your tummy?"

"Of course," she answered with a smile, "both me and my tummy will come. Together."

The fateful day arrived. I arranged to meet Sara at the entrance to the rabbinate offices. She was already there when I arrived. We hugged. She took my hand in hers and we strode into the room hand in hand. One of the rabbis looked up in surprise.

"Who's this woman?" he asked.

"A good friend," she answered.

"And why, 'good friend,' have you not been here until now?" It was impossible to miss the note of contempt in his question.

"Women's matters kept me away, Your Honor," she said with a smile, and without fear.

The judge looked down and shuffled the papers in front of him. After a few minutes he looked up and said, "Well, today we are winding up the discussions. Is there anyone who'd like to say something else?"

The room was completely quiet. Suddenly, Sara stood up and said that she wanted to say a few words.

"Are you a relative?" the judge who sat in the middle asked.

"No," she answered.

"Only a family member can speak at this stage," he ruled.

Sara tried to say something, but he didn't let her talk. It was clear to all that "the family members law" had been invented at that moment. The judges wanted to end the discussion as quickly as possible. The ruling had been written, and now they were to declare it. All those present looked at the judges and waited for them to speak. Suddenly there was a creak, and the door to the hall opened. Everyone turned at once toward the noise, to see who was disturbing the proceedings. In the doorway stood Menachem Mendel's mother. She stopped, looked around, as if to check that she had arrived at the right place, and then walked with her heavy legs toward the stand. I looked at her in surprise, not understanding what she was doing. Like me, her husband and son looked at her in shock.

Her husband was the first to regain his composure. "Chana, *was macht du*[31]?" he asked her from his seat.

Chana ignored him and stood by the stand, leaning on it, as if she couldn't support her own weight.

The judge who had silenced Sara before looked up and asked her in the same way, "Who are you?"

Menachem Mendel's mother looked forward toward the judge. Her face was blank when she said, "Chana Friedman, Menachem Mendel's mother."

"And what might you be doing at the stand?" he asked with the same tone he had used before with Sara.

"I would like to provide testimony," she said, and her heavy breathing echoed in the tiny hall.

"And why did you not coordinate your testimony with the rabbinical pleader at the appropriate time? Today we are announcing the ruling."

Chana didn't answer. She continued to stand where she was in silence. Suddenly the voice of the third judge was heard, the one who had been quiet most of the time. "Mrs. Friedman, please speak, we're listening."

His partner judges turned to him in complete surprise. They wanted to tell him something, but he raised his hand firmly and quieted them.

Chana began to speak. "Honorable judges, Perele is a good girl. I was surprised that her parents had her marry my son, Menachem Mendel, who

---

31 What are you doing here?

is known to be violent. Right from the beginning he hit her. Once she almost died. She even lost the baby because of him."

There was rustling beside me. I turned my head toward Menachem Mendel and his father and saw them whispering.

His father's hands, which lay in his lap, were clenched into fists. They moved uncomfortably, and I saw that Mr. Friedman was trying hard to adjust his sitting position so that he could catch his wife's eye. But Chana did not turn even a bit and continued to look forward. She continued to speak slowly but confidently, like someone who had decided that nothing was going to keep her from saying what she had to say. I suddenly saw her in a completely different light. Maybe she had also rediscovered herself.

"Perele tried as hard as she could to make a peaceful home. She would prepare food and always served him when he arrived home. She was a good wife, but he was never satisfied, he always had objections. Even when she was in the hospital, near death, he didn't go to visit her. He doesn't care about her at all."

The quiet judge sat up in his chair and looked straight at her. "And how do you know all this? Did Menachem Mendel tell you?"

"Tell me? Of course not, Your Honor. Menachem Mendel told me nothing, but I heard him speak with my husband and tell him. After all, even if I'm next to them they think I'm deaf or stupid and understand nothing. But I heard them very well. I heard everything he did to her, and I heard his father tell him how to behave to her so that she wouldn't rebel and would be obedient."

"And why didn't you say anything? Why didn't you intervene?" asked the judge who had conducted the hearings.

Chana Friedman smirked, and in a voice as cold as ice said, "How could I intervene, after all, I'm obedient and not rebellious. I'm deaf and dumb and stupid."

Silence. The judges looked at each other. Menachem Mendel's rabbinical pleader sat with his head down, and Sara took my hand in hers and squeezed it. Suddenly, Menachem Mendel's father got up. With a quick step and his head down, he left the room. A second later, Menachem Mendel left too. Chana didn't move her head. She continued looking forward toward the judges, and her folded arms rested on the stand. But something in her face caught my eye. Her indifferent expression had disappeared, and now there was something softer. The wrinkles on her cheeks straightened a bit and a hint of a smile pulled at her lips. It was clear to me that a very heavy burden had been taken off her shoulders. What a great woman, I thought, what courage.

The judges told us to wait outside while they discussed the case. I sat with Sara on the bench. Chana left the room last. She walked by me, and I went over to her. She took my hands in hers and I said thank you. She kissed me on both cheeks and when her face was close to my ears, she whispered, "I did that for myself," before she let go of my hands, turned her back, and strode out of the rabbinate building in her clumsy black shoes. A short time after that I was called inside. On the elongated stand sat only the quiet judge. The other two left via the side door, and he was the only one in the hall. With his finger, he directed me to approach the stand.

"Soon you'll be summoned to the divorce-receiving ceremony," he said and gave me a bundle of pages.

"Thank you," I said, "thank you for insisting on hearing what Mrs. Friedman had to say."

"I'd hoped she would come," he whispered and then rose, collected his papers and left from the door behind the stand.

I was dumbfounded. What had he meant by that? Did he know her?

On my way out, I took another look back and hoped with all my heart that I'd never see that place again. The questions about what happened in this discussion gave way to thoughts about the future. I had just one more stage. Only then could I feel completely released. Until then I would restrain myself.

When I got to the apartment, I went out to the balcony with a cup of coffee. I could see other buildings, old ones. Below, me, children were playing soccer. They'd set up goalposts for themselves with boards they'd found. Farther from the building, workers were refurbishing another building. There was noise all around me, but the cries of the children, the workers who shot instructions at each other, and the sound of the cars that came from the front of the building assimilated one into the other and became a monotonous tumult. My thoughts went back in time. I remembered the figure of Mr. Friedman leaving the hall, and I knew that the shame he felt then would remain for a long time. I wondered what would happen with Chana, his wife. It seemed on the surface that she had become reconciled to the life that she lived. But maybe a chance had been born that her husband would change his ways now that his weakness had been discovered.

And Menachem Mendel? I had mostly pity for him, but also rejoiced in his failure. The moment the family's secret had been revealed was also the moment his weakness was discovered. The weakness of not being able to shake off what he had experienced. He had grown up in a house where the mother was a servant, and the father was an all-powerful ruler. If he'd had courage, he could have defended his mother, but since he didn't, he'd chosen to stick to the ways of his father, to feel like he was worth something.

Suddenly, without any warning, I could see the figure of Dan. Until that day, I'd never dared think of him, sure that it'd be considered an infidelity. Even now I avoided it. Until I had the ceremony that released me completely from Menachem Mendel, I wouldn't do or think of anyone or anything that wasn't related to the life that I knew. But sometimes plans are disrupted.

TWENTY-THREE

It was a Saturday morning. Sara had invited me to spend Shabbat with them, but I preferred to stay in my apartment. I woke up later than usual and decided to spend the day doing whatever I felt like. I drank my coffee on the balcony, enjoying the cool breeze. No one was around. There were no children, and no construction workers. People slept or leisurely spent Shabbat in their homes. Thoughts came and went in no particular order. They were just random thoughts, of someone nice who'd asked me for help at the library, and when I'd found the book he was looking for, he bowed exaggeratedly and said, "You've made me a fan."

The neighborhood grocer also came into my head; he always reminded me that I could run up a bill with him and didn't always have to pay right when I bought something. Or the neighbor who lived on the floor below me, a woman who was a little older than me, who the previous morning I'd seen with a young man on his way out of her apartment, standing and kissing in the doorway. I chuckled at the embarrassment I'd felt, as if I were in her place. I also thought of a girl I had met at the beach a few weeks before and made a decision. I got up, put the coffee cup in the sink, arranged my scarf on my head, and left the apartment.

Outside, it was a sunny mid-winter's day. People in white shirts were returning from the synagogue, prayer books in hand. They were hurrying home for lunch. A woman was walking alone with a baby in a carriage. Maybe she was letting her husband sleep and was occupying their noisy baby. A few cars drove by on the street, the traffic lights changing colors. And I moved along slowly, feeling a strange happiness in my heart. I'd never gone out alone without being concerned or scared about something. Even now I sometimes stole a look to the side, to be sure that Menachem Mendel wasn't following me. Living with him had caused me to be vigilant. The reminder of his ability to get to me under any circumstances had achieved its goal. Anywhere I went, I was always scared that he would be behind me and see everything I did. Anywhere I was, I anticipated that he could appear suddenly and do something to humiliate or hurt me.

I got to the beach. I took off my shoes and walked barefoot on the seashore. Or almost barefoot. My thick stockings were a barrier between my body and the sand. But it was still a new feeling for me. Just a few people were on the beach. Most were just walking around, like me, and there were a few others in bathing suits trying to absorb the warmth of the winter sun. No one looked at me, no one stared. A bit farther from me sat a group of people listening to music. I vaguely heard their carefree laughter. Some were smoking, some were eating. The sight seemed so natural that I wondered if I would ever be able to act like that. To sit with friends, laugh, eat. To do things without looking around with worry or fear. I decided to continue on my way and pass by the group. When I got closer, their conversations became clearer. I heard someone say that he had been abroad and found exactly what he'd been looking for. Someone else told him, "Okay, bro, whoever has enough money can buy whatever and however much they want." The rest laughed. Apparently they were brothers and felt comfortable with each other. I got really close to them. Then I looked forward and continued walking.

"Perele?"

It seemed like someone had called my name, but that wasn't possible, so I continued walking.

"Perele!" I heard again, and he was already next to me. "What are you doing here?"

"Walking," I answered.

"Alone?"

"Yes, why?"

"Do you want to join us?"

I turned my head and looked at the group of men. They seemed curious about Dan's meeting with the religious girl. I guessed he hadn't told them about me. Some of them looked up and stole a look at us.

"No, I don't think so," I answered.

"So can I join you?"

"Your brothers won't be angry if you leave them?"

"My brothers?" he asked in wonder and then continued with a smile, "They'll get over it."

He made them a sign that he was continuing with me and we walked side by side along the shore.

"Do you come here often?" he asked.

"Yes, of course," I smiled and added, "every Shabbat I'm here, strolling along the beach."

He didn't know if I was being cynical or serious. When I saw the expression on his face I clarified, "This is the second time in my life that I've been at the beach."

He suddenly reached out his hand toward my face to move a lock of hair that had come out from behind my scarf. His sudden hand movement caused me to flinch in panic.

"Sorry," he said, "I didn't mean to scare you."

I saw that he felt bad. How could I explain to him that a hand heading in the direction of my face was a hand of punches, not caresses? "I'm sorry," I said. "I was just a little frightened," I tried to soften my response.

We walked for a while in silence.

Suddenly, with no warning, he asked me, "Can I buy you a cup of coffee?"

"What do you mean?"

"What do I mean? To sit at a café and have something to drink."

"And that's it?"

"I don't understand you, Perele."

"I've never sat at a café and drunk coffee. You can drink coffee at home. I've never understood why people have to sit outside and drink."

"You've really never been to a café?"

"Never."

"I see," he mumbled to himself. "Actually, I don't understand. I see lots of religious people sitting at cafés and restaurants enjoying themselves. I see religious people at the movies, going hiking, and doing all kinds of fun things."

I thought for a moment. How should I answer him? All religious people were the same to him.

"You know, not all religious people are the same. It's like... like, let's say, tablecloths. They're all tablecloths, but some are cotton, and some are satin, and some are tightly woven, and others not. And there are all kinds of colors and shapes. Short ones, long ones, round ones—"

"Got it. So there are also all kinds of religious people."

"Right. You've heard of the ultra-Orthodox, right?"

He nodded and suggested we sit on the sand because we were getting closer to a really dirty area.

"Here?" I asked, surprised, "Just like that, with clothes on the sand?"

He had a mischievous smile on his face and then said in a voice that tried to imitate mine and was a bit high-pitched, "Yes."

The expression on his face and the slightly chirpy voice that came out of his mouth made me laugh out loud. "That's what I sound like?"

"Something like that," he answered and sat down where we were standing. I hesitated another minute and then I sat like him on the moist sand and pulled my skirt down so it would hide my disgusting thick stockings.

"Okay, I'm listening, tell me everything."

For a second I thought he was joking, but when I turned to look at him, I saw that his face was completely serious.

"Okay, so here goes," I started. "There are all kinds of groups of religious people. There are national religious, ultra-Orthodox, and Hassidim. The Hassidim are actually part of ultra-Orthodox society. There are two other groups that belong to ultra-Orthodox society, the Litvaks and the Haredi Sefardim. I belong to the largest group of Hassidim, which started in Poland. There are other types of Hassidic groups, each one having a rebbe or spiritual leader of its own, and each is run independently. An important characteristic of our Hassidic group is the principle of sexual asceticism. The rebbe stressed to us the saying, 'Sanctify yourself in what is permitted to you.' The idea is to avoid things that are permitted, in order to curb the sexual inclination and get to a state where you are able to control it.

Meaning, to stay away from anything related to sex, even more than Jewish law requires."

"Wow," I heard him say, "that's harsh."

"Right."

"Give me an example of behavior that's supposed to chase away thoughts about sex," he said and then added with a shy smile, "maybe I'll learn something."

"You really want to know?"

"Sure."

"I, before I got married, didn't know anything. All my life they'd told us to stay away from the opposite sex. Before marriage, we don't know anything related to relations between a man and a woman. And then, a few days before the wedding, they tell you that you need to let your husband do all kinds of things to you." My face felt hot, and I knew that my cheeks were red. Dan did not look away from me, and though I was sure he could see I was embarrassed; he didn't say anything. I took a deep breath and continued. "When I went to the counselor who teaches what you need to do with your husband on the wedding night, I was in complete shock. Everything she said was against everything I'd heard my entire life. I thought she was lying or trying to test me for some reason. I even vomited from the stress and anxiety. It was awful."

"But after you get married it's different, right?"

"Not by much. For example, husband and wife. They're not allowed to touch one another in public. They need to keep a distance from each other to avoid temptation. Temptation is the source of all sins. So a husband and wife wouldn't walk down the street next to each other. The wife would always walk behind him. Or if the husband wants to pass their baby to his wife, he won't do it directly, but through someone else, so there won't be any touch that arouses thoughts of temptation. We minimize participating in family events, because the mixing is also liable to arouse the evil inclination."

"So you wouldn't go to family events?"

"Very rarely."

"I don't understand, there's separation between men and women at those events, so how could there be temptation?"

"Right. Even so."

"Wow," he said, and scratched his head. "And what's the meaning of 'the evil inclination?' What's so wrong with such a drive, especially if it's between husband and wife?"

His question confused me. "Inclination between husband and wife is good?" I asked.

"Obviously. It's a good inclination, not a bad one."

"How?"

"Because if a husband and wife love each other, then there are all kinds of inclinations aroused. They want to touch each other, feel each other, make love."

"Make love?"

"Perele, you've never made love? But you're married."

"Everyone who's married makes love?"

He started to laugh. His laugh got louder, and I watched him, embarrassed and confused. From laugh to laugh I heard him say, "You're right, not everyone who's married makes love."

The next day I worked at the library. Between shelving the books and answering people's questions, I thought about my conversation with Dan. I also thought about how I'd walked next to a man, shoes in hand, and we had a relaxed everyday conversation, what I once felt would never happen. I thought mainly about what he had said regarding love. I didn't understand what he meant when he said that a husband and wife made love. Love seemed to me like something good and unachievable, though I didn't know exactly how to describe what love was. Between Menachem Mendel and I there was no love, not even affection or any other positive feeling. After all, I hadn't gotten to know him well enough to have any positive emotion toward him. We'd never had a true conversation; we'd never exchanged ideas. I'd never gotten any idea about what he thought about all kinds of things. I wonder, I asked myself if there's love between Sara and her husband, Yedidya.

The next day, Dan came to the library. I saw him when he came in. He went up to Sophie at the desk, and she pointed in my direction with her hand.

"Hi," he said when he was near me.

"Hi."

"When do you finish work?" he asked.

"In about an hour."

"So I'll wait for you."

"Why?"

"I want to talk to you about something."

"Aren't you supposed to be at work now?"

"I'm supposed to be, but this is more important."

"This?"

"I'll come back in an hour," he said and walked toward the exit.

The hour passed by incredibly slowly. I couldn't concentrate on my work. I put books in the wrong places, I didn't answer people who approached me, and I found myself standing without moving and staring at a row of books on the cart. Finally, I saw him come in again. I put the cart to the side, grabbed my bag from the back room, and we left the library together.

Outside he asked if it would be okay to sit and talk in his car. I said that I'd prefer to sit in an open place.

"Okay. There's a public park near here, we can sit there."

We walked side by side in silence. Occasionally his shoulder touched mine and lit my skin on fire.

We got to the park and found a free bench. The park was almost empty, as it was around noon. Here and there, people walked by us. On a bench not far from us, a caregiver was feeding an elderly woman in a wheelchair. A young woman sat on another bench. She rocked a baby stroller with her foot and held a mobile phone to her ear. I pulled my sweater around my body and felt the cold penetrate my bones.

"Are you cold?"

"No, I'm fine," I lied.

There was silence again. He seemed to be weighing how to start the conversation.

"Perele, what am I to you?"

"What?"

"Don't be scared," he tried to explain, "I'm just totally confused and am trying to put things in order."

"In order? What things?"

"My thoughts, emotions. Since I've met you, something's been happening to me. I find myself thinking about you nonstop. I know that we come from two distant worlds, but that doesn't keep me from thinking about you, wanting to see you all the time. Do you know how hard it is that you suddenly disappear for long periods?"

"Sorry," I mumbled.

"No, you don't need to apologize. It's clear that you're going through something, and I just wish that you'd trust me enough to share it with me. On the one hand, I feel as if I know you. Feel you. On the other hand, I know almost nothing about you. I've told myself many times to stay away from you. To not look for you. But then my emotions just erase any logical thought and I look for you in the field or the library. It's good you never told me where you lived, because then I'd appear there too."

"I'm getting a divorce," I said.

"What?"

"I'm getting a divorce. During the last few months, I've been at hearings at the rabbinical court, and soon they'll summon me to the divorce ceremony."

He leaned back, stretched his arms out on the bench and said nothing. His eyes were fixed on a point on the horizon, and he sat like that for a long time, quiet and thinking.

"Dan," I called him, but he didn't hear.

"Dan," I said again. He turned toward me, and I saw that he was far away. He squinted his eyes and returned.

"Because of me?"

"What because of you?"

"You're getting divorced because of me?"

"No! You saw me once." I reminded him that he'd seen me when my face was bruised and wounded. "He never changed. But it wasn't only because of him. It's connected to the lifestyle, the way of thinking, to the fact that I'm sick of being constantly afraid that I'm committing a transgression. Always thinking what they'll say if... The fear of temptations and punishments, warnings and illogical rules. I'm tired of putting my head down just because I'm a woman. I'm sure that there are other things in this world, and I want to get to know them, taste them, try things out."

"And maybe you won't like what you find?"

I thought for a moment before I answered, and then I said that I just wanted to expand my options in the world and that I was sure that there would be some things I wouldn't like, and some I would, but at least I could choose what was right for me and what wasn't.

"Do you think there's a chance you'll want to return there?"

"No, never. My loathing of that life didn't begin yesterday or the day before, and it also wasn't a result of my marriage. It was a process that had been happening within me for many years. Actually, since I was a child. I'd always been different; I'd always thought differently from most of the people around me. Many times I argued with my parents because I didn't want to do what everyone else did. Even as a little girl I kept my eyes open. I rode on the bus and didn't look down. I saw people in the street dressed and behaving completely differently, and that really intrigued me. Instead of being disgusted by it, as many in my community were, I was drawn to the outside world. Deep down, I'd decided a long time ago to check out what was happening outside of the familiar life, but not until recently did I have the courage to do anything. I'd needed to mature along with my thoughts. I apparently also needed to suffer," I added, thoughtful.

"What do you mean?"

"Even with all my difference and contrariness, I was still very young, and not ready to get up and leave. Apparently I needed to be beaten to find the courage to make a change."

"You don't really mean that."

"Yes, I do. Sometimes you need to be so desperate to reach the decision to change your life. After my mother died, there was no one left on my side. You could say that I'd been left alone. In some sense that made it easier for me. That way I wouldn't have to take anyone else into account. It wouldn't bother me that I was hurting anyone."

"I didn't know that your mother died," he said and made a movement in my direction, but then caught himself and moved back. "I'm sorry," he said quietly.

"Thank you."

"But what about your father?"

"My father?" I said, and sadness came over on me, "My father is deep inside his own life. He's pretty sick of my rebellions. He'd prefer me to be far away. Besides that, he'll probably get remarried soon. Already the matchmakers are buzzing around him and trying to set him up with someone to replace my mother."

"I'm sorry," he said again, "that probably really hurts."

We sat in silence for a few minutes. He was immersed in his thoughts, and I was thinking about how that was the first time in my life that I'd spoken so much about myself with a man, and with such candor. What surprised me even more was how natural it had felt to open up my heart to him. I wasn't feeling as if I'd broken any type of law or committed any type of sin. I wasn't feeling different. I was feeling equal, and that was something new for me. He did not give me the feeling that I was doing something forbidden. He really listened to me, he was interested, he identified with my pain, and he did all that even though I was a woman.

Something new was happening in my life. The constant fear that dwelled in the depths of my gut had gotten lighter. It was still there, but it weighed less. I looked forward to the day I'd no longer feel it at all. To the day when my body would be clear of this misery, and I'd say what I thought without worrying that the sky would fall on me or some other disaster would happen to me.

"Come, let's go," he said and got up from the bench.

"But what did you want to tell me? I spoke the whole time and I didn't let you talk at all."

"That's okay, Perele, I understand now that it's too early to talk about the things I'd wanted to. We'll have time to talk about them later on. But I do have one request."

I looked up at him and waited.

"Don't disappear. It's hard for me when you suddenly disappear and I don't know what's happening with you."

"So what can I do?" I asked and suddenly I realized that I knew almost nothing about him. He hadn't told me anything about himself. On the other hand, I'd never asked him.

"Let's exchange telephone numbers. Give me yours and I'll give you mine," he suggested, "and when you feel like talking to me, call me."

I smiled and he asked, "Can I shake your hand?"

I hesitated for a moment and then I reached out my hand.

After we said goodbye, I felt as if I had butterflies in my stomach. A light feeling filled me and was with me the next day, but two days later the sky fell on me and shattered any hope that everything was already behind me.

TWENTY-FOUR

The days started to get warmer and longer. Stubborn rays of sun penetrated the windows of the library and projected a strong light in the hall. The warming sun brought with it more people to the library. There were many books to shelve and more people and children came and went. I loved having so much work. It was interesting and the time flew by. People who already knew me stopped and exchanged a few words. I remembered well how when I first started working, I would hide behind the bookcases. The people in the hall scared me. I was afraid they'd want to talk to me. Later I started to walk around in the hall, nodding my head hello, sometimes waving, smiling and even asking "How are you?" of the regulars that I knew.

That day it was so hot outside that I decided on the way out to take off my top layer and walk around in the short-sleeved shirt I'd been wearing under it. At first I wanted to put the top layer back on, because I felt as if I were undressed, but I forced myself not to. I decided I'd give myself a few minutes to get used to it. I waited a few minutes, and when I realized that no one was staring at me, I continued on my way. It was a strange sensation, to feel the heat of the sun on my arms. I stroked my arms and took pleasure in the new, unfamiliar sensation. Nothing happened, the sky didn't fall, and I even got home in peace without getting hurt.

I climbed the stairs, holding onto the metal banister, and felt exhilaration. Until I got to the door of the apartment. I put my hand in my bag to find the key, and when I looked up, my eyes saw a word sprayed in black paint all over the door. "Prostitute." My body began to tremble uncontrollably. I sat on the top step and leaned my back against the beams of the banister. I breathed heavily until I thought that I was having a heart attack. I looked at the door again and started to cry. I'd been so naive, I thought. It turned out that everything was not quite behind me. After I'd calmed down a bit, I got up and went inside. I took a rag and started to clean off the dirty word. I scrubbed the door as hard as I could, trying to get rid of any trace of the hurtful word, until the original paint also began to peel off. I decided to buy new paint and repaint the door myself. I decided I wouldn't let him break me. After all, it was only a word, I tried to persuade myself. I wouldn't attribute any meaning to it, and it wouldn't hurt me.

The next day was my day off. I could stay at home and read or go to the beach, to which I was drawn so much. Finally, I decided to visit Dan at the garage. I passed the field and got to the garage where he worked. I looked in and saw no one. The place was open and deserted. Suddenly I heard muffled voices coming from the other end of the garage. I went in, following the sounds. Inside, I found a small room with five men sitting around a table. Dan looked at the doorway, and when he noticed me, he got up smiling.

"Perele, what a surprise!" he approached me, his face focused on mine and he smiled in a way that no one in the world had ever before. And then he stood next to me in front of the others and said, "Guys, I want you to meet Perele, she will be visiting us often." When he said that, I felt both embarrassment and pleasure at the same time.

"Come," he said, "I want to show you something."

At that moment, I saw his hand rise to hold mine, but then he reconsidered, and put his hand back down. I wondered for a moment how it would feel to have his hand in mine. The truth was that I very much wanted to feel his hand, but the habit of being afraid of such a thing overcame my curiosity. I followed him until we got to the place where I'd seen for the first time the car they had been working on.

"Ta-dam," he sang and pointed proudly to the car that looked completely different from the first time I'd visited the garage. It looked perfect. The paint was smooth and shiny, the door handles gleamed. The tires looked completely new, and everything was clean and sparkling.

"Look inside," he instructed.

I bent down and looked inside. Seats had been installed; the dashboard was immaculate. All the parts that had been missing were now in place. One thing was still missing, but for a moment I couldn't tell what. And then I noticed that there were no seatbelts in the car.

"What about the seat belts?" I asked.

"Good for you," he complimented me. "Installing them is really all we have left to do. We are debating how to connect them."

"Why, what's the problem?"

"The problem is that this car has a turbo engine."

"Turbo?"

"Yes. This engine is more powerful than a regular one, and for that we need to adjust the seating so it will be safe in a high-speed ride."

"So?"

"So that means that the belts must be attached at four points instead of three as with a regular car, so that the belt protects both shoulders and the lower portion of the body."

"So what will you do?"

Dan smiled at me before he answered, "Hmmm, let's see if you can figure out a solution. Think where it's possible to attach them."

"Can I sit inside?" I asked.

"Sure."

I sat in the driver's seat and held the steering wheel. It was a strange feeling. Would I ever be able to drive a car? I asked myself. I felt so at home in that moment. I was sure that if someone taught me to drive, I would be a great driver. The seat was exactly the right hardness. I leaned back. My feet went forward and touched the pedals. It seemed as if every part of my body knew where to be. The precision reminded me of the game of blocks we used to play with when we were little. There was a drawing on each side of each block, and we had to choose the correct drawings to make one full picture out of them. If we did it wrong, the final picture would be distorted. But when we did it right, the picture was perfect, exactly how the parts of my body fit the car.

"So, what do you say?" Dan brought me back to the present.

"I think…" I said, "I think you can put a hole in the seats, a neat well-designed one, through which you could put the belts and attach them somehow onto the back seat."

I heard applause next to me. Until that moment, I hadn't noticed that one of the men had joined us and was also waiting to hear what I had to say.

"Great, wow!" called Dan. "That's exactly what we were thinking too."

I got out of the car and stood up straight. Dan looked at Motti who was standing next to him.

"So what do you say?" asked Dan.

"Fantastic, you did amazing work!" I marveled.

"Yes, we worked on it nonstop," he said and stroked the body of the car. For a moment I thought about what would happen if his hand would touch my body that way, but I immediately shelved that idea as it was a sinful thought.

"So what's the next project?" I asked.

"In a week, the frame of a car from the 1970s is supposed to arrive. An old car. The buyer wants us to make it into a sports car."

"What does that mean?"

"The plan is to restore the outside of the car exactly as it was originally, with the internal structure based on advanced sport technology."

I stared at him, waiting for him to continue. I didn't want him to stop talking. I wanted him to tell me more and more about what they were doing.

"The plan," he explained, "is to install new pistons, specially built engine heads, a stronger and lighter crankshaft, stronger and lighter connecting rod, a computerized engine, exhaust pipes and turbo systems."

I understood none of what he said, but the words my ears heard were like a wonderful song in a foreign language.

"The owner is an old customer of ours." He continued, "I think this is the fourth car he's sent us. It's his hobby, antique cars. He likes fast cars with special accessories. He has a lot of money. He visits here a lot; he likes to keep an eye on the work. If you come here often, you'll certainly meet him." And then he stopped, turned around to me and added, "So we'll be seeing you here?"

I blushed, and didn't know how to answer, so I started to walk toward the door.

"Hey, where're you going?" he called after me.

"Outside to warm up. It's cold inside," I answered.

"Motti," he called to the other guy. "We're going outside for a while." And to me he said, "there's a workers' restaurant here. Let's get something to eat."

"Didn't you just eat?"

"Yes, but you didn't."

When we got there, I told him that I wasn't so hungry, though my stomach kept growling.

"It's kosher, you can eat here."

I smiled at him gratefully and was happy that he understood without my explaining.

"So how was your week?" he asked after we sat at a table with paper tablecloths that were quickly replaced after the last people had finished eating and left.

His question reminded me of the day when I had found that word that was smeared on my door in black paint. "What happened, Perele? You're sad all of a sudden."

I debated whether to share what had happened with him and then decided that I would. "The day before yesterday, when I came home from the library, someone had written a terrible word on my door with black spray-paint." It was hard for me to say the word.

"What did they write?" he asked.

"It's hard for me to say the word, but it's very hurtful."

"Why didn't you call me?"

"I don't know; I didn't think of it."

"Who do you think did that?"

"My husband, Menachem Mendel," I answered without hesitation.

"You told him where you lived?"

"No, but he found out anyway."

He sat up straight and his face became serious. "Why would he do that?"

"He wants to humiliate me."

Dan thought for a minute and then said, "I guess he doesn't want to get divorced."

"It's much more complex than that."

"What do you mean?"

"It's a long story and you have to go back to work."

He took his telephone out and put it to his ear. "Motti, listen," he spoke into the phone. "I'm not coming back today. You lock up. Everything's okay. No. No. I have it. Tomorrow. Thanks, bye." And then he looked at me and said, "I have all the time in the world."

I hadn't planned to tell him, certainly not then, and for sure not at that place. But sometimes stories are woven when it's least expected, and apparently at that moment, at that place, in that atmosphere that had been created between us, it was right. So I told him everything, from the day my parents told me they'd found me a husband, until the decision to leave the marriage and live alone. I tried to organize the thoughts and events that were running around my head so I could tell the story with a beginning, middle, and end, like the stories that have a logical order.

The time mingled with my life story. I told him everything, almost everything. At a certain point I forgot he existed. I spoke nonstop. I felt I was opening up my personal life before him, like an oyster opening its armor, because I was letting out for the second time in my life all the pain and thoughts I had been carrying with me since my marriage. I told him about the first time Menachem Mendel had broken things and continued to the times I had been hospitalized after being beaten by him. I finished up by describing the last hearing at the rabbinate when my mother-in-law had testified in my favor. Dan was quiet the whole time. He didn't take his eyes off my face or ask any questions. Sometimes I saw his face change. Sometimes it was hard and sometimes soft.

I was completely immersed in reconstructing the most recent years of my life, I didn't stop for a moment, except to take deep breaths now and then. There were times when I felt I was suffocating and imagined as I was talking that Menachem Mendel had gagged me. I swung between imagination and reality but never stopped talking. I spilled everything that had been sitting inside of me for all those years, like drain water flowing out into the sea. It was already twilight when I'd finished talking. We were the only ones in the restaurant. The owner was busy cleaning, people came and went, but neither of us noticed them. Every once in a while we heard doors slamming, a sign that the businesses had also started to close. I didn't know how long we'd sat like that, me straight-backed, and him bent over and listening carefully.

Finally, I said, "So that's my story."

Dan remained quiet. He lifted his hands to his face and sighed. And then he put them down and said something I didn't expect. "If he were here now in front of me, I would kill him." Without any warning, he reached out and grabbed my hands which were resting on the table. At first I wanted to remove my hands from his, but he squeezed them and made it hard for me to pull them away.

"Perele, I only want to hold them, and that's it."

His soothing voice, a bit pleading, affected me. I left my hands in his and let my muscles relax. I was surprised to discover that the contact didn't frighten or threaten me. I knew for sure that the hands holding mine wouldn't turn into punching fists. Their touch was warm and comforting.

"I'm angry at myself," he said suddenly.

"For what?"

"That I didn't ask you, that I didn't insist you tell me."

"How would that have helped?" I asked.

"I don't know," he answered honestly, "but at least I would have been with you, I would have listened. Held your hand. And then killed him!"

It seemed like my story really hurt him, and that surprised me. Never before that had anyone felt the pain of my life. Not Rabbi Weiss, not my parents, not Menachem Mendel's parents, not the judges of the rabbinical court. And there I sat, with a person, a man who was not part of my family, and he was upset after hearing the story of my life. It was a strange feeling for me, but not unpleasant.

"So what now, Perele?" he asked, his hands still holding mine.

"Now," I said, from within my deep thoughts, "now, every day is a new day for me. I'm trying to get used to living without fear. But it's hard," I admitted in a whisper. He tightened his grasp of my hands. "I'm sure that the writing on the door is only the beginning. He won't let me go so easily. I hurt his ego and that's the worst thing to do to him. It's the reason for his beating me. He has such a small personality, that the only thing that he can do to survive, in his understanding, is to bash me up. Because without that, in his twisted thinking, he's worth nothing."

"I'm worried, Perele. I don't know these people, because I grew up in a completely different environment, but I'm worried for you."

His words touched my heart. It couldn't be, I thought, that they had taught us to believe that all people who weren't religious were either prostitutes or uncontrollable men. I was there sitting with a man who was warm and concerned, a man who cared. It couldn't be that underneath his cloak of concern hid a lustful monster waiting for a chance to pounce.

When I got home later, I felt exhausted, as if I'd been carrying a heavy load all day. The verbal reconstruction of my life aroused emotions I'd sought to forget. I felt once again the beatings, the threats, and especially the fear. It was with me all the time, in every place, though I thought I'd managed to drive it away. Any talk of the past returned me to the cold apartment, to the tension I'd felt every day before he came home. To guessing what mood he would be in, and what I could expect as a result. The fear was an inseparable part of me. And maybe it had always been there. I'd always had a reason to be afraid. Sometimes it was of my parents' reaction, sometimes of the neighbors, sometimes of the stares, of the social isolation, of my differentness, of my brother's steps on his way to my room. Fear. Fear. Fear. And to all that was added the fear of the physical pain, of my husband's punches. I had been pretty naive to think that with the divorce from Menachem Mendel would come peace of mind. Menachem Mendel wouldn't let that happen so easily.

Twenty-five

A few days after that conversation with Dan, my father called and asked me to come over for Friday dinner. He said we hadn't seen each other in a long time, and it was time for me to visit them. Indeed, I hadn't seen my father for three months. I agreed and asked if he wanted me to come early and do some cooking. "No need. Everything's all set up, just come," he answered cryptically. The days following passed quickly. I was busy at work. Sophie had asked me to work more that week, so most of the days I returned home late in the evening and fell into bed exhausted without eating supper. I noticed that my clothes hung loose on my body. I had lost a few kilos. I was in any case always considered rather thin, but at this point I was even more so.

On Thursday I went shopping. Usually, I cooked the food I would eat for the week on Friday morning. I would freeze some of the food and defrost what I wanted. Though my father said it was all organized, I decided to make something that he liked. I wanted to make him happy, to make up for my long absence. I prepared his favorite kugel and added the dried fruit compote that my mother had always made for the end of the meal. I hoped to surprise him, to show him that I knew how to cook, and was getting along fine, even though I lived alone.

Friday arrived. I got up early, cleaned the apartment, did some more shopping, and an hour before the time to light the Shabbat candles, I went to my parents' apartment. Ten months had passed since my mother had died, and the thought that I'd get there and she wouldn't be there was still strange and painful. Since her death, I'd visited my father two or three times, and the pain that I felt was unbearable. It was like praying in a synagogue when the rabbi wasn't there. My mother was home for me. She always wore an apron, and the familiar smell of her cooking greeted me when I came in. She moved around the kitchen like a ruler and didn't like people helping her. She'd only ever allowed us to serve the food to the table that she'd previously set.

I went up the stairs and could already smell the food. But it was different. Not the familiar smell that I had been looking forward to. I could still identify the dishes, but another aroma was added to them. I felt sadness. I missed her so much that I could feel it physically, really. My frustration, her withholding what I needed from her—it was as if they had never existed. I was willing to accept her exactly as she had been, despite the differences between us. I rang the bell with my free hand. The door was opened by a woman I didn't know. I figured she was the one who was cooking my father's meals, as a man wouldn't stand around the kitchen and cook. The Hassidic community helped widowers both with cooking meals and with the children. I smiled at her and wished her *Gut Shabbos*[32]. She smiled back at me and invited me in exactly when my father came out of his room, dressed in his Shabbos clothes, wrapped in his *kapota*[33] with the *spodik*[34] on his head. Under the robe was a white shirt and *hoyzn zakn*[35].

"*Gut Shabbos*," he greeted me. My little brothers and sisters sat around the table and smiled at me. "Come, sit," my father invited me to the table and sat at its head. After he made the blessings on the wine and the bread, the woman brought the food to the table. I was surprised when she didn't leave immediately, as surely she had a family waiting for her. After she finished serving, she took off the apron and left the apartment without saying anything. I looked at my father, confused. I didn't understand what I was seeing. My father, who noticed me staring at him, cleared his throat and said, "Perele, that was Nechama. She will be moving here in two months, at the end of the year following the death of your mother, may she rest in peace."

---

32 Shabbat Shalom, customary greeting on the Sabbath

33 Robe of shiny silk fabric

34 Large fur hat

35 Pants whose ends are put inside the socks

"*What?*" I said in complete shock, "What do you mean?"

"Nechama and I are engaged, and we're getting married in two months," he answered and asked me to pass him the salad plate. I looked around. My siblings were hiding their heads in their plates and eating quietly. When I looked around the table, I realized that all my father's favorite foods were there. Nechama already knew his taste and preferences and behaved as if she were in her own place, like she was his wife, and her conduct made me feel terrible anger and pain. At that moment, I felt that I preferred Menachem Mendel's fist over the spectacle that was taking place before my eyes. I couldn't stand it. I got up and left the apartment. In the background, I heard my father calling me.

I sat down on one of the stairs, and just burst out crying. I felt like my mother's life had been sealed. As if she'd never existed, as if she'd left nothing behind. I'd always believed that the connection between my parents had been warm and close, but in light of my father's haste to replace her, that idea was completely shattered. I continued to sit on the stairs in the dark for a long time. From the other apartments, I heard Shabbos songs. I imagined the other families sitting around the table, the holy atmosphere, the warm foods, and I wondered if that's how the world worked. Someone dies, and a short time later someone else takes his place. A year hadn't even gone by since she'd passed away, and my father had already found her a replacement. Had the connection between them been based on convenience? With all my heart I hoped I was mistaken, but what I saw smashed what I had always believed.

The plan had been for me to spend Shabbos at my father's place, but now I would have to walk about an hour and a half back to my apartment. When I finally reached home, I went straight to bed, and fell asleep within minutes. I woke up early in the morning and saw that I'd fallen asleep in my clothes. I went over what had happened, and what echoed most strongly in my mind was my father's reaction; he hadn't even bothered to run after me. He let me go and continued eating as if nothing had happened.

The wedding took place two months later, and I preferred not to attend. My father called once to invite me but didn't insist that I come. I haven't visited him since. It was still hard for me to handle the sight of another woman in my mother's kitchen. Every once in a while, we would have short phone conversations. He wouldn't mention the name of his new wife, and I wouldn't ask about her. Kind of an unspoken agreement we were both careful to keep.

One day, on my way out to empty the garbage, I met a young woman who lived in my building. The one who I had seen kissing the young man in her doorway. She wore a thin leopard-print tank top, her hair gathered up in a barrette.

"Hi," she said, "You live above me, right?"

I nodded, and wanted to go back home, but she continued. "Do you live alone?"

"Yes."

"Me too. Maybe you want to come over some time? We can watch TV together."

"TV?"

"You know, the box with lots of people talking inside it, and you can shut them up when you want to," she said with a smile. When she saw me hesitate, she added, "You know what? We don't have to watch TV. We can just sit and talk."

I was about to refuse, but then a sentence came out of my mouth that surprised me, "Okay, I'll come."

"Tomorrow?"

"Tomorrow," I promised.

"Great! We'll meet in the evening. I come home from university around seven." She started to walk away, and then turned and said, "I'm Tamar."

"Perele," I yelled after her.

The next day, I went downstairs. There was a sign on the door that said, "Bless Tamar's mess."

"Hi, come in," she opened the door, "I'll come and join you in a second. Sit in the living room."

I had no problem figuring out where the living room was, as our apartments were identical. I looked around as I waited. The style of our furniture was also similar. She too collected things others had tired of. Here and there I noticed new things, but there weren't many of them. On the brown sofa with wooden armrests calmly sat two pillows covered with black and brown leopard fabric. Her living room differed from mine mainly due to the TV that was broadcasting the news. Until then, I'd seen a TV only in store windows and at kiosks that I'd passed by. I'd never stopped to look at the programs they broadcast, but I was very curious to see what was on that wonder device. Tamar took a while, and I sat down by the TV. The newscaster was providing details of a terror attack in Jerusalem, and the pictures ran so quickly that I had a hard time following them. I got close to the screen, and concentrated on it, trying to take in everything that was happening. I suddenly heard Tamar call me. "Hey, you," she said and burst out laughing. "I've been standing here a few minutes, and you're just riveted to the screen."

"I'm sorry," I said. "It's the first time that I'm actually seeing a TV show."

"Really?"

"Yes."

"You can also watch other things; you don't have to watch depressing news."

"What else is there to see?"

"Movies, TV series, sports. Whatever you feel like."

I didn't understand how it was possible to choose what to watch. I'd thought there was just one thing to watch. I had so much to learn.

Tamar turned off the TV and sat down with me. She served me a cup of coffee, and said she preferred to turn the TV off so that we could talk and get to know one another. The time flew by. I couldn't believe that I could sit and have such a long conversation with someone. Tamar told me about herself with an openness I'd never experienced. She came from a town in the north. Her parents had divorced when she was a little girl, and she had lived with her father. Her mother had schizophrenia and she visited her every once in a while. Her words flowed with contagious naturalness until I found myself telling her about my life. I told her about my mother's death, about the pain that my father had found another woman instead of her so quickly. I told her about the problems I had when I was young because of my modern character, and also about my decision to find a new life outside the community.

Tamar listened with great interest. Her eyes didn't leave mine for a moment. She didn't even change the way she sat. When I stopped talking, she bowed her head for a moment and then picked it up again and looked me straight in the eye. "I understand that you don't want to tell me about your marriage. I see the ring. But that's okay, when you're ready to talk about it, I'll be happy to listen." As time went on, I got used to her directness. With her, there were no misunderstandings. She always said what she thought or felt. At first it was hard for me to be with her, but in time I appreciated her directness and candor. We became friends. The meetings with her were usually spontaneous. She wasn't someone who made plans in advance. She just like to "go with the flow," an expression I learned from her. Sometimes she came over in the evening and asked if I was free, sometimes she opened the door and called me to come down, and often we met in the morning, when she was rushing off to school and I to the library.

One time we ran into each other in the morning and planned to meet in the evening for coffee. She kissed my cheek and hurried to catch the bus that had arrived at the stop. It was a gray and gloomy winter day. The sky cast darkness on the world. Outside, it was very cold. I got to the library. It was also dark there, despite the fluorescent lighting. Only a few people had come that day. The weather induced a gloomy atmosphere for us all. Sophie barely left the desk. Usually she walked around the hall, spoke with people, and came over to me. This time she occupied herself with the computer and, except for getting up to go to the bathroom, she sat there the whole day. In the afternoon, the hall was almost completely empty. Sophie called me and said she was planning to close the library early that day. "It doesn't seem like anyone will come in this weather. You can go if you want," she suggested.

I also wasn't in such a great mood. I couldn't stop thinking for a second about the event I needed to attend the following week: I'd received a notice about the time of the divorce ceremony at the rabbinical court after several months' anticipation. For some reason, though I certainly wanted to end the process, I felt increasing tension. I had no explanation for this feeling, but it became worse as the date approached. "Do you want me to help you straighten things up before closing?" I offered Sophie, but she assured me there was no need and encouraged me to go home.

"This is weather for sitting at home with a cup of hot tea," she said with an encouraging smile.

There were only a few people on the bus on the way home. Everyone was wrapped in their coats, protected from the bone-chilling cold. It was just about six o'clock and outside it was almost completely dark. I approached the building. I hoped that the light would go on fast, because too often the switch didn't work, and I had to walk up the stairs in the dark. When I pressed the switch, the light went on for a second and then off, and I was left in the dark. I started to climb the stairs. I got to the first floor when suddenly I saw unclear shadows of figures. I saw three of them. Someone grabbed my arms and pulled me back, so that I couldn't defend myself. Another figure approached me and whispered in my ear, "Promiscuous slut."

A fist landed square on my face. I thought I heard my nose break. I felt like I couldn't breathe. I wanted to scream for help, but no sound came out of my mouth. Despite the pain, I started to move my body from side to side. I kicked my legs in the air, and it seemed to me that one of them had fallen backward because I heard a brief cry of pain. I continued to move around wildly. All the fear that I carried, all the tension and dread, all the desire to end the connection with my terrible husband went out in wild swings and in a long scream that finally came out of my mouth. Suddenly I heard a door open and after it cries of pain, "Aii, aii, that burns." And then running, and after it, silence.

Arms grabbed me, holding me tightly. It was Tamar, who whispered soothing words in my ear. "Everything's okay now, Perele. Lean on me," she sat me gently on the couch and leaned my head back. I heard her mumble, "Good thing I don't go anywhere without pepper spray." She disappeared for a moment and came back with a wet towel that she put on my nose.

"I think it's broken," I said in pain.

"I don't think so," she said, "but it's bleeding a lot."

It took a long time for the blood to stop, and then I calmed down.

"We must report this to the police," I heard Tamar say. "This neighborhood is messed up. This is not the first time I've heard of women being attacked on the staircase. I'd cut off their balls one by one, those rapists."

"They're not rapists," I said in my voice that had returned.

"What? How do you know?"

"They're messengers on behalf of my husband."

"I don't understand."

An hour later I finished telling Tamar my life story. I didn't skip a single violent incident I'd been through. I told her everything, without beautification or refinement. She was horrified.

"How come you haven't told me this until now?" she wondered.

"I was ashamed," I answered honestly.

"You were ashamed? Of what?"

"That I didn't leave him sooner ... I was so weak."

"You're talking nonsense," she exclaimed. "He's the coward that should be ashamed and not you. I'm sure that his father also hit his mother."

"How do you know?"

"Because that's what usually happens. Violence is passed down from generation to generation. His father was despicable, and he's despicable too." She spat in anger. "So who attacked you?"

"Messengers on his behalf, apparently."

"Sure, he doesn't have the courage to stand in front of you, so he sends someone to do the work for him. I told you, despicable."

Through the pain, a smile emerged on my lips. I wasn't used to Tamar's way of talking, but she didn't put me off. Her words described exactly what I felt toward Menachem Mendel and others like him.

"Now get up a minute," she instructed. She held my hand and led me to her room. "I want you to look at yourself in the mirror," she positioned me in front of my swollen, distorted face. "First, so you can see what your face looks like, and so that you won't be startled later on. And besides that, if you look more deeply, you'll see the heroine reflected in the mirror. A heroine with a smashed face," she laughed, "but a true heroine."

I didn't contradict her. There was no point in telling her that just then I saw only a bruised face and nothing more. The thought of being a heroine had never crossed my mind. She helped me get to my apartment and treated me like a baby. She undressed me and lay me down in bed. Before she left, she gave me a painkiller and then asked again if I wanted to file a complaint with the police. When I said no, she said, "That's what I thought."

During the coming days, she visited me every day and took care of me like a close sister. Two days before the date of the divorce ceremony, she told me she wanted to come with me to the rabbinate offices, but I knew who needed to be with me there and asked for her understanding. I called Sara and asked if she'd want to join me. She'd given birth a few months before, and I figured she couldn't come with me, but her answer surprised me. "Of course I'll come. Little Aharon and I will come together," she answered immediately.

The day I'd been awaiting finally came. Sara met me at the doorway, by the stairs. She looked pretty and well-groomed, as if she hadn't given birth just four months before. Though her face was made up, I saw a few small wrinkles around her eyes, which apparently indicated a lack of sleep.

"You're so pretty," I told her.

"Thank you. Pretty and tired, but content," she answered. "May it soon happen for you, Perele."

I smiled and stroked her hand. We walked together with the baby carriage clearing the way for us and went into the hall. The judge was already waiting there. Menachem Mendel sat on the bench in the center of the room and waited for the ceremony to begin. I looked around. In the corner of the hall sat an older woman that I didn't recognize at first, but when she lifted her head, our eyes met and held each other. It was Chana, Menachem Mendel's mother. She stayed in her place during the entire ceremony. I noticed that since she'd entered the hall, she hadn't exchanged a word with her son. The ceremony was short and infuriating. Only when I heard the words, "Divorced, divorced, divorced," did I understand that my nightmare was over.

The rabbi left the hall, and to my dismay, Menachem Mendel left the room after him without gracing his mother with a look. I approached her and touched her arm. Chana got up and surprised me by opening her arms and holding me closely to her chest. After she released me, I said to her, "Thank you for coming!"

She surprised me again, saying, "I didn't come for you, I came for myself." When I raised my eyebrows questioningly, she continued, "You've filled me with hope, and hope is a very important thing." Then she kissed me on my cheeks and blessed me, "You should have a good life, Perele." I smiled, my eyes following her when she left the hall in slow heavy steps.

"Poor woman," mumbled Sara when I joined her, and we started to leave.

"Maybe," I said pensively, "but she's brave. It's not simple to do what she did, to come out like that, in public, against your husband and son. I wonder what her life will be like now."

"Right. But what's important now is *your* life."

I smiled at her.

"What are your plans now, now that you were released from this man whose name will not cross my lips?"

"I don't know. I have to get used to the feeling that I'm not tied to the man whose name I also don't want to say." I laughed, and she did too, and then suddenly I suggested without thinking, "Do you want to come to my apartment?"

Sara stopped and then said, "I have to get home to put Aharal'e to bed. Another time."

"Sure. Thanks for coming with me today. It was very important to me."

"Me too." She leaned toward me, hugged me, and went on her way.

I'd put her in an awkward situation. If she'd come to my apartment, it would have been as if she'd accepted my way of life. Actually, until that day she hadn't expressed an opinion on the subject, and I didn't know what she really thought. She'd never said anything about my living alone outside of the neighborhood, or that I worked in a place with people who are not religious. On the other hand, she'd supported me and been with me during my most difficult times, and that's no small thing. Maybe in the future she'd have the courage to cross the bridge to my side, if only for a very short time.

On my way home, I thought about everything I'd been through the past year. Leaving my husband, renting an apartment, living by myself, a new friend, a new man friend, I'd been attacked and continued my life, and now I was divorced. I'd cut the ties to the man who'd made my life miserable in recent years. But not just that. I'd cut other ties that weren't connected to him. I'd broken away from my differentness. I'd broken away from the fear of the evil inclination, of the super-strict rules, of the threatening and disdainful looks. The divorce meant the end of my previous life. I felt that I was in a kind of corridor between two doors. One had closed behind me and the other was opened slightly, calling me to try and open it further.

TWENTY-SIX

I entered the library and, as usual, passed by Sophie's desk and said good morning to her. Sophie was busy with some task. She looked up, mumbled, "Good morning," and then I heard her call in a voice she'd never used in the library, "Perele?"

I turned around and she was already next to me.

"Is that you?"

"Yes, it's me," I laughed.

"I don't believe it! You're so pretty," she said, grabbed me by the arm and pulled me behind the bookcases. "What happened? Why did you do that? I mean, it's nice, you look great. But why?"

"The divorce is final."

"What?"

"That's it, the Menachem Mendel era is over."

"Thank God," she said and hugged me tightly. "Well, that's a cause for celebration. Today we're going to celebrate. After work, we're going to raise a cup of coffee in a toast."

When she saw my hesitation, she added, "At a kosher place, of course." And then she hugged me again, and on her way back to the desk I heard her murmur, "How wonderful."

While arranging books and answering people's questions, I contemplated what had happened since my decision until I had carried it out. I had made the decision even before the divorce was final. I just had to do something that would symbolize my breaking off from the harsh world of "holiness." Something powerful that made a clear declaration. Something that everyone could see, especially me. And what could be more apparent than a change to my appearance?

After I returned from the rabbinical court, I stood in front of the mirror in the bathroom. I looked at myself for a long time and told myself out loud, "Perele, it's over. You are now yourself, and not who they tell you to be. Now you need to get to know yourself and love yourself. Because you are pretty and smart and good," and without looking away from the reflection, I continued to tell myself things. When the tears ran down my face like a waterfall, I reached up and slowly removed the scarf from my head. My hair was liberated and fell onto my shoulders like whipped cream flowing from the container it had been trapped in. I took a pair of scissors and cut my hair until my scalp was left with sharp spikes. As I progressed in this task, I distanced myself further from the familiar Perele, and in her place appeared a strange figure I had never met. Her features were familiar, but the expression on them was foreign to me.

"Who are you?" I asked out loud, and immediately answered, "I am the new Perele."

"And who is the new Perele?"

"She is a brave, determined, stubborn young woman."

"What else?"

I stopped for a second and continued with the conversation, unsure if it really happened or was only in my head. I'm also ambitious, curious, and I want to learn new things, I told myself. I want to meet new people. I want to love, and I want to be loved.

The next time I saw myself in the mirror was in the morning. I found myself waking up in my bed in a panic. I didn't remember how I'd gotten to bed, and I didn't remember at first what I had done the previous night. But bits of cut hair on the pillow reminded me of the meeting I'd had with the reflection in the mirror. I immediately went to the bathroom and looked at myself again, to decide whether I had been dreaming or if what I'd imagined had actually happened. The reflection was already a little more familiar than it had been the night before. "Hi," I said to the figure, and she smiled back at me. I stroked my head and felt the spikes. I loved the feeling on my palms, and gradually I started to love the face in the reflection. I showered, got dressed, and left the house with my head uncovered.

At the end of the workday, when silence echoed in the library and darkness lovingly enveloped the endless mysteries on the shelves, Sophie and I went out to a kosher café. Sophie put her arm in mine. My heart was full of expectation and excitement for something new: to sit with a friend at a café and talk. The three hours we spent there together showed me a different Sophie than the one I thought I knew. For some reason, I had imagined her life totally different from what it really was. I imagined her as a mother of children, married for many years to the same man, living in her own home. I had been jealous of her orderly life, that she had a regular job that allowed her peace of mind. I imagined her coming home and hugging her young children, warming up food that she'd prepared for them in the morning, helping them with their homework, sighing with relief on Friday after working in the kitchen and finishing all her tasks ahead of the weekend, and spending Shabbat mainly sleeping and resting. But in reality, her life was completely different.

Sophie had been married to the same man for almost thirty years. As time passed, they'd realized that they didn't have very much in common and decided to continue living together but separately. Each one lived their life as they wanted. "Sometimes," she said, "he doesn't come home at all at night, or returns a day or two later." They hardly communicate, except for what relates to their three children. "I learned to live alone," she said. "It's even convenient for me. I conduct my life as I see fit, and don't have to report to anyone. The kids are already grown and have their own lives, so my life is completely my own."

"I thought that you had young children."

"Yes, they're young."

"I meant children, who are still of school age."

"No, they're already university students."

"But you look really young."

"I married very young and was very young when the eldest was born."

We continued to chat, and as time passed, I found out more and more about Sophie. Suddenly I saw her in a completely different light. From someone in charge of the library, giving instructions and conveying self-confidence in what she does, a woman with weaknesses was revealed; a person who's sometimes disappointed, excited, frustrated, and often lonely. Maybe that's what connected us, the loneliness, I thought. At nightfall, we parted, but not before we promised each other to get together more often.

On my way home, I thought about the hours that had passed. I thought how in recent years I'd been busy with myself, and I hadn't managed to look around me, never having asked Sophie about her life. I had just been involved in her interest in me, and I'd not thought to be curious about her. For a moment, I thought about Sara. Was Sara really happy and content, or was her behavior, like mine in the past, hiding another life?

It was already eight in the evening when I turned on the light in the staircase. I started to climb up to my apartment, and then I heard a rustling, and after it a cry of shock. "Perele, is that you?" I turned and encountered the amazed look on Tamar's face. "Is that you? I don't believe it; what did you do?"

I laughed and turned to her while stroking my cropped head. "Yes, it's me," I promised her.

"Wow, how pretty you are!" She climbed up two stairs and came towards me, reached out and rubbed my head. "Ouch, it's sharp," she laughed. "You're amazing, it looks so good on you." She grabbed my hand and pulled me into her apartment. "You have to tell me everything."

"There's nothing to tell," I mumbled, "I just decided it was time for a change."

"You're great. We have to celebrate. Wait."

Tamar disappeared for a moment and returned with two glasses of wine. She handed me one of them and called out, "Salut."

"L'hayim!" I answered.

At eleven I went home. I had never had such a day. I'd spent time with two friends, with one at a café and with the other at her home, over two glasses of wine. My head was spinning but I was exuberant, though possibly a bit too much. As I brushed my teeth, I looked at myself in the mirror and laughed for no reason. I couldn't stop laughing. I kept trying to stop, but I couldn't. My laughter had a life of its own, and it increased uncontrollably. Toothpaste ran out of my mouth like soap from a sponge. I said something unclearly and burst out laughing again, and the toothpaste mixed with my saliva, ran onto my shirt and from there to the floor. The laughter wouldn't die down. It sounded like a barking dog. I sat on the bathroom floor with my legs apart and leaned my head on the wall.

When I finally opened my eyes, it was already light out. At first, I couldn't remember why I was by the shower and not in my bed, but then I started picturing what had happened the night before. I understood that the wine I drank at Tamar's place had confused me. Maybe also the sentence "You're so pretty!" didn't really help me stay balanced. I got up to rinse my face and saw white toothpaste all over it. I smiled at my reflection in the mirror, showered, and got into bed.

When I woke up, it was already noon. I was supposed to be at the library about a half hour later, and I was ten minutes late. Sophie looked up at me and smiled. She said nothing about my being late. I walked around the library with the cart. I gathered and shelved the books. I straightened books on the shelves and moved others that were out of place. The whole time, a song was playing in my head. A song without words, with a tune I'd invented myself. For a while I heard myself hum out loud, and then I was quiet and scolded myself.

At six in the evening, I felt tired and asked Sophie if I could take a break. Two hours remained of the shift. I assured her that all the books were back in their places on the shelves, and the cart was empty. I went to the back room and sat on the chair I'd used in the past, when I'd read books secretly. There were no books on the table. No more tower with a note with my name on it. I had no need to prove to anyone that I existed. I could walk freely to any shelf in the library and pull out any book that I wanted to read, without worrying about sin or punishment. It seemed as if I had naturally and easily gotten used to life without fear, but sometimes, for no apparent reason, I was stricken with fear and thoughts that Menachem Mendel would come to hurt and humiliate me. The feeling was so palpable that I had to sit to calm my breathing. It was hard for me to let go of the fear, and it was even harder for it to let go of me.

There was a knock at the door. Before I could answer, it opened slowly, and a familiar head looked in. "Oh, sorry, I'm looking for... Perele?!" He took a step inside. "Is that you?!"

I nodded.

"Perele?" he repeated my name.

"Yes," I laughed, "it's me."

He stepped inside, all the while looking at me. "I don't believe it," he murmured, pulling over another chair to sit across from me. He looked at me and didn't say a word. He had a strange smile on his face. We sat silently and looked each other straight in the eye. Finally, he asked, "Can I touch it?" and before I managed to say no, he reached over and touched the top of my head. "It's nice," he said, and added, "you're beautiful."

My cheeks flushed, and I bowed my head so he wouldn't see.

"You're blushing," he said, "and that looks good on you too. And also, I like to embarrass you," he added and laughed cheerfully. I joined his laughter, and something relaxed inside of me.

When we'd stopped laughing, he asked what had caused me to make the change. I told him that my divorce was finalized and saw how his body straightened on the chair. His eyes penetrated further into mine.

"So because of that you didn't want us to meet," he said.

During the previous weeks, he had called several times and asked if we could meet. I'd told him I couldn't, and each time gave him a different reason for the refusal.

"Now I understand," he said, and was quiet. Then he asked, "And how do you feel now?"

"Kind of liberated."

"Kind of?"

"Yes, I'm still getting used to the new status. It's strange for me. I need time to get used to not being scared."

Then he asked, "Do you have plans for this evening?"

"No."

"I'll wait until you're done here, and then I'll take you to a nice place."

My first impulse was, as usual, to refuse, but I stopped myself. Why not? I thought. What terrible thing could happen from sitting and talking with a man?

At eight, he was waiting for me outside the library. "Come, New Perele," he smiled and then put out his hand to take mine.

"Not yet," I said and hid my hand behind my back.

"Not yet," he repeated and added, "that gives me some hope."

He smiled and led me to his car, which was parked nearby. It was the second time I'd sat with him in a car. I told myself that I wasn't doing anything bad. He's driving, and I'm just sitting next to him. Every once in a while, I stole a look at him, but he was keeping his eyes on the road. We rode in silence. Dan didn't tell me where we were going, and I was concentrating on my internal struggle.

Finally, he stopped the car and said, "Come." We got out of the car, and in measured steps, climbed the steep hill side by side. I found myself on the top of a hill, and the sea spread out before us like a star-studded blanket. The light of the moon played with the waves and generated random sparkles of light and shadow, like fireflies at night. In my imagination, the sea and the moon interacted playfully like old friends, knowing they had an audience. They teased and exchanged glowing winks, and their arrogance was also the source of the admiration by those looking on at them.

"This is amazing. It feels as if the whole world is the sea, except for the hill and us."

"I told you I'd bring you to a nice place," he boasted.

We gazed out at the sight in front of us. Suddenly he said, "How was it to ride with me alone in the car again?"

I looked at him. He smiled, but also looked serious. "You knew it was hard for me," I said.

"Yes, I knew."

"And still you asked."

"Yes. And it went okay, right?"

I smiled and looked back out toward the horizon.

TWENTY-SEVEN

My father called me one day and asked me to come for the Passover meal. Since I'd been home and met his then-future wife, I'd avoided going back. We'd spoken briefly on the phone now and then, but nothing beyond that. I hesitated and told him I'd think about it and get back to him. I had no plans for Passover. My father was the only one who'd invited me, and I really didn't want to be alone for the holiday. A few days later, I called him and told him I would come. That seemed to make him happy.

A few days before the holiday, I decided to come to the dinner with some of my father's favorite dishes; a peace offering for my absence and coolness last time we'd met. I bought the things I needed at the grocery store, and two days before the dinner, I began to cook. I boiled water, washed vegetables, kept track of my hands that knew how to do the work themselves and allowed me to sail off and think about questions that remained unanswered. Like for example, why was it so important to me to make my father happy? Did I have anything to apologize for? Was there any justification for all my guilty feelings related to him and to my family in general?

As the questions arose, I felt uncontrollable anger growing inside of me. Anger at my father whom I'd so needed and who had chosen to distance himself rather than help. A father that in my eyes did not do his job, to defend and accept his children unconditionally, as I thought should be. And yes, he was also a husband who had closed the chapter of his life with my mother so quickly and so callously, without preparing, sharing, or explaining. My busy hands stopped suddenly and turned off the gas. Then they poured the cooking vegetables into the garbage, and instead of standing in the kitchen in an apron, I straightened my clothes, grabbed my bag, and went out.

The wide smile on Dan's face when he saw me immediately made the distress I'd felt on the way over disappear. I went inside, and like a photo in an album commemorating a particular moment, so he stood with his friends, bent over like the other times, around the car. They exchanged a few words, shook their heads, and made gestures with their hands. I saw the men's surprise at my new look. Motti, the friend I'd gotten to know more than the others, came up to me and said, "You look nice." I mumbled an embarrassed "thanks" and waited for Dan. One of the guys, whose head was under the hood, asked him a question, but Dan ignored him and walked up to me with the smile that widened as he got closer.

When he was really close to me, he said, "Can I kiss you?"

"What? Where'd you get that idea?"

"On the cheek," he promised.

I thought to myself, what does it give him, to kiss me on the cheek? But I didn't move when he brought his head close and planted a kiss on my cheek. For a moment, I wondered if the kiss had left a mark that would let anyone passing me by know about my sin.

"Come, Perele," he coaxed, and naturally lay his hand on my back.

He didn't know that every such movement—his hand on my back, his arm rubbing my arm, or his pushing hair away from my face—all those gestures that were so obvious from his point of view, were a reminder of what I had left behind. On the one hand, I was afraid, but on the other hand, I took pleasure in the very daring. His hand on my body gave me goose bumps, but also created fear of violating the prohibition against touching, which was so ingrained in me. We sat again at the same workers' eatery we had been to before. I put my hand on the table, and he, who sat across from me, took them in his hands. I tried to pull them back, but he held them tightly and didn't allow me.

"Perele, I can't keep from touching you," he said, his eyes not leaving mine.

I was quiet for a few seconds, and then I confessed, "I'm not used to this."

"You never held hands or touched each other, even when you were first married?"

"Of course not. I hardly knew him when we got married. In our community, you don't show affection in public. It's just not done."

"Not even a husband who loves his wife?" he wondered.

"Not even."

"But why?"

"Because that way we'll fix the permissive and lascivious world," I said mockingly.

He didn't hear that I was making fun, and asked, "You really believe that?"

"I don't, but most of the community does."

"Then it's really forbidden for you to show affection, hug, kiss?" he asked in amazement.

"In public for sure. But I would imagine that there are married people who do that at home."

Gradually I released my hands from between his.

He sat back and was quiet for a few moments. "I don't understand how it's possible to train someone not to feel, not to love, and not to show love. I really don't understand."

"Look, they don't teach us not to love or feel. Of course not. But in our community, love is measured in different ways."

"How?" he asked, continuing to look at my face in expectation of an answer.

"Mainly in that women lift all burdens from their husbands and leave them free to deal with spiritual matters. We keep a distance between men and women. We are like two separate groups, each with its own way of life. Each group has its role. The men need to deal with learning and spiritual issues, and the women need to help them, so they aren't disturbed by anything connected to the running of the house. The women take care of the children, cook, clean, and all that. There are even those who believe that women, in the way they were created, were born with a love of cooking, while men were born to hate it."

"But what if a woman hates cooking and would rather learn, or as you put it — 'deal with spiritual issues'?" he asked innocently.

I smiled at his question. No one in the community would ever ask such a question. "You're speaking about equality," I commented quietly.

"Oh, yeah…" he mumbled, and then added, "Why should a woman not be able to choose what she wants to do? She could do something that she likes and still enable her husband to learn."

"Look," I took a deep breath and I knew that what I was going to say wouldn't convince him or change his mind. "Equality the way you perceive it is different from the way we see it. For us, fairness is precisely in the differentness. The opposing sides make up the whole. There's order to the world. Like the sun rises in the east and sets in the west, like on Rosh Hashanah we eat apples dipped in honey, on Sukkot we shake the palm branch, and when Shabbos ends, we say the Havdalah prayer. There is an order to the world, and it's totally unconnected with equality or inequality. The order is determined by God, who assigned a role to everyone. And everyone who has a role must work as hard as possible to fulfill that role, and not compare himself with anyone else. That way, the world will be orderly and complete. And besides that," I added, "women are the ones who pass down the values and education to the next generation. Without them, it wouldn't happen."

In the process of explaining it to him, though I had no idea why it was so important to me that he understand, I realized that I was actually showing the people and the community I had left in the best possible light. For some reason, it was important to me that he understand the logic in that way of life. I wanted him to know that it wasn't just a whim, but that there was a whole rationale that had been constructed many years before to protect a different type of life that engages in spirit, out of true and deep faith. From his expression, I could tell that he wasn't convinced. Finally, he asked, "How do you make different people all act the same way?"

"With rules and regulations whose aims are to protect us from anything that might distract us from dealing with spiritual matters and fulfilling commandments." I took a deep breath. "It's like training a puppy not to run into the street or relieve himself in the house. Our whole life we have teachers and supervisors who make sure that we don't transgress any of the rules of 'holiness.' We are taught to believe that mixing of genders is a sin. That it's against the way of the Torah and the community, and therefore we must do everything possible to avoid it. There is no touching of any kind, family events are avoided so as not to succumb to temptation, even a fleeting glance. Men look down when they pass a woman. I've even heard about someone who when he travels by bus takes off his glasses, so he won't see the women that board. They always stressed to us the importance of concentrating on learning and other spiritual activities."

"And what about sex or subjects like that, they never spoke to you about them?"

I smiled. "Of course not. That's not something that's discussed unless someone has some kind of problem."

"What does that mean, problem?"

I felt I was being swept to a place I'd never been. I'd never discussed these things with anybody. Even if I'd wanted to, there'd be no one to do it with. These subjects were taboo.

"It's a little difficult to speak about that," I confessed.

He was quiet and waited for me to decide if I wanted to continue or not.

"Let's say, someone, someone who...who... satisfies himself." I stuttered, and it seemed like he was doing his best to not turn his smile into laughter. "Then if someone told on him to the rabbi or counselor..."

"But it's something natural."

"But for us, it's forbidden. It's distracting. You always need to be dealing with spiritual things and not physical things. Not to submit to the impulse, rather to take control of it."

"Wow. That's not easy when you love someone and she loves you. Even for us, the 'lowlifes,' it's forbidden to let impulses control you, because that can lead to bad things happening. But a man and woman who love each other and are attracted to each other—it's the nicest thing that can happen," he said with deep conviction.

"It could be, I wouldn't know," I whispered.

"You'll learn," he said with confidence.

TWENTY-EIGHT

It was the day before the holiday. In the morning I decided to pamper myself and bought myself a white dress with colorful flowers. I thought it was special and just right for a holiday. Usually I wore dark clothes, black or gray, like many of the other women in the community, as we had grown similar in dress and in lifestyle. I put the dress on and a white jacket over my shoulders. I put on light pink lipstick; it was a present from Tamar, and I'd wondered then if I would ever use it. I knew that my father wouldn't be happy with my appearance, and to reduce his objection, I put on my old wig. I made my way to my parents' place an hour before the holiday started.

Nechama, my father's wife, greeted me. I still had a hard time seeing her as his wife. It was easier for me to think of her as someone who had come to cook, clean, and take care of his children. I smiled at her and gave her the present I'd brought for the holiday. A white tablecloth with golden fringes. Nechama smiled back at me, not a warm smile but a polite one, that of someone who had to offer hospitality to an undesirable guest. I walked by her and went inside. My younger siblings greeted me with somewhat shy smiles, and my father, on his way toward me, stopped suddenly. He looked me over, and like an open book, I could read the dissatisfaction and anger in his face at my appearance,

"Happy holiday, Perele," he said formally, and sat at the head of the table.

Before I sat down, he'd already taken the Haggadah and started to conduct the *Seder*. His wife didn't move from her spot until it was time to begin the meal, and then she got up and started serving the food. I got up after her to help, but my father, in a restrained voice, commanded me to sit.

"I want to help, Tatte."

"It's not necessary," he answered curtly, "Nechama can manage by herself."

Nechama came and went, putting things on the table and returning to the kitchen, over and over.

I fought with myself not to defy him, but finally, I couldn't stand it anymore. I got up and helped her serve the food. Nechama said nothing and my father ate the chicken soup silently. The children, who felt the tension, also remained silent.

When we sang a song at the very end of the *Seder*, I felt that I could no longer sit there. I got up and started to wash the dishes.

"Sit down, Perele!" my father ordered in a tone that could not be misunderstood.

How was I going to manage being there until the following evening? I thought to myself. My father had changed so much. He'd once shown tenderness in his face. Even when he was angry, reading a holy book, or praying, his mouth would have been in a small smile when he looked at any of us. Now there seemed to be rigid grooves on his cheeks, and his expression was serious and uncompromising, like a marble statue. He'd never been to my apartment, and usually avoided inviting me to their place altogether. On the rare times I'd come to visit him, he'd tried to maintain as pleasant an atmosphere as possible. Now it seemed as if he didn't care about anything. He was stiff and distant, and his attitude erased the good memories of him from my childhood. It was as if he wanted to let me know that there was no more reason for me to visit.

Somehow, I lived through the evening. The next morning, I decided to visit Sara. We had spoken before that and she'd implored me to come visit her when I was at my father's. Many people in white shirts were walking around the street. Children played on the sidewalk in holiday clothes, and the spring weather was clear and pleasant. Sara was standing out on her balcony when I arrived at her building. She called down to me to come up. I started up the stairs and felt how my heartbeat accelerated. I hadn't been there for many months. I slowed down and tried to calm myself, but my body, which hadn't forgotten, reacted in fear. I put my hand on the banister and continued climbing. I kept stopping to catch my breath. Would it always be like this? I wondered. Would I ever manage to free myself of these feelings of fear? Would just the mention of Menachem Mendel's name always arouse the terror that I was feeling?

As I got closer to the floor where I'd lived, I felt my legs get heavier, as if made of cement. I pulled myself up using the banister. Another stair and then another, and I was almost there. Another two stairs and I would be there. To get to Sara's apartment, I had to pass the old accursed apartment and turn right, to the door opposite it. When I got to the top of the stairs, the door opened, and he was standing there. I don't know if he'd heard Sara calling my name, or if it was just by chance. Either way, I stood still and couldn't continue. I couldn't breathe. He looked at me with his penetrating gaze, and his eyes flashed with malice. The familiar smile spread over his face and revealed teeth yellowed by nicotine.

"So you thought you'd escape from me, huh? You thought you were a big hero?" he hissed.

I was stuck to the spot. Like a scream unheard in a dream, my legs did not hear the command to continue. I stood in front of him dumbstruck.

"Have you nothing to say? I see you're shaking with fear. Good. It'll always be like that. You'll never get rid of the fear because I'll always appear in places you'd never even imagine. You'll never be rid of me."

With these words, with the smile still smeared on his face like tar on the street, he passed to the left of me and his arm pushed my body, as if by chance. He walked by me and went down the stairs.

"Perele, what's happening?" I heard Sara's voice. Since I didn't answer, she came out into the hallway toward me. When she saw my expression, she asked, "What happened? Why are you like that?"

I couldn't answer and started crying.

"What happened?" she asked again in concern.

"Menachem Mendel." I managed to say.

"You met him?"

I nodded.

"What, now?"

"Yes," I managed to emit, between sobs.

Sara put her arms around my shoulders and led me inside. She sat me on the couch in the living room and continued hugging me until I stopped crying and started breathing normally.

The next day, in my little apartment, I went over what had happened in the last two days. I felt safe there and wondered about the great fear that had attacked me, even though I was just moments before, so confident of the steps I'd taken and saw myself in a completely different place. Even though I could actually picture the increasing distance between me and the little girl fighting her internal demons, it was clear to me that I still had a long way ahead. But I knew I'd get to where I wanted to be. I was so sure of myself, at that moment that I wanted to get up and go to the old apartment and tell him that he didn't scare me anymore, that I wasn't afraid, that he could say whatever he wanted and nothing would affect me. But of course I continued sitting where I was. It was enough to feel the confidence at that moment. I told myself that I didn't need to prove anything to him. That in time, he would understand that his words had lost their devastating power over me, as his orange bearded face and narrow lips were just the features of his face and nothing more.

There was a knock at the door. "Hi," Tamar burst in full of energy, ponytail jumping sassily on her head.

"Where were you?" she asked, and I felt that there was tone of complaint in her voice.

"I went to my father's for the holiday, why?"

"Why? Because I was bored."

"You didn't go to your father's?" I wondered.

"No. He went overseas with his girlfriend."

"Really?!"

"Why are you so surprised?"

"Because I think it's strange that people travel overseas for the holiday instead of spending it with their family."

"It's not strange at all. Lots of people do it."

"So you were alone?"

"No, I was at my brother's for dinner and then I came back."

"Great," I said. I couldn't find anything else to say.

"Wait, wait, I just thought of something," she said with a big smile. "Why didn't I think of it before?" she continued.

"Of what?"

"That you and Ido have to meet."

"We have to?"

"Yup. He's so cute and you're really cute, and I think it could work out between you."

"Work out what?"

"Oh, Perele, really. I want you to meet him."

"Why?" I still hadn't understood.

"Earth to Perele. I want you to meet him, so you can go out together, spend time together, and maybe something will develop. Maybe you'll fall in love. Wow, that could be great, you and Ido," these last words she said to herself.

I smiled at her without saying anything. She wanted to fix me up with her brother. I had just gotten out of solitary confinement, and she wanted to put me into another one.

"So what do you say?" she asked while removing the cork from the bottle of wine she had brought with her.

"I say no!"

She turned to me in surprise. "Wow, such determination," she mocked, "why not?"

"Because I only just now got out of prison and you already want me to go back?"

"What are you talking about? My brother is as close to Paradise as you could get. Totally not prison." I could feel the insult in her voice.

"I'm sorry Tamar, I didn't mean that. I'm just not ready yet." I hesitated before I added without meaning to, "And besides—"

"And besides what?"

"Never mind," I tried to avoid answering.

"Besides what?" she didn't give up.

"The truth is, it's nothing. Just that I met someone and—"

"Perele, you met someone? And you're going out and everything?"

"Calm down, Tamar, we just talk. We're not going out or anything."

"But—"

"Listen, I just got out of a terrible relationship. The last few years have been really tough. I was with someone I despised, who hit and humiliated me, and there was no one around me to support or help me. Not even my parents, whose status in the community had been damaged because of me. My mother died, and my father married another woman, and with everything I have going on, I can't think about anyone, or any kind of relationship at all."

My words sounded very convincing at the time. I almost convinced myself. But later on, when I was alone in my apartment and my thoughts began to wander on their own, I realized I hadn't been completely honest. Not with Tamar, and not with myself. Dan had come up in my thoughts without my wanting him to during the past months. On the one hand, I believed I had to experience the growing distance between me and my former life alone, but on the other hand, I wasn't able to control the thoughts and feelings of confusion and awkwardness, the strong desire to be with him, but also the resistance I had at the same time.

The next day he called. "I bought tickets to a movie," he said naturally. "Should we go?"

"To a movie?"

He didn't respond, waiting for a response.

"I don't know, and I've never been to the movies."

"I know," he said in a calming voice, "that's why I want us to go."

I fought with myself. Was it time to go to the movies and sit in the same theater with men? What if a man sat next to me? What if someone saw me or asked me something? What if in the movie there were men and women together, doing forbidden things on the screen? The questions shot at me like deafening blows on a *shofar*[36]. After a long silence, I heard him say, "I'll pick you up at seven. Be ready, sweetheart."

"He's picking me up? 'Sweetheart'?!" No one had ever called me that, and certainly not in such a soft voice. I felt as if I were within a rubber frame that was shaking me back and forth, right and left. Should I go or

---

36 A hollow wind instrument usually made of a ram's horn. On Rosh Hashanah, the *shofar* is blown as part of the prayer services.

back off? Should I give myself more time, or was it time to shatter the glass protection I had surrounded myself with? The questions didn't leave me, and continued to rock my thoughts, like a ship whose rudder was gone, and it was at the mercy of the waves. What was right and what was wrong? Should I follow my heart, or listen to my brain that was telling me to wait, that it wasn't time yet?

Dan came at seven. I sat in his car and the thoughts were still running around my head.

"Perele, everything will be all right. If you feel uncomfortable and want to leave, just tell me, and I'll take you home."

How could he read my mind? That was scary but also soothing. The fact that I had the option of returning home at any time slowed the pace of my thoughts.

We went into the theater, which was already dark. On the screen were advertisements for products, some of which I wasn't familiar with. I looked around. There were shadows and unclear facial features of people looking towards the screen - they were not interested in me at all. The anonymity made me feel better. It was the complete opposite of the net I'd been trapped in in my previous life, in which there had been no distinction between the public and the private. The rabbi, the supervisor, and the counselor all knew about everything that was happening in our house, and it was totally legitimate for them to make demands and change things.

I survived the movie, though I only started to pay attention to it sometime after it had begun. Dan was silent throughout, and I was very thankful for that. When we left the hall at the end of the screening, I expected to feel his hand on my back, but he kept his distance until we got outside.

"How was it?" he asked.

"The movie?"

He smiled. "Yes, the movie too."

I thought for a moment, and then I said, "It was okay. At first it was strange, but after that it was fine."

"Should we go get some coffee?"

We sat at a café near the theater and ordered coffee and pastry.

"So, what was so strange?"

"The situation was a bit weird for me. To sit among men and women that I don't know and watch a movie. It was an unfamiliar situation for me, but I was surprised to find out that I'm not angry at myself now. I'm not saying to myself, 'What have you done?' I'm not afraid at all, as if I'd been to movies many times."

"You're a brave girl," he said.

I felt my cheeks get hot. "Why do you say that?"

"Because I know that what you're going through is not easy. I read a bit about your community and I understand a little more now. At first I thought you were religious, and that's it. You know, for us, the secular people, all the religious people are the same. Now I know it's nothing like that, especially in your community. So I now think you have a lot of courage to do what you're doing, and I promise not to rush you. I promise to help you make the transition change at your pace unless you ask me to do otherwise."

His words moved me so much that I wanted to take his hand and squeeze it in mine. And that's what I did. I reached out both my hands and took hold of his. He was surprised at first, but then his special smile appeared, and I felt as if I had come a long way and reached my destination in one piece.

Twenty-nine

Av was an especially hot month. There was no air conditioner in the apartment. I cooled it with a fan I bought at the beginning of the summer, but it didn't help that day. I was working at the library from the early afternoon. I had asked Sophie if I could come in earlier because I couldn't stand the sweat on my body. Time passed slowly. Few people came to the library, but among them were some high school students sitting in a group looking for material for the project they were working on. Here and there I had to go over to them and ask them to be quiet. They tried, but it never lasted very long. They seemed so carefree. Sometimes one of the boys would muss the hair of one of the girls sitting next to him. She would laugh and continue reading out loud from the book in front of her.

It seemed like such a nice and natural sight, but 180 degrees from the world I had come from, where such behavior was completely impossible. From the time we were very young, we had been trained that any contact with the opposite sex was bad and prohibited. That the very proximity might, God forbid, lead to terrible things. From an early age, my brothers studied in *cheder*, elementary school for boys, under the authority and supervision of the rabbi. Then they went to elementary school *yeshiva*, and after their bar mitzvah, they went to boarding school. They were always under supervision, and their daily study schedule was busy and full of activity. In boarding school, they studied until almost nine at night, and at ten, they had to get into bed and turn out the lights. They never had any free time or option of engaging in anything besides studying more Torah. They never wasted any time, and only sometimes they sat around doing nothing and talking about this and that, and they certainly never mixed with girls.

They even taught them and us girls to avoid worldly vanities and contact with the opposite sex, even from those in our family, like cousins and other relatives. We had to monitor our hands, eyes, and thoughts. The main thing was to avoid temptation. I was standing in a corner, just a bit away from the center of the hall and saw how boys and girls sat around a table laughing and looking at each other without fear. I wished I could be like them. I wanted to sit like that with people, without fear, to smile without concern that I was doing something terrible, or feel that if someone wanted to move a curl from my cheek, he could do it and I would smile at him without being scared.

When I got back home, it was almost eight in the evening. Outside the last rays of light were fighting over their right to shine a little longer, but the obedient sky started to swallow them and covered the world with a thin blanket of darkness. I started up the stairs and stopped in front of Tamar's apartment. It was quiet. She apparently hadn't returned yet, I thought. Maybe she had gone to visit one of her siblings? As I got near the door to my apartment, the light in the staircase shut off automatically. I felt blindly along the rough wall until I found the switch. I turned on the light and screamed. A black shape was leaning against the door. When it saw me, it jumped to its feet in panic. It was my brother Benjamin, who'd been sitting leaning against the door.

"Benjamin, what are you doing here?"

"I'm sorry, Perele, I didn't mean to scare you. I just dozed off."

"But what are you doing here? Did something happen to Tatte?"

"No, no, don't worry, everything's fine," he said.

"Then what are you doing here?" I repeated my question. "How did you know where I live?"

"Can I come in, Perele? I'm thirsty."

I opened the door and let him in. But I was still anxious. Lots of questions were going through my mind. What was he doing at my apartment? Who'd sent him to me? Had he come to threaten me to get me to return? Had someone seen me at the movies with Dan? I gave him a glass of water and suggested we go out to the balcony. He looked around the apartment quickly and followed me outside. We sat on the two chairs on the balcony, and when I looked at him, I saw that the hand holding the glass was trembling.

Benjamin was almost nineteen and was supposed to be married the following month. Among my siblings, he was the only one that I had any contact with, though it was pretty scant. It mainly consisted of his nodding at me when I came to visit my parents' place. The rest of the older siblings ignored me completely. When we were little, I'd sometimes joined the group of neighborhood boys he'd played with. Though they always tried to get me to leave, Benjamin would smile and try to stop them from bullying me. He always smiled, except when he sat next to my father and they debated one of the verses of the Torah. Then he was serious, and his usual smile faded in his attempt to impress my father.

He lowered his head to the glass and sat that way for a long time. I waited and didn't push him to explain what he was doing at my apartment, but when I realized he wasn't planning to talk, I cleared my throat. Benjamin looked up at me. Since his bar mitzvah, he hadn't looked at me so directly.

"What happened, Benjamin?"

"I can't take it anymore," he mumbled.

"What can't you take?" I asked and moved my chair over to his so I could hear his voice.

"I can't go on."

"I don't understand."

"I don't want to marry her," he finally said.

I leaned back. He sat bent over, his chin on his hand. He was avoiding looking at me directly. It seemed that he suddenly understood what he'd done. Maybe he regretted having come, or that he'd said what he'd said so directly. Silence. I didn't know how to react to what he'd said and waited for him to continue.

After a long silence, he continued talking.

"Perele, I don't know her at all. I barely saw her twice. And if God forbid I won't love her? And if she's stupid or lazy? And if she's not a *balebuste*[37]

---

37 A woman who manages the home efficiently and diligently

like her parents say?" And then he whispered, "And she's also not so pretty."

"So why did you agree? Why didn't you tell Tatte that you didn't want to marry her?"

"Because Tatte was so excited. In any case, there weren't that many options," he said in defeat.

I bowed my head and said, "That's because of me, right?"

He didn't answer, but I knew that our family was considered defective, and that my siblings' chances to find a good match had dropped since I'd left.

"Perele, how's your life?" His question surprised me. I wondered if he was really interested, or if he was asking for some other reason.

"All right," I answered noncommittally.

"I mean, are things good for you? You have no regrets?"

"No, Benjamin, I have no regrets at all. Things are hard, but not hard enough that I'd want to return."

"I'm also thinking of leaving," he said.

"What? Really? Because of the wedding?"

Benjamin was the last one I'd have thought would leave. He was an outstanding student. He kept the commandments strictly. He always tried to follow the path my father had set for him, sometimes seeming to be even more pedantic than my father. When we were young, he would criticize my clothes or my avoiding doing certain things, sometimes with a look, and sometimes reviling me with nasty words.

"It's not because of the wedding. I've been thinking about it for a long time."

"But why? You've always been so thorough, you've always asked the right kind of questions, shown great interest, been sure to do what you were supposed to do. What happened?"

"It's true, I made sure to do what I was supposed to, asked the right questions, stayed in the dormitory more than I had to. I was always the last one to leave the classroom. But that was all so that I wouldn't have time to think sinful thoughts. When I was alone, my thoughts immediately ran in other directions. I tried not to be alone, and to always be busy. But now I feel that I can't lie to myself anymore, especially after the whole deal with the wedding."

"When did this start, Benjamin?"

"A long time ago, Perele, a long time ago."

"What's a long time ago? When?"

"I think since I was little."

"Since when, Benjamin?" I insisted and saw that he couldn't look me in the eye.

"Since we were both little," he stuttered.

I waited for him to look up, but he stayed in the same position and rolled his hat in his hands.

"You knew, right?"

There was an awkward silence and then he nodded his head.

A lump of disgust rose in my throat. I felt like a wild animal whose prey was larger than its throat.

"And you said nothing?"

"I was a little boy, Perele."

"But later?"

"What about later? You also never talked about it. Besides, no one spoke."

"Who's no one? Who else knew?"

He hesitated before answering. "We all knew, Perele."

"And no one said anything? No one tried to stop it?"

"Momme finally stopped it."

"Yes, after a year," I retorted.

I got up from the chair and went inside. I couldn't stand looking at his face which represented the face of my other brothers who had all remained silent. And not only their faces, but the faces of my parents who chose to lock the door rather than do something that would pull me out of the dark pit that I continued to fall into. The door was locked, and so the problem was solved. Only Perele was left behind, with a monument of memories that would never be erased. Little Perele was brought as a sacrifice to protect the good name of the Fisher family. And then I went back to the balcony and stood over my brother.

"Tell me, did you know about Menachem Mendel?"

"Everyone knew."

"Who's everyone?"

"Everyone," he repeated in a whisper.

"Who's everyone, Benjamin?" I raised my voice.

"I don't know, the brothers, the neighbors, the people at the synagogue."

He lowered his head and arranged his black socks. Suddenly, I could no longer stand looking at him.

"Benjamin, get out of here."

"What?"

"I want you to leave."

"But Perele, I wanted to speak with you," he said, pleading.

"But I don't want to. Leave!"

He got up heavily from the chair. When he walked by me, he lowered his head and walked quickly to the door. He opened it and walked out without closing it after him.

Two weeks passed since Benjamin's visit. That day, I finished working in the library in the afternoon. As I was walking to the bus stop, my mobile phone rang. My father was on the other end of the line. "Perele, I want you to come to us for Shabbos," he said, without any "Hi, how are you." Thus he informed me and expected me to fulfill his command without appeal. I thought about refusing but decided to comply.

I got to my parents' place. It was almost Shabbos. Outside was a veil of sanctity that created an atmosphere of anticipation of something good. Nechama opened the door. When I greeted her *Gut Shabbos*, she didn't answer but turned around and went into the kitchen.

My father nodded at me and mumbled a blessing for washing hands. I sat at the table. Benjamin sat across from me. He kept his head down and avoided making eye contact with me the entire meal. The rest of my siblings ignored me, as usual. Only my seven-year-old twin brothers looked at me once in a while and giggled together. Nechama said not a word to me the whole evening. My sister-in-law, who was married to my brother a year older than me, asked me how I was and then she too lost her words.

After the meal, my siblings started to go their own way. The married ones who lived nearby left. Nechama hurried the twins off to bed. Benjamin asked my father for permission to leave and go to the *yeshiva* for a while. I stayed with my father in the living room. Nechama disappeared into one of the rooms. I was surprised that she didn't stay in the kitchen and wash the dishes. I got up and took the bread plate off the table and went in to straighten up the kitchen.

"Perele, come sit," my father said.

"In a second, I'll straighten things up in here and then come in."

"Leave the dishes and come sit here," he said and pointed at the sofa. He remained seated at the head of the table, so he was a bit higher than me.

"I understand that you met with Benjamin," he said calmly.

I was surprised but I nodded and said that Benjamin had come to my apartment.

"And how did he know your address?" he asked innocently.

"I don't know. I thought you'd told him."

"No, I didn't tell him. And what did you tell him when he came?"

"Tatte, what are you getting at? Why all these questions? I don't understand."

"Interesting, Perele," he started, and his voice became tough and angry, "it's not enough what you did, now you want to pull out Benjamin after you."

"What are you talking about? He came to me."

My father stood up and in a loud voice I wasn't used to, said, "Perele, you shamed your family. You caused us so much heartache, your mother may she rest in peace couldn't stand it anymore."

I was in shock. "So now you're also blaming Momme's death on me?" I yelled.

When she heard that, Nechama came out of the room she was hiding in and said, "Don't yell here!"

I stood up, looked at her, and then looked at my father. We looked each other in the eye until I lowered my head. He just stood there and said nothing. Nechama stood next to him, and both of them looked at me in defiance. There was no mercy in his face, nor any other emotion I'd expect to find there, in the father who had once bought me little presents and took my hand in his on the way to the market. I put my hand on my head, and in a sharp movement, took off my wig and threw it at him. I left it behind and left his apartment.

THIRTY

On Tuesday, 11 Shevat 5770, I wore jeans for the first time. For a long time, I'd wanted to try wearing pants. The month before, I'd bought pants at one of the stores downtown. The saleswoman sent me to the fitting room, but I told her I'd take them without trying them on. Later, I finally stood in front of the mirror and looked at my legs wrapped tightly in the pant legs. It was a strange feeling, as if someone had wrapped my legs in plastic wrap and wasn't letting them breathe. I pulled the fabric to the sides with my hands to allow for more space between my skin and the pants, but the fabric revolted and returned to its place. I tried to walk, but I felt as if I were walking on stilts, or like a baby learning to take its first steps. My first impulse was to take the pants off and get back into the skirt, whose boundaries were familiar to me and maybe even more comfortable.

I walked around my little apartment in the pants, and, as was my habit, spoke to myself. "Perele, you just have to get used to it," I tried to persuade myself. But it was a lot more than that. Our way of dressing in the community expressed the values we had grown up on. The value of modesty, hiding the body, respectability. The bigger or thicker the covering, the more ideal the woman was perceived to be. They even told us which fabrics to use, and which not to. That it was prohibited to use see-through or tight fabrics, denim, or any fabric that God forbid would emphasize the contours of the body. Now I looked at my body, and my shapely legs looked back at me. My imagination ran wild. One leg said how beautiful my body was, my legs long and well-built, and there was no reason to hide them, while the second was angry at my daring and implored me not to be part of this fashion rebellion which was temporary, empty, and pathetic.

Through all this, I moved around the rooms of the little apartment and tried to get used to the new feeling of my body. I kept pulling at the fabric on my legs as I continued to walk around, staying in the pants that whole day and sleeping in them as well. The next morning, there was only a touch of the battle that had taken place the previous night left within me. I put on a red shirt, with long sleeves but tighter than the shirts I was used to wearing and left for the library. When I went inside and said my "Good morning," Sophie looked up.

"Perele!" she called. When I turned to her, she smiled and said nothing.

I received similar reactions from the usual library patrons, who had become my friends over time. "Wow, you're gorgeous! That looks great on you," one of the girls said. "Where have you been hiding all this time?" said someone and smiled at me with big white teeth. I even received whistles of admiration. I smiled at everyone and felt how the tension pent-up inside of me dissipated and how its place had been taken by a sense of untroubled exhilaration. During work that day I felt like a feather in the wind. I flew from shelf to shelf and rested the volumes in their place. Not one book fell, and each one of them stood exactly as I had put it down. The cart that tended to rebel against its crooked wheels submitted to my authority. The feeling that enveloped me reminded me of the dandelions in my field in spring. The ones whose leaves fell and on their elderly heads remained soft white seeds that flew off with every gust of wind. Even the time, which sometimes insisted on moving slowly, passed quickly. The reactions I received that day encouraged me to board the bus that would bring me downtown, and not the one that would bring me home.

I walked around the stores that had never before merited my glance. I found myself moving among them, stopping to look at the well-shaped mannequins and the clothes they displayed. I entered the first store awkwardly. In the next one, I approached the saleswoman and asked for help. And at the next store, I conducted myself freely. I tried things on and took them off, tried to figure out what to take, and even asked the saleslady her opinion. After some two hours I headed home, my arms carrying bags full of clothes I had bought for myself.

One day at the end of the summer, I wore jeans and a turquoise t-shirt. My feet were adorned with silver sandals studded with small turquoise stones. The library patrons were already used to seeing the new me, and it seemed that their attitude toward me had changed as a result, as if the fence separating us had collapsed. Their comments were lighter, and sometimes a bit intimate. At first I didn't know how to take that, but with time I learned to respond lightheartedly, so that our relations remained in the friendly zone and not beyond. One day, I arranged with Dan that he pick me up from work, after we hadn't seen each other for a long time, and had only spoken by phone. Our previous meeting, where he'd come to the library by surprise, had been engraved in my mind for years as an event that reflected the changes I'd made in my life.

Dan waited for me outside the car, as he always did when he came to pick me up. He always made the effort to get out of the car. I left the library and walked over to him. My hair had grown a bit and fell playfully onto my shoulders. Dan leaned on the car and was concentrating on his cellphone. He suddenly looked up and his eyes fell on mine. He didn't recognize me and went back to his activity on the phone. But he immediately looked up again and stared at my body. When I was really close to him, he stood up straight and tense, his eyes not leaving mine. We stood facing each other in silence. My cheeks burned. I felt heat flooding my body but didn't know why. Dan just stood there for a time that seemed like eternity to me and didn't say a word. This time I didn't look down and continued looking at him confidently.

"Perele," he said finally, "you've changed."

I laughed happily and said, "Yes, I've changed my wardrobe."

"I don't mean the jeans," he said. "That too, but not only that. You've really changed," I waited for him to explain what he meant.

"Your face, the expression. It shows confidence that wasn't there before. As if you've found out something new about yourself."

"What do you mean?"

"I don't know. As if you've changed the way you see yourself. What you saw as flaws, you now see as positive traits. Even the way you stand is different. It's firm, not limp. Your legs are planted firmly on the ground, and it seems that even if someone tried to push you, he wouldn't be able to move you at all."

"And you see all that because I'm wearing jeans?" I teased.

Suddenly he put his arm out, pulled me to him, and kissed me on the lips. I was surprised. Mainly at myself. I would have expected myself to panic and run, but my body stayed in place, as if what had happened was expected, and what I felt was completely natural. It seemed that he was also surprised at my response. He'd also expected that I would push him away. But when he saw that I didn't move, he looked into my eyes and put his lips on mine in a long soft kiss that took me to dreams I'd had in my other life. When we separated, he smiled at me and said, "You've changed, there's no doubt that you've changed. And how I love that change."

When we sat at the café, we had the feeling that another divider between us had fallen. The conversation flowed. There were no awkward silences. There were silences, but they were different. They were relaxed and comfortable.

"What caused you to replace the skirt with pants?" he asked casually.

"It was time, no?"

"I don't know. You tell me."

"Every day I stand in front of the mirror before I go out the door. And one day I didn't like what I saw reflected back at me. I looked at myself and saw a limp, like you said, graceless old woman. So I bought myself a few pieces of jewelry and put them on, but they didn't change the look that had started to become repulsive to me. Then I thought of my sisters and sisters-in-law and other women, and they all looked old to me. I thought about how because of the weaknesses of men, because they cannot resist temptation, we, the women, have been sentenced to cover ourselves with thick fabric and cover up any hint of sensuality or femininity. I think that was the moment that gave me the courage to buy pants made of fabric the community had prohibited us from using."

"You look wonderful," he said. "The turquoise matches your blue eyes."

"Thank you," I said shyly.

Dan put out his hands to mine and placed them against his mouth. I didn't pull back.

When I got home and sat on the balcony with a cup of coffee, I remembered that once, in what seemed like an eternity, a couple had passed me on the street arm in arm, and I'd asked myself if I would ever experience something like that, serenity, closeness, intimacy. At the same time, I didn't dare imagine myself that way, but I remember well the longing I had for love that came from familiarity, desire, and a joint decision—all things I didn't have.

A week later I called Sara. I'd been wanting to invite her over for a long time. I remembered that when she came with me to the rabbinate building, I offered her to come and see my apartment, but she avoided with some pretext. I hadn't been completely convinced whether her response at that time had been honest or evasive. When I called, she said that it was about time we got together, and that she missed me very much.

"So come to my apartment," I suggested.

"What?" she asked, and I had the feeling that she was stalling for time.

"Come to me. You promised you'd come see my apartment."

I was pressuring her to come and didn't know why. I knew exactly what she was thinking. Yet I still insisted. In retrospect, I thought that maybe I'd wanted to prove to her that I was doing fine. And maybe in my invitation there was a degree of defiance against the life she represented for me. A life I'd chosen to leave. Either way, I didn't leave her many options and finally she agreed, so we planned for her to come the next day. I didn't work that day. I made a list of food I wanted to prepare, and I went to the grocery store with products known for their strict level of kashrut (kosher food). I remembered that she'd told me that her favorite dish was her mother's chicken soup, with noodles and soup almonds. I spent the entire morning in the kitchen. I prepared each dish carefully, so that it would be exactly as it would have been at my mother's house. My kitchen was kosher, so there was nothing special to be done about that. It was important to me that she feel comfortable and confident enough to eat what I served her without apprehension.

At one in the afternoon, there was a knock at the door. Sara came in, breathing heavily. "You didn't tell me that you had so many stairs," she sat down sprawled on the couch. When she looked at me, her eyes opened wide in wonder. "Wow, Perele," she burst out.

I involuntarily put my hand on my hair and mussed it with my fingers.

"You look like... like... a secular girl." There was no irony in her words.

"Yes," I said.

"It's strange for me to see you like that. But it looks very nice on you," she added with a smile.

Sara looked well put together, as always. Her black skirt was exactly the right length. She was wearing a beige shirt, and around her neck was a gold necklace, adorned with shiny black stones. The combed wig sat exactly on her beautiful head, and her black shoes also looked new and expensive. She even had on light makeup. Many women in the community avoided ornamentation, lest it be considered immodest or overly proud. Sara was among the more modern women in the community. Whenever she left the apartment, even to the grocery store or to run errands, she always looked like a million bucks. She was always tidy and dressed neatly.

When she had recovered a bit, she looked around. "Cute," she said. "Tiny," she added.

"Yes, but for one person, it's enough," I said, a bit apologetic. "I thought you'd bring Aharal'e with you."

"Yedidya came home, and he'll watch him until I return."

"Do you want to see the apartment?"

"Of course."

I finished giving the tour in a minute. "Come sit," I invited her to the table. I'd put out a colorful tablecloth and white plastic plates I could buy on my budget. I went to the stove to serve her the soup she loved.

"I'm not so hungry," I heard her say.

I turned and said that I'd just bring her a bit, in that case. I told her I'd prepared the soup with the noodles and croutons that she liked.

"Thank you, Perele. I'm sure that it's yummy, but I'm really not hungry at all."

"Not even a bit? Just to taste?"

"No, really not. Thank you."

I was very disappointed, and that apparently showed on my face.

"But I'll take a glass of water," she said.

I filled her a glass from the faucet. She took it in her hand and said, "I'm sorry, Perele, but you know how we are. Stricter than strict." She got up, sat next to me, and added, "But I'm really happy I came. You have a very sweet apartment."

"How did Yedidya respond when you said you were coming to me?"

She hesitated a moment before she answered. "At first he wasn't so happy, but after I told him it was important to me to see where you lived and that we're good friends, he agreed."

"And you also promised him that you wouldn't eat anything," I continued her words.

"Right," she admitted, and nodded her head.

"You know what, Sara? It's okay, I understand."

"Really? You're not angry?"

"No, I'm not angry. The main thing is that you came."

She seemed relieved, then she took my hand in hers and said, "Now I want to hear everything that's happened in the past few weeks. If there's something really interesting, tell me right away."

After we'd cleared the air, it was much easier. Time flew. We didn't stop talking, mostly me. I told her about my work at the library, about the regular patrons that had become like friends. I told her about one of them who came almost every day, and always picks up the same book. When I asked him once why he always reads it, and doesn't take a different book, he answered that he preferred to know a lot about one subject, and not a little bit about many subjects.

Sara laughed out loud. "Strange man," she said.

"Right, he's really strange, but harmless. He always says hello to me and asks how I am." I didn't mention Dan at all. "And what about you, what's new with you?" I transferred the spotlight to her.

"Me? You know, there's nothing much new. Except that..." she debated whether to continue or not, looking down for several minutes. I sat next to her silently and didn't push her to continue. Finally, she said, "I'm thinking of starting my own business."

"What?" I was very surprised. A woman that chooses to start an independent business was considered too liberal, and that was likely to generate

234 | L.S. EINAT

unpleasant comments. In the future it could even harm her children's chances for a good match.

"I know what you're thinking, but these days it's a little different in our community. There are women who have all kinds of jobs. It's true that most are either nursery schoolteachers or schoolteachers, but there are also those who do other things."

I noticed how she said "our community." It was a declaration or recognition that I didn't belong to it anymore. Sara recognized that I was no longer part of the community and had still come to me and sat with me in my apartment, outside the boundaries of the Hassidic community. At that moment I felt strong affection for her. Despite everything, she hadn't given up our friendship, and her not eating my food was negligible compared with my appreciation for her. I turned toward her and encouraged her to tell me about her decision.

"Well, I decided that I wanted to be self-employed."

"But what do you want to do?"

"I want to design and sell clothes," she said.

"That really suits you."

"Really? Why?"

"Because you have good taste in clothes. You really know how to put together outfits. You know how to ornament clothes with a piece of jewelry, and you look fantastic. I'll buy clothes from you!" I promised.

"I'm not sure that you'll like my clothes," she said with a narrow smile.

I looked at myself in the tight jeans and burst out laughing. Sara joined me, and together we filled the small apartment with laughter; the apartment holding within it the story of both our lives. For a moment, I also thought that Sara and I weren't really that different from each other. We were both rebellious, each in her own way. I rebelled out of a sense of suffocation from a rigid way of life, from ways of thinking that seemed to be illogical and archaic. Sara rebelled against the rules which apparently felt old-fashioned to her. But her choice was to do it within the Hassidic community and not outside, which seemed much more courageous than the decision I'd made. I threw out my arms spontaneously and hugged her tightly. "I'm so proud of you!" I told her. She returned the hug, and we remained in the embrace, each one reading the other's thoughts.

When I closed the door after Sara left, it was with a smile of happiness. I was happy I had her, and I knew that our friendship was stronger than the way of life either of us had chosen.

THIRTY-ONE

The air smelled of soot, and a thick fog covered the earth like a cadaver's shroud. Cars drove carefully with their hazard lights on. I finished my shift at the library and decided, despite my feeling of asphyxiation, to go visit Dan at work. He wasn't expecting me, but I knew he'd be happy to see me. A new path had been paved around the field, so I didn't have to walk in the mud and get my shoes dirty. When I got to the garage, he greeted me with a big smile, and the others nodded at me. He took my hand and led me to the center of the garage, and then, as always, told me what they had been working on. He said they'd had a mechanical problem that they hadn't managed to solve, and therefore they'd contacted another garage in the USA. After speaking with them, they'd understood their mistake and ordered the part that would solve the problem.

The more he spoke, the more I felt that my entire body was tense, listening with great interest. Every time I came to the garage, something changed in me. The world outside disappeared and left my mind. I felt a tremendous spurt of energy in me. Every word they exchanged became a source of interest for me. The silent car was waiting patiently for diligent care, to be reborn. I'd never had such feelings. I had a million questions that I wanted answers for, but on those visits, I was content with the electrifying atmosphere. At first, I hid these feelings, and did not understand them. But in time, I realized that I was attracted like a magnet to the challenge of turning a dead body into a living one. The need to think, to try, to err, and to try again, swept me and my thoughts. Sometimes I felt the puzzled looks of both Dan and the men.

"Do you want to get something to drink?" he asked, and started to walk toward the sink, to wash his blackened hands.

"No, I prefer to stay here, if that's okay," I answered and approached the car, my eyes trying to absorb in one look all that was already there and whatever was still missing.

Dan turned his head and I saw his amazement. "Really, you want to stay here?"

"What are all those cables?" I asked, ignoring his question. The hood was open, and many cables dangled from it in different directions.

"We're building the electrical system," he answered.

"Alone? It came without an electrical system?"

I saw that he and Motti exchanged smiles, "Our garage is the only one in the country that has people with all the different specialties. We have an electrician, a mechanic, and an auto body mechanic and painter. We have everything we need under one roof. There's no other garage like this in the country."

"Really?"

"Really," he assured me.

"And which are you?"

"I'm a mechanic, but I also have knowledge in automotive electronics."

"I see. And are you successful?" I asked without thinking.

Dan burst out laughing and the others who'd heard my question joined in.

"Let's just say that we all manage to make a nice living from the work," he said after the laughter died down.

I didn't really understand how long-term work on one or two cars could earn a living for so many families.

"Now let's get out of here. I can't stand looking at their faces anymore," he begged me as a rag flew toward him and hit him on the end of the nose. "You see what I have to put up with here?" he laughed and went to wash his hands.

When we left, it was even more murky outside. We got in the car and headed downtown. Dan stopped the car near a small, dimly lit café. The streets were desolate, and the café was empty, except for a man sitting by one of the windows in the corner, drinking from a mug and reading a newspaper. When we entered, he looked up and looked back down. I thought to myself that if I'd been wearing the clothes I used to wear, he would have looked at me longer, but now we looked just like any other couple. Just like anyone else, normal and unobtrusive.

Dan ordered coffee and I ordered tea. I hugged the mug with my hands to warm them. Dan was quiet.

'Why are you so quiet? Did something happen?"

"No, nothing happened."

Something in his tone made me uncomfortable. His silence continued and filled my stomach with a strange bad feeling.

"Dan?"

"I want you to come to my place," he finally said.

"Why?"

"Because it's time, and I want you to get to know my life."

"You want me to meet your parents?"

"My parents? I live in my own apartment. You see, you don't know anything about my life. I want you to see where I live. I want you to ask what I like to eat or what I do in my free time. I want you to ask me about my childhood. I want you to ask about my family. I just want you to show some interest in me."

"Okay, let's go to your apartment."

He looked at me for a while, and then asked for the check. In the car on the way to his apartment, we said nothing. Each one was deep in his own thoughts. It was foggy out and he drove slowly and carefully. The drive took about twenty minutes. He parked the car in a neighborhood I had never been to before. The buildings were new and well-kept. Each apartment had a balcony. Despite the darkness, I could see a patch of grass adjoined the front of the building, and there were rows of colorful plants on either side of it. Low-sitting light fixtures lit the entry path, and when we got near the wide glass door, he pressed the buttons and the door opened into a lit lobby area.

"A new place?" I asked.

"Yes, I've been living here for about a year."

Something was standing between us. A strange awkwardness. Dan made no effort to conduct a conversation, and I was too tense to start one. I'd never been in an apartment with a man who wasn't my husband before. I tried to tell myself that I wasn't doing anything wrong. I'd known Dan for a long time, and I'd come to see where he lived. I was acting interested in him, as he'd requested.

We took the quiet elevator up to the tenth floor. When he opened the apartment door, the gray sea was laid out in front of me in all its glory. The window to the west had no curtain, and created an endless continuation to the living room, which was already quite large. Dan touched the switch and a soft white light filled the room. I'd had no idea his apartment would look like that. I expected something small and modest, more like my compact apartment. But I'd been wrong. Dan's apartment was large, spacious, and well-lit.

"Wow!" I said in admiration.

"You like it?"

I nodded.

"Come see the rest of the rooms."

He took my hand and led me through the apartment. It had three rooms besides the living room. First he showed me what he called the "workroom." There was a table that was pushed to the wall, under the window, on which large papers containing drawings were scattered. There was also a computer there with a printer beside it, exactly like in the library. Another room had no furniture, just closed cardboard boxes on the floor. Finally, he showed me his bedroom. It had a large double bed, covered in white sheets.

"Nice," I said and fled immediately to the living room. The white bed in the bedroom reminded me of incidents I'd preferred to forget. For me, a bedroom was a disgusting, hateful, and painful place, even if it was all in white.

Dan followed me to the living room. "What happened?" he asked, worried.

"Everything's fine," I evaded the question.

"You don't like bedrooms," he stated seriously. "Perele," he continued, "not everyone is Menachem Mendel. Most aren't."

"I know." I was about to cry.

"I wish I could take away your fears," he said and sat next to me on the blue couch. "Listen," he began, while moving a lock of my hair behind my ear. "I know that I can't understand what you went through. But I want to hear about it. I want you to trust me and share it with me. I want to understand better. I know that you had a violent husband and I admire the courage you had to leave him and that way of life. But what else happened there? I feel that you haven't told me everything. And I want to know."

"Why? Why is it so important to you?"

I wasn't used to people for whom it was so important to know things about me. I had mainly gotten used to people examining and criticizing my actions. From my parents and siblings through my neighbors and people in the synagogue. I was used to stares and stolen glances, whispering and distancing. I had experienced alienation and hurtful comments. In the world I had come from, no one had ever asked me how I felt, what I was going through, what was hurting me. But maybe it had been my fault, as I'd never shared with people what was going on in my mind. Only much later had I started to dare tell some of what was happening with me, but I still did so very cautiously.

"You're important to me," I heard him say.

"Why?"

"Again why. I don't have a clear answer; I can only tell you that I think about you a lot. That when anything happens to me, I talk to you in my head and tell you about it. When I see you suffering, it really hurts me. What else can I tell you to get you to trust me? I really want you to be happy, to manage to liberate yourself from the demons inside of you."

"I also want that," I whispered.

"Tell me why the bedroom scared you so much."

"It's hard."

"I know."

"Darkness also scares me."

"Why?"

"Because bad things happen in the dark," I said and stopped talking. Dan was also silent.

"When I was around eleven, my brother would come into my room and do all kinds of things to me. At that time, I didn't understand what he was doing. Only after I got married did I understand."

"What did he do?"

"I can't talk about that."

"You can, Perele, you need to. What did he do to you?"

I turned away from him and said, "He would lie down behind me and rub against me. He would take his hands and touch all kinds of parts of my body until he had reached satisfaction, and then he would leave the room and close the door behind him.

"How long did that go on for?"

"For about a year."

"Did anyone know about it?"

"I told my mother about it and she was very angry with me, but she also made it stop."

"She was angry at you?"

"Yes. In our community, they don't talk about things like that. I guess she was angry at the way I told her about it. But I was just a young girl, and I totally didn't understand what he was doing. I sensed it was something wrong, because he didn't speak about it during the day, and did it at night, in the dark, when everyone else was sleeping."

"Turn and look at me," he requested.

"I'm embarrassed."

Dan leaned over and hugged me. Gradually, he made me turn around, until my face was in front of his. "There is nothing for you to be ashamed of," he whispered with his mouth to my ear. "You did nothing bad. The person who did something bad was your brother, and also your mother who didn't talk to you about it, and made you feel guilty."

"Even now, I don't know what I could have done besides tell my mother."

"It's good that you told her, because despite her anger, she made it stop."

"I also feel sorry for him," I said.

"For him? Why?"

"Because I don't think he knew what he was doing either. You need to understand that our whole lives they'd told the boys to keep away from the girls. Not just physically, but in their thoughts. Every such thought was considered wasting time that could be spent on Torah study and was forbidden. We were given no information related to anything that happens with boys' and girls' bodies. We only knew that it was forbidden and that we needed to stay away from each other to avoid sinning. In a book that I'd read at the library, I learned that during adolescence, the sexual drive is aroused. I guess that that's what happened to my brother, and he didn't know what to do with it. We had a concept called 'observing the covenant' that means that it's forbidden to spill semen for no reason, except inside the wife's womb."

"And masturbation is prohibited?" he asked.

"Prohibited. It's considered unnecessary spilling of semen."

"But how can you control that? It's something natural."

"The rabbis and mentors at the dormitories speak with the boys and explain to them how they can avoid doing such things. I don't know exactly, but there are rules at the boarding schools, what's allowed and what's prohibited to do, so as not to create temptation that would lead to that."

"Wow, this whole idea is directly opposed to human nature. I don't understand how they want to control human nature. It's impossible. I'm sure that most of the boys don't manage to keep these rules and hide what they do."

"Or do things to their siblings," I added.

"Right; or do things to their little sisters."

THIRTY-TWO

"And Menachem Mendel?" he asked.

"What about him?" I played dumb.

"Tell me about him."

"He was a violent person."

"I know, you told me."

"So what do you want to know?"

"I want you to talk about what happened between you at night."

"Why?"

"Why? Because I think it'll help you. I think that if you get that out, you'll feel better and stop hiding it, as if you'd done something wrong. I think that when you start talking about things, they become more manageable."

What he said sounded logical, but it was still hard for me to speak about it. What happens in the bedroom is not usually spoken about, except when a rabbi asks questions if there is a problem. I was also afraid that if I'd bring things out, I wouldn't be able to put them back inside.

Dan could see my dilemma. "Start talking," he encouraged, "and see how you feel."

I took a deep breath and started talking. At first I spoke haltingly, weighing every word, but as I went on, I felt that I could talk. Dan's presence instilled confidence in me and my speech became continuous. At a certain point, I forgot that he was there, and I spoke into space or to myself. In the middle of speaking, I experienced moments from the past. There were even times when I felt a pain in the pit of my stomach, as I'd felt then. I went all the way into the black hole where I'd lived for many long months, feeling powerful hunger for a soft touch, a kind word, affection; everything I hadn't gotten then.

I told him that the sexual relations had been mechanical. That they were done in complete darkness, with clothes on, except for certain places that had to be exposed. I told him about the words that Menachem Mendel would say during intercourse. That he sometimes didn't manage to penetrate, and then he blamed me and cursed me during his attempts. I told of the physical pain I felt every time, and how my husband ignored it. I also spoke about how he asked me to do things to him, but when we went to the rabbi, he said that it was I who had demanded them of him. All the physical and emotional pain I'd felt then came up. I couldn't stop myself. I went into detail that if I had been aware of them at that moment, I would have stopped myself. I went through that painful life all over again. I felt the tremendous disappointment that I had allowed myself to put up with evil for so long and cried over the lost time. I also cried over my world, which had revolved around punches, pain, hate, enmity, humiliation, and fear.

When I finished talking, there was silence. The wind outside blew and whistled. Dan got up, stood over me, and offered his arms. I stretched out my arms toward him and he pulled me up. When we were standing, he pulled me close and hugged me. Just like that, without talking, without saying a word. We stood for a long time leaning on each other, as if trying to draw strength. And maybe he only wanted to thank me for trusting him and telling him my most intimate experiences. For me it was the first time ever that I'd received and given a hug out of true feeling. We were so close that I felt his heartbeat in my chest. Finally, he let go and only said, "Thank you."

Later he prepared a light meal and we spent time together in the kitchen, as if that's what we did every day.

"So we're not going to meet your parents today?" I teased.

He looked at me and laughed his familiar carefree laugh. "That too will come," he said. I was wondering if he was just joking, or if he really meant it.

A week later, he invited me to the garage to light Hanukkah candles with them. "It's our tradition. Every year we light Hanukkah candles together the second night," he said. I agreed, of course. I took advantage of any opportunity to visit the garage. If I could have, I would have gone there every day.

One of his work friends put a yarmulke on his head and said the blessings on the candles. They darkened the garage completely, so that only the candles and another little light they'd left in a corner lit the place. It was a bit surrealistic. Five men and one woman standing around the *menorah* in a dark garage singing the traditional Hanukkah song *Maoz Tzur*. I felt strange among the men, but another stronger feeling told me that I was in exactly the place I should be. My eyes kept wandering to the car on the left side of the garage. I wondered if the electric cables were still hanging from the motor. I was curious to know whether they had received the part they'd ordered and if it had been installed, and also what they planned to work on after that and whether they had a new problem that needed solving. I was thinking about all this while they sang another Hanukkah song.

"What were you thinking about?" Dan asked me afterward. "Your head was in a totally different place."

"Did you get that part you ordered from overseas?" I asked, ignoring his question.

"Now I understand." he said. "Come see."

We went to the other end of the garage. Dan turned on the light, and I felt my muscles tense. I looked at the motor, and the cables were gone.

"You solved the problem?" I asked excitedly.

"For now," he answered just by the way.

"What's that supposed to mean?"

"It means that the specific problem we had was solved, but there's another problem."

I waited for him to continue.

"Well, it's not a problem," he corrected. "We need to think how we can expand the capacity of the engine, its power. Do you have an idea?" he asked me.

I thought for a moment and said that I didn't right then, but I'd think about it at home.

"Good, let's go," he said.

When we turned to leave, I saw that we'd been left alone. The rest of the guys had already gone.

Thirty-three

A few days later, I had a bad day at the library. It could be that if I'd been concentrating better, I would have understood that what happened at the library was a hint of things to come. "Sometimes there are days like that," Tamar would tell me later, "you get up in the morning, and everything goes to shit."

When I got to the library, there was a power outage. The hall was dim, and people had started to lose patience. Some left, and others waited in the hope that the problem would be fixed quickly. It took about an hour for the electricity to return, but every once in a while, there'd be short outages, and the light kept going on and off. One of the patrons came up to me and asked when the problem would be fixed. I answered that I didn't know, but that I hoped it would be soon. He came up to me again a short time after that, this time angrily, and said that he couldn't study like that, and that we had a lot of nerve not to take care of the people sitting there.

"You have to put pressure on the electric company," he said, putting his face close to mine, and then adding, "it's a damn library!"

The third time he came up to me, I saw his face was red with anger. His voice thundered through the hall. "Have you called the electric company?" he yelled, "Of course not. You don't care about us."

Then he went over to the book cart and started throwing the books all over. Sophie could see what was going on from the desk. She got up quickly and tried to calm him, but he didn't listen to her, and after he'd finished emptying the cart, he went to one of the shelves and continued throwing books on the floor.

At that moment, I felt that I couldn't restrain myself anymore. I went over to him and yelled, "Stop that now!"

The man was surprised by my action. He stopped for a moment and looked amazed.

"Get out of here, or I'll call the police!" I continued to shout at him.

The man stood for a moment without moving, and before he managed to say another word, I raised my voice again and yelled, "Now!"

From the corner of my eye, I saw Sophie standing and staring at me. The man went back to the table he'd been sitting at, gathered up his things, and walked quickly out of the library.

"Good job!" I heard Sophie next to me.

From the end of the hall, a few people were applauding. Suddenly the light went on and the few stubborn people left in the library breathed a sigh of relief.

On the way home, I had to wait a long time for the bus. Two completely loaded buses passed by without stopping. Only the third bus, which was full, stopped and picked up the people who had gathered at the stop. The ride was annoyingly slow, and people bumped into each other every time the bus stopped. Finally, I got home. I was supposed to meet Dan in another hour. I showered, put on black jeans and a white sweater, brushed my hair which was now below my shoulders, and waited for him. When he arrived, he said that he'd heard about a new coffee house on the south side of town. He suggested we go there to get a drink and talk. When we arrived and got out of the car, someone called his name. Dan turned his head and said, "Oh, it's Jonathan."

They met and hugged. Dan introduced me as his girlfriend, and they continued talking. When I realized the conversation would continue for a while, I started walking away. I stood by one of the store windows and bent down to read the price tag on one of the garments. What happened after that was completely unexpected. Someone grabbed my arm tightly, and before I saw his face, I heard his voice, full of venom. "You're looking for clothes, you slut, huh?"

He clamped down tighter on my arm until I felt as if one of my bones were breaking.

"Walking around at night by yourself. What are you looking for, men?"

He brought his face close to me until our eyes collided. His face twisted toward me, full of burning hatred. His familiar mustache came even closer to me. I was flooded with a mixture of feelings. First it was the familiar fear, but then the fear changed to something else, not courage, but a decision that this man wouldn't threaten me anymore. That I wouldn't let him intimidate me anymore. I shook out my arm and pushed him back hard. He hadn't been prepared for such a response.

He lost his balance and fell down backward. Surprise mixed with fear was smeared on his hateful face. I stood above him and looked down. "Don't you ever come near me again," I said to him in a determined voice. "I'm not afraid of you. You're worthless. You're nothing. You're weak, just like your father. If I ever see your face again near me, the whole community will know exactly who you are."

I wanted to say lots of other things, but suddenly a man's hand grabbed him and lifted him up. Then a fist hit his face, and it seemed to me that I heard a bone pop. Dan stood beside me and wanted to continue punching him, but I stopped him. "It's not necessary," I told him in a confident voice, "he won't come near me again."

At that moment I knew that the Menachem Mendel phase of my life had come to an end. His terrified face said everything. He slowly got up from the ground, his hand on his bloody nose. As he distanced himself from the range of Dan's arms, he turned and started to run for his life.

"Are you okay?" Dan asked with concern and hugged me tightly.

"If you release me, I'll be able to answer you," I said and smiled.

At that moment, I felt great. Not because of Menachem Mendel's petrified face, and not because of the fist that wanted to protect me, but because of the feeling of internal liberation that I felt. As if my organs had been tense, or I had been locked up in a dark cell, and now my clenched organs had lengthened and flexed, the cell had opened, and a bright light pulled me out. The fear I'd been so used to was gone. In its place was a sense of pride. Pride at the words I'd said, and my decision of *"no more."* And yes, I'll honestly admit that I also felt malicious joy at the fear I'd seen in his eyes. Fear that had moved from me to him. I, little Perele Fisher who had walked around frightened for so long, had found the words that released me from the prison of fear I'd spent so much time in.

"I'm fine," I answered Dan's question.

"Are you sure?"

"Totally."

"If I ever see him again, I'll kill him," he said.

"You won't see him anymore," I promised.

"Why are you so sure?"

"Because he's a coward."

Dan pulled me close to him again, this time gently, to his chest. "Perele, I love you," he said simply.

I hugged him back hard, and we stood leaning against each other, each one lost in their own thoughts, until we turned, holding hands, toward the place we originally intended to go.

The days after that evening passed by in a calm routine. The distance between me and my old world increased. Almost every day I tried something new and unfamiliar. I learned new words, strange slang. One day Tamar suggested we go out to a pub. We sat at the bar, and every once in a while, someone would come and talk to her. When I commented that she had so many friends, she burst out laughing and said that I was killing her.

"I'm killing you? Why?" I asked with concern.

"No, I didn't mean you were literally killing me, you're just so funny. I don't know those people, they're not my friends."

"They're not?"

"They're just trying to pick me up," she laughed.

"Pick what?"

She explained that "to pick me up" meant to try to get to know her and spend time with her... Who'd ever heard of anything like that in our community?

One time she came to me and asked, "Do you feel like binge-watching a TV series?"

"Do I feel like binge-watching?" I answered, puzzled, and again she burst out laughing.

Later I learned not to be so shocked by her strange language, and I only asked that she explain to me what she meant.

I'd worked at the library for almost two years. As the days passed, I began to feel bored. Though I could read books and take some of them home, it was the same work, day after day. I had no possibility of developing myself or learning new things. Sophie could see this, and one day suggested that we go out together after work. When we sat together, she with a cup of coffee and me with tea, she told me that she felt that something had changed in me.

"The excitement that you had when you started to work at the library has disappeared. What happened?"

I looked down and thought hard how to answer. I didn't want to sound ungrateful, as she had accepted me for the job even though I'd had no experience or knowledge in the field, during the most difficult period of my life.

"The problem is," I began, "I feel that I can do more."

Before I finished the sentence, she cut me off and said, "You're right."

"Really?"

"Yes, I myself wanted to tell you that I thought you'd gotten all you could from working at the library. Unfortunately, I have no possibility of promoting you. There's no other position I could offer you."

"You wouldn't be angry if I left?"

"Of course not, I'm just sorry that I wouldn't see you as often as I do now. But you won't disappear on me, right?"

"Of course not," I promised sincerely.

I was very fond of Sophie. She was the kind of person that accepts people as they are. Without criticism or judgment. She never tried to change me or push me toward anything. She was sensitive to my situation and enabled me to go through the process at my own pace, in a way that was good for me. Above all, she'd helped me loads by giving me a job that allowed me to rent an apartment and support myself with dignity. We decided that I would start to look for another job and, in the meantime, I'd continue working at the library.

The urge to find another job increased. As soon as I knew I was leaving, each day at the library became a difficult chore. Deep down, I knew exactly what I wanted, I knew what would make me happy, but I was also aware that my heart was inclined toward an occupation that wasn't customary in my new world, and certainly not in the world that I'd left.

The next day, I called Dan and asked that we go to that café in the south of the city. I don't know exactly why. When he got to the apartment to pick me up, he came up to me and kissed me on the lips. For him that was a completely natural gesture.

"How are you, my pearl?" he asked, and the sweet smile I had so gotten used to was directed entirely at me. "And you're still blushing," he stated.

I smiled back at him.

"What do you say we stay here instead of going out?"

"Here, in the apartment?"

"Yeah."

At first I panicked, but then I told myself that there was no difference between my apartment and his, as there I had also been alone with him. And anyway, what could happen?

I made us coffee and suggested we sit on the balcony.

"Why are you so tense?" he asked.

"I'm not," I quickly answered. "Yes, I am." I corrected myself.

"Did something happen?" his voice sounded worried. He looked down toward me and brought his face close to mine.

"No, no, nothing happened, but I wanted to speak with you about something important to me."

"I'm listening," he said after he'd moved away and leaned back.

Sitting across from him and anticipating his response to what I had to say reminded me of one of the few times that I'd sat with my mother for a serious discussion. I was about sixteen, a high school student. The girls had distanced themselves from me because I was considered too modern. Independent. Someone looking deeper meaning. They had been instructed by their parents to reduce contact with me to a minimum. I returned home that day with a heavy heart and a feeling of deep loneliness. I asked my mother to sit with me a bit, because I wanted to talk with her. At first she tried to get out of it by saying that she had to finish making lunch for the kids who were coming home any minute, but I insisted. Finally, she wiped her hands on the kitchen towel and sat with me on the couch. My mother didn't like this kind of discussions. She was usually busy with talks about recipes or some neighborly gossip. Conversations with me made her tense, because with me, my family thought, things were never easy and were always related to problems.

I told her what was happening to me at school. I even cried. At school I acted as if I didn't care at all, but at home, I fell apart. I asked her to speak with the girls' parents, and convince them that I wasn't dangerous, that I wasn't a bad girl. I asked her to do something for me, but nothing I expected from her ever happened. She gave me a lecture, said my behavior was not acceptable, and that I had to change. I remembered the pain well. The recognition that there was no place in the world where I could find comfort. Where someone would hold me and say that he understood and would try to do something for me. So even facing Dan's warm look, I was afraid that what I expected of him wouldn't happen either. That he too would say that my request was unacceptable and impossible, and he would try to persuade me to choose something else and push me to compromise. The pain of disappointment and frustration that I'd felt in the past with my mother threatened to burst out again.

"I'm leaving the library," I informed him and waited to hear what he had to say.

Dan didn't move his eyes from me and didn't say anything. I was very tense. Apparently the tension was visible on my face, because he leaned toward me and said, "Relax, everything's fine." Then he leaned back on his chair and waited for me to continue talking.

"I feel that I've gotten all I can from the work there, and Sophie said I had nowhere to advance." I swallowed and continued. "I want to do something else. I want to do something that I love, even if this something is not a normal job for women to do." I continued to twist and turn with the words, pushing off the moment that I would tell him exactly what I wanted. It seemed like I saw a little smile appear on his face, but I ignored it and tried to prepare him gradually for what I wanted to say. I prepared arguments in my head against his arguments, which I knew would certainly come. I wanted to tell him that my entire life I'd been forced to take the pre-set path but in my heart I knew wasn't meant for me. I meant to tell him that even if he didn't agree with me, I wasn't going to give up. And then I heard him say, "I've already spoken with Motti about that."

"About what?"

"About you coming to work with us," he said as if we'd already agreed on everything.

"What? I don't understand."

"Perele, are you sure this is what you want to do?"

I nodded my head. At that moment I was dumbstruck.

"If so, then it's agreed. When to you want to start?"

"Wait a second. Wait, I don't understand, how did you know?"

"By the light in your eyes every time you come into the garage. Nothing interested you more than looking at the car and thinking what could be done. Sometimes, when I spoke to you, you didn't hear anything. For a long time I've known that that's what you wanted, maybe before you knew."

"So why did you let me twist and turn for so long?" anger stole into my voice.

"It was fun," he laughed.

His laughter melted the tension that had built up inside of me since I'd decided to speak with him about my wanting to work in his garage. The pain and disappointment that I'd felt in the past were swallowed up into the feeling of happiness that filled me.

"Come here," he said.

He got up from his chair and stood next to me.

"I'm angry at you," I said in a not very convincing tone.

"I know," he said and started to kiss me in places I didn't think you were allowed to touch.

A few minutes later we were in my narrow bed, and what happened after that bore no resemblance to anything I'd known before. Instead of darkness there was light, instead of pain there was gentleness, instead of silence there were sighs of enjoyment, and instead of concealing clothes, there was complete nakedness that exposed all the vulnerability that had been hidden in the past underneath the cloak of modesty.

His hands moved freely all over my body and aroused in me little flames that flickered on and off. My legs intertwined with his without embarrassment, and my lips hungrily accepted his mouth. I never even knew that such kisses existed. I'd never known that touch I felt on my skin. Everything that happened that night was new and unfamiliar, but also stirring and awakening. His liberty was contagious. I accepted him inside of me without reservation. Everything that had been pent-up inside me disappeared like melted ice. I was eager to receive and at the same time to give.

After we made love, I fell asleep immediately. My body needed rest to absorb the experience. I slept deeply. But the morning arrived and did not spare me the turbulent thoughts running through my head. What had I done? What had I done? I asked myself over and over.

Dan left for work and allowed me to sleep, and I was left exposed to the gap between what was ingrained in me and the liberty that had dominated my actions the night before. Menachem Mendel was right when he said I was a slut. I'd slept with a man who wasn't my husband in the most indecent way possible. If my father knew about it, he would mourn for me as if I were dead. My entire life they had warned us about the evil impulse and I, who had let that impulse fly, proved that everything they'd taught us was the absolute truth. Maybe I deserved Menachem Mendel? Maybe he's the payback for my sinful thoughts, for my hidden desires that were revealed to God. I even thought of getting up and going to Menachem Mendel to fulfill what had been decided upon up above.

That day, I did not get out of bed. I was sure that if I got out of bed, something bad would happen to me. The sky would fall on me, I'd get hit by a passing car, I would fall and get hurt, maybe I would die. A disaster would happen, that I was sure of. I put the thin blanket over my face and stayed like that all day, hiding from the world and from myself. The telephone rang, but I ignored it. I figured that Dan was looking for me, but I couldn't speak with him. What could I tell him, that I regretted the whole thing? I preferred to ignore the call.

During the following days, I avoided speaking with him. I informed Sophie that I wasn't coming to work, and early in the morning I left home and walked around the streets, trying with all my heart to cope with the dissonance between the old world and the new world. It weighed heavily on me. As if I had experienced the death of someone close. Feelings moved inside of me in circles like a crazy uncontrollable dance. I tried to understand them, to calm myself. After all, it was with full consciousness that I had chosen a different way of life. With a clear head, I had moved away from the way of life that had caused me suffering, that I couldn't stand anymore, so why, why did I feel so dirty, so bad?

One day I couldn't stay alone, so I knocked on Tamar's door. She opened the door cheerfully and greeted me with a hug. One look at my face caused her to become serious.

"What happened?" she asked, with true concern in her voice. "What happened, Perele?" she asked again after she didn't get an answer. She sat me on the sofa and hugged me. I started to cry and saw that the worry on her face had turned to trepidation. "Perele, you're stressing me out. Tell me what happened. Did he come here, your despicable husband? Did he do something to you?"

I shook my head and started crying harder.

Tamar went to the kitchen and brought me a glass of water. "Drink!" she instructed. "And calm down," she added.

After a few minutes, I felt my breathing return to normal and I could talk. "I slept with Dan," I said simply.

There was silence.

"What? And that's why you're like this? That's it?"

I nodded.

"You're nuts. I thought something had happened to you. I was sure that someone had attacked you or I don't know what. I swear, you're crazy."

"But it's forbidden, I'm not married to him," I said and felt like I was about to start crying again.

Tamar took a deep breath and moved away from me. "Who said it's forbidden?" she said and tried to maintain composure, though I saw that she wanted to scream.

"The Torah, the rabbis," I whispered.

"Yes, right, the ones you left. The people who think in ways that even in the Middle Ages would have been considered dark. You're talking about the rabbis that forced you to marry and stay married to a man who hit you and abused you. You're talking about those who get into your underwear as if it were their complete right. That's who you're talking about?"

I didn't answer, and I continued to sit quietly. Tamar continued. "I want to tell you about my God. He thinks that you need to get married for love. He thinks that if a man and woman love each other, they need to express it, and not hide it. To hug, kiss, and yes, make love. Because love for Him is the most important thing. It inspires you; it lets you feel appreciated and wanted. It gives you energy and causes you to smile and be happy. And I'll tell you something else about my God. He believes that a woman can learn, achieve and make choices according to what's suitable for her, and that she too deserves to achieve her dreams without someone telling her there's a problem with it. My God believes in women, and I believe in Him.

"You left that God because he subjugated you," she continued passionately. "He hit and abused you. If it had been good for you, you would have stayed. And now you're afraid because things are good for you and you're not used to that. Someone loves you and accepts you as you are, and that makes you scared, because how could it be, you tell yourself, that someone loves you as you are, modern and independent? They always told you that you were bad, that you had to change, because if you didn't do that, no one would want you. And finally, they married you off to someone bad and violent, and you think that's exactly what you deserve. A Menachem Mendel. So wake up, Perele, and decide who your God is. Is He the one who oppresses or the one who loves you exactly as you are? Now you need to choose." She was quiet, and then suddenly she asked, "Now tell me how it was."

"What?

"How was it with Dan? Tell me."

"You're out of your mind," I said.

"Right, that's how I am, but God loves me like that."

THIRTY-FOUR

Two more days went by, during which I tried to take in the things that I'd heard from Tamar, until I called Dan. He answered me right away.

"Perele?"

"I'm sorry."

Silence.

"I didn't mean to cut myself off from you like that. I needed time to digest and understand."

Silence.

"I panicked. Suddenly all the thoughts that I'd thought had left me already, returned. Everything that they told me once, everything came back to me. As if someone had opened a box and the life that was in it jumped out. I was sure that I'd done something terrible, that a disaster would happen to me because of what we did."

When the silence continued, I asked, "Are you angry?"

He cleared his throat and then he said quietly, "I was angry."

"And now?" Fear that I didn't manage to hide snuck into my voice.

He sighed and said, "Now less so."

Now I was quiet.

"Look," he started, "I'm trying to understand you. Really. But it's also not so easy for me. Just when I think that everything is good between us, suddenly you disappear or ignore me. Sometimes it's hard for me to get into your head, as much as I try. I understand that you're scared, that this life is new for you, but it's hard for me to accept it when you don't share what bothers you with me and choose to run away."

"So what should I do?" I asked helplessly.

"Talk to me. Don't close up. Even if you're scared or don't understand something, just talk to me. Share your thoughts with me. I want you to learn to trust me."

He's right, of course, I thought. During my life until then, people that I'd trusted had disappointed me. My parents, my friends, and actually everyone around me, including myself. It took me too long to pick up the pieces and leave the life of fear. I was forced to develop a defense mechanism to help me deal with the crises expected in the future, but this mechanism was now my undoing. It caused me to push people away from me. I couldn't distinguish between those who wished me harm and those who wished me well. I was cautious with everyone. I was almost twenty-one years old, and it was hard for me to believe that there was someone in the world that really cared about me and whose actions were only for my benefit. Even Dan's good intentions, consideration, sensitivity, and gentleness with me made me wonder what made him act like he did. It couldn't be that someone really loved me, without expecting anything in return. How could I change everything now, and believe in people without suspecting that there were conditions for their nice treatment of me? Was it at all possible? Did I have the capability of giving Dan what he was looking for?

And then I said, "I'll try."

"Good," I heard him say, "I'm coming." And he hung up.

When he arrived, we sat on the balcony and he said, "I thought about our conversation. I think that some of your lack of trust in me is because you don't know me well enough. You're so busy with what you've been going through that it's hard for you to be interested in others."

"I'm sorry."

"Don't be sorry, you can fix it." His face showed both seriousness and mischief.

"I want you to meet my parents. I want you to see where I grew up."

"It's not too early?" I cut him off.

"Too early?"

"To meet your parents." I mumbled in embarrassment.

He laughed, and my embarrassment increased. I got up and went inside. I poured myself a glass of water and gulped it down. This zigzag left me emotionally exhausted. First I was in one world, and then I was thrown back to the world I had come from. Would I ever be set free of the ways of thinking of my past? Would I always feel grotesque and out of place? Was it my fate to be torn between two worlds? I was pretty discouraged at that moment. Dan and Tamar symbolized the new world for me. He in the choices he made for himself, in his peace of mind and his ability to tolerate me, and she in her energy, the lifestyle she had chosen for herself, and of course her relaxed way of talking. I was out there somewhere, moving in a dark space without direction, getting thrown back and forth and not finding my place.

Dan, who didn't know what was taking me so long, came in and asked, "Is everything okay?"

When he saw my face, he came over and put his hands on my shoulders. "I know that you're very confused, but you'll manage to get through it. I'm sorry I laughed at you, just sometimes I don't understand the world you came from."

"Are you sure it'll end?" I asked in disbelief and apprehension.

"I'm completely sure, it'll just take time. Look at new immigrants. For example, the ones who came from Ethiopia. They came to a totally different world from the one they'd lived in. They needed to get to know it, to get used to the norms of life and new values, to a strange culture. It takes time, lots of time. You made a really big change too. You crossed a bridge and went from one world to another, worlds completely different from each other. Give yourself time to get used to it. I believe you'll always have some traces left from the previous life. Be patient. Don't expect everything to change overnight. Don't get angry with yourself, and don't push yourself too hard. It'll come. You'll see."

His words helped a little, but the bad feeling remained in my tummy.

A week later, I realized that something he'd said was right. Tamar came to me in the evening and was very upset. She told me that her friend, the one she'd had relations with, had decided to end their relationship. He said something about her not being able to give all of herself, that she was suspicious and untrusting.

"And what did you tell him?"

"What could I tell him? He was right. I'm always like that. I'm suspicious of everyone. I don't let anyone get too close to me. I keep my distance."

"But why?"

"Do I know why? Maybe I'm just like that, or maybe it's because of my parents' terrible divorce. My father cheated on my mother and she took it very hard. We took it hard too, me and my brothers. We couldn't believe he had done that. He'd always showed love and affection toward her, but it turned out that he was also having an affair with someone from work. Classic story."

"So you can't trust anyone either?"

"It's hard for me. I'm always looking for signs of cheating. I ask questions, investigate, sometimes check calls on the telephone."

"I didn't know that," I said quietly.

"I'm not proud of it. I know it's stupid, but I can't free myself of that feeling."

It turns out, I told myself after Tamar had left, that I wasn't the only one carrying baggage from the past. She too, who always seemed happy and easygoing, was having troubles with her own demons. So maybe I wasn't so different or crazy.

The next day Dan called and said that his parents had invited us to Friday night dinner.

"What, they know about me?" I asked in panic.

"Of course," he answered. I felt that he didn't understand at all why I was upset.

"What did you tell them about me?" I asked and tried to hide the tension I felt.

"Not a lot," he answered. "I said that I'd met someone who was amazing and very modest that wants to marry me and because of that she wanted to meet them."

"What?!" I yelled, "That's what you told them?"

"Relax, Perele, I'm just teasing you." His laugh was light and bubbly.

"So what did you say?" I didn't give up. The bad feeling that had melted somewhat started to swell up in my stomach.

"I said that I'd met someone really cute and that I wanted them to meet her."

"And that's it?"

"I also said that you were becoming nonreligious," he said in a confident voice.

"Okay."

"Great, I'll come pick you up at seven."

What I experienced that Friday evening was very strange and completely different from anything I'd ever known before. It started as soon as we went inside. His mother pulled me to her chest and said that she was really happy to meet me. I didn't know what to do with my arms, and they stayed hanging at my sides. Then she insisted I sit next to her. Dan's brother and his wife were also there. He shook my hand and she hugged me gently. In the days before this get-together, I'd never stopped thinking about what would happen at the meal. It was obvious to me that Dan's parents would want to meet me, and certainly they would ask questions about my past, my family, my plans for the future. I'd rehearsed my answers. I invented questions and answered them, sometimes one way and sometimes another way. I planned what I'd say and what I'd hide. I was under tremendous pressure.

And then it was Friday, and I was sitting at the table with a family I didn't know, that had received me warmly, and no one asked me anything. The conversation was pleasant. They spoke about an event that had occurred a while back and their opinions were divided on it. His father talked about a work colleague that everyone knew, whose wife had become seriously ill. The conversation flowed naturally, and it seemed like everyone felt comfortable. Only I sat quietly and looked at each person who spoke.

Suddenly I felt a hand on my arm. It was Dan's mother, Shira. She smiled at me warmly and squeezed my arm. I smiled back. She had a nice face. Her skin was smooth, and except for light brown lipstick, she wore no makeup. She was a pretty woman. Once in a while she stood up and brought another course to the table. When we got to dessert, a wonderful cake full of chocolate and halvah, Dan's sister-in-law told Dan's father, Oded, that she wanted the recipe for the cake. I didn't understand why she said that to him and not to his wife. It took me a while to understand that the person who had made the cake was Oded, the husband, the man. I'd never heard of a man who baked or cooked. In our community, there was a clear division of labor. The woman was in charge of the home, cooking, the children and their education, while the husband's job was to earn a living and learn. And there I was sitting at the Shabbat table listening to a man explain how to make yeast cake. For me, it was as if they'd taken the world and shook it so that everything had gotten mixed up and a new order was created.

After we finished the meal, Shira suggested we move to the living room. Dan sat next to me and put his hands around mine. I tried to pull my hands from him, but he didn't let me. Then Dan's sister-in-law, Ella, asked me what I did. I got confused. The serenity I'd felt when they had discussed things besides me was violated. I felt my muscles tense. I cleared my throat and with a hoarse voice said that I was planning to study.

"Really, what?" she asked, and everyone looked at me.

I was sure that Dan felt my awkwardness and I expected him to save me, but like all the rest, he was looking at me, waiting for my answer.

"Uh, auto mechanics," I shot out the answer as if spitting out something bitter.

At first there was silence, and then I heard applause, and someone said, "That's great, good for you!"

Shira got up and sat down next to me.

"Move, give me space near her!" she ordered her son. She separated me from Dan and sat beside me. "Perele, I'm so proud of you! That's great," she said.

"Thanks," I whispered.

"Don't be embarrassed. It's wonderful that you chose something that women don't choose every day. You should be proud of yourself and not be ashamed."

"Really?"

"Of course. Very few women are engaged in that field. It's considered a masculine field and it's about time that women got into it."

"Mom, calm down. Perele is not a revolutionary. She just wants to work in something she likes," Dan said. He stopped her enthusiasm and then explained to me, "My mother lectures women's groups on their right to equality, or something like that. Right, Mom?"

"Yes, indeed, I especially lecture about something like that," she smiled.

"Sometimes she exhausts us with her battles and the fervor and the demonstrations and the signs and the gatherings and... and..."

I wanted to stop Dan. I felt he was embarrassing her in the way he'd explained what she did, but when I turned to look at her, I saw that she was smiling and looking at him with loving eyes.

The rest of the evening was relaxed. The conversation flowed. I was quiet most of the time. Sometimes I saw that Shira sneaked a look at me. Once she smiled at me when our eyes met. As the time passed, I felt more and more comfortable. It was late when we left. Shira and Ella both hugged me. Oded said that it would be nice to see me again and Dan's brother Michael smiled at me. I left their house with a completely different feeling than when I'd arrived.

"How do you feel?" Dan asked when we were in the car.

"Good," I answered without hesitation. That was how I summed up the first meeting with his parents.

Later, in bed, I went over the evening in my head. My conclusion was that despite all the pain, alienation, violence, the distancing from my family that I'd experienced—I was lucky. I knew that many people that left the Hassidic community felt lonely and were forced to cope alone with the transition and the obstacles along the way. I had Dan, and his family.

That night I slept well, deeply, and dreamlessly.

But the following week my world was upended again.

Thirty-five

That afternoon, when I returned from the supermarket, and started to put everything away, there was a knock at the door. Tamar was still at school and Dan was at work. I cautiously asked who was at the door. There was no answer. I became suspicious and decided not to open the door. Though many months had passed since I'd left my old world, I was still anxious that something might happen.

I moved away from the door and then I heard a soft voice. I moved back to the door again, and asked in a trembling voice, "Who's there?"

"It's me, Benjamin."

I opened the door and was shocked to find Benjamin without his hat. His shirt tails were out of his pants, and his pants were out of his socks. He'd always been careful to put them into his socks, but his pant legs were fluttering around his ankles.

"What happened?" I asked, worried, as he came in and sat on the chair in the kitchen.

He leaned his head on his hands and I thought I heard him crying.

"Benjamin, answer me, what happened?"

When he didn't say anything, I grabbed his arm and asked warily, "Tatte?"

"Tatte?" he repeated. "Tatte went nuts," he said and continued to withdraw into himself.

"Benjamin, talk to me, what happened?"

"I told Tatte that I wanted a divorce," he blurted, his head still in his hands.

"And what did Tatte say?"

"He said that it was your fault."

"Mine? Why?"

Benjamin looked up at me. "He said that everything was because of you. That you are a bad influence on us. That you talked to me and persuaded me to get a divorce."

"What? That's what he said?"

Benjamin nodded his head.

"And what did you tell him?" I could feel my fury intensifying.

"I told him that he was wrong. That I'd never spoken to you and I hadn't seen you. But he didn't believe me. He got it into his head that you're to blame for everything."

"But why?" I asked again, "Why should he think like that? I haven't been in touch with him for months, and I hardly speak to you guys at all. Why does he think that I have such an influence on all of you?"

"I think that he just can't handle it, and it's easier for him to blame you than to look inside and see what's actually happening."

"What do you mean?"

"Two months ago I went to him and told him that it wasn't good with her. I think there's something wrong with her. But Tatte forced me to go home and pray. He said that I needed to pray with full focus and intensity and pay attention to my deeds. And when I told him I'd done nothing bad, that we just didn't get along, he answered that he didn't want to hear about it. A month later I came to him again and begged him to listen to me. But since he was appointed head of the *yeshiva*, he won't listen to anything that doesn't fit in with his way of doing things."

"I didn't know that he was head of the *yeshiva*," I mumbled.

After a period of silence, I asked, "Where's your hat, why do you look like that?"

"I don't know. I've been walking the streets for hours. I didn't know what to do. I don't want to go home."

"So what will you do?" I asked, concerned.

Benjamin waited and then he looked into my eyes and said, "Maybe you can talk to him?"

"Me? Are you crazy? He thinks that you want to end the marriage because of me. How could I talk to him? Besides, he probably wouldn't even open the door for me."

"Perele, he always admired you. Even though you were... like you were."

"Yes, he appreciated me and threw me out of the house," I said ironically.

"Please, Perele, I can't go back there."

His pleading made me come around.

"Will you come with me?" I asked.

"No, I prefer to stay here."

I went to the closet and pulled out some old clothes. I put on a long-sleeved shirt, long skirt, and thick stockings. I put on a wig that I'd always had in the closet. When I looked at myself in the mirror, I saw a girl I didn't know. I thought to myself that if Dan or Tamar could see me, they would have thought I'd changed my mind or lost it. I grabbed my bag and left.

Benjamin's miserable look stayed with me the whole way, until I reached my parents' place. It was already evening. I hoped he'd be at home. I didn't want to wait for him with Nechama walking around me suspiciously. I arrived at the neighborhood where I hadn't been in a long time. I looked around, and it seemed as if time had stood still. The same people, the same uniform dress, the same announcements plastered on trees and walls that time had gnawed on their corners, but they still sounded a warning, threatening, and promising trumpet. On one of the signs, they were looking for merciful Jews to donate money for a sick little girl that needed a liver transplant in New York. On another, they were announcing the death of a righteous man who had brought many back from wrongdoing, and he was "from a race of angels and heavenly stones."

At the entrance to my father's street, there was a notice calling for an assembly to be held at the holy forefathers' graves in Hebron on the night of the Fast of Esther, to stop the mass murder of Jews by evil wrongdoers. Whoever came to the assembly would receive all the salvation in the world, and would be blessed with all the blessings, and would achieve all the wonderful things in the world. I stopped for a moment and looked around. People passed me by and saw me as one of them, but I knew there was a giant abyss between us. I felt like a stranger on the street that had once been my home. I looked at people in wonder at their ways, their clothing. I read the notices and the language seemed strange to me, ornate and flamboyant. I wanted to retrace my steps and get out of there, but Benjamin's pleading pushed me forward.

I knocked on the door that had once been mine. I heard feet dragging and the door opened and there was Nechama. She didn't recognize me at first, as I hadn't been there in a long time. But as soon as she identified me, she stood there with her hands on her hips.

"Yes?" she asked, as if she had always been the woman of the house.

"Is Tatte home?"

"No," she answered curtly.

"When will he be back?"

"Late."

My first impulse was to turn around and leave, but the ownership she'd demonstrated, and her humiliating treatment made me angry, so instead of turning around, I walked inside. Before she had a chance to say anything, I sat on the couch and told her that I would wait for my father to return. Nechama didn't even offer me a glass of water. She got to work cooking in the kitchen. I closed my eyes and imagined that it was my mother's hands rattling the pots and dishes. I got up from the couch and went into the kitchen. Nechama lifted her eyebrows, as if to ask what I was doing in her territory.

I ignored her as she'd ignored me. I opened one of the cabinets and took out a glass. I went to the faucet and took some water. If looks could kill, she would have done so happily. That whole time she stood in one place without moving, until I walked out of the kitchen. I turned around and went back to sit on the couch. I smiled to myself with a certain childish satisfaction. I wouldn't let her humiliate me. She should know that this was my home before it became hers. My feeling of satisfaction did not last long. The door opened and my father entered. At first he didn't notice me. Nechama approached him and made gestures with her head. When he looked up at me, his face changed.

"Perele, what are you doing here?" I felt that he was barely controlling his anger.

For a moment, I lost my confidence. "I want to talk to you," I said finally.

My father turned his head back to Nechama, and then returned his face to me. It seemed as if he were hesitating, but then he sat on one of the chairs, at a bit of a distance from me.

"What do you want?" he asked in a voice that was cold and businesslike.

"I wanted to speak with you about Benjamin."

Before I could continue, he burst out, "I knew you were involved in that."

"I am not involved in that," I cut him off. "I knew nothing about it until he came to me today."

My father was silent, and I could see that he was struggling with himself, whether to believe me or not.

"Continue!" he commanded.

"Look, Tatte. He's not happy. He's suffering." I tried to speak to his emotions. I hoped that maybe Benjamin had a different place in his heart from the one I had.

"Benjamin needs to try harder. Do you think that things were always good between your mother and myself? Everyone has his crises." I saw that he was trying to stifle his anger.

"Yes, that's true. But for him it was like that from the beginning. He said that something is wrong with her. Maybe you should speak with him yourself and see."

"In our family, we don't give up," he said, as if reciting a verse from the Torah that was not to be questioned. "He needs to put more of himself into his learning, into spiritual matters, and not be looking for enjoyment. He should spend many hours learning in the *yeshiva* and return home only in the evening. What's the problem? He has two options. Either he'll live well with his wife or badly by himself." Then he stopped for a moment and added, "Like you. There's no other option."

"But Tatte, lots of people get divorced, it's not so terrible."

"My family doesn't get divorced," he said emphatically, and stood up.

"But I got divorced!" I yelled at him.

He turned toward me, looked me straight in the eyes, and said the sentence that brought an end to any hope I'd had. "But you're not mine anymore."

"Tatte!" I called after him, but he had already left the living room and was out of earshot.

I left the apartment in great anguish. The man that had stood before me, the one who had let me go, was different from the man I'd known in childhood. I remembered him as a warm and loving man. Sometimes he'd taken my hand, bought us presents, smiled and joked around. When had he become a cold and detached person whose children's welfare was no longer of interest to him? Was that my fault? Had what I done hurt him so much that he'd changed completely and lost his capability to love and show compassion?

I left the neighborhood and, on the way, took off the wig. I held it in my hands and then threw it in the closest dumpster. I hurried home and found Benjamin sound asleep in my bed.

THIRTY-SIX

When I woke up in the morning after having slept folded up on the armchair, I found Benjamin awake, sitting in my bed, with his hands covering his face.

"Benjamin?" I whispered.

He lifted his head and it looked as if he'd been crying.

"What's happening, Benjamin?" I asked and got up from the chair.

I straightened my clothes and went to make us a hot drink. My heart went out to him. I knew exactly how he felt, but I didn't know how I could help. He asked me how the meeting with Tatte went and I shook my head.

"I don't know what to do," I heard him say.

There was silence, and then I asked, "What do you want, Benjamin? But really, what do you want?"

He answered immediately. "To get divorced!"

"So get divorced!"

"But how? Tatte will never agree," he whimpered.

I didn't answer. I let him think for himself about his way of doing things, without causing him to be influenced by mine. He had to think for himself of the price he might pay and decide if he was ready for that. It was his decision and his alone.

"So what should I do, Perele?" he begged.

"You have two options. Either get divorced or continue living with her. You must decide what you prefer, and what price you're willing to pay for whichever choice you make."

"I know," he mumbled. He started to collect his belongings.

"Thanks for letting me sleep here."

I nodded and let him leave. I felt bad for him. He had a very tough decision to make. Whatever he decided would affect his life, especially his relationship with our father.

Tatte. What an effect he had on us. I started to wonder what was happening with my other siblings. Were they all conducting their lives according to what was right for Tatte? If so, I pitied them. What a waste, I thought, to live someone else's life and not yours. I smiled to myself. I understood the long way I had come, to the point that even my automatic thoughts had changed. Like a smokescreen that had started to clear and revealed the landscape as it really was. The life I had chosen for myself seemed clearer and right for me. I was on a train that had started out crawling and slowly gaining speed toward a destination that at first had been unclear, but as it advanced, the destination had become clear and certain. I hoped that Benjamin would also have the courage to choose the right destination for himself and go with it.

In the afternoon, a few weeks after Benjamin's visit, there was a knock at the door. I was startled, but then I heard Tamar's impatient voice, "Perele, open up already."

I opened the door and as was her way, she burst inside. "Listen, I've wracked my brain to come up with a way for us to celebrate my birthday."

"Wracked your brain?" I was afraid, "What happened? How?"

"Ohh, Perele, cut it out."

"Why? What did I do?"

Tamar roared with laughter. "You're so funny, I'm mad about you."

"Tamar what happened? Why are you mad? What have I done?" I was upset. I thought I had done something to make her mad. I only heard "wracked my brain" and "mad." Beyond that, I understood none of what she was saying, because instead of looking sad and pained, she looked cheerful and jubilant.

"Calm down, Perele. That's just how I talk. 'Mad about you' means that I love you. That's the meaning. It's just slang." She started laughing again.

"You're crazy," I said, "do you know how much you scared me? I thought you'd really destroyed your brain, that you were mad."

Tamar sat next to me and took my hand. "One day you'll learn my language. Everything's fine. Nothing bad happened," she calmed me. "Exactly the opposite, I want to have a fun birthday celebration, and I keep thinking about what to do. Do you have a suggestion?"

"No, not now."

"Okay, so now you have homework, to think of a birthday celebration for Tamar. Tomorrow I'm going to visit my mother for the weekend, and when I get back, I want to hear your idea," she commanded.

I smiled and said, "Of course."

That whole weekend I looked for an original idea how to celebrate Tamar's birthday. I thought about an invitation to a café, a nice present, or a trip together to the beach. Finally, I ruled all that out, and decided on something else.

It was Thursday. I'd asked Tamar to come to my place at eight in the evening. When she entered in a leopard-print miniskirt, a low-cut black shirt, and long earrings, we were all ready and waiting for her.

I went and took her hand. "Tamar, I want you to meet the important people in my life, about whom you've heard so much. This is Sophie, the library director, who was always very kind to me, and thanks to her I have this apartment. This is Sara, my friend, that, though I left the Hassidic community, she did not give up on me." Then I dragged her to the other side of the room and said, "And this is Dan."

"Da-an," she said, elongating the word. "Finally! She brought you out into the light."

Dan smiled at her and answered, "I'm also happy to meet you. Finally."

Tamar immediately felt comfortable around people that had been complete strangers a few minutes before. She moved around the room as if she were the host. She served the food I'd prepared, moved from one to the other, and had no problem talking to any of them. Sara came over to me and whispered, "She's adorable." I was happy. I'd debated a long time whether to invite Sara. I was afraid she wouldn't feel comfortable around people with such a different lifestyle from hers. In the end, I let her make the decision. To my surprise, it seemed that she felt very comfortable. She talked with Sophie and laughed at Tamar's remarks. She kept her distance from Dan, but that was fine with me.

When everyone seemed to have had enough of the food I'd prepared, I asked them to sit. I told them that I wanted to read something in honor of Tamar. Sophie returned to her place next to Sara and Tamar brought a chair over and sat next to Dan. I cleared my throat shyly and told how I'd met Tamar. How she spoke a language that was so strange to me that sometimes I didn't understand her at all. About her directness that was also strange to me, until I'd learned from her to be a little like that too. And I also spoke about her kind heart, her help, and support. Tamar blew a kiss at me, and I took what I'd written and read it out loud:

I once met a girl; Tamar was her name.
We spoke pretty different and didn't dress the same.
One day she's chilling and the next she's laying back.
It changes so fast that I can't keep track.
She is cool and funny,
One day she called me "Honey,"
Do you need "honey?" I asked.
She smiled and said, "You' re the best."
She told me her birthday was coming soon,
And ordered me to plan a party in the afternoon.
I mumbled to myself, "Drat,
Who has time for that?"
Eventually I thought, why not?
She is important to me and I love her a lot.
She's my sister in crime,
And was there for me in difficult times.
For a moment I started thinking,
That whoever invented language, would probably be weeping.
But what's that compared to my sweet friend,
Whose strange language became my own in the end.

When I finished reading there was silence, and then Tamar jumped from her chair and smothered me with hugs and kisses. "You're the best, Honey," she laughed. Everyone else laughed too. My eyes met Dan's. He smiled, and his brown eyes expressed a strong feeling that I was afraid to call by name. I smiled back at him with all the warmth I felt for him at that moment.

"You've changed," Sara said to me when the others were busy talking. And then she added, "For the better."

"Yeah?" I asked.

"You're completely different from that frightened submissive child that you were with Menachem Mendel."

"Right," I agreed. "I'm not the same person. To Menachem Mendel's credit, it can be said that he pushed me to change. He brought me to the point that I had to do something. Today no one could give me orders or degrade me." And then I changed the subject and whispered in her ear, "I'm so happy that you're here. I wasn't sure you'd come."

"I talked about it with Yedidya. He understood that it was important to me to keep in contact with you and he agreed."

"Thank him for me," I said seriously.

Suddenly there was a knock at the door. I looked at Tamar and asked if she'd invited anyone. She shook her head. I went to the door and opened it cautiously. There was my brother Benjamin. He was wearing his usual clothes but had a different look in his eyes.

"I got divorced!" he announced victoriously. He didn't see the people in the room because I was hiding them with my body. "Can I come in?"

Before I managed to answer, he had already come in. When he saw I wasn't alone, he turned to me with a questioning look on his face.

"Benjamin, come meet my friends," I said.

He bowed his head and was about to take off his hat to use it to block his view of the women in the room, but then he thought better of it, picked up his head, and smiled weakly at everyone.

"This is Tamar, my neighbor, it's her birthday."

He mumbled, "Mazel tov."

"This is Dan," I pointed at him without describing our connection. "This is Sophie. I work with her in the library. And this is Sara, a neighbor from my old apartment."

Sara managed to cause him to raise his eyebrows, but he didn't ask or say anything. Dan went to the table where there was some food left and offered him a piece of cake. Benjamin was going to refuse, but I nodded at him and he took the plate from the hands of my partner.

The rest of the evening was very pleasant. I looked around once in a while and saw that my friends were comfortable with each other. Dan stood and talked with Benjamin who looked relaxed. Sara fit in well and I heard her tell Tamar and Sophie about the business she'd started. They both sounded excited and asked her millions of questions. I detached myself a bit from the group and leaned my back against the kitchen counter, looking at the human beehive around me. A Hassidic man dressed in pants gathered into his socks, and a black robe covering his clothing standing next to a girl in a little leopard-print miniskirt and a revealing shirt that left very little to the imagination. A handsome man with brown eyes and straight nose talking with a short librarian about their love of books. And another woman, elegantly dressed and clearly religious was listening with great interest to the conversation between the two, though clearly she had never read, and would never read, the books they were discussing. This mixed crowd created magnificent harmony, without borders of religion, lifestyle, or worldview. At that moment, I felt blessed.

Dan deserted Sophie and left her with Sara to continue their conversation without him. He came over to me and said, "Great job!" He put his thumb on my face and gently removed a morsel of food. And then, I don't know why or how it happened, I put my lips on his and kissed him softly. He was surprised too, but immediately recovered and kissed me back. We smiled at each other, and from the corner of my eye, I could see Benjamin staring at us.

When everyone had left, Tamar told me on her way out that it was the best birthday she'd ever had. Benjamin and I remained alone in the apartment. He told me that he'd gone through with the divorce despite my father's opposition and had taken the chance that he wouldn't want any contact with him. The divorce process had been quick. He'd left the joint apartment and was living at the *yeshiva*. To my surprise, he asked suddenly if I was getting married.

"What? Why do you ask?" I asked back.

"Because I saw you kissing the guy that was here."

"Ohh, no, I'm not getting married."

It looked like he wanted to ask something else but decided not to.

"Tell me," I turned the conversation back toward him, "does Tatte know you got divorced?"

"Yes. I went to him before the ceremony and told him."

"And...?"

"He said nothing. Not for or against. He remained silent, and I left his apartment."

"And the others?" I asked, referring to my other siblings.

"Yossele and Baruch spoke with me, and Leah also called." It seemed that something had changed in him. His face showed no misery or desperate need to receive approval from others. He showed confidence and strength to cope with what the future would bring. Benjamin slept over that night, but he slept in the armchair and I in my bed. In the morning he got up early and went to the *yeshiva*.

I got up with a song in my heart. The memory of the night before filled me with joy. I knew that I had come a long way since I'd married Menachem Mendel, whose name came up very rarely. In another two weeks, I was to start my studies. Sophie suggested I continue working at the library as long as I could, so that I could keep the money I'd saved for another time.

My daily schedule was about to change. The classes I'd registered for would take place three times a week. On the other days I would be in the garage and would learn by watching. That's what I'd agreed with Dan who'd received the approval of his colleagues. A new era was dawning, and I was so excited. I knew I had followed through with what I wanted to do. I knew that even among secular people there were very few women who worked in the business I was planning to work in. I could never compromise. I'd already done that. The time had come to not give in to compromise. That's what I told myself every time doubt poked at me. I was very worried about what was to come, the uncertainty of my actions and my future, but on the other hand, I was full of excitement and anticipation. I innocently hoped that from then on only good and exciting things would happen to me. But someone had other plans for me.

THIRTY-SEVEN

It was the first day of my classes. I woke up with the feeling of being born again. I put on clothes I'd bought the weekend before. I even went to get my hair styled. It was the first time a strange man had touched my hair. Surprisingly, I didn't feel awkward and sat straight and relaxed in the chair. I even made small talk with him, something I'd never done. I wondered when I'd ever stop comparing my two worlds. Would I ever accept my new world without needing to compare it to the old one to get support for what I was doing? I put the question aside for the time being and hoped that in time I'd accept the choice I'd made completely, without doubt.

Dan was with me the evening before. We sat at the narrow kitchen table.

"Are you excited?" he asked.

"Extremely."

"You're totally sure about it?"

"Totally," I answered without hesitation.

"I remember myself the moment I decided that that was what I was going to do. The truth was that my parents, though they are very liberal and open, had expected me to study at university. But I knew long before they did, that I was going to do something else."

"How did they react when you told them?"

Dan got up, turned on the kettle, and sat down again.

"On the one hand, they weren't so surprised, but on the other hand they'd hoped that I would somehow change my mind, though they knew there was no chance. When I looked for a place for the garage, and I made a partnership agreement with Motti, they already knew that their son would not study at university and would instead do dirty blue-collar work."

"So they didn't say anything? They didn't try to persuade you? They didn't threaten you?"

"Threaten?" he laughed out loud. "You can't threaten me. They knew I was sure of myself and that there was no chance of my giving up."

"And now?"

"Now?"

"Do they say anything? Make any comments?"

"Of course not. They're happy that I'm working at something I love, and besides that, I'm not doing badly at all, so there's no reason to stop or change anything. Every day I learn something new. It's the kind of work that requires lots of thought, attempts, failures."

Dan continued talking and I disengaged completely from what he was saying. Shamefully, my thoughts had wandered to the bed next to the wall. I wanted to make love with him. I wanted to stroke his face. I wanted to feel his weight on me. His talking was a kind of background music to the thoughts that filled my head. I was ashamed of myself and my thoughts, and I tried to make my face look like I was listening, but I suddenly heard him ask, "Perele, where are you now?"

I returned my attention to the table and to his face awaiting my answer. "I...I... was thinking about something else," I whispered.

"I noticed. What were you thinking about?" he asked quietly.

"I... it doesn't matter, about something..."

Dan got up, walked around the table, and stood by me. He put out his hand and helped me get up. "So what exactly were you thinking about?" he whispered in my ear and rubbed his stubbly cheek on mine.

"I don't remember."

The kettle button clicked off, and the water in it was forgotten.

Dan started to undress me slowly. I felt as if my body had grown small bulbs that made it rough. I shivered and Dan wrapped me in his arms and pulled me toward him. Even the fluorescent light shining in the room didn't scare or threaten me because of the unforgivable sin I felt I was committing. I was completely in the moment. For me it was like the first time. Love that comes true without fear of the morning after. I was like a ripe fruit open to anything the world had to offer. I caressed his face and body without embarrassment. I kissed him as if we had met again after a long separation. I put my hands everywhere I wanted to touch. My head was clear of thoughts of punishment, disaster, beatings, degradation. Of my father. The only thing that was important at that moment was Dan. Any other thing in my world was reduced to the need for me to feel him with me. Inside of me. When we were lying down next to each other, I looked at him and saw him smiling in satisfaction.

"What?"

"Listen, Perele, if I'd known you were like this, I would have moved things along faster a long time ago," he said and kissed my nose.

"Me too," I said in defiance and he laughed loudly.

"Shameless being that you are. Come to me, come, let's make up for lost time."

We hardly slept the entire night. When I woke up, he wasn't in bed. I almost forgot it was a special day for me. The day I'd meet something knew, a world that had always attracted me and only recently had I found out I could become part of it. I was thrilled. I pressed the button on the kettle and then I saw on the cutting board a note written in sugar granules, "Good luck."

I put on my new clothes and some makeup, took a deep breath, and went outside, right foot forward, of course. When I got to my first class, I saw I was the only girl with ten guys. When I entered, they whispered among themselves and stole glances at me. It seemed they felt even less comfortable than I did. I sat in the front row and they kept their distance from me, as if I would give them some kind of disease. I decided to ignore that and concentrated on the teacher. As the days passed, they started to get used to my being there, and one day, someone asked my permission and then sat down next to me. A few days after that, they even approached me and asked questions about what we were learning. With time, we became a tight-knit group and the walls between us fell, to the point that sometimes I thought they'd forgotten that I was a woman. We were a varied group of people of different ages and backgrounds. I was "the girl." When they spoke about me, they said, "the girl said this," "the girl explained that..."

There was no doubt that I'd found my place. I got up every morning with a feeling of joy and returned home every evening with a feeling that I'd learned something else. Not only in the field of mechanics but also about people. People that if I hadn't left the Hassidic community, I would never have had any contact with. There were men with families where they were the sole breadwinners. There were two smart young men who'd decided to open their own garage. There was another guy who spoke little, but once in a while he dared to ask me a question. One of the men was a religious guy who didn't talk to me for a long time, but as the days passed, he started to feel more comfortable, and sometimes we'd talk about our personal lives during breaks. He told me that he was about to marry a girl he'd loved since they were in high school.

My world expanded. Life became varied and interesting. Being with Dan in the garage also extended my knowledge and my world. Dan tried to make sure I felt comfortable around his work friends, and after a while, they stopped being careful around me. In the garage, I dressed like them in blue coveralls and didn't cringe at anything that needed to be done, even if I had to pick up something heavy or get my hands dirty. The days were busy. At first I worked a few hours a week at the library, but as time passed, I found myself running to the garage any free moment I had. Sophie understood and we decided I would stop working at the library.

One day, after working at the garage, I took off the coveralls, washed my hands, and changed my clothes. Dan said that he needed to stay at the garage and asked if that was okay for me to take the bus home.

"Sure," I answered. I kissed his cheek and left.

It was summertime. The sky turned blue over the dry earth. Here and there white clouds decorated the heavens. It was six in the evening and still light out. In a flash, I decided to cross my old field that I hadn't walked through in a long time. My hair was very long. I gathered it into a ponytail that bounced on my short-sleeved red shirt, tucked into my black jeans. I walked across the field and expected to feel great excitement in the place that knew all the secrets of my life. The field that had taken me into its arms that changed according to the seasons and accepted me unconditionally. A place where

I'd cried over my pain and despair, and because of which I'd met Dan. But the excitement didn't come. No pounding heart, no desire to keep walking there. Nothing. The field had become just a field. Prickly, dirty, full of piles of garbage, from which poked headless and drooping weeds. I continued to walk around, but I remained completely indifferent. How had I attributed such importance to that field? I asked myself. And the answer came to me immediately. The field was replaced with my new life, a life full of meaning. The thorn bushes that had hugged me, I'd replaced with the real hugs of a man I'd fallen in love with and he loved me. I had no need for a field or a beach to be able to sense myself and soothe my pain. The real life I'd created for myself filled me with meaning. The field was only a field.

I crossed it and passed the neighborhood I'd once lived in. It too left me indifferent. I walked and looked at people, stores, mothers pushing strollers alongside other children. Suddenly, out of all the people passing me, I saw my father walking toward me. He seemed to be deep in thought. The distance between us was getting shorter. He saw me, but still hadn't identified me as his daughter. We gradually approached each other, and only when we were a few meters from each other did he recognize me. For only a second did he stop walking, but then he took his black hat off, tilted it to hide his face from me, and continued walking.

When he passed me, I called him, "Tatte," but he didn't stop. I turned my head back in the hope that he would decide to stop, but he moved faster until he was swallowed up in the crowds walking in the street, some of whom looked just like him. I squinted so as not to lose him, but he had already disappeared. Like many others who avoid meeting the look of an unknown woman, that's how he acted with me, and he continued as if I were just another silhouette walking past him. I stood where I was; I couldn't move. I felt as if my face had been slapped hard, and my entire body trembled. My father, who had brought me into the world, had made me a stranger to him.

I arrived home and burst into tears. The insult was searing, but the farewell hurt me even more. During the previous months, I'd convinced myself that the separation from my father had been temporary, that his love for me would overcome his anger. I was sure that's what would happen. But now reality had knocked me fiercely in the face and forced me to recognize that his anger had won. That his lack of desire to accept my different lifestyle had conquered the love, the blood relationship. I'd become an orphan. The hope, which was the last thread that tied me to him, had faded. My father had decided to tear me from the home I'd known. He'd decided to disown me.

My crying subsided and I was filled with deep sadness. Sadness over the death of hope.

Thirty-eight

On the days after that, I walked around dazed. Flashing before my eyes was always the sight of my father hiding his face from me. Every time I saw that picture, I felt a deep stab in the pit of my stomach. A real physical pain. In the first days, I felt sorry for myself. Sometimes I cried and didn't want to get out of bed. As time passed, the pain turned to anger. I asked myself how a father could do such a thing to his daughter? I was angry that he had chosen the easy way out instead of contending with the issue, and then I convinced myself that I didn't need him. That if that's what he'd chosen, so be it. In my thoughts, I started to distance myself from him. I had to act that way, because otherwise the pain wouldn't let me move on.

The time that passed took the edge off the feeling of desertion. I pushed myself to get used to being an orphan at such a young age. The more I distanced myself from my father and childhood home, the closer I became to Dan and his family. In time, it became mine. His parents opened their arms to me. One day, Dan and I were sitting at his place. The supper dishes remained on the table, with all the leftover food. Dan moved his chair from the table and stretched his legs out. He seemed relaxed and content.

"What are you so pleased about?" I asked and threw an olive pit from my plate at him.

"What am I so pleased about?" he repeated my question. "The calm." he answered. "The peacefulness."

When I raised my eyebrows, he continued. "Our relationship makes me feel good. Until a year ago, my life looked different. I spent most of my time at the garage, sometimes until the middle of the night. I would come home and go straight to bed, wake up early in the morning and go back again. I didn't leave myself any free time for anything else.

"And women?" I shot out without thinking.

"There were," he said, "but nothing serious."

"Nothing at all?"

"There was someone, but that ended," he said vaguely.

There was silence. I very much wanted to hear the story, but I didn't want to seem too keen.

"Her name was Sharon," he suddenly began, "we were together almost a year. At first everything was really great. We spent a lot of time together. We enjoyed being together. We spoke a lot; sex was good. Everything seemed almost perfect."

As he continued to speak, I felt a lump climb higher in my throat. I wanted and didn't want to hear the story of the love he'd had. Every sentence he said made me wonder about our relationship. Did he also think the sex was good with us? Did he enjoy it, was he happy, unhappy? I was thinking and not listening. Until I heard the sentence, "And then things began to change."

"What changed?" I asked.

"She would sometimes make comments about my work. She asked if that was what I wanted to do my whole life, if it didn't bother me to work and get dirty, and why didn't I go learn something. At first I answered her questions, but then I understood that it really bothered her. That she wanted to change me. When I asked her directly if my profession was a problem for her, she evaded the question but ultimately admitted that it was. She preferred that I study at university, get a degree and work in something clean and prestigious."

He was quiet for a few moments and I thought he wouldn't continue, but then he said, "When I understood what she was getting at, I ended the relationship."

"It wasn't hard for you?"

He hesitated and then answered, "Actually, no. I guess the breakup had begun before that. The actual separation was just the final stage. No, it wasn't hard."

"Did your parents like her?"

He lifted his head and looked seriously at my face. "My father liked her very much. My mother less. She always said that she felt that Sharon wasn't happy with what I did, but I dismissed it and convinced her—and mainly myself—that she was wrong.

"How did your mother know?"

"Look, my mother had a difficult life. Her choice to get involved with the advancement of women came out of the pain she'd felt at home when she was young."

He stopped for a moment and there was silence. I very much wanted to ask him what his mother had experienced, but I restrained myself. I decided to let him tell me at his own pace. He hunched over the table, using his fork to peck at the remains of an egg on his plate. Leaning back again, he continued softly, "My grandparents, my mother's parents, were very different from each other. He was a strong man, loud and domineering, and she, who was a very smart woman, played herself down, and instead of developing herself and doing something, she stayed at home and took care of the kids."

"You think that staying at home and taking care of the kids isn't good?"

"It's not good if it comes out of fear and not out of true choice."

"What does that mean?"

"My grandmother wanted to get out of the house. She was interested in lots of things. She learned fast and had a fantastic memory. But every time she brought up the subject of going to work or study, he would direct her to stay at home and raise the children, such that it wasn't really her decision. It was carried out in fear and obedience, and not by choice. That's what I'm referring to."

"Was he violent? Did he hit her?" I asked in a trembling voice.

"Not physically," he answered immediately. "But he beat her psychologically. He suppressed her ambitions, belittled her, made nasty comments, ridiculed things she said. Gradually, she stopped expressing her opinion and sat silently at the table."

"And no one tried to stop him or encourage her?" I asked in pain.

"My mother tried, but he shut her up too."

"And what happened to them?"

"She died of a heart attack, and he was left alone. A year after she died, a growth was found in his vocal cords. He slowly started to lose his ability to talk, until he couldn't talk at all and then he eventually shut up too." Dan chuckled to himself.

"And your mother?"

"After his death, she swore she wouldn't let anyone suppress her desires. I remember her in my childhood, fighting for everything. As if she were looking for reasons to fight, to influence, to prove to herself that she was strong and unbendable. With time, she became more moderate, but her opinions remained solid and stable. To this day, she won't put up with injustice, especially when it comes to women."

It was one in the morning when we cleared the table. I slept over, but we didn't make love that night. It seemed that each of us needed time to take in what had been said. I saw his mother in a different light. A woman who'd experienced difficult displays of psychological violence and submission, who decided to fight her mother's war. Each woman she fought for was a reflection of the mother she loved.

THIRTY-NINE

Benjamin came to visit. His visits had become a regular thing. He would come about once a month with no advance warning; he'd knock on the door and enter. Sometimes Tamar would join us and the three of us would sit and drink and chat. At first, he felt a little uncomfortable around her, but in time, he learned to respect her and even seemed to like her. I kept disposable dishes for him in one of the kitchen cabinets, and he would use them when he came. But that day, I felt tension in his movements. He walked around the room and didn't sit down. Sometimes he would stroke his beard, pensively.

"Did something happen?" I asked.

"No, no, nothing," he said, evading the question. He sat on the armchair in the living room and then got up again.

"Benjamin, what happened? Why are you so restless? Did something happen to Tatte?"

"No, no, Tatte is fine. Actually I was at his place yesterday."

I felt a pang in my heart. "Did Tatte mention me?" I whispered.

"No, Perele, he didn't. I'm sorry."

"So what's the problem?" I asked.

"I spoke with Baruch this week," he answered and looked me right in the eye.

The mention of my second brother's name caused me to flinch. "He told me, Perele."

I bowed my head. I couldn't meet his eyes. "What did he tell you?" I finally asked.

"He told me what he'd done to you when you were little."

"But you already knew."

"I knew, but not really."

I felt my cheeks burning. I couldn't look up. At that moment I was an eleven-year-old girl again, lost and confused.

"He's so sorry, Perele."

I said nothing and he continued. "All these years, he's been suffering because of it. He says he didn't know at all what he was doing, and only when he got older, after the conversation with the counselor before his wedding, did he understand the terrible thing he had done to you. He's hated himself since."

"So why hasn't he come to me?" I whispered with my head down.

"He can't face you. He's ashamed. He told me that he's wanted to come to you many times, but he was afraid. He didn't know how you would respond or whether you'd be willing to talk to him or listen to him. He said that he's come to your apartment a few times, come up the stairs but then ran away. He didn't have the courage to knock on the door."

"And I thought that he didn't even remember," I murmured.

Benjamin cleared his throat, and then he said something that surprised me very much. "I think that it's the reason he has no children."

"I don't understand, what's the connection? Did he tell you something?"

"He didn't say anything explicitly, but he hinted somehow that he didn't have relations with his wife the way they're supposed to."

"Really?"

Benjamin nodded. "Maybe you'll speak with him, Perele?"

I sighed and said I didn't know. "It's hard for me. I don't know if I can. It's also embarrassing for me. And besides, I'm still angry at him. He should have come to me a long time ago. He should have overcome his fear and come to me and not sent you to speak for him."

"You're right. He should have come. But now he's in a mental prison. He's surrounded himself with walls of silence, lives within the agony of his thoughts and his guilty conscience. That's how he's lived since he understood what he did."

I got up and got myself a glass of water. I wanted to feel anger, I wanted to hold on to the fear that I felt then, at that time. The insult, the pain that didn't let me rest so many years. But I didn't feel any of that. The only thing I felt was pity. Not for myself. For Baruch, my brother. Though I had moved on despite what happened, he'd stayed stuck in place. Baruch was one of many who didn't know what to do with their sexuality. Who moved constantly between a natural inclination and the rabbi's regulations. No one prepares them at that age to deal with the feelings and thoughts that flood them with their sexual development. They move between the natural lack of control of emotions and inclinations and the demand for complete self-control.

I came back and sat with Benjamin.

"So, what do you say, Perele?"

"I say that I need to think about it all," I answered curtly.

Benjamin let out a sigh and got up to go. "Perele," he turned to me again, but I stopped him and asked him to give me some time. He gave in, said "*Gut Shabbos*" and left.

When Dan came for supper the next day, I told him about the meeting with Benjamin. Right away he asked how I felt.

"I'm okay," I answered.

"What does that mean, 'okay'?"

"I mean that I'm not sad anymore. The pain that I felt then has faded, and sometimes I don't feel it at all. Of course I'll never forget it. The deed will be etched in me forever, but I'm not angry, I don't hate him."

"I'm happy."

"Happy? Why?"

"Again with the why?" he said with his sweet smile, and then he became serious and said it was hard to live with anger and hate. That those are feelings that stop you, that don't let you develop and move forward.

"Since when did you become so smart?" I brought him down to size.

"I always was," he said and laughed as he took my arm and sat me on his lap. "So what do you say 'Why,' will you come live with me?"

"What?"

"Don't you think your rent is a big waste of money? And besides, I need someone to clean and cook, and do the shopping."

At first I thought he was serious, but then I looked up and saw the twinkle in his eyes. "Get a maid!" I retorted.

"We'll get a maid," he corrected himself. "So you'll come live with me?" he asked again.

"I need to think about that," I answered but deep down, I already knew the answer.

A month later I moved my things to his apartment.

Getting used to living together was quick, as if it were exactly the right time to do it. As the days passed, we created a routine that was suitable for both of us. On the days I didn't have classes, we drove together to the garage and spent the day there. While there, we maintained only work relations. Each of us did what we were supposed to do. We left intimacy for home. On the other days, I went to college, and when I returned home, I continued to study by myself. Sometimes I felt a strong need to be in the garage and get my hands dirty, and then I would suddenly appear there. I was always happily received by Dan, and with indifference by his friends, who learned to see me as part of the regular team.

Tamar was sorry I'd left the apartment above her. She said that she was really upset because she couldn't just come and visit me spontaneously in slippers and pajamas. But she was also happy for me. She liked Dan very much and always said he fit me like a glove.

One day I came back early from class. Outside there was a sandstorm and my eyes burned. The blinds in the apartment were open and there was a thick layer of dust on the furniture. I decided to clean. I changed my clothes and rolled up my sleeves. I closed all the blinds to prevent the dust outside from coming in, and I cleaned the whole place thoroughly. I had a feeling of intoxication. I felt liberated, and the movement of the mop in my hand became a light and happy dance partner. I scrubbed and rubbed, wiped down all the furniture and polished everything until there was an atmosphere of cleanliness and fragrant freshness. Dirty sunrays penetrated the closed windows, dimly lighting the living room. I put all the furniture back in place and took a shower. I allowed myself to enjoy an extended time in the water that flowed on my body and removed the remainder of the dust that had stuck to me. When I left the bathroom, I found Dan sitting and nibbling on a giant sandwich he'd made for himself. "I was really hungry," he apologized.

"That's okay, I'm not so hungry."

Dan put the sandwich on the table and asked me to sit with him. He put his face near mine and sniffed me like a dog. "Mmmmm... what a nice smell," he said with his mouth by my earlobe.

"You're giving me goosebumps," I laughed at him.

"Very good," he answered and continued to kiss my neck, my exposed shoulder and onward.

"Good, you convinced me," I said huskily.

"That's how I like to come home," he said after we'd laid down together on the sofa in the living room.

"Me too," I admitted.

"So what do you say? Should we make it legal?"

I took a deep breath and said, "I'd like that very much."

Dan stroked my hair and then whispered to me, "So let's sign on that with love."

We made love all afternoon and evening. From the living room couch we moved to the bedroom, where we fell asleep completely exhausted, until the next morning. I heard Dan get out of bed and take a shower. The monotony of the water flowing put me back to sleep, until he returned to the room and stood above me.

"Do you know what time it is, sweetie?"

"What time is it?" I asked in a purr.

"Ten in the morning."

"Ten?"

"Yes."

"I was supposed to be at the college two hours ago!" I shouted.

"Right, and I was supposed to start work three hours ago. But if that's what happened, maybe we'll take advantage of the day and spend time together. What do you say, my sleeping beauty?"

I nodded and fell back asleep. I awoke to the smell of warm pastry. I showered, got dressed and left the room. Dan was reading the newspaper and there were some bread rolls, hard-boiled eggs and cut up vegetables on the table.

"You made us breakfast?" I marveled.

Dan nodded. The picture flashed through my mind of a *yeshiva* student with an orange beard, sitting at the table and waiting for me to serve him lunch. I shook my head to erase the picture and sat on Dan's lap. I planted a warm kiss on his lips, and he said, "Payment lovingly received."

The months since our decision to get married and the wedding ceremony flew by. We decided to have a modest event, with just family and close friends. I told Dan I wanted to have a rabbi at the ceremony, and he agreed immediately.

When we went over the guest list, I realized that Dan had many friends, but my list was very short.

"What about your family? Are you going to invite them?" he asked one day.

"I'm debating it," I admitted.

I wavered over inviting everyone, and whoever wanted to would come, or to invite only those that I had contact with. The biggest dilemma was whether to contact my father and invite him. I was very afraid of my disappointment should he refuse. Finally, after much deliberation, I called Benjamin and asked him to come over.

"Benjamin," I said after he'd sat down on the chair, with a paper cup of black coffee in his hand. "I'm giving you invitations for everyone. Give them out, and whoever wants to come can come. Whoever doesn't, won't." We both knew about whom I was thinking especially.

Benjamin promised to give out the invitations for me.

FORTY

We set the wedding date for 14 Sivan. Almost four years after my first marriage. According to the rabbis, it was a good day for a wedding. Though the event was supposed to be small, the preparations were many. Dan's mother, Shira, came with me to make all the arrangements. At the dress fitting, I saw myself in the mirror and burst into tears. The longing for my mother flooded me at that moment, and I felt I couldn't go on. I looked at my reflection and saw my sad face. That was not how a bride should look before her wedding, I thought to myself. In my heart, I called to my mother and told her it didn't matter what had happened between us, I wanted her with me, now! Shira noticed my change in mood and came over and hugged me. It seemed like I didn't have to explain anything to her. She understood me.

The date was approaching. One day, Shira asked me who from my family was planning to come.

"I don't know," I answered honestly. "No one's called me."

"In any case, we'll keep the room divider between the men and women," she promised.

"Thank you," I said quietly and kissed her cheek.

Dan was very stressed the days before the wedding.

"Why are you so tense?" I asked him one day when we were at home. I was reading and he was pacing back and forth restlessly.

"I don't know," he answered. "This is the first time I'm getting married; I don't know what it's like. The second time I'll know what to expect."

I threw the book on the floor and went over to him. "Don't even say that in jest!" I warned him.

"Okay, okay, I didn't mean anything," he laughed at my seriousness. "Come, come to me, my soon-to-be wife. Come and comfort me."

We were happily engulfed in the love we felt for one another. Sometimes just one look from him would arouse me. As much as I loved him, that's how attracted I was to him.

The wedding day arrived. Unlike the preceding days, Dan seemed relaxed. I was totally stressed out, mainly because I didn't know if any of my family would be there to celebrate with me. I was worried how their demonstrative absence from my wedding would affect me. I imagined the loneliness I'd feel, the finality, the pain that would be stronger than the obvious happiness of my marriage. Benjamin had not been in touch since I'd given him the invitations, and I saw that as a sign that none of my brothers or sisters would be coming. I tried not to think about it, but I was not very successful. I saw myself standing alone at the entrance to the hall, hoping to see someone familiar come in, dressed in holiday clothes, and then I imagined the disappointment shattering my hopes.

The guests started to arrive. First was Dan's close family. His brother Michael and wife Ella and their new baby. The garage crew came up to me and introduced their wives. I smiled at everyone, but my heart was submerged in tears. Dan tried to get me to come inside, but I told him impatiently that he should go in. "I'll come in soon," I added. I prayed to God, "Please, God, have at least one of them come. Don't let them leave me alone." The tears were welling at the corner of my eyes and threatened to stream down my face. "Please, God, please."

Suddenly a hand took my arm. "Come, Perele, you need to come inside already." It was Shira, gently urging me to just go into the hall.

"Soon. I'll be there soon."

She let go of my arm and walked away.

Then it seemed like I noticed someone with a tall hat among the guests making his way into the hall. I went forward to see better, and our eyes met. We stood in our places like statues and didn't move. He looked down at first, and then slowly lifted his head until our eyes met. His gaze was as embarrassed as mine, but our eyes did not let go of each other's. I guess that at that moment we were both thinking of the exact same thing. His face hardened and his eyes narrowed. He got up the courage to come closer to me. There was fear in his eyes. He didn't speak, he just tried to read my face. The guests flowing inside saw what was happening. Two or three of them congratulated me but didn't try to talk and continued on their way.

Finally, I heard him say, "Mazel tov, Perele."

I swallowed, cleared my throat, and answered, "Thank you, Baruch, I'm very happy that you came."

At that moment, his expression changed. The muscles of his face softened, and a slight smile came to his lips.

"Thank you, Perele, thank you," he said with great emotion.

He looked forward and made his way to the hall. Suddenly, like fireworks in the sky, more and more people dressed in black walked in, their silk robes sparkling in the darkness. Benjamin arrived and then all my brothers and sisters and their spouses. There was Shmuel and Aharon and Leah and Esther with their partners, and my younger brothers, Yossele and Yakov. The women kissed me on the cheek and the men nodded their heads and said, "Mazel tov, mazel tov!" The tears freed themselves and poured down my face. The makeup smeared on my face, but I didn't care at all. My happiness beat all the concerns I'd had before.

Just one person hadn't come. My father. His absence hurt me, but the pain was dulled by the presence of the rest of the family.

I went into the hall and Dan, who came toward me, was shocked by my face. "What happened? Why are you crying?" he asked with concern.

"They came, Dan, they're here."

He wrapped his wide arms around me and pulled me to his heart. "I'm so happy, my beloved," he whispered. "What do you say we go get married for a second and then you can continue crying with happiness?"

"Just a minute." I stopped him and ran to the corner of the hall to hug Sara, who looked wonderful. She returned a warm hug. "You look fantastic!" she complimented me.

"Thanks, my dear, you too."

"Can you believe it?" I asked her. "After everything?"

"I believe it, Perele. You deserve it after what you've been through. I'm proud of you."

"Proud of me? You're not angry?"

"Angry? Why? Why?"

"That I left, that I'm living my life differently."

"Of course not. I respect your decision and I'm proud that you followed through, and I'm happy that now you're happy, that you found love. You deserve it."

Sara had opened the business that she'd planned. She managed it together with a partner, had a marketing man, and advertised her company in the ultra-Orthodox sector. She said that there were a few people in the community that didn't like what she was doing, but many others had wished her success. Her customers were well-dressed women who invested in their appearance. She had also started designing clothes that she loved. She was in the later months of her second pregnancy, and her business partner was picking up the slack. She hugged me tight and I told her I loved her.

"And I you."

"Wait a second, I also deserve a hug!" I heard Tamar behind me who had come in a long leopard-print dress, of course, and looked like she'd just stepped out of a fashion magazine. She had a little too much makeup on for my taste but was prettier than ever. She wore a black jacket over the low-cut dress, and large round earrings.

"Of course you deserve a hug, a big one!" I answered and she crushed me to her heart and said, "You look stunning."

"Thank you, neighbor."

"Not anymore," she corrected me.

I smiled at her with great affection. Tamar had finished her studies and was going on job interviews. She'd started going out with "someone cute," and it looked like it might be serious. A few months later her lease ended, and she moved to another city.

"I met the librarian outside," she informed me.

"Sophie? I'll go find her."

"No need, I'm here, behind you."

"Sophie! I'm so happy to see you."

"Me too, my dear," she said and hugged me. Dear Sophie. I'll never forget how she took me in with open arms and helped me in the days when I was totally lost. Once she told me that she loved routine and feared change. She'd continue working at the library for many more years and would live in the same apartment.

Dan suddenly reappeared. "My almost-wife, do you want to be my wife or not? The rabbi already wants to go, and I've barely managed to convince him to stay." Then he said to my friends, "Hi, ladies, I'm taking her for a minute to get married. She'll be right back."

"Wait, where's the photographer?" I called.

"Afterward, sweetie pie, come let's get married first."

"No, now!" I insisted.

"Photographer!" roared Dan, and everyone turned around. The photographer came over warily.

"Take their picture and fast," Dan directed.

Sara, Tamar, Sophie, and I stood close together, with our arms around each other's shoulders and big smiles on our faces, and we screamed, "Mazel tov!" The framed photo has a place of honor on our sideboard. Every time I feel a little depressed or sad, I look at my friends who were there for me in the days when even my own legs couldn't bear me.

And my father? The years never softened him. When my first son was born, I invited him to the bris[38]. I didn't know if he would respond to my invitation. He didn't come. Since he'd cut off contact with me, I retained a glimmer of hope that ultimately he'd soften and reconnect with me, but the years passed, and he didn't budge. When my second son was born two years later, I invited him again, but he didn't come then either. I wanted him to be my son's godfather. If he had come, I would have forgotten everything and given him the biggest possible honor. I so wanted him to come, but he disappointed me again.

The passing years never extinguished the spark of hope in me. From time to time, I asked my siblings how he was and if he'd asked about me, but I always received a slow nod of the head and a sympathetic look. The years passed and the figure of my father has remained engraved in my heart like writing on a tombstone. Sometimes I imagined him coming to the bris of

---

38   Jewish circumcision ceremony

one of my sons, including a conversation between us. I saw him holding my son tenderly, looking at his closed eyes, and then looking up at me and smiling as he shook his head proudly. My heart overflowed at that moment and tears ran down my cheeks. After the *mohel*[39] finished his job, I imagined my father putting the baby into Dan's arms, coming over to me and saying, "Things worked out well for you."

"Right, Tatte."

"Are you happy?" he asked me in the dream.

"Yes," I answered without hesitation.

"*Nu*, it should be with good luck," said my imaginary father, and left.

The dream recurred every time we had a happy occasion to celebrate. Without thinking, I would look at the door and imagine him standing there with the *spodik* on his head, and a warm smile on his face. But none of that ever happened. The missing note in my song would be absent forever. I gave birth to two sons and a daughter, and my love for them is boundless. Dan and I opened another garage and we manage it together. The past is always present in my life, in my thoughts, feelings, and involvement with my children and husband. My brothers and sisters and I are in contact, with some more and others less. I have a family. One from the past and the other from the present, and both together complete my world.

Almost.

---

39   The person who performs the Jewish rite of circumcision.

Acknowledgments

It was the middle of the day, Purim. I remember that it was very hot. My friend and I decided to travel to a city close to where we lived and walk around streets we had never been to. We knew that various Hassidic families lived in the area, and our curiosity pulled us there.

Within twenty minutes we arrived in a world completely different from our own. Some women in wigs hiding their hair, others with scarves on their heads, and men in different types of hats—and everyone dressed modestly. Only my friend and I wore jeans and t-shirts. Suddenly, a man in a shiny black robe and fur hat came up to us and invited us to his house. Curiosity continued to draw us in, and we accepted his offer. We went into his house and were immediately asked by his wife to put on a hat and ritually wash our hands. The woman invited us to sit down at the dining table that was covered with a white tablecloth, and over it a sheet of transparent plastic. She gave us a light meal and drink, and she spoke with us as we ate. We asked whether they belonged to a specific Hassidic community that we were familiar with from the media, but she chuckled and said no. That community was very radical and they would never have brought us into their home. Before we left, we realized that the man of the house, the same *yeshiva* student who had invited us to his home, was giving out money to people who visited him. It is a mitzvah on Purim to distribute money to the poor, his wife explained to us.

That visit, though it had been short, left me thinking, mainly about the woman's response regarding the Hassidic community we had asked about. I

Googled for more information. As I looked into it, I realized that Hassidism was different from what I'd thought I'd known. My curiosity increased. I started to look for people in the community who would agree to speak with me and tell me about their lifestyle. Unfortunately, I didn't manage to convince anyone in the community to meet or even correspond with me.

The decision to write a book about the curious Hassidism had been coming together slowly inside of me even before I was conscious of it. At the next stage, I contacted the Hillel organization, which helps people who leave the religious community. The path these people take into the secular world is usually extremely difficult. The community they come from sets up very difficult obstacles for them. Some of these young people commit suicide as a result. Many find themselves on the street, penniless. These are young people who have no idea about the world beyond their Hassidic community. They lack basic education, especially in math and English, which are mandatory subjects in Israel. They don't know how to manage on the most basic level, how to do things like open a bank account, look for a job, make social connections, etc.

The Hillel organization helps them in all these areas, and the members also helped me by introducing me to young people who were willing to tell me about the difficult process they had undergone.

I want to thank all the brave people who followed their hearts despite the dangers, threats, and obstacles placed before them.

I want to give special thanks to a wonderful man who prefers to remain anonymous. My dear friend, you provided me with knowledge worth its weight in gold. I still contact you with questions, and you, with your good heart send me exact answers. And if you're not sure of them, you ask others and get me the precise information I need.

Rivka Arzon, such a wonderful and brave woman. You were my inspiration for writing the book as it is. The meetings with you were fascinating and I especially appreciate your courage in sharing your difficult life with me. I'm happy for the good place you are in today.

Thanks to all the others who spoke with me on the phone and told me about what they went through, and what they are still going through today. I cherish you greatly.

To Dr. Nava Wasserman, thank you from the bottom of my heart for enriching my knowledge of the Hassidic world, both in conversation and in your excellent book *I Never Called My Wife*, which became my bible as I wrote.

Big thanks to you, Motti Ashkenazi, my dear, funny brother-in-law, for your patience and the information you provided to an ignoramus such as myself in everything related to technical information on cars in general and specifically restoration of collectibles. You're an amazingly talented person.

To my first readers, for all their comments: Shula Eliahu, my dear sister, for the thorough reading and welcome comments on what needed fixing. My beloved sister Zivi Neuman, for the comments and constant encouragement that strengthened my faith that I was doing the right thing. Thanks to both of you, my loves.

Iris Senior, Dorit and Rafi Chen, Ayala and Shaul Gini, Nechama Gamliel. Thanks for daring to read the preliminary drafts, sometimes more than once, so that the writing would be exact and correct.

Marissa Shua my dear friend, you are for me a safe place for consultations on English. For every question and dilemma, you were a deep and patient help. You never gave up until we found the exact word.

Benny Carmi, my agent from eBook Pro and the entire wonderful team that works with you. Thanks for the calm, professional support. You became a family to me.

Susan Treister who translated the book from Hebrew to English. It was a pleasure to work with you. We worked very well together. And it appears that together we reached a wonderful result. You are amazingly professional.

Last and most important of all, my dear beloved husband, who walks with me hand in hand along the winding writing path. Thank you for your infinite love and support.

My beloved wonderful daughters, Ortal and Reut. Loving thanks for the respect and appreciation you constantly demonstrate. Thank you for the help that you provide me for every dilemma and difficulty during the writing. You are the fuel that powers my writing hands.